The most popular sf movie of all time was definitely not named *Star Peace* . . .

"Unfortunately, war sings its own siren-songs, with an appeal which, given the right conditions, can be almost universal. . . . War promises a release from the drudgery of the paddy-fields, the dull repetitiveness of the assembly line and checkout stand, the endless tedium of a thousand other mechanical and intellectual treadmills. To the statesman and commander especially, it holds out an intellectual challenge. It offers rewards—real, symbolic, sometimes imaginary: the satisfactions of promotions and command, of comradeship in discipline, of self-mastery and self-esteem, of aggressive drives legitimized, self-sacrifice and loyalty, the promise of the thrill of victory and of the power to subjugate—*and always drama.*

"No, this does not mean that war is *good*. But it does tell us a great deal about the human race—about ourselves."

Reginald Bretnor
from his *Introduction*

THE FUTURE AT WAR

POUL ANDERSON,
ROBERT HEINLEIN,
JERRY POURNELLE

Edited by
REGINALD
BRETNOR

VOL. I: THOR'S HAMMER

BAEN BOOKS

THE FUTURE AT WAR, VOL. I: THOR'S HAMMER

Copyright © 1979 by Reginald Bretnor

A Baen Book

Baen Publishing Enterprises
260 Fifth Avenue
New York, N.Y. 10001

First Baen printing, March 1988

ISBN: 0-671-65394-6

Cover art by Eddie Jones/RGP Agency

Printed in the United States of America

Distributed by
SIMON & SCHUSTER
1230 Avenue of the Americas
New York, N.Y. 10020

ACKNOWLEDGMENTS

The Long Watch by Robert A. Heinlein
Copyright © 1949 by *The American Legion Magazine;* © 1976 by Robert A. Heinlein. Reprinted by permission of Robert A. Heinlein.

Old Woman By The Road by Gregory Benford
Copyright © 1979 by Gregory Benford. First published in *Destinies I*. Reprinted by permission of the author.

Moon Rocks by Tom Purdom
Copyright © 1973 by Condé Nast Publications Inc. First published in *Analog Science Fiction/Fact*, April 1973. Reprinted by permission of the author and his agents, Scott Meredith Literary Agency Inc., 845 Third Ave., New York, NY 10022.

Marius by Poul Anderson
Copyright © 1957 by Street & Smith Publications, Inc. Originally published in *Analog Science Fiction*, March 1957.

Scenario For The Fall Of Night by Roger A. Beaumont
Copyright © 1979 by Roger A. Beaumont. Published by arrangement with the author.

The Spell of War by Randall Garrett
Copyright © 1979 by Randall Garrett. Published by arrangement with the author.

The Man In The Gray Weapons Suit by Paul J. Nahin
Copyright © 1979 by Paul J. Nahin. Published by arrangement with the author.

Just An Old-Fashioned War Story by Michael G. Coney
Copyright © 1977 by Michael G. Coney. First published in *Ascents of Wonder* [edited by David Gerrold]; reprinted by permission of the author and his agent, Virginia Kidd.

The Private War Of Private Jacob by Joe Haldeman
Copyright © 1974 by Universal Publishing & Distributing Co. First published in *Galaxy*. Reprinted by permission of the author.

Training by David Langford
Copyright © 1979 by David Langford. Published by arrangement with the author.

CONTENTS

INTRODUCTION

The Future at War is to be a three-volume anthology. This volume, *Thor's Hammer*, is the first. It deals with future warfare on earth and in near space.

The second, *The Spear of Mars*, will be concerned with war in our solar system and a bit beyond, and with invasions of the earth itself.

The third, *Orion's Sword*, will venture farther out, into interstellar and intergalactic space.

This does not mean that *The Future at War* will argue *for* future warfare. But war is not a natural phenomenon apart from man—like a tornado, a tsunami, a meteor shower. It is something men *do*, something we have been doing since long before recorded history. Today, in many areas of a world still more or less at peace, savage wars are being fought; most of them with advanced weaponry produced by civilization's science and technology.

They are being fought in spite of the ritual dances our statesmen and our mass media have been performing so dramatically for so many years: the Disarmament Dance, the One World Dance, the Non-Aggression Pact Dance, the Human Rights Charade, and (with a very few cheering exceptions) the grotesque mummery of the so-called Emerging Nations. At the moment, barring a quantum jump in political intelligence or the sudden appearance of a world leadership capable of something better than dancing ritual dances, it seems highly likely that these wars will continue and will escalate.

In the meantime, the dances are continuing, and a constantly increasing share of the world's resources is going into maintaining the ever-accelerating curve of weapons development and preparation for war.

Unfortunately, too, war sings its own siren-songs, with an appeal which, given the right conditions, can be almost universal. (The most popular sf movie of all time was definitely not named *Star Peace!*) War promises a release from the drudgery of the paddy-fields, the dull repetitiveness of the assembly line and checkout stand, the endless tedium of a thousand other mechanical and intellectual treadmills. To the statesman and commander especially, it holds out an intellectual challenge. It offers rewards—real, symbolic, sometimes imaginary: the satisfactions of promotions and command, of comradeship in discipline, of self-mastery and self-esteem, of aggressive drives legitimized, self-sacrifice and loyalty, the promise of the thrill of victory and of the power to subjugate—*and always drama.*

Consider the role of war in literature. Who, having seen it, can forget Shakespeare's *Henry V* and the *Field of Agincourt?* Who, having read *War and Peace, The Red Badge of Courage, For Whom the Bell Tolls, All Quiet on the Western Front,* or even *Gone With the Wind* can forget their drama and their power? No, this does not mean that war is *good.* But it does tell us a great deal about the human race—about ourselves.

This being so, how is it that so many of us—in the West, at least—have accepted the wishful myth that most of the world's people *actively want peace;* not just for themselves but for all other men—and that the ambitions and passions and madnesses of their leaders are the sole cause of wars? If this were indeed so, there would be no wars; for no amount of propaganda, no exercise of charisma or police power, could make them fight or work to support their leaders' wars.

As matters stand, war is a habit to which the human race has become addicted, the damaging effects of which, over the centuries, many intelligent and sensitive men have tried to ameliorate—but you can't kick a habit by blaming it on someone else. The Communists, for instance, have very glibly blamed war on the bourgeoisie, on capitalists, on imperialism. They still do, despite the fact that in Czechoslovakia and Hungary they launched campaigns of aggression against dissident *Communist* governments, despite their repeated skirmishing on the Russo-Chinese frontier, despite Vietnam's invasion of Cambodia and China's subsequent attack against Vietnam. The Communists certainly haven't kicked the war habit—and, where the Third World is concerned, well, the less said the better.

The world we live in is a chaotic world, at best a precariously balanced world, a world in which the instruments for our self-destruction are appalling. Is it any wonder, then, that ever since H. G. Wells wrote *The War of the Worlds,* much science fiction has been devoted to the future at war? For science fiction is the literature of *what if,* and the *what ifs* of war are quite as important, quite as fascinating, and certainly more urgent than those of peace. By now, certain themes have become standard fare and have been explored from many different standpoints. The three volumes of *The Future at War* will present a selection of them—a selection which cannot hope to be complete. (The one major theme which will not be included is that of utter mutual atomic destruction; not because I consider it impossible—quite the contrary—but because it has been developed so often and in such detail that any restatement of it would be redundant.)

More than any other form of literature, science fiction can show us the alternatives we conceivably may face, as well as the decisions we may conceivably have to make; and, because of its concern with the science and technology so rapidly and drastically changing the face of war, it can perhaps help us to confront the alternatives and decisions of war and peace. Whether we like to admit it or not, at times, war has contributed to the progress of mankind and, paradoxically, to the security and peace of men and nations. It is possible that war can never again play either of these roles, that its toys have finally become too terrible. If so, then the time has really come for mankind to kick the habit.

Many years ago, Élie Faure, himself a combat soldier in World War I, wrote of war:

> Man is above all an artist. He only rejects those forms of art that are exhausted. The desire of perpetual peace will not kill this form of art unless the conditions of peace involve a new method of warfare, with the same sudden and collective intoxication, the same shining responsibilities, the same creative risks, the same atmosphere of voluntarily accepted tragedy.*

*Quoted by Havelock Ellis, *The Philosophy of Conflict, and Other Essays in War-Time* (London: 1919).

Faure's statement tells us a great deal about the nature of mankind; and perhaps, during the space adventure on which we have barely embarked, men will find conditions of peace involving that same intoxication, those same risks and responsibilities, and a similar atmosphere of willing tragedy and well-earned triumph, all without mutual slaughter.

Perhaps. Let us hope so.

Reginald Bretnor
Medford, Oregon

In 1948, when Robert A. Heinlein published this powerful and moving story in the American Legion Magazine, only three years had passed since Hiroshima and Nagasaki, and our first concern still seemed to be to protect the "secret" of the atomic bomb. (There was a year to go before the Russians detonated their first atomic device in September 1949.) No one except science fiction writers and a few scientists gave much thought to the possible military importance of space.

Indeed, only a few weeks after that first Soviet harbinger of a new age of confrontation, Dr. Vannevar Bush published a consoling book entitled Modern Arms and Free Men; it dealt with the atomic bomb, the guided missile, and such weighty subjects as "the nature of total war." Dr. Bush had been chairman of the National Defense Research Committee, later enlarged into the Office of Scientific Research and Development, of which he became director. He was also director of the Advisory Committee on Uranium. "In no other country," says the publisher's blurb in the book, "has a scientist ever been given the wartime powers or the funds which were at Dr. Bush's disposal . . ."

Is it any wonder that in its time the book was considered authoritative? Therefore it is doubly interesting to look at some of Dr. Bush's views today: (a) he took a rather dim view of guided missiles because of their expense and inaccuracy; (b) he thought even less of the possibility of using atomic energy to power war vessels; and (c) as far as my reading could discover, he didn't mention space at all.

Bush's view of future possibilities may be compared with Heinlein's. The ability to see too far ahead for comfort is far less perilous than the failure to foresee at all.

Robert A. Heinlein
THE LONG WATCH

"Nine ships blasted off from Moon Base. Once in space, eight of them formed a globe around the smallest. They held this formation all the way to Earth.

"The small ship displayed the insignia of an admiral—yet there was no living thing of any sort in her. She was not even a passenger ship, but a drone, a robot ship intended for radioactive cargo. This trip she carried nothing but a lead coffin—and a Geiger counter that was never quiet."

—From the editorial *After Ten Years*,
film 38, 17 June 2006, Archives of
the *N. Y. Times*

Johnny Dahlquist blew smoke at the Geiger counter. He grinned wryly and tried it again. His whole body was radioactive by now. Even his breath, the smoke from his cigarette, could make the Geiger counter scream.

How long had he been here? Two days? Three? A week? Time doesn't mean much on the moon. He let his mind run back: the last clearly marked time in his mind was when the Executive Officer had sent for him, right after breakfast—

"Lieutenant Dahlquist, reporting to the Executive Officer."

Colonel Towers looked up. "Ah, John Ezra. Sit down, Johnny. Cigarette?"

Johnny sat down, mystified but flattered. He admired Colonel Towers, for his brilliance, for his ability to dominate, and for his battle record. Johnny had no battle

2

record; he had been commissioned on completing his doctor's degree in nuclear physics and was now junior bomb officer of Moon Base.

The Colonel wanted to talk politics; Johnny was puzzled. Finally Towers had come to the point: it was not safe (so he said) to leave control of the world in political hands; power must be held by a scientifically selected group. In short—the Patrol.

Johnny was startled rather than shocked. As an abstract idea, Towers' notion sounded plausible. The League of Nations had folded up, so had the United Nations; what would keep the Federation from breaking up, too, and thus lead to World War IV? "And you know how bad such a war would be, Johnny."

Johnny agreed. Towers said he was glad that Johnny got the point. The senior bomb officer could handle the work, but it was better to have both specialists.

Johnny sat up with a jerk. "You are going to *do* something about it?" He had thought the Exec was just talking.

Towers smiled. "We're not politicians; we don't just talk."

Johnny whistled. "When does this start?"

Towers flipped a switch. Johnny was startled to hear his own voice, then spotted the recorded conversation as having taken place in the junior officers' messroom. A political argument, he remembered, which he had walked out on . . . a good thing, too! But being spied on annoyed him.

Towers switched it off. "We've started," he said. "We know who is safe and who isn't. Take Kelly—" He waved at the loudspeaker. "Kelly is politically unreliable. You noticed he wasn't at breakfast?"

"Huh? I thought he was on watch."

"Kelly's watch-standing days are over. Oh, relax; he isn't hurt."

Johnny thought this over. "Which list am I on?" he asked. "Safe or unsafe?"

"Your name has a question mark after it. But I have said all along that you could be depended on." He grinned engagingly. "You won't make a liar of me, Johnny?"

Dahlquist didn't answer; Towers said sharply, "Come now—what do you think of it? Speak up."

"Well, if you ask me, you've bitten off more than you can chew. While it's true that Moon Base controls the

Earth, Moon Base itself is a sitting duck for a ship. One bomb—*blooie!*"

Towers picked up a message form and handed it over; it read: I HAVE YOUR CLEAN LAUNDRY—ZACK. "That means every bomb in the *Trygve Lie* has been put out of commission. I have reports from every ship we need worry about." He stood up. "Think it over and see me after lunch. Major Morgan needs your help right away, to change control frequencies on the bombs."

"The control frequencies?"

"Naturally. We don't want the bombs jammed before they reach their targets."

"What? You said the idea was to *prevent* war."

Towers brushed it aside. "There won't be a war—just a psychological demonstration, an unimportant town or two. A little bloodletting to save an all-out war. Simple arithmetic."

He put a hand on Johnny's shoulder. "You aren't squeamish, or you wouldn't be a bomb officer. Think of it as a surgical operation. And think of your family."

Johnny Dahlquist had been thinking of his family. "If you please, sir, I want to see the Commanding Officer."

Towers frowned. "The Commodore is not available. As you know, I speak for him. See me again—after lunch."

The Commodore was decidedly not available; the Commodore was dead. But Johnny did not know that.

Dahlquist walked back to the messroom, bought cigarettes, sat down and had a smoke. He got up, crushed out the butt, and headed for the Base's west airlock. There he got into his space suit and went to the lockmaster. "Open her up, Smitty."

The marine looked surprised. "Can't let anyone out on the surface without word from Colonel Towers, sir. Hadn't you heard?"

"Oh, yes! Give me your order book." Dahlquist took it, wrote a pass for himself, and signed it "by direction of Colonel Towers." He added, "Better call the Executive Officer and check it."

The lockmaster read it and stuck the book in his pocket. "Oh, no, Lieutenant. Your word is good."

"Hate to disturb the Executive Officer, eh? Don't blame you." He stepped in, closed the inner door, and waited while the air was sucked out.

Out on Moon's surface he blinked at the light and hurried to the track-rocket's terminus; a car was waiting. He squeezed in, pulled down the hood, and punched the starting button. The rocket car flung itself at the hills, dived through and came out on a plain studded with projectile rockets, like candles on a cake. Quickly it dived into a second tunnel through more hills. There was a stomach-wrenching deceleration and the car stopped at the underground atom-bomb armory.

As Dahlquist climbed out he switched on his walkie-talkie. The space-suited guard at the entrance came to port-arms, Dahlquist said, "Morning, Lopez," and walked by him to the airlock. He pulled it open.

The guard motioned him back. "Hey! Nobody goes in without the Executive Officer's say-so." He shifted his gun, fumbled in his pouch and got out a paper. "Read it, Lieutenant."

Dahlquist waved it away. "I drafted that order myself. You read it; you've misinterpreted it."

"I don't see how, Lieutenant."

Dahlquist snatched the paper, glanced at it, then pointed to a line. "See? '—except persons specifically designated by the Executive Officer.' That's the bomb officers, Major Morgan and me."

The guard looked worried. Dahlquist said, "Damn it, look up 'specifically designated'—it's under *'Bomb Room, Security, Procedure for,'* in your standing orders. Don't tell me you forgot them again!"

"Oh, no, sir! I've got 'em." The guard reached into his pouch. Dahlquist gave him back the sheet; the guard took it, hesitated, then leaned his weapon against his hip, shifted the paper to his left hand, and dug into his pouch with his right.

Dahlquist grabbed the gun, shoved it between the guard's legs, and jerked. He threw the weapon away and ducked into the airlock. As he slammed the door, he saw the guard struggling to his feet and reaching for his side arm. He dogged the outer door shut and felt a tingle in his fingers as a slug struck the door.

He flung himself at the inner door, jerked the spill lever, rushed back to the outer door and hung himself on the handle. At once he could feel it stir. The guard was lifting up; the lieutenant was pulling down with only his low Moon weight to anchor him. Slowly the handle raised.

Air from the bomb room rushed into the lock through the spill valve. Dahlquist felt his space suit settle on his body as the air pressure in the lock began to equal the pressure in the suit. He quit straining and let the guard raise the handle. It did not matter; thirteen tons of air pressure now held the outer door closed.

He latched open the inner door of the lock. As long as it remained open, the lock could not operate; no one could enter.

Before him in the room, one for each projectile rocket, were the atom bombs, spaced apart to defeat any faint possibility of spontaneous chain reaction. They were the deadliest things in the known universe, but they were his babies. He had placed himself between them and anyone who would misuse them.

But now that he was here, he had no plan to use his temporary advantage.

The speaker on the wall sputtered at him. "Hey! Lieutenant! What goes on here? You gone crazy?" Dahlquist did not answer. Let Lopez stay confused—it would take him that much longer to make up his mind what to do. And Johnny Dahlquist needed as many minutes as he could squeeze. Lopez went on protesting. Finally he shut up.

Johnny had followed a blind urge not to let the bombs—*his* bombs!—be used for "demonstrations on unimportant towns." But what to do next? Well, Towers couldn't get through the lock. Johnny would sit tight till hell froze over.

Don't kid yourself, John Ezra! Towers could get in. Some high explosive against the outer door—then the air would whoosh out, our boy Johnny would drown in blood from his burst lungs—and the bombs would be sitting there, unhurt. They were built to stand the jump from Moon to Earth; vacuum hurt them not at all.

He decided to stay in his space suit; explosive decompression didn't appeal to him. Come to think about it, death from old age was his choice.

Or they could drill a hole, let out the air, and open the door without wrecking the lock. Or Towers might even have a new airlock built outside the old. Not likely, Johnny thought; a *coup d'état* depended on speed. Towers was almost sure to take the quickest way—blasting. And Lopez was probably calling the Base right now. Fifteen minutes

for Towers to suit up and get here, maybe a short dicker—
then *whoosh!* the party is over.

Fifteen minutes—

In fifteen minutes the bombs might fall back into the
hands of the conspirators; in fifteen minutes he must make
the bombs unusable.

An atom bomb is just two or more pieces of fissionable
metal, such as plutonium. Separated, they are no more
explosive than a pound of butter; slapped together, they
explode. The complications lie in the gadgets and circuits
and gun used to slap them together in the exact way and at
the exact time and place required.

The circuits, the bomb's "brain," are easily destroyed—
but the bomb itself is hard to destroy because of its very
simplicity. Johnny decided to smash the "brains"—and
quickly!

The only tools at hand were simple ones used in handling the bombs. Aside from a Geiger counter, the speaker
on the walkie-talkie circuit, a television rig to the base,
and the bombs themselves, the room was bare. A bomb to
be worked on was taken elsewhere—not through fear of
explosion, but to reduce radiation exposure to personnel.
The radioactive material in a bomb is buried in a "tamper"
—in these bombs, gold. Gold stops alpha, beta, and much
of the deadly gamma radiation—but not neutrons.

The slippery, poisonous neutrons which plutonium gives
off had to escape, or a chain reaction—explosion!—would
result. The room was bathed in an invisible, almost
undetectible, rain of neutrons. The place was unhealthy;
regulations called for staying in it as short a time as possible.

The Geiger counter clicked off the "background" radiation, cosmic rays, the trace of radioactivity in the Moon's
crust, and secondary radioactivity set up all through the
room by neutrons. Free neutrons have the nasty trait of
infecting what they strike, whether it be concrete wall or
human body. In time the room would have to be abandoned.

Dahlquist twisted a knob on the Geiger counter; the
instrument stopped clicking. He had used a suppressor
circuit to cut out noise of "background" radiation at the
level then present. It reminded him uncomfortably of the
danger of staying there. He took out the radiation exposure film all radiation personnel carry; it was a direct-

response type and had been fresh when he arrived. The most sensitive end was faintly darkened already. Halfway down the film a red line crossed it. Theoretically, if the wearer exposed himself enough in a week to darken the film to that line, he was, as Johnny told himself, a "dead duck."

Off came the cumbersome space suit; what he needed was speed. Get it done and surrender—can't hang around in a place as "hot" as this. He grabbed a ball hammer from the tool rack, paused to switch off the television pick up, and got busy. The first bomb bothered him. He started to smash the cover plate of the "brain," then stopped, filled with reluctance. All his life he had prized fine apparatus.

He nerved himself and swung; glass tinkled, metal creaked. His mood changed; he began to feel a shameful pleasure in destruction. He laid into it, swinging, smashing, destroying!

So intent he became that he did not at first hear his name called. "Dahlquist! Answer me! Are you there?"

He wiped sweat and looked at the TV screen. Towers' worried features stared out.

Johnny was shocked to find that he had only wrecked six bombs. Was he going to be caught before he could finish? Oh, no! He *had* to finish. Stall, son, stall! "Yes, Colonel? You called me?"

"I certainly did! What's the meaning of this?"

"Uh, I'm sorry, Colonel."

Towers' expression relaxed a little. "Turn on your pickup, Johnny, I can't see you. What was that noise?"

"The pickup is on," Johnny lied. "It must be out of order. That noise—uh, to tell the truth, Colonel, I was fixing things so that nobody could get in here."

Towers hesitated, then said firmly, "I'm going to assume you are sick and send you to the Medical Officer. But I want you to come out of there, right away. That's an order, Johnny."

Johnny answered slowly, "Uh, I can't just yet, Colonel. I came here to make up my mind and I haven't quite made it up yet. You said to see you after lunch."

"I meant you to stay in your quarters."

"Yes, sir. But I thought I ought to stand watch on the bombs, in case I decided you were wrong."

"It's not for you to decide, Johnny. I'm your superior officer. You are sworn to obey me."

"Yes, sir." This was wasting time; the old fox might have a squad on the way now. "But I swore to keep the peace, too. Could you come here and talk it over with me? I don't want to do the wrong thing."

Towers smiled. "A good idea, Johnny. You wait there. I'm sure you'll see the light." He switched off.

"There," said Johnny, "that should convince you I'm a half-wit—you slimy mistake!" He started to use the few minutes gained.

He stopped almost at once; it dawned on him that wrecking the "brains" was not enough. There were no spare "brains," but there was a well-stocked electronics shop. Morgan could jury-rig control circuits for bombs. Why, he could himself—not a neat job, but one that would work. Damnation! He would have to wreck the bombs themselves—and in the next ten minutes.

But a bomb was solid chunks of metal, encased in a heavy tamper, all tied in with a big steel gun. It couldn't be done—not in ten minutes.

Damn!

Of course, there was one way. He knew the control circuits; he also knew how to beat them. Take this bomb; if he took out the safety bar, unhooked the proximity circuit, shorted the delay circuit, and cut in the arming circuit by hand—then unscrewed *that* and reached in *there*, he could, with just a long, stiff wire, set the bomb off.

Blowing the other bombs and the valley itself to Kingdom Come.

Also Johnny Dahlquist. That was the rub.

All this time he was doing what he had thought out, up to the step of actually setting off the bomb. Ready to go, the bomb seemed to threaten, as if crouching to spring. He stood up, sweating.

He wondered if he had the courage. He did not want to funk—and hoped that he would. He dug into his jacket and took out a picture of Edith and the baby. "Honey chile," he said, "if I get out of this, I'll never even try to beat a red light." He kissed the picture and put it back. There was nothing to do but wait.

What was keeping Towers? Johnny wanted to make sure that Towers was in blast range. What a joke on the jerk! Me—sitting here, ready to throw the switch on him. The

idea tickled him; it led to a better: why blow himself
up—alive?

There was another way to rig it—a "dead-man" control.
Jigger up some way so that the last step, the one that set
off the bomb, would not happen as long as he kept his
hand on a switch or a lever or something. Then, if they
blew open the door, or shot him, or anything—up goes
the balloon!

Better still, if he could hold them off with the threat of
it, sooner or later help would come—Johnny was sure that
most of the Patrol was not in this stinking conspiracy—and
then: Johnny comes marching home! What a reunion!
He'd resign and get a teaching job; he'd stood his watch.

All the while, he was working. Electrical? No, too little
time. Make it a simple mechanical linkage. He had doped
it out but had barely begun to build it when the loudspeaker called him. "Johnny?"

"That you, Colonel?" His hands kept busy.

"Let me in."

"Well, now, Colonel, that wasn't in the agreement."
Where in blue blazes was something to use as a long lever?

"I'll come in alone, Johnny, I give you my word. We'll
talk face to face."

His word! "We can talk over the speaker, Colonel."
Hey, that was what he wanted—a yardstick, hanging on
the tool rack.

"Johnny, I'm warning you. Let me in, or I'll blow the
door off."

A wire—he needed a wire, fairly long and stiff. He tore
the antenna from his suit. "You wouldn't do that, Colonel.
It would ruin the bombs."

"Vacuum won't hurt the bombs. Quit stalling."

"Better check with Major Morgan. Vacuum won't hurt
them; explosive decompression will wreck every circuit."
The Colonel was not a bomb specialist; he shut up for
several minutes. Johnny went on working.

"Dahlquist," Towers resumed, "that was a clumsy lie. I
checked with Morgan. You have sixty seconds to get into
your suit, if you aren't already. I'm going to blast the door."

"No, you won't," said Johnny. "Ever hear of a 'dead-man'
switch?" Now for a counterweight—and a sling. He'd use
his belt.

"Eh? What do you mean?"

"I've rigged number seventeen to set off by hand. But I put in a gimmick. It won't blow while I hang on to a strap I've got in my hand. But if anything happens to me—*up she goes!* You are about fifty feet from the blast center. Think it over."

There was a short silence. "I don't believe you."

"No? Ask Morgan. He can inspect it, over the TV pickup." Johnny lashed the belt of his space suit to the end of the yardstick.

"You said the pickup was out of order."

"So I lied. This time I'll prove it. Have Morgan call me."

Presently Major Morgan's face appeared. "Lieutenant Dahlquist?"

"Hi, Stinky. Wait a sec." With great care Dahlquist made one last connection while holding down the end of the yardstick. Still careful, he shifted his grip to the belt, sat down on the floor, reached out and switched on the TV pickup. "Can you see me, Stinky?"

"I see you," Morgan answered stiffly. "What is this nonsense?"

"A little surprise I whipped up." He explained it—what circuits he had cut out, what ones had been shorted through, just how the jury-rigged mechanical sequence fitted in.

Morgan nodded. "But you are bluffing. Dahlquist. I feel sure you haven't disconnected the 'K' circuit. You don't have the guts to blow yourself up."

Johnny chuckled. "I sure haven't. But that's the beauty of it. It can't go off, *so long as I am alive*. If your greasy boss, ex-Colonel Towers, blasts the door, then I'm dead and the bomb goes off. It won't matter to me, but it will to him. Better tell him." He switched off.

Towers came on over the speaker shortly. "Dahlquist?"

"I hear you."

"There's no need to throw away your life. Come out, and you will be retired on full pay. You'll go home to your family. I promise."

Johnny got mad. "You keep my family out of this!"

"Think of them, man."

"Shut up. Get back to your hole. I feel a need to scratch and this whole shebang might just explode in your lap."

* * *

Johnny sat up with a start. He had dozed; his hand hadn't let go the sling, but he had the shakes when he thought about it.

Maybe he should disarm the bomb and depend on their not daring to dig him out? But Towers' neck was already in hock for treason; Towers might risk it. If he did and the bomb were disarmed, Johnny would be dead and Towers would have the bombs. No, he had gone this far; he wouldn't let his baby girl grow up in a dictatorship just to catch some sleep.

He heard the Geiger counter clicking and remembered having used the suppressor circuit. The radioactivity in the room must be increasing, perhaps from scattering the "brain" circuits—the circuits were sure to be infected; they had lived too long too close to plutonium. He dug out his film.

The dark area was spreading toward the red line.

He put it back and said, "Pal, better break this deadlock or you are going to shine like a watch dial." It was a figure of speech; infected animal tissue does not glow—it simply dies, slowly.

The TV screen lit up; Towers' face appeared. "Dahlquist? I want to talk to you."

"Go fly a kite."

"Let's admit you have us inconvenienced."

"Inconvenienced, hell—I've got you stopped."

"For the moment. I'm arranging to get more bombs——"

"Liar."

"——but you are slowing us up. I have a proposition."

"Not interested."

"Wait. When this is over I will be chief of the world government. If you will cooperate, even now, I will make you my administrative head."

Johnny told him what he could do with it. Towers said, "Don't be stupid. What do you gain by dying?"

Johnny grunted. "Towers, what a prime stinker you are. You spoke of my family. I'd rather see them dead than living under a two bit Napoleon like you. Go away—I've got some thinking to do."

Towers switched off.

Johnny got out his film again. It seemed no darker, but it reminded him forcibly that time was running out. He was hungry and thirsty—and he could not stay awake forever. It took four days to get a ship up from Earth; he could not expect rescue any sooner. And he wouldn't last four days—once the darkening spread past the red line, he was a goner.

His only chance was to wreck the bombs beyond repair, and get out—before that film got much darker.

He thought about ways, then got busy. He hung a weight on the sling, tied a line to it. If Towers blasted the door, he hoped to jerk the rig loose before he died.

There was a simple, though arduous, way to wreck the bombs beyond any capacity of Moon Base to repair them. The heart of each was two hemispheres of plutonium, their flat surfaces polished smooth to permit perfect contact when slapped together. Anything less would prevent the chain reaction on which atomic explosion depended.

Johnny started taking apart one of the bombs.

He had to bash off four lugs, then break the glass envelope around the inner assembly. Aside from that the bomb came apart easily. At last he had in front of him two gleaming, mirror-perfect half-globes.

A blow with the hammer—and one was no longer perfect. Another blow and the second cracked like glass; he had tapped its crystalline structure just right.

Hours later, dead tired, he went back to the armed bomb. Forcing himself to steady down, with extreme care he disarmed it. Shortly its silvery hemispheres too were useless. There was no longer a usable bomb in the room—but huge fortunes in the most valuable, most poisonous, and most deadly metal in the known world were spread around the floor.

Johnny looked at the lethal stuff. "Into your suit and out of here, son," he said aloud. "I wonder what Towers will say."

He walked toward the rack, intending to hang up the hammer. As he passed, the Geiger counter chattered wildly.

Plutonium hardly affects a Geiger counter; secondary infection from plutonium does. Johnny looked at the hammer, then held it closer to the Geiger counter. The counter screamed.

Johnny tossed it hastily away and started back toward his suit.

As he passed the counter it chattered again. He stopped short.

He pushed one hand close to the counter. Its clicking picked up to a steady roar. Without moving he reached into his pocket and took out his exposure film.

It was dead black from end to end.

Plutonium taken into the body moves quickly to bone marrow. Nothing can be done; the victim is finished. Neutrons from it smash through the body, ionizing tissue, transmuting atoms into radioactive isotopes, destroying and killing. The fatal dose is less than a tenth the size of a grain of table salt—an amount small enough to enter through the tiniest scratch. During the historic "Manhattan Project," immediate high amputation was the only first-aid measure.

Johnny knew all this but it no longer disturbed him. He sat on the floor, smoking a hoarded cigarette, and thinking. The events of his long watch were running through his mind.

He blew smoke at the Geiger counter and smiled without humor to hear it chatter more loudly. By now even his breath was "hot"—carbon-14, he supposed, exhaled from his bloodstream as carbon dioxide. It did not matter.

There was no longer any point in surrendering, nor would he give Towers the satisfaction—he would finish out this watch right here. Besides, by keeping up the bluff that one bomb was ready to blow, he could stop them from capturing the raw material from which bombs were made. That might be important in the long run.

He accepted, without surprise, the fact that he was not unhappy. There was a sweetness about having no further worries of any sort. He did not hurt, he was not uncomfortable, he was no longer even hungry. Physically he still felt fine and his mind was at peace. He was dead—he knew that he was dead; yet for a time he was able to walk and breathe and see and feel.

He was not even lonesome. He was not alone; there were comrades with him—the boy with his finger in the dike, Colonel Bowie, too ill to move but insisting that he be carried across the line, the dying Captain of the *Chesapeake* still with deathless challenge on his lips, Rodger Young peering into the gloom. They gathered about him in the dusky bomb room.

And of course there was Edith. She was the only one he

was aware of. Johnny wished that he could see her face more clearly. Was she angry? Or proud and happy?

Proud though unhappy—he could see her better now and even feel her hand. He held very still.

Presently his cigarette burned down to his fingers. He took a final puff, blew it at the Geiger counter, and put it out. It was his last. He gathered several butts and made a roll-your-own with a bit of paper found in a pocket. He lit it carefully and settled back to wait for Edith to show up again. He was very happy.

He was still propped against the bomb case, the last of his salvaged cigarettes cold at his side, when the speaker called out again. "Johnny? Hey, Johnny! Can you hear me? This is Kelly. It's all over. The *Lafayette* landed and Towers blew his brains out. Johnny? *Answer me.*"

When they opened the outer door, the first man in carried a Geiger counter in front of him on the end of a long pole. He stopped at the threshold and backed out hastily. "Hey, chief!" he called. "Better get some handling equipment—uh, and a lead coffin, too."

"Four days it took the little ship and her escort to reach Earth. Four days while all of Earth's people awaited her arrival. For ninety-eight hours all commercial programs were off television; instead there was an endless dirge— the Dead March *from* Saul, *the* Valhalla *theme*, Going Home, *the* Patrol's *own* Landing Orbit.

"The nine ships landed at Chicago Port. A drone tractor removed the casket from the small ship; the ship was then refueled and blasted off in an escape trajectory, thrown away into outer space, never again to be used for a lesser purpose.

"The tractor progressed to the Illinois town where Lieutenant Dahlquist had been born, while the dirge continued. There the casket was placed on a pedestal, inside a barrier marking the distance of safe approach. Space marines, arms reversed and heads bowed, stood guard around it; the crowds stayed outside this circle. And still the dirge continued.

"When enough time had passed, long, long after the heaped flowers had withered, the lead casket was enclosed in marble, just as you see it today."

Robert A. Heinlein is, indisputably, the dean of American science fiction writers, but that statement scarcely does justice to his significance, to his influence on readers and on other writers. From the publication of his first story, "Lifeline," in Astounding *in 1939, he has continued to be the most innovative writer in the field, developing new themes, devising new techniques and approaches, constantly renewing his own concepts in the light of the changing world around him. This continual refreshment has enabled him to anticipate, not only new inventions, but new societies. It enabled him to become the first writer to break into the major general magazines of the '40s and '50s with true science fiction, undisguised as something else, and in the '60s—with novels like* Stranger in a Strange Land—*to introduce science fiction to a new audience of many millions, most of them young and many of them with no previous idea of what science may mean to the future of man.*

Robert Heinlein was born in Kansas in 1907, and graduated from the United States Naval Academy in 1929. In 1934, he was retired from the Navy for physical disability; however, in World War II, he served with the Navy in aeronautical engineering. After the War he resumed his writing, and the rest is history—some of it his own Future History, the carefully planned succession of stories that continued to grow and develop even as he was bringing them into being.

Mr. Heinlein has received many awards, including the Grand Master Nebula of the Science Fiction Writers of America. Yet these must inevitably be understatements, our way of recognizing his real reward: his works.

His 43rd novel was published on his recent 80th birthday— the day his 44th novel was started.

The course of every major modern war has been determined largely by someone's failure to foresee the full influence of science and technology on weapons, on other instruments of war, and on the vulnerability of nations and their armed forces. The failure to understand the negative effect of firepower on tactical mobility, and the positive effect of railway and motor transport on strategic mobility, led to the terrible Western Front stalemate of World War I. The failure to understand the menace of the submarine and develop effective countermeasures almost defeated Britain in World War II, and indeed would probably have done so if the German High Command had not failed to appreciate the full potential of the submarine until too late.

The impact of science and technology on the conditions and instruments of war must always be proportionate to the ever-accelerating curves that describe scientific and technological progress. The steeper the curve, the greater the impact. So it is essential to our survival to foresee these mighty changes; and this is especially true where space warfare is concerned, for the militarization of near space (and treaties not withstanding, space is already being militarized) can and will radically alter the value of every factor in the major equations of war. The simple fact of earth's gravity increases our vulnerability to attacks from space vehicles and bases, and correspondingly makes it more difficult and more expensive for land-based vehicles and weapons to counter such attacks.

In this challenging article, G. Harry Stine discusses what is happening, what may happen, and what we ought to do to cope with it.

G. Harry Stine

DEFENDING THE THIRD INDUSTRIAL REVOLUTION

By the year 2015 A.D., space utilization will have progressed to the point where there are many large multipurpose communications/information satellites in geosynchronous orbit, a wide variety of space manufacturing facilities in various earth and lunar orbits, as many as two dozen or more huge solar power satellites beaming power from geosynchronous orbit to both earth and the various space industrial facilities, and several lunar outposts set up to mine lunar materials. This is all part of "the Third Industrial Revolution," the utilization of space for the benefit of people on earth. This Third Industrial Revolution is now the subject of intense study and planning by both government agencies and private enterprise in several countries around the world.

The Third Industrial Revolution is already under way. It began on April 6, 1965 with the launching of "Early Bird," the world's first commercial communications satellite. The 1970s is the decade of the communications satellite; the 1980s promise to usher in the development of space processing—the manufacture in earth orbit of the first of many industrial products that can be made only in the weightlessness of earth orbit. The 1990s should see the first solar power satellites.

Both domestic and international private enterprise is involved. Already the Soviet Union has conducted intensive experimentation in space processing aboard various *Soyuz* and *Soyuz-Salyut* missions. They continue as of this writing.

The Third Industrial Revolution is going to create two

18

areas of concern and interest to military planners in the next thirty to fifty years.

One of these is new technology that will create new problems of defense and military operations. Space industrialization will produce new and less expensive space transportation systems. Space industrialization will produce radically new materials that will have military implications in terms of increased strength, decreased weight, and various other physical properties. Space industrialization will also produce very large energy collectors and transmission devices in space.

The second area of concern involves the fact that the Third Industrial Revolution will create property of value in space—communications satellites, information-handling satellites, manned space laboratories, manned and unmanned space factories, solar power satellites, lunar mining stations and outposts, lunar and orbital catapults or "mass drivers," and other facilities. There will be human activity in space connected with each of these. These facilities will also have commercial value, property value, and even military threat value. Where there exist arenas of human activity and interrelationships and property, there will be disagreements and conflict. We cannot expect these aspects of human nature to change in the next fifty years.

Therefore, as we go into space, we will have to take our highly evolved cultural heritages and societal organizations with us to forestall disagreements and to resolve conflicts. There are the rules, codes, regulations, laws, and treaties that we have individually and collectively agreed to observe. But they are effective only when the majority of people involved agree to abide by them, and when means exist to enforce compliance with them.

These means of enforcement include the military/police organizations. There is a very fine line of distinction between a military organization and a police organization. In some cultures and nations, the distinction cannot be drawn at all. In our Anglo-American culture, the police handle the affairs of internal compliance while the military organization handles the enforcement of transnational agreements including protection of property from seizure or destruction by other nations.

Therefore, the Third Industrial Revolution is not only

going to require military/police protection of space property but will present military organizations with new technology. Both of these involve new military doctrines for use in earth-luna space . . . or cislunar space, that being the portion of space that exists between the Planet Earth and the orbit of its satellite, the Moon.

Protection of space property is very dependent upon the basic military rationales, doctrines, and operational realities of cislunar celestial mechanics. Celestial mechanics involves the way objects move in space with relationship to various gravitational fields. It is no longer a subject for mere academic discussion or scientific utility in aiming space probes. Celestial mechanics becomes the cornerstone of space strategic and tactical doctrines.

There will be military operations in space above and beyond those necessary for protection of space properties.

Historians Will and Ariel Durant have pointed out, "In every century the generals and rulers (with rare exceptions like Ashoka and Augustus) have smiled at the philosophers' timid dislike of war. . . . War is one of the constants of history, and has not diminished with civilization or democracy. In the last 3,421 years of recorded history, only 268 have seen no war."

Anthropologist Dr. Carleton S. Coon has succinctly summarized the prevailing philosophy of the majority of the peoples (and therefore their governments) of the world in what he terms the "Neolithic philosophy: You stay in your village and I will stay in mine. If your sheep eat our grass we will kill you, or we may kill you anyhow to get all the grass for our own sheep. Anyone who tries to change our ways is a witch and we will kill him. Keep out of our village!" This Neolithic philosophy was successful for its time as an attempt to cope with a world where shortages and outright lack of basic survival necessities have been the norm. It created the "Attila Syndrome," a least-effort way of acquiring what one wants and does not have: "Take it by force."

The rational antithesis of the Attila Syndrome has existed only briefly in recent history. It came into being about 250 years ago as a philosophical buttress to the First Industrial Revolution and it was a better least-effort solution: "Make it, don't take it, and everybody has more." This may be termed "The Industrial Syndrome."

Until the Neolithic philosophy of Coon disappears from the human race (if it ever does; it may be an important long-term survival trait), it would be folly to believe that mankind will disarm and settle all disputes by negotiation. The arts of diplomacy and politics are not yet rigorous enough to prevent us from killing each other all of the time . . . just some of the time. It is a very delicate evolving system that requires the lubrication of learned responses and manners. It is very susceptible to sand thrown in the works by charismatic leaders, "men on horseback." Its effectiveness is supported only by the veiled threat of physical force that could or might be brought to bear should diplomacy fail.

Until we manage to eradicate the Neolithic philosophy and its Attila Syndrome from the majority of the human race—if we ever do—there will be military implications to everything we do, like it or not.

This led the late pioneer futurist, Dandridge M. Cole, to formulate in 1960 his famous "Panama Theory" of the military utilization of space. This theory is briefly stated:

"There are strategic areas in space—vital to future scientific, military, and commercial space programs—which could be excluded from our use through occupation and control by unfriendly powers. This statement is based on the assumption that in colonizing space, man (and/or other intelligent beings) will compete for the more desirable areas . . ."

When this is applied to military space operations in the Earth-Moon system, the prime strategic doctrine is that of the "gravity well."

The gravity well is a concept first put forth by Dr. Robert S. Richardson, then of Mount Wilson Observatory, and reported by Arthur C. Clarke in his pioneering 1950 book on space, *Interplanetary Flight*. Because of Earth's gravity field, our planet can be considered as being at the bottom of a tapering well some 4,000 miles deep. Near the bottom of the well, the walls are very steep; as one reaches the top of the "gravity well," the sides become less steep until, at the top of this funnel, we have reached a nearly flat plain which is dimpled by another, smaller, shallower gravity well some 240,000 miles away, the gravity well of the Moon. While this is a simplication, it conveys the concept of the gravity well.

To climb up the gravity well from the planetary surface requires a great deal of energy. Partway up the gravity well, it is possible to maintain the position of an object by making it spin around the surface of the funnel rapidly enough so that centrifugal force neatly balances the gravitational force tending to pull the object back to the planet at the bottom of the funnel. To get away from the Earth, one must project an object such as a space vehicle up the side of the gravitational well at an initial speed of 7 miles per second; it then climbs the walls of the well and, if its direction and speed are just right, crosses the nearly level plain at the top until it falls into the gravity well of the Moon. Or goes on outward into the Solar System, in which case our gravity well model must be expanded to include the very powerful gravity well of the Sun. But since we are considering only the Earth-Moon system herein, the simple model will suffice.

The strategic implications of the gravity well in military space operations require that one be at the top of a gravity well or at least higher up the well than the adversary.

The planet-bound analogy to this is the doctrine of the "high ground." In naval tactics during the age of sail, it was the "wind gauge"; or getting upwind of the enemy.

The salient feature of the gravity-well doctrine is the fact that it provides both an energy advantage and a maneuvering advantage to the person on the high ground. It requires far less energy in the form of propulsion and propellants to operate high on the gravity well, and it is possible to maneuver with relative ease and flexibility at or near the top of it.

A simple analogy indicates the basic military advantage: Put one man at the bottom of a well and the other at the top of a well. Give them both rocks to throw at each other. Which man is going to get hurt? Which man has more time to see his opponent's rocks coming and more opportunity to get out of the way? Which man has the greater opportunity to do something about the oncoming rock?

In Earth-Moon orbital space, the person having a base of maneuvering on top of a deep gravity well or in a more shallow gravity well than his opponent has a definite military advantage in terms of surveillance capability, energy required to affect a strike, maneuvering room, and the ability to activate countermeasures in reasonable time.

The logical consequence of the gravity-well doctrine leads inevitably to the most important military fact of the late 20th century and the early 21st century: with improvements in space transportation available and with the technology in hand to maintain long-term military positions in space, the control of the Moon means control of the Earth. In a like manner, according to this doctrine, *control of the L4 and L5 libration points in the lunar orbit means control of the Earth-Moon system*.

Control implies that one is able to regulate the flow of spacegoing commerce and other traffic, to protect one's own facilities in space, to deny the use of other critical military *and/or* commercial orbital areas to others, to launch strikes against *any* target on the surface of the Earth *or* the Moon or in any orbit in the Earth-Moon system, or to detect any oncoming threat and take counteraction in time.

The gravity-well doctrine dictates the general considerations for space weapons systems that would be most effective. However, one must first take a careful look at the basic concept of a weapon.

A weapon can be broadly defined as a means of imposing one's will upon another. Thus, a weapon need not have a physical reality; the threat of the use of a weapon is itself a weapon—if the opponent believes the said weapon exists and will be used.

Heinlein defines a weapon as a machine for the manipulation of energy. But it has a broader definition than that. The following categorization of weapons may be useful in determining those that would be most useful in various operational zones of the Earth-Moon system and may also provide a key to the discovery of new and heretofore unsuspected space weapons that could be developed and used with the technology of the Third Industrial Revolution.

Mass manipulators: Produce damage through the use of the basic inertial characteristics of mass and the conversion of energy of position (potential energy) to energy of motion (kinetic energy): mass projectors, penetrators, detectors, and decoys.

Energy manipulators: Produce damage through the application of high energy density or the sudden release of large amounts of energy: projectors, concentrators, releasers, screens, and detectors.

Biological manipulators: Produce damage to organic lifeforms or other chemical agents: gases, poisons, disease vectors, etc.

Psychological manipulators: Produce alteration of the mental state of the enemy in a desirable fashion that reduces the will or capability to resist: propaganda, counterintelligence, brainwashing, covert manipulation of the information media, mood-altering drugs, consciousness-altering drugs, mind-altering drugs.

Some weapons are a combination of one or more of these basic types, and some require a vehicle to transport them to the point of use or application.

Use of these weapons in accordance with the strategic doctrine of the gravity well requires in turn that we consider the Earth-Moon system to consist of a series of definite military operational areas. These are basically zones within the gravity well or, for a better mental view, a series of concentric spheres with the Earth at the center. These are not so much well-defined spheres with distinct boundaries, but rather zones of operation that fade into one another. In a sense, they resemble the energy levels of electrons around an atomic nucleus. Briefly, these zones may be defined as:

Near Earth Orbit (NEO) extending from an arbitrary level of 50 kilometers above the Earth's surface to approximately 200 kilometers—well below the lower limits of the Van Allen radiation belts.

Cislunar Space (CLS) extending from about 200 kilometers above the Earth's surface to the geosynchronous orbital altitude of about 39,000 kilometers.

Lunar Surface/Orbit (LSO) extending from geosynchronous orbit to the lunar orbit about the Earth and including the *Near Lunar Orbits* with an arbitrary altitude of about 100 kilometers from the lunar surface.

Translunar Space (TLS) extending from the lunar orbit out to an arbitrary distance of approximately one million kilometers from the surface of the Earth at which distance an object can be considered to be in orbit around the Sun due to the much greater influence of the solar gravity field at that distance.

Each operational area has unique military considerations that affect tactical doctrine, tactical operations, and weapons systems within each area.

Near Earth Orbit is a valuable military operational area for earth-launched, earth-oriented activities, and of course is already being used as such; it is an area that is easily reached from the Earth's surface by spacecraft capable of attaining velocities of about 25,000 feet per second. So far during this decade, at least six nations have begun conducting reconaissance and surveillance operations there— and at least two nations possess the capability of operating manned spacecraft in the area. In the years to come, NEO could be used for quick-look and high-detail surveillance, satellite hunter-killer operations, a staging area for manned surface-to-surface troop strike transports, and "quick dip" hypersonic skimming into the upper atmosphere for surveillance, reconaissance, or offensive purposes. Thus, NEO is basically a tactical scouting area for Earth-centered operations and a maneuvering area for surface-to-surface operations. It is also the area through which surface-to-surface ICBMs must travel during the ballistic portion of their flight and therefore the area in which they are most vulnerable to intercept by orbital-launched interceptors or orbital beam weapons. Although NEO is reasonably far up on the sides of the gravity-well funnel in terms of the energy requirements needed to reach the area from the Earth's surface, current technology permits the deployment of rapid-ascent satellite interceptors. Thus NEO is an area where it is difficult to respond to threat: a nearness to counterweapons on the surface or in orbit, and large energy expenditures are required for maneuver in the area. The possibility of basing a large manned military space station in NEO should be dismissed; it would be a very large target in a predictable trajectory and would be destroyed in the opening moments of any war in which its presence could be a factor.

Cislunar space, however is a more valuable zone of maneuver and reconnaissance. Not only is less energy required for maneuver but geosynchronous orbit lies in CLS, making it a prime location for surveillance, navigational, communications, data transfer, meteorological, and energy satellites. Geosynchronous orbit is already crowded. As of mid-1977, there were more than a hundred unmanned satellites located in geosynchronous orbit. Because of orbital crowding and the possibility of frequency interference caused by beam overlapping, these numerous small satellites will be replaced in the late 1980s and the 1990s with large, multipurpose platforms which will be militarily vulnerable.

However, facilities in CLS are more secure from Earth-launched offensive operations because of the time required for vehicles to climb the gravity well. Various location and detection systems sited in NEO and CLS may be used to identify any potential threat with sufficient early-warning time to permit initiation of counteractivities.

The primary consideration of CLS from the military point of view is the strategic importance of the trojan libration points in the lunar orbit. More of this later.

Lunar surface/orbit has quite different military characteristics. Because of the mass of Luna, it is a prime location for a military base on or probably beneath its surface. It is the prime location for one of the most important space-weapons systems we can now foresee, a weapon system that is basically very old. This device is the catapult, usually referred to in current terminology as a "mass driver." Whatever term is used to identify it, it is a rockthrower. The Moon is the best site in the Earth-Moon system for such a device because the mass of the Moon provides ample ammunition for the mass driver as well as a very large and stable base to improve its accuracy. Launching very large masses at speeds of a mile per second or more produces some massive reaction forces which would misalign or reorient any mass driver located on its own in orbital space.

The lunar mass driver is a critical system requirement for the overall industrialization of the Earth-Moon system. Although an Earth-based mass driver is a potential commercial cargo transportation system for terrestrial materials launched into space, the energy requirements are very large because of the Earth's atmosphere and the very deep gravity well; the lunar mass driver is the most economical cargo transportation device now envisioned for providing materials for space industrialization, including the materials to construct large space structures. It will undoubtedly be built in several locations on the lunar surface for providing lunar materials for deep space operations in the Earth-Moon system. However, it has a military utility that cannot and must not be overlooked.

A large lunar mass driver capable of hurling masses of up to one ton can be converted into an earth bombardment system. It is a non-nuclear weapon and not subject to existing UN treaties! The results of the sudden dissipation of large amounts of kinetic energy should not be lightly dismissed. The Barringer Meteor Crater in Arizona was created by the impact of an estimated 80-foot in diameter nickel-iron meteorite; the impact was roughly equivalent to the detonation of 2,500,000 tons of TNT—read that as a 2.5 megaton bomb.

Small lunar mass drivers can be used as weapons systems against space facilities. Such small mass drivers can be considered as space Gatling guns. Such a small mass driver is envisioned as throwing a mass of a couple of kilograms, but throwing such small masses in very rapid succession. The impact of a one-kilogram mass travelling at several miles per second can do considerable damage to a space facility—such as when several hundred or thousand such masses impact a solar power satellite, the iridescent solar panels of a reconnaissance satellite, or the pressure hull of a manned space station.

No explosives are required for such space weapons; the conversion of kinetic energy to heat is quite sufficient.

The military capabilities of mass drivers built and used for commercial purposes are such that they will require protection against seizure or destruction, wherever they are built and operated.

The area of military operations beyond the lunar orbit that we have tagged "Translunar Space" is a zone of maneuver and rendezvous for military space vehicles with very large propulsion and maneuvering capabilities. There is a location in this area, however, that could be used as a military staging point. Beyond the Moon's orbit along the Earth-Moon line lies a zone in space where the gravity fields of both the Earth and the Moon balance one another; this is known as the L2 lunar libration point. Anything placed at the L2 point will stay there, hidden from view of anyone on the surface of the Earth or on the earthside of the Moon.

There are two other locations in the Earth-Moon system that are of the utmost military importance. These are the so-called "trojan" lunar libration points. They are the result of a special and unique solution to the classical "three-body" problem in celestial mechanics. There is a zone in the Moon's orbit 60 degrees behind or following the Moon in the orbit and 60 degrees ahead of the Moon; these are stable points where the gravity field of the Earth and the Moon are balanced or equaled out. An object placed in either of these two libration points—labeled L4 and L5 for convenience—will stay there. L4 and L5 are the two most stable of the libration points in the Earth-Moon system.

The importance of the L4 and L5 libration points from a military viewpoint is the fact that neither has a gravity well and both sit at the top of the gravity wells of both the Earth and the Moon. From the L4/L5 points, one can control the gravity wells of the entire Earth-Moon system.

These libration points have no gravity wells. A zero-gravity well means the greatest capability for maneuver with the minimum amount of energy and denies the use of a gravity well to an adversary for his purposes.

At L4/L5, one sits on top of the hill, so to speak. These points are the most difficult places to reach in the Earth-Moon system from the energy expenditure point of view. They are therefore the best places to site any military bases because they are defensible. They are the best locations for small mass drivers and high-energy beam weapons.

L4/L5 are proposed as the locations of large future space settlements by O'Neill and the L5 Society. Nowhere in the extensive literature about this proposal is there to be found any discussion of the military implications of these L4/L5 sites. If the military implications were considered, they were either dismissed as unimportant or simply ignored for philosophical/ideological reasons.

There is no guarantee that any space settlements at the L4/L5 locations—or on the Moon either, for that matter—will remain peaceful industrial or commercial activities. Writers such as Heinlein and Bova have already speculated on scenarios involving revolutions and seizures of such space settlements. There are any number of grievances that can and have triggered military uprisings. There are any number of reasons or lessons from history wherein an industrious, hard-working group of close-knit people have taken a sharp turn in their external affairs to become a military threat.

And there are any number of scenarios that can be developed around the seizure and takeover of a large L4/L5 space settlement for military reasons. Three reasons might include control of the settlement's product of value— energy or materials—or straightaway military control of the facility to exert military pressure on nations on Earth.

There are therefore two roles for military space operations involving the space settlements at L4/L5: (a) military protective force or presence, similar to that of the U.S. Army in the American West following the Civil War, for the purpose of protecting the settlements against takeover or prevention of the use of military force by the inhabitants of the settlements, or (b) straightforward use of part of the L4/L5 space settlements as an admitted military base of operations for control of the Earth-Moon system.

This last will be argued vehemently. However, are we very certain that the space settlements under consideration will be built or even occupied forever by the sort of hard-working, industrious, peace-loving Anglo-American types now envisaged as populating these settlements by advocates?

One must point out that there are social characteristics of many basically militant Oriental cultures that would make their people optimum space settlers; characteristics such as the ability to live in high-density quarters with little or no privacy, subjugation of the individual to the group, highly structured manners and other interpersonal interfaces, and unquestioning willingness of the individual to follow the directives of authority figures. The military in these cultures now lies barely beneath the surface of the culture, hidden from recent conquerors in some cases.

How will this situation be handled? The author can only point to the problem. It will take the best minds and the most careful diplomacy of the next fifty to one hundred years to begin to find workable solutions to the basic problem.

The L4/L5 points may be declared demilitarized international zones; this may work for a time, but from a historic point of view, treaties are rarely inviolate for as long as fifty years and practically never in force a century after their signing.

By international agreement, a balance-of-power situation may be established with adversaries controlling the two lunar libration points in a carryover into space of the current USA-USSR balance of strategic power.

We may also find that the Third Industrial Revolution takes into space many of the current industrial security activities that surround most business operations in a quiet, unobtrusive, but highly effective manner. The military may indeed be present in space as they already are. There may also be another type of organization in space connected with space industrialization: a police force, the security guard, and company cops.

It is often easier to get into a secure military base than it is to gain access to a factory. Industrial security is much more stringent than military security; this is a statement of observed fact.

We may find that firms involved in space industrialization would rather hire mercenaries than depend upon military protection from a government. Firms such as Brinks, Wells Fargo, Purolator, and other private security organizations may end up in space along with many of the industrial firms they presently protect.

Each advance of humanity into new and different environments has created new types of social organizations to handle the new problems presented by the advance. Our expansion into space in the Third Industrial Revolution is no exception. We are beginning to see the development of new types of social organization to handle the knotty problems of raising large amounts of capital to finance high-risk, long-term projects such as solar power satellites. The Third Industrial Revolution presents other difficult problems, as we have seen. We must therefore anticipate the development of new types of military organizations that might evolve to handle the very difficult problems arising from the military implications of our expansion into space.

We cannot ignore the reality of the military implications of space any more than we can ignore the reality of our home-town lives by disbanding the town police force. We can attempt to build a universe of law where matters of human conflict can be solved by judgment, arbitration or negotiation. But this universe of law must be backed up by the means to enforce the rules through application of physical coercion. This will always be the case as long as the Attila Syndrome exists in the human race . . . and that may be for a very long time to come if we meet, Out There, another species that is as mean, as nasty, and as highly competitive as we are.

But that is another story.

BIBLIOGRAPHY

Bova, Ben. *Colony*. New York: Simon & Schuster, 1978.

Clarke, Arthur C. *Interplanetary Flight*. New York: Harper & Bros., 1950.

Cole, Dandridge M. "Strategic Areas in Space-The Panama Theory." Los Angeles: Institute of Aerospace Sciences, March 15, 1962.

Coon, Carleton. S *The Story of Man*. New York: Alfred A. Knopf, Inc., 1962.

Durant, Will and Ariel. *The Lessons of History*. New York: Simon & Schuster, 1968.

Heinlein, Robert A. *The Moon Is A Harsh Mistress*. New York: G.P. Putnam's Sons, 1966.

Levitt, I. M. and Cole, Dandridge M. *Exploring The Secrets of Space*. Englewood Cliffs, New Jersey: Prentice-Hall, 1963.

Stine, G. Harry. *The Third Industrial Revolution*. New York: G. P. Putnam's Sons, 1975. Revised Edition, New. York: Ace Books, 1979.

G. Harry Stine is a science-fact and science-fiction writer. He is also an engineer, a high-technology marketing consultant, and one of the founders of the concept of space industrialization. He received his B.A. in physics from Colorado College in 1952 and immediately went to work on rockets at White Sands Proving Ground. He was one of the first futurists, working for an aerospace company on future space programs as early as 1957 before the launch of Sputnik-I; and on the Tenth Anniversary of the launching of Explorer-I, the first U.S. satellite, he was awarded a silver medal as one of fifty American space pioneers by the Association of the United States Army.

Because of his early association with this nation's military rocket programs, he has written about the military implications of space for nearly a quarter of a century. He is a Fellow of the Explorers Club and the British Interplanetary Society, an Associate Fellow of the American Institute of Aeronautics and Astronautics, and a member of the New York Academy of Sciences. He has published more than twenty books on science and technology, including three sf novels. His science fiction has appeared under the pen name of "Lee Correy," and he is presently writing a series of four robot war novels.

And what may happen if and when the Third Industrial Revolution becomes a fact? When colonies have been established in near space? When old Earth, in one way or another, becomes dependent on them, and they in turn cease to depend totally on Earth? What may happen if, under these conditions, men remain unchanged by space?

In this story, Gregory Benford presents one answer— one which wars on Earth have made only too familiar.

Gregory Benford

OLD WOMAN BY THE ROAD

An old woman in a formless, wrinkled dress and worn shoes sat at the side of the road. A soft wind sighed through the pines crowding the white strip of road, and I was panting from the fast pace I was keeping. The old woman was sitting there, silent and unmoving. I nearly walked by before I saw her.

"You're resting?" I said.

"Waiting." Her voice was dry, and when she breathed out, there was a sound in her throat like rustling leaves. She was sitting on a brown cardboard suitcase with copper latches. It was cracked along the side, and white cloth stuck out.

"For the bus?"

"For Buck."

"The copter said the bus will stop up around the bend," I said. "On the main road."

"I know."

"It won't come down this side road."

I was late myself and I figured she had picked the wrong spot to wait.

"Buck will be along." Her voice was high and had the back-country twang in it. My own voice had some of the

33

same sound, but I was keeping my vowels flat and right now her accent reminded me of how far I had come.

I looked down the long curve of the sandy road. A pickup truck growled out of a side road and into the deep ruts of white sand. People were riding in the back along with some boxes and trunks and a 3D. They were taking everything valuable they could, but the Outskirters hadn't given us much time.

"Who's Buck?"

"My dog." She looked at me directly, as though it was obvious who Buck was.

"Look, the bus—"

"You're the Bishop boy, aren't you?"

I looked off up the road again. That set of words *the Bishop boy* was like a grain of sand caught between my back teeth. My mother's friends had used that phrase when they came over for an evening of bridge, before I went away to the university. There never seemed to be any way to avoid admitting it and then putting myself in a little slot in other people's heads. There hadn't been any way then and there wasn't one now. I said, "Yes, I am." The words came out precisely.

"Thought so."

"You're—?"

"Elizabeth McKenzie."

"Ah."

We had done the ritual so now we could talk.

"I knew your grandmother real well."

"Mrs. McKenzie—"

"I strictly believe I saw you once, long time ago. Out at one of your grandmother's fish fries. You and some little boys were playing with the nets down by the water. My husband went to shoo you away from the boats. I was cleaning flounders, and your grandfather was tending the fire. It was down at Point Clear."

"I think I remember that. Mrs. McKenzie, there's not long before the last bus."

"I'm waiting for Buck."

"Where is he?"

"He ran off in the woods."

I worked my backpack straps around on my shoulders. They creaked in the quiet.

There wasn't a lot of time left. Pretty soon now it would start. One of the big reflecting mirrors up in synchronous Outskirter orbit would focus its light on a rechargable tube of gas. The gas would cycle through its molecular phases and be excited by the incident light. Then the lasing process would begin in the long tube, excited molecules cascading down together from one preferentially occupied quantum state to another lower state, the traveling wave jarring more photons loose as it swept down the tube. The photons would add in phase, summing in an intense wave, growing in amplitude. The beam that came out of the hundred-meter-long tube would slice down through the atmosphere and through the cloud cover above us. And instead of striking an array of layered solid-state collectors outside Mobile, the beam would cut a swath twenty meters wide through the trees and fields around us.

"The bus is coming," I said.

She looked at me.

"I'll carry that suitcase for you."

"I can manage it." She squinted off into the distance, and I saw she was tired, tired beyond knowing it.

"I'll go along with you, Mrs. McKenzie."

"I'm not going until Buck comes on back."

"The bus . . . *Leave* that dog, Mrs. McKenzie."

"I don't need that blessed bus."

"Why not?"

"My children drove off to Mobile a few hours back with their families. They said they'd be coming to pick me up."

"My insteted radio"—I gestured at my temple—"says the roads to Mobile are jammed up. You can't count on them getting back."

She moved her thin legs on the suitcase. "My children left early."

"Well—"

"They're dropping off a lot of the things they had from that new house of theirs. Then they'll come back and get me. They said so."

"How'll they know where you are?"

"I tole 'em I'd try to walk to the main road. Got tired, is all." She blinked at the sun. "They'll know I'm back in here."

"Just the same, the deadline—"

"I'm all right, don't you mind. They're good children, grateful for all I've gone and done for them."

"I think it's better if you get on the bus, Mrs. McKenzie."

"I'm not going without Buck. Buck has been with me since he was a . . ." She didn't finish, and I looked around at the pine woods, blinking back sweat. In among the pines were some oak, their roots bulging up out of the sandy soil and knotted. There were a lot of places for a dog to be. The land around here was flat and barely above sea level. I had come down to Baldwin County to camp and rest. I'd been here five days, taking skiffs down the Fish River, looking for the places I'd been when I was a boy and my grandmother had rented boats on the river and lived in an old rambling fisherman's house. The big mysterious island I remembered and called Treasure Island, smack in the middle of Fish River, was now a soggy stand of trees in a bog. The steady currents had swept it away. There was thick mud there now, and the black water tasted like a weak leaf tea. But it was all fine, the inlets and the deep river currents that pulled on the skiff. I'd been camping down on the point where the Fish River snaked around before running down in a straight line into the bay. The helicopter that came over in the morning blaring out the alert woke me up. The Outskirters had given four hours' warning, the recording said. This forty-klick square in southern Alabama, and two others in Asia, had been picked out at random for a reprisal. The big cylinder communities circling Earth would use their laser systems, designed for power transfer from orbit, to slash and burn. The carving would go on until Earth granted the cylinder worlds real independence. But there was no real balance of power there. Once the Outskirters had a free hand, they could hold the leash on Earth. They had the economic and now the military power. And maybe that wasn't so bad; they were the best people Earth could produce.

I had been thinking about that a lot while I was down on the point. It was hard to figure which side you should be on. There were fine people up in orbit, and they were a lot like me. A lot more than the people in Baldwin County, anyway, even though I'd grown up here. I'd worked on laser tech systems for a while now, and I knew the real future was up in orbit. The Outskirters were smart, and they knew when to act.

"Where's Buck?" I said decisively.

"He . . . that way." A weak wave of the hand.

I wrestled my backpack into the shoulder of the road where the creeper grass took hold. A car wheezed its way out of a rutted side road. Pale, crowded faces with big eyes looked out at us. Then the driver hit the hydrogen and they got out of there.

I went into the short pines near the road. Sand flies jumped where my boots struck. The white sand made that soft *skree* sound as my boots skated over it. I remembered how I'd first heard that sound down here as a kid, wearing tennis shoes, and how I'd finally figured out what caused it.

"Buck!"

There was a flash of brown over to the left, and I went after it. I ran through a thick stand of pine, and the dog yelped and took off, dodging under a blackleaf bush. I called it again. The dog didn't even slow down. I skirted to the left. He went into some oak scrub and I could hear him getting tangled in it and then getting free and out the other side. By that time he was fifty meters away and moving fast.

When I got back to the old woman, she didn't seem to notice me. "I can't catch Buck, Mrs. McKenzie."

"Knew you wouldn't." She grinned at me—a grin with real mirth in it. "Buck is a fast one."

"Call him."

She smiled vacantly and raised her hands to her mouth. "Buck! Here, boy!"

The low pine trees swallowed the sound.

"Must of run off."

"Now Mrs.—"

"You scared him. He doesn't come when there are some around he don't know."

"There isn't time to wait for him."

"I'm not leaving without ole Buck. Times I was alone down on the river at the old McAllister place and the water would come up under the house. Buck was the only company I had. Only soul I saw for five weeks in that big blow we had."

A low whine. "I think that's the bus."

She cocked her head. "I hear something all right."

"Come on. I'll carry your suitcase."

She curled her lip up and crossed her arms. "My children will be by for me. I told them to look for me along in here."

"Your children might not make it back in time."

"They're loyal children."

"Mrs. McKenzie, I can't wait for you to be reasonable." I picked up my backpack and brushed off some red ants crawling on the straps. "You walked this far from the McAllister place?" I swung the pack onto one arm and then the other.

"I did."

The old McAllister place was a good five klicks away. So she had gotten exhausted and sat down here to rest.

"You Bishops was always the reasonable ones." She narrowed her eyes. There were a lot of memories in her face.

"That's why I want you to go now."

"Your grandma was always talking about you." She glanced skyward. "You been up there, hadn't you?"

"Yes. Yes, I have."

"An' you're goin' back. You were down here on vacation." I looked down the road, deserted now.

"It's your people, up there."

"The wrong group seems to be in control."

"Same people as always." She sniffed.

"Mrs. McKenzie, there's the bus." The turbo made its high whirr as it wheeled off the blacktop highway around the bend. "It's the last one."

"You go along." She sat back heavily on the suitcase. I reached out to take her arm and her face changed. "Don't touch me, boy."

I saw that she wouldn't let me coax or force her down that last bend. She had gone as far as she was going to, and the world would have to come the rest of the distance itself.

Up ahead, the bus driver was probably behind schedule for this last pickup. He was going to be irritated and more than a little scared. The Outskirters would come in right on time, he knew that.

I ran. The sand gave way under me. I saw I was more

tired than I thought by the running and walking I had done to get here. I plowed through the deep ruts. The whole damned planet was dragging at my feet, holding me down. I went about two hundred meters along the bend, nearly within view of the bus, when I heard it start up with a rumble. I ran faster and tasted sweat. The driver raced the engine, in a hurry. He had to come toward me as he swung out onto Route 80 on the way back to Mobile. Maybe I could make it to the highway in time for him to see me and slow down.

I knew everything depended now on how fast I could move, so I put my head down and ran. Ran.

But there was the old woman back there. To get her the driver would have to take the bus down that rutted road in the sand and risk getting stuck. All that to get the old woman with the grateful children. She didn't seem to understand that there were ungrateful children in the skies now; she didn't seem to understand much of what was going on, and suddenly I wasn't so sure I did either.

Gregory Benford is Associate Professor of Physics at the University of California, Irvine. He received his Ph.D. in theoretical physics from the University of California, San Diego, in 1967. He has published over forty scientific papers and has been a Woodrow Wilson Fellow. He was a Visiting Fellow at Cambridge University, England, in 1976. His research interests include solid state physics, plasma physics, and high energy astrophysics. His astronomical research centers on the dynamics of pulsars, violent extragalactic events, and quasars. He has also published numerous articles in Natural History, Smithsonian, New Scientist *and other major periodicals.*

Gregory Benford's fiction includes several dozen short stories and three novels; Jupiter Project *(1975)* If the Stars Are Gods *(1977), and* In the Ocean of Night *(1977). In 1975, he received the Nebula Award of the Science Fiction Writers of America for short fiction. He lives in Laguna Beach, California.*

Or perhaps . . .

Robert Frazier

ENCASED IN THE AMBER OF ETERNITY

From the vantage of my cabin porch,
I see the flames as waves lap along the coast,
and the Torchships fall like comets,
dancing a St. Vitus dance;
fireflies hovering over the pyre of Portland.
Every major city on the continent has crumbled,
sticks of charcoal and lumps of eraser gum.
Power plants are melted into slag,
paint squeezed from the tube.
Telephone poles stand uselessly in bunches,
brushes shorn of their bristles.
The art of devastation is as subtle as the Florentine
    flood.
In the countryside the vineyards of the living go
    on,
but the wine is flat.
Blank televisions stare back at the blank faces,
a poetry of truly blank verse.
Yet here in my mountain retreat only time has
    changed,
crystallized into honey,
as I stock up for a long winter.
Its length stretches out before me
like the glow of an eternal sunset
spread out over the dark silhouettes of Oregon
    pine.
The snows are coming;
white pages of a new history
falling upon itself.

Robert Frazier has been involved in many aspects of poetry in the science fiction field—an area which offers unlimited challenges to the poetic imagination, and one in which too little has as yet been done. He has been an editor, a member of an awards committee (CAS Award), and has read papers on science fiction poetry at conferences and conventions. And of course he writes it.

His latest sale (prior to this one) was to Jerry Pournelle for his anthology Endless Frontier. He has had two poetry collections in 1987, Perception Barriers and Co-orbital Moons, and his recent fiction sales include Twilight Zone, Amazing Stories, Isaac Asimov's S.F. Magazine, and In The Field of Fire anthology by Jack and Jeanne Dann.

On Earth, we have had brutal wars of extermination, wars fought ruthlessly and efficiently for territory or dominance, wars waged largely as a sport, and wars for very limited objectives fought with deliberate restraint by military professionals.

Which of these will we fight in orbit—among the asteroids, or on the Moon?

Tom Purdom

MOON ROCKS

The rocks have been lying on the Moon for two and a half billion years. Twenty-five million centuries before Joseph Davino was born, a small asteroid scraped the lower slopes of the lunar Apennines and smashed into the southern edge of Mare Imbrium. Rocks and boulders flew across the surface of the Moon and sat there in perfect, undisturbed silence until a machine rolled across the dusty landscape and flashed a message at its controllers on Earth. Rocks of high-grade gold ore are lying on the surface of Mare Imbrium near the border of the region dominated by the European Economic Community. There are no tracks within five kilometers of the site. No one in the EEC knows the ore is there.

"You'll be inside their radar range a hundred kilometers before you reach the site," Colonel LeFarge says. "You'll have to pick your way through the foothills until you're almost on top of it. You'll have a double supply of consumables, and I'll have Wild Bill take a supply caravan out and pick you up at Base Six. I thought about sending out a diversion but I decided you'd have a better chance if we set things up so you could take your time in the foothills."

Major Joseph Davino is a pleasant, cosmopolitan man who still feels warm and nostalgic when he thinks about

42

the books about space travel he read when he was a child—books in which it was generally agreed that no one would ever fight wars over gold mines on other planets. His three-year tour of duty will be up in four months, and he already knows Washington is planning to follow the normal program and replace him with a new volunteer. His work on the Moon has been competent but undistinguished, and he has one black mark on his record: he let an enemy combat team slip past a perimeter he was guarding and they managed to pick up six hundred pounds of unrefined gold ore and cripple a million dollars' worth of high-grade equipment. Colonel LeFarge is handing him a difficult, nerve-wracking job but they both know the colonel is giving him a break, too. The automated exploration vehicle has stumbled on a strike that looks like it may be one of the biggest finds in the history of lunar exploration. If he can sneak into the EEC's turf and snatch it away from them under their noses, the computer jockeys in the Pentagon will probably listen to the colonel's recommendation and give him the only reward he wants—three more years in which he will be two hundred and forty thousand miles away from dirty skies, dirty wars, short rations, and all the violence, frustration, and despair that seethe across the beautiful globe hanging above the lunar landscape.

Major Joseph Davino executed his mission with superlative skill and an outstanding exhibition of the qualities that make an officer suitable for combat on the lunar surface. His intelligence and his careful attention to detail demonstrate that he is the kind of tested officer we need in our forces on the Moon. It is recommended that his request for a second tour of duty be approved . . .

Major Davino hates planes, guns, and all the nit-picking restrictions of military life. He spent ten years in the Air Force after he graduated from college, however, and he transferred to automated ground vehicles and spent two years in a grueling training school when it became obvious the United States didn't need any more jet pilots on the Moon. Every year he spends on the Moon is one more year he doesn't have to spend on Earth. If he can win another tour of duty on the Moon, he may even be able to stay on the Moon until he retires.

There is also a woman—a doctor who has a permanent berth on the Moon because she is a leading expert on lunar physiology. She won't go back to Earth with him if he has to go, and Major Davino doesn't blame her.

Three days after leaving his home base, Major Davino is still creeping across the surface of the Moon. Four fully armed robot vehicles are spread out around his command vehicle in a large semicircle. Four screens are lit up on his control panel. Each robot vehicle has to be maneuvered through the foothills as carefully as he is maneuvering the command vehicle.

The foothills are a jumbled mass of rocks, craters, and low hills. The terrain can hide him from the EEC radar if he is careful, but the Europs will know he is coming as soon as he lets them pick up one blip on the screen mounted on the slope of Mount Ampere. Anything that moves stands out on the lunar landscape like a ship on an empty ocean. Robot scouts will start forming a circle around the place where the radar picked up the blip. The nearest European combat team will start moving into position. Electronic detectors will start hunting for tracks that contain recent traces of exhaust fumes and vented CO_2.

The robot vehicle on his left passes behind a rock. The screens blank. The muscles in his back and legs tense.

The vehicle on his left is Gun Buggy Three. It is about five hundred meters away and it is the only gun buggy he can see. All the signals traveling between him and his squadron have to be relayed through Three. His vehicles are all traveling on automatic until Three creeps past the rock and resumes contact.

A well-placed enemy observer would know he is now out of contact with his squadron. He has fought six hundred missions in the computer simulator and he has usually picked a moment like this when he has been the ambusher. His emotions responded with a rush of pleasure every time he hit the main link in his opponent's commo chain during a temporary blackout. His simulated gun buggies swept in before his opponent could reestablish the chain and the simulated enemy squadron was destroyed in five minutes.

He is not afraid he will die. No one has ever died in a

battle on the Moon. The struggle on the Moon is a limited, courtly warfare in which men withdraw or surrender
when they are outmaneuvered. Someone may die by acci-
dent sooner or later, but death is not his major worry.

The screens clear. He taps the halt button and the
screens freeze while he studies the landscape. Four will
have to move thirty meters to the right and peer around
that medium-size crater on his left. Three will have to
drop back twenty meters and hold position so it can maintain the commo chain. Two and One—

He taps out his orders on the computer keyboard
mounted on the left side of his control panel. The computers on the gun buggies verify the orders with the computer in the command vehicle and five green lights flash
on the control panel. He presses the start button, and the
whole squadron creeps forward.

He has been moving through the foothills like this for
two Earth days. The whole squadron stops every hundred
meters, and he plans the next move for all five vehicles.

The four screens blank again. He turns his head and
searches the landscape for Three. There was nothing between him and Three when he set the course. Two of the
buggies will lose contact in about seventy-five seconds,
but Three is supposed to stay in contact until he reaches
the next halt point.

The screens light up again. Three rises out of the ground.
It had slipped into a depression he didn't see. It blanked
out before its computer could react to the new situation
and raise its antenna.

The other two buggies lose contact right on schedule. Their
screens come on again thirty seconds later, and he stops at
another halt point. He pulls a plastic bottle out of a compartment and rolls two tiny drops of liquid down his tongue.

Warm, pleasant sensations spread through his body. His
brain is still functioning, but every important muscle in his
body is relaxing for forty-five seconds. He is a muscle
cramper when he gets tense. Three sips on the bottle
during his working day can fight off fatigue better than any
energizing drug on the market.

He is only eighteen kilometers from his ultimate destination. If he can keep on moving without stopping to rest,
he will be there in about eight hours.

He puts the bottle back in its compartment and studies the screens. Orders go out to the gun buggies. They move forward thirty meters, and the screens blank once again.

His hands tighten on the steering wheel. He searches the terrain on his left and sees a thin cloud of dust moving across the area between two small craters. Three has rolled into another shallow depression before its computer can raise its antenna. The sun is approaching its maximum altitude above the horizon and he is having trouble seeing the smaller variations in the surface.

Three's black and white framework rises out of the depression. Two screens light up on the console. The other two screens are still blank.

The halt order leaps out again. His fingers tap out more orders. Gun Buggy Four rolls away from its position and starts creeping along the bottom of the big, rolling hill directly in front of him.

The two blanked-out screens belong to the two buggies spread out on his right. Gun Buggy One is supposed to send its signals to Two, and Two is supposed to relay its signals through Three. Two is the buggy the Europs will probably hit first if they're ambushing him. Knock out Two and One will be isolated. The first shot in the battle will leave him with two working gun buggies in contact with the command vehicle.

His eyes dart across the screens and the landscape outside his windows. Electronic probes leap out from every vehicle. He moves Three closer to the command vehicle and guards his left flank.

Four rolls its front end around a boulder at the bottom of the big hill. Its camera pans across low rises and small, shallow craters.

There is no danger he is going to die. The bottle in the compartment is looming in his mind as if it is as big as Mount Bradley, but there is no danger he is going to die. The stakes are high, but the Europs know they will be exposed to retaliation if they actually kill someone.

The stakes are high, but they are not decisive. One hundred overpopulated, technologically advanced nations are jockeying for position in the world economy, and bigger gold reserves can give a country a stronger currency and a temporary, marginal advantage over its competitors. You cannot eat gold and you cannot use it to power your machines—but you can use it to back up your currency and make the other guy give you a little more of his goods for a little less of yours.

You don't even have to transport the gold back to Earth. It costs only seven dollars and fifty cents to ship one pound of payload back to Earth, but the gold can be buried in a base on the Moon and be just as useful as gold buried in Fort Knox. Five other major powers have bases on the Moon, and the gold can be transferred from base to base if actual transfers of real metal are deemed necessary. Two of the smaller countries on the Moon have even discovered they can back up their currency with unmined gold and save themselves all the trouble of actually digging the stuff up and turning it into neat, shiny bars.

A red and yellow flare rises above the horizon on his right and arcs across the black sky. Gun Buggy One has been attacked. It kept moving forward after the commo link was cut, and it is reacting according to its automatic program. Its sensors have picked up enemy machines, and it has verified that the machines are operating like hostile gun buggies and not automated scouts.

Davino's fingers dance across his console before his emotions can react. Six hundred engagements in the simulator take command of his reflexes. Gun Buggy Four changes course and takes up a position between the hill in front of him and a low crater on his right. Three moves left two hundred meters and trains its camera on the left side of the hill.

They have eliminated two of his gun buggies, but they still don't know where he's going. He can still slip by them if he can knock out the other guy's gun buggies when they close in. No country on the Moon has more than a dozen combat groups. They will try to trail him, but there is still a good chance he can slip through their net and reach the site.

He will have accomplished something even if he just destroys their equipment and returns to his base. He has lost fifty percent of his equipment, but the colonel will still give him a good report if he destroys more of theirs. Two

other comb.. ...ms are waiting in reserve. Somebody else
may slip through their net if he weakens it.

A red alarm light flashes on the control panel. A fuzzy,
brownish shape rolls across Three's screen. Three's gun
turret swings toward it, and it disappears behind a crater
before the radar sight can lock on.

Two more flares rise on Davino's right. Gun Buggy One
is still evading its assailants and trying to reestablish contact with the command vehicle. Its automatic program is
advising him it is definitely being attacked by two enemy
gun buggies.

Davino repositions Three's gun. A little pulse of hope
slips through the lid he has clamped on his emotions.

He now knows where three of the Europ's gun buggies
are located. The Europ's command vehicle and his other
gun buggy have to be located somewhere between them.

There is a very good chance, in fact, that one of the
Europ's vehicles is hiding behind the hill in front of Davino.
There has to be something in that general area if the
Europ is still in contact with all his buggies.

The buggies he has located can all be operating on
automatic, of course. The Europ could have sent them
into action and hidden his fourth buggy somewhere else.
But he knows that isn't very likely. All three enemy buggies are engaging in aggressive actions; he knows the two
buggies on his right are trying to destroy One, and he is
pretty certain the buggy he saw on Three's screen was
trying to sneak around his left flank. A gun buggy can
engage in evasive action on automatic, but nobody in his
right mind is going to let a buggy attack by itself. Suppose
it shoots at a manned command vehicle by mistake?

Davino has always taken big chances when he has worked
with the simulators. Sometimes he has won, sometimes he
has lost. Aggressive guys do O.K. sometimes, and cautious
guys do O.K. sometimes. There are no hard and fast
rules—but his six hundred battles in the simulator have
taught him one important lesson. When they catch you in
an ambush and knock off a big chunk of your firepower,
you may as well be aggressive. You may lose anyway, but
you don't stand a chance if you lie still and let them draw
the noose around you. Five buggies will close in on him

from five different directions as soon as the Europ pulls his troops off One. They may be closing in on him right now.

He taps out another series of orders on the console. Gun Buggy Four starts rolling around the right side of the big hill. Three starts rolling up the slope.

The command vehicle rolls up the hill thirty meters behind the dust and rocks arcing away from Three's back wheels. A shallow, unexpected depression catches Davino by surprise. All four wheels leave the ground in the low gravity and come down with a soft bump that makes the cockpit rock from side to side like a cradle. The gun buggies are traveling at their top combat speed—thirty kilometers per hour—and they are leaving the ground and sailing through space every twenty or thirty meters.

He speeds up the command vehicle and catches up with Three as he approaches the top of the hill. The command vehicle sails over the top of the hill with Three on the left and Four racing around the bottom of the hill one hundred meters below.

He is looking down a long, gentle slope that stretches away from him for several hundred meters before it merges into the rolling lunar landscape. There is a beat-up, heavily cratered boulder field at the bottom of the slope, and there is another big hill on his right, about five hundred meters in front of him.

A red and white vehicle is parked between two small craters on the top of the other hill. It has an armored, bubble-shaped cockpit, and there is a big blue cross on the front end.

His eyes sweep across the boulder field. A flash of reflected light grabs his attention. An enemy gun buggy has been stationed inside a jumble of craters and boulders near the front of the field. The boulders are taller than the buggy, but there are big gaps in the jumble, and he can see the top of the antenna and part of the framework near the middle of the buggy.

A moving cloud of dust catches his attention on the left. A small four-wheeled vehicle is rolling across the slope toward Three. It is about one meter long, and the square, black box on its front end is a warhead containing several pounds of the latest development in high explosives.

A gun buggy crawls around a crater near the bottom of the hill. Its gun turret swings toward Three. Two more wheeled torpedoes drop off the arms on its sides and race up the hill. The gun buggy in the boulder field rolls out of its hiding place and turns its gun toward Three.

Davino's hands leap into action. Six hundred hours in the simulator have made his responses as automatic as the actions of his gun buggies.

Magnetic latches release the torpedoes mounted on Three. Homing devices lock on their target and send three torpedoes rolling toward the European buggy on the left. Three swerves forty-five degrees and turns its gun turrret toward the buggy in the boulder field.

Guns flash on the enemy buggies. A silent explosion erupts near Three's back end. A crater spreads across the lunar surface as if someone is blowing into a box of sand.

A light on his control panel tells him Three has fired its main gun. Another cloud of dust and rocks sails into the sky. Another shell slides into the chamber of Three's gun.

Three's machine guns open on the torpedoes closing in on it. The European buggy on the left swerves away from a torpedo and rolls behind a crater. The buggy in the boulder field fires another shot.

Davino's hands have been hopping across the console as if he has been playing two melodies on the piano at the same time. He has been guiding Four through the bumps and craters on the side of the hill at the same time he has been handling Three. Four has been sailing over dips and swerving around craters at top speed, and it is now racing toward a point at which it can open fire on the boulder field.

The Europ has seen Four coming around the hill. The buggy in the boulder field is turning its turret toward Four, but the Europ has miscalculated by at least ten seconds. A big, ragged hole blossoms in the front end of the buggy. The front end skids to the left. The wrecked buggy comes to rest with its gun lying across the side of a gray boulder.

Davino turns toward the other enemy buggy. The lights on his control panel tell him two of his torpedoes are still active and are still rolled into a network of craters, but he can still see the top of its turret.

Davino twists a dial on the control panel. The command vehicle swings to the right and rolls down the hill with the two gun buggies racing along with it. Electronic fingers leap at the European command vehicle parked on the other hill. Gun turrets swing toward their target.

Trumpets ring in Davino's mind. The Europ could have backed up and disappeared over the hill if he had reacted fast enough, but now it's too late. His sights are locked on the bastard's cockpit, and nobody can deny it. The other enemy gun buggy is on the other side of the boulder field, and it will be at least thirty seconds before it can work its way through the boulders and train its guns on Davino's vehicle. Surrender or die—and nobody dies in this war. You go back to your base with your command vehicle stripped of its weapons, or they take you and your vehicles prisoner and exchange you later. But nobody expects you to fight when the enemy has the drop on you. This is the Moon, gentlemen, not some crummy jungle in South America.

He can disarm the Europ and push on to his destination. He can radio LeFarge and have them send in the reserves while he patrols this area with his two gun buggies and keeps his prisoner incommunicado. It isn't the kind of victory he was hoping for, but LeFarge knows they gave him a rough assignment. LeFarge will give him a good report. Everybody in Washington will know they snapped up the prize because Major Joseph Davino outmaneuvered an ambusher and tore a big hole in the enemy's defense system.

Movement catches his eye. Two red and white buggies are parked on his right with their guns trained on his cockpit. The two buggies that have been pursuing One have come up in time, after all. They have been maneuvering through the craters while he has been fighting the Europ's other buggies, and the Europ has brought them into action with seconds to spare.

Davino's fingers rest on the buttons that will send three shells flying toward the Europ's command vehicle. Nobody will ever know if he pushes the buttons and fires on the Europ in cold blood. Nobody has died so far, but accidents can happen. One of the shells will probably hit the Europ's command vehicle before the Europ can fire the guns on his two buggies. The Europ may even be getting ready to kill him before he kills the Europ. How long can you fight a war for high stakes before somebody cracks?

The snotty computer jockeys in the Pentagon will never forgive him if he lets that find get away. LeFarge will know it has been one of those things, but LeFarge won't be able to help him. He took this job because he knew he needed a big success, and now there's only one way he can get it. Nobody in the Pentagon is going to reward him for making a good try. The orders that will send him back to Earth are already being processed in Washington. Nobody is going to pat him on the head and tell him the Pentagon has a kind heart and everybody knows he and Dr. Cunningham are a wonderful couple and shouldn't be torn apart.

He will never see Annie again. He will live out his life on a cramped, crowded, smelly, poisonous world where you have to fill in a form to look at a mountain.

The two guns on the enemy buggies turn away from his cockpit at the same time his own guns turn away from the Europ's command vehicle. The gun barrels swing around until every gun is pointing at a spot on the horizon that is at least one hundred and twenty degrees from the nearest target.

A light flashes on Davino's console. He presses a button and static fills his earphones.

"I will back off two kilometers south," a voice says in his earphones. "Will you back off two kilometers east?"

"I will back off two kilometers east," Davino says.

"Thank you. I think you fought most gallantly. I would have been completely defeated if my two gun buggies hadn't come up faster than I had any right to expect."

"I thought your ambush was very well planned. I didn't know you were anywhere near me until you attacked."

"We picked you up on the radar only once. My commanding officer said you were one of the most skillful drivers he had ever seen. I am Captain Anton Olivini."

"I'm Major Joseph Davino. It's been a pleasure meeting you."

"It's been a pleasure meeting you also, Major. May you have an easy trip home."

"The same to you, Captain Olivini. Good luck."

"Godspeed."

The six vehicles back away from each other with their guns carefully pointed backward. Davino wishes he can feel noble, but he soon realizes he can't.

Tom Purdom started publishing in 1957, and since then he has published five novels and a long list of short stories and novelettes, as well as nonfiction about such subjects as disarmament and arms control, nuclear policy, and education. He has taught at Temple and Drexel Universities, and has handled PR work for several Philadelphia organizations.

Purdom's keen interest in military policy and history is reflected in much of his fiction, such as his novel Reduction in Arms, *and his nonfiction. He served two years in the Cold War Army, has watched the veterans come home from three wars, and is keenly aware that he may be alive today because his parents were kind enough to see that he was born in 1936, and not, say, 1923, 1932, or 1950.*

He lives in Philadelphia with his wife, Sarah Wescoat Purdom, and one son.

Unfortunately, recent developments in the weaponry of space hold out little hope for such chivalrous encounters as that in Tom Purdom's story; and that weaponry, in certain of its immediate and most important aspects, is foreshadowed in this article by Jerry Pournelle. It was written three years ago; it was highly pertinent then, and what he has to say about it today emphasizes its present pertinence:

"I wrote this article in 1976 as a column for Galaxy, *shortly after rumors of a new Soviet beam weapon appeared in the technical press. Since that time, the official position of the U.S. Department of State is that the infrared phenomenon was caused by a break in a natural-gas pipeline in Siberia. High-ranking U.S. Air Force officers remain skeptical, pointing out that the "fires" were never recorded by weather and other optical wavelength observation satellites.*

"Except to add the above and the brief comments at the end of the article, the column has not been revised."

Especially in view of recent developments in the High Frontier space defense program—in which, incidentally, Dr. Pournelle has been instrumental—this article is singularly prescient.

Jerry Pournelle, Ph.D.
LASERS, GRASERS, AND MARXISTS

As I write this, there is confusion about just what happened in the Soviet Union last summer and fall. According to one report, the Soviets have developed a powerful laser system capable of blinding our infrared detection satellites; according to another, there was a large gas fire in Siberia and everyone got excited over nothing.

No matter. Whatever happened in 1975, there is no secret that the United States and the USSR are engaged in a technological race to develop large laser weapons. The death rays of 1930s science fiction are coming, and someone will develop them. Let's take the opportunity to look at lasers, grasers, nasers, masers, and such other devices.

First, all these gadgets have one thing in common. They produce coherent radiation through stimulated emission. That sounds elementary to about half my readers and incomprehensible to the rest, so at the risk of boring some of you (we know of at least one Nobel prizewinner who regularly reads *Galaxy*) I'd better explain.

Imagine a mob leaving a football stadium after a game. You could say that the stadium is radiating people. They walk at different speeds with different lengths of stride, and they go in different directions. Their motion is outward from the stadium, but otherwise unpredictable: it is incoherent.

Now imagine that they all issue from the same stadium door; they march in step, each stride the same length, and they all go in the same direction. Coherent radiation is like that. It's all the same frequency (and thus if it is visible light, it is a very pure color); it goes in the same direction. Think of light as waves, and all the waves have their peaks and valleys at exactly the same time. The result is a very powerful beam.

This is done by stimulated emission, and that takes a bit of explaining. All electromagnetic radiation involves photons. A very small part of the electromagnetic spectrum is visible light. When the frequency gets too high, the light is no longer visible, and we call it ultraviolet. Higher frequencies yet are X-rays, gamma rays, and finally what are called cosmic rays.

Below the red end of the spectrum is, not surprisingly, infrared, which we can detect as heat. At lower frequencies still are radio, radar, and television. In theory, at least, a "laser" could be built which operated in any frequency from cosmic rays down through gamma rays (grasers) through visible light (lasers), down into the infrared (IR), through the radio frequencies (masers), and finally down to the frequencies we use to send power through wires. However, since a 60-cycle wave (which sometimes you hear as a hum if you put a cheap radio set near an electrical wire) has a wavelength something like 3200 miles long, it's unlikely that anyone will ever want to build a device to stimulate radiation at that frequency.

In practice we don't know how to build stimulated emission devices at all frequencies. One of the Navy's big problems is developing a powerful blue-green laser. Obviously such a device would be useful, because that's the frequency of light that best penetrates ocean water, and would let submarines look a long way ahead without giving off the characteristic "ping" of a sonar. There are, however, lasers at a number of visible light frequencies, masers which work the same way but in radio frequencies, and IR lasers which operate at the low edge of visibility.

They work this way: Take some atoms that have the desired characteristics. Excite an electron, so that it jumps to a higher energy state. It absorbs a photon when it does that. Now "stimulate" the atom so that the electron will jump back to the lower energy state, giving up the captured photon as it does. That photon comes out at precisely the same frequency each time. Now get a lot of those atoms to do that at the same time, confine the photons so they can't get out except when going in exactly one direction, and you've got a coherent beam. Its frequency will depend on the kind of atoms you've excited.

Note what we've done. We haven't created any energy. Instead, we've put in energy and got it out again. Since no process is 100% efficient, we've lost some of our input. On the other hand, the energy we put in wasn't coherent, and the output was.

The energy input process is called "pumping." The first lasers, and many of those for sale commercially, are pumped by light. There are, however, a number of other ways to pump a laser. You can use electromagnetic energy by surrounding the laser device with coils of wire and putting juice through them. You can also pump the laser directly through nuclear radiation, and we'll come back to that. If you want a portable laser, you might also come up with a mirror system that gathers sunlight, focuses it into your device, and converts it to laser energy. That's not too useful for military weapons unless by agreement you won't fight in the shade, but it could be a valuable technique.

However you pump the laser, and whatever the frequency you're using, the result is a beam each of whose elements is exactly (well, almost exactly) parallel. One space-tracking system sends out a beam that hasn't fanned to more than a few meters at satellite altitudes. Thus you've concentrated a lot of energy into a very narrow beam, and that is why all the military interest.

Of course there are a number of other applications that have nothing to do with war and destruction. Laser beams bouncing off the reflector Neil Armstrong left at Tranquillity measure the Earth-Moon distance within fractions of a centimeter, and *that* allows tests of great importance to cosmologists—one cosmological theory says that the universal constant of gravitation (G) isn't constant at all, but changes with time. Since the masses of Earth and Moon don't change much, a good test of whether or not G is changing is just how stable that Earth-Moon distance is. Incidentally, the last I heard the experimental results indicate that G is not changing, but stay tuned; there's just enough error in the observations to let a few cosmologists hang onto the G-is-changing theory. Most, however, seem to have given it up.

We've all heard about some other civilian uses for lasers, such as communication, surveying instruments that need no flagman and are a thousand times more accurate than the old transit-target-and-chain system, satellite tracking devices, laser surgery to burn out just the cells the physician wants killed without harming those on either side (and yes, lasers can be focused *that* small), and all the rest. Lasers are one major reason for retiring the slide rule: laser accuracies allow manufacture of the electronic chips that are the heart of pocket computers. (It seems unfair, since the laser's inventor was a slide-rule addict, but there's nothing to be done about it. Dietzgen has gone out of the slide-rule business, and there you are. Progress.)

So. We have a source of narrowly focused energy. Obviously, if we can get enough energy focused into a narrow enough beam, we have a death ray. Add more and we have a disintegrator. The military advantages are enormous. No longer is there a time-of-flight problem. For all practical purposes, your shot hits the instant it is fired, which means you don't need to track the target, whether it's a tank or an ICBM; just locate it, and zap! it's dead. Also, you've launched nothing, and you can refire your weapon as fast as you can pump up its atoms. You haven't contaminated your defense environment by blowing off

chemical or atomic weapons and thus producing smoke or
ionization or something else you can't see through.

It shouldn't be any surprise that military people sponsor
a very great deal of laser research. Most of it is secret, and
it takes a lot of digging to find out how well they're doing;
but from hints that turn up here and there, laser weapons
are doing quite well. A few years ago there were rumors
that lasers were used to knock fist-sized holes in army
tanks at about a hundred feet. A year ago last fall, I was
told by a usually reliable source that the airplane-eating
laser was proved to be practical. Now we have the rumors
of the Soviet laser blinding our IR satellites. Even if it
didn't happen, it wouldn't be too surprising.

As I write this, there aren't very many details known.
According to *Aviation Week (AW)* a publication not generally known for being wrong, on several occasions the U.S.
IR-watching satellites were suddenly blinded by a very
great deal of IR-frequency energy coming into their recep-
tors. That could happen in several ways. One, there was
just a lot of IR coming up out of the Soviet Union. A *very*
large fire, for example, would do it. Another way would be
for a smaller amount of IR to be focused exactly onto our
satellite. Nothing could do that but a laser.

Again according to *AW*, when this first happened, U.S.
weather satellites were called on to show us the fire in
Siberia. They hadn't seen one. USAF also launched one of
their lower-altitude spy satellites (I don't know what they're
called nowadays; they used to be called SAMOS, and
there was a SAMOS project listed in the Pentagon phone
book, but if you dialed the number someone answered
"Weather Observation") and *it* didn't find any fire. The
AW article stirred up a fuss ("panic" was one of the milder
words used to describe reactions in the aerospace industry) and there was subsequently a Department of Defense
statement to the effect that nothing had happened, and
someone else reported that it was all a big false alarm over
a natural gas fire in Siberia, and if you take DOD's word
for everything they tell you—you do, don't you?—then
that's all there is to the story.

If you have an abnormal distrust in DOD flacks, you
might react as did a USAF general officer friend, who
pointed out that the early-warning satellites—they're sup-

posed to watch for the IR flare of Soviet rockets, including ICBMs—are at synchronous altitude, and if you can shine enough energy on them at *that* altitude you're a long way toward burning holes into something at, say, ICBM reentry altitudes. At that point, the hackles start rising on the back of your neck, or they do on mine, and if you're not scared, maybe you'd better rethink the problem.

And here I've got to say a few words about politics, and I hope I don't lose too much of my readership.

In this era of "overkill," surely no one but a madman would risk nuclear war. One hears that said until it becomes a part of one's mental furniture. Unfortunately, it isn't true.

One need not be mad to begin nuclear war. One may quite rationally do it. Perhaps "rationally" is the wrong word. Perhaps I should say "logically" instead. It all depends on whether or not you regard Marxism as "rational." Certainly good Marxists do, and in fact every Soviet university student is required to take some forty semester-hours of courses in the subject; and one of the tenets of Marxism is not only that it is rational, but that it is the *only* rational political philosophy.

Marxism claims to be an objective science of history with predictive powers. Like Hari Seldon's Plan in the old Asimov *Foundation* series, Marxism doesn't pretend to be exact. Variations are possible, and even errors are possible; but Marxism is, say the Marxists, the *only* objective science of history, and in its broad predictions it is infallible. Marxism rejects any religiously derived values and ethics and goals for the human race; Marxists have only one source of ethical values: to further progress, which is defined as moving toward the ultimate social order, namely the classless society. That which brings us nearer that goal is progressive and good. That which puts off man's final state is regressive, reactionary, and evil. No individual person is important; indeed, concern for individuals in preference to the ultimate historical goal is mere bourgeois sentimentality.

This most emphatically does not mean that Marxists are villains or that they do not love their families and friends; only that to allow love for friends or families to stand in the way of progress is, by definition, regressive, reactionary, bourgeois, and condemnable. Therefore no Marxist could in conscience refuse to start World War III so long as he could be certain that (1) the human race would survive it, and (2) the outcome would be the world revolution and the triumph of socialism. It is as if a convinced Christian were truly to believe that he could only bring about the Second Coming by starting Armageddon.

Now naturally no one is going to start WW III on a suspicion, a rumor, or sloppy calculations. One precept of the Leninist branch of Marxism (one which I suspect Karl Marx would condemn, but I may be wrong) is "Do not endanger the homeland of Socialism." This allows Marxists to be good Russian patriots and certainly tempers reckless adventurism. However, it is not required for *all* of the Soviet Union to survive WW III, so long as enough lives through to bring the Revolution and its attendent benefits to all mankind. What is enough might in theory be a scientific question (to Marxists all social problems are scientific questions) but in the real world any decision is likely to be affected by the normal sentiments of mankind, or at least one sincerely hopes so. Note, though, that such influence is intellectually condemned, and that the more educated the Soviet citizen, the more intellectual training in Marxism he has enjoyed.

So. Have we demonstrated that it would be rational to begin WW III provided only that the military authorities could assure the Presidium that (1) the Soviets would survive, and (2) there would be no effective opposition to communism throughout the world; and that this is entirely independent of the level of casualities the Soviet Union and the rest of the world might sustain? Now, I am not insane enough to think that most Soviet citizens, or even most party members, think that way; but they are *supposed* to think that way, they teach their university students to think that way, and some of them talk as if they really think that way; and there is no intellectually acceptable argument within the confines of Marxism to refute the proposition.

Thus, what happens if one morning the Marshal of the Soviet Union reports that "If the war begins tomorrow, we will lose 40% of our population. We will retain at least

50% of our industry. The Red Army will occupy all of Europe to the Atlantic coast within three weeks. The United States, Canada, Australia, and New Zealand will effectively cease to exist and certainly will have no military power whatever. China will be neutralized, and if it becomes necessary, will be reduced to the Stone Age. What are your orders?"

In my judgment that would not be a safe world to live in because *someone* in the Presidium might well find it tempting—and would the others have effective arguments? Be powerful enough to halt the truly convinced Marxists? It seems to me a bad gamble, and far better for all of us that we never give the Suslovs of this world such a temptation.

Nonsense. Idiocy. Etc. Pournelle has finally gone off his rocker, and probably was deranged all the time. In the first place, no one could imagine keeping national power after losing 40% of their population.

But they took losses of over 30% in WW II and emerged infinitely more powerful when the war ended than when it began.

Even so. There's no way to hold casualties that low. The U.S. has millions and millions of megatons, and everybody knows that WW III would end civilization and indeed very nearly exterminate mankind; certainly it would end that technological civilization that you, Pournelle, are so proud of and from which you expect such great things.

I wish I believed that. Unfortunately I know better. There is a way to fight strategic nuclear war. There is a war plan that will neutralize most of those U.S. weapons. I'm giving away no secrets by describing it.

First, suppose we get rid of the airplanes, or at least don't replace the poor old B-52s which were, after all, designed in the post-WW era and were built in the 50s. Second, note that of our missile subs, many are in harbor at any given time, and can't get out on less than a couple hours' notice. Scratch half the sub force, killed in harbor.

Next, imagine that the Soviets have many more subs than we do (and in fact according to *Jane's* they do) and that they routinely send them out to follow our missile boats around (as, I am told, they now do). Scratch more of the sub fleet. If we're lucky, maybe ten subs will get off their birds. That's about 150 missiles; not an impossible number to intercept if you've got laser weapons. We'll come back to that in a moment.

But there are all those Minuteman and Titan missiles. Yes: 1,052 in all, 52 Titan and 1,000 Minuteman. All land-based. All in locations mapped precisely down to the last inch. (I could obtain such maps with a few hundred dollars and a summer of work; and if I could, we may be sure the Soviets have done it.) The land-based missiles can be dealt with.

The technique is called pindown, and it works this way. First, blind the IR satellites, so that the first indication that anything is coming out of the Soviet Union is from B-Mews at Fairbanks, Gander, Thule, etc. If you want to be really sneaky, fire the first shots from submarines. In any event, with MIRVs (Multiple Independently-targeted Reentry Vehicles) you need only one bird to drop a warhead at each Minuteman and Titan complex. Explode the warheads at optimum burst height.

Repeat every five minutes. One warhead explodes over each missile's farm.

I don't know the exact time of powered flight for Minuteman, but it's easy to show that it has to be more than four minutes, and Titan has about the same rise time. The birds are very vulnerable during boost-phase. It doesn't take a lot of disturbance to knock them *way* off course—after all, a tiny nudge at this end is miles and miles after intercontinental flight. Not one of those birds is going to hit its designated target.

Meanwhie, behind that train of one-every-four-minutes pindown missiles, there comes a wave of ICBMs which will finish the job.

Insanity? Yes, in the sense that it's hard to imagine sane people doing it. No, in that it makes perfect sense if you believe the only destiny of man is to achieve the classless society, and the United States is the only obstacle in the way of eternal peace and happiness for all.

What evidence have we that anyone might do this? Only that when the U.S. decided we had "enough"—that is, had achieved nuclear sufficiency—we stopped building birds. We haven't put a new missile into a silo in a decade.

It was thought that one reason for "international tension" was that the Soviets felt strategically inferior to us. They were nervous because *we* might be contemplating preventive or preemptive war. All that would vanish when they achieved parity. Therefore, we stop building strategic weapons and let them catch up.

They caught up.

They kept going. They've got a *lot* more birds than we do, and as best I can tell, they're building them still. What for? It's a costly effort and of no rational value—unless you define rational as I just have.

So now what? Should the U.S. spend a great deal more money on nuclear weapons? Increase our overkill capability? (Note that if you assume you'll lose part of your force because you intend to let the other guy attack first, you *need* "overkill" in order to have "sufficiency". Note also that the Soviets have long since gone past us in "overkill" capacity, and are still pouring concrete and filling silos with birds.)

I won't pretend to have knowledge of optimum strategic mix. I'm far out of date and intend to stay that way—I don't want a clearance. I'd rather be able to say what I want without worry. It's certainly possible that we need some new strategic offense weapons, and to update those we have.

I do, however, have strong feelings about concentrating *entirely* on offensive weapons. Air Force generals have long downgraded strategic defense. Air-war strategists are taught "nobody ever won a war by protecting himself" and similar maxims. Defensive weapons are no doubt a fine thing, but mostly they suck up scarce defense funds that should be going into weapons we can use to knock out the other guy before he can do any harm to our people. Given a good enough strategic offense, we won't *need* defensive weapons because either we will have deterred the other guy so he doesn't start the war in the first place, or he will be knocked out quickly and effectively if he does. So say a number of generals. I have never agreed.

I don't agree now. I believe a *defensive* arms race makes enormous sense. Yes, and I supported the now-discontinued ABM system, too, even though I knew full well that Spartan wasn't likely to be worth a hoot in hell.

Why?

Well, because the really expensive technology and the really tricky problems of ABM have nothing to do with Spartan. Don't get me wrong. The kill mechanism is the key problem to effective anti-ICBM weapons. Until you have something that will deliver lethality, you can't shoot down ICBMs. On the other hand, even if you have a marvelous kill mechanism, you can't use it unless you can detect and locate your target.

That was the expensive part of our now-defunct ABM system. Detection and tracking. Hardened radars. Phased-array radars, which look like solid concrete barns, have been known in theory for a long time, but in practice they're hideously complex. They work this way.

In the old-fashioned radar, the antenna moved. A big dish was steered mechanically, and your tracking computer "knew" where the dish was pointed at the time it received the blip returned from the target. The antenna was vulnerable to enemy weapons—even chemical weapons, sabotage, and small-arms fire—and the mechanical parts caused terrible errors unacceptable at thousand-mile ranges.

Phased-array radars have thousands of small antennae buried in a lump of concrete. Nothing moves. Instead, the various antenna elements are excited in a precise computer-controlled sequence and the returns monitored by computer. The whole thing is expensive in money, and a few years ago expensive in terms of needed research to get it working.

We got that much out of our dead ABM. Presumably we have the antennae and computers, and need only a kill mechanism.

The laser is the obvious answer to that. What kind I leave to the experts. The theoretically best would be X-ray or gamma-ray (graser) frequencies since those would penetrate atmosphere best and deliver the greatest lethality per beam cross-section. Missile-killing lasers are likely to be large—very large—and we need a great deal of work on them.

They may need a new form of pumping. We have now a few nuclear-energy pumped lasers—that is, a small unshielded reactor pours neutrons and other high-energy nuclear particles directly into the laser, which transforms their energy into useful coherent radiation. (It is even proposed for the future that nuclear-pumped lasers be put into orbit to light cities at night and keep streets warm in winter. Possible, but I'd think unlikely.)

Certainly the efficiency of lasers needs work. When you pump enough energy in to kill missiles at great distances, you'd best not waste much in your laser lest you melt your own system. Methods of steering the mirrors must be developed.

None of this, though, looks all that difficult. There was a time when really big lasers were "theoretically impossible," but them days is gone forever. *Somebody's* going to do it. And we will be in a new military era.

There are also enormous civilian benefits. Really big lasers can put mass into orbit, cutting down on the costs of entering the Third Industrial Revolution. I do want to emphasize, though, that I'm not arguing for laser development as ABM merely as a sneaky way to get space industries.

No. Big lasers, coupled with already-developed phased-array radar technology, will yield an ABM system capable of handling a few hundred incoming missiles. It may be chauvinistic of me, but I'd rather we had that capability and the Soviets didn't.

That's highly unlikely—especially so if what our IR satellites saw was *not* a Siberian gas fire—so I'll settle for both of us having the ABM. Strategically that would make the pindown attack impossible, and any first-strike war plan hideously complex. The resulting bipolar world has its problems, but it's one we could live in.

What I really wouldn't like to see is too much temptation put in the way of the Party Theoreticians over there. Maybe it isn't likely—reverently, I hope to God it isn't likely—but might they believe what they've been teaching the last forty years?

This article has not needed revision. As mentioned in the opening note, there remains controversy over what was observed in 1975. In reality, it hardly matters. Two major points are relevant:

1. The Soviet Union is known to have made a number of scientific breakthroughs in beam technology. This includes not only lasers, but also particle beams. They have apparently tested devices which beam the energy from a small nuclear explosion. Nicolai Basov, their Nobel Laureate in beam physics, is justly credited with numerous advances in the state of the art.

We lack information on current operational capabilities, but there is no doubt of Soviet scientific capability in the critical field which Stefan Possony calls "beamology."

2. The reentry and disintegration of a Soviet satellite, with pieces falling in the Canadian north woods, resulted in a surprising discovery: the Soviets have nuclear satellite power sources considerably larger than any we have ever flown. This is a known operational capability which came as a complete surprise—and was learned by studying an obsolete satellite which had been up so long that its orbit decayed. Current Soviet capabilities remain unknown.

If a country intends to employ some kind of beam weapon in space, the ability to carry a large operational power source is critical. There is no reason to assume that this is the sole reason the Soviets developed a nuclear satellite power system, but the fact remains that they have developed this technology.

Finally: this morning's mail brought me the current year's The Military Balance, *an authoritative annual study issued by the International Institute for Strategic Studies in London. The Soviet strategic (nuclear) missile delivery establishment has once again increased in both numbers and overall capability.*

The U.S. strategic missile force remains essentially unchanged.

—*Jerry Pournelle*

Dr. Jerry Pournelle holds advanced degrees in operations research, mathematics, psychology, and political science. He worked in space research and was active in both the Mercury and Apollo programs. He was also Chief of the Experimental Stress Project in the Boeing Human Factors Laboratories and was involved in the qualification tests for the original astronauts.

A former professor, he now writes full time and has been President of the Science Fiction Writers of America. His many articles on new developments in science and technology have appeared in Galaxy, Analog, Destinies, *and elsewhere. In 1972, he won the John W. Campbell Award, and is the author of* A Spaceship for the King *and* The Mercenary. With Larry Niven, he wrote the Hugo-nominated *The Mote in God's Eye, as well as* Inferno *and* Lucifer's Hammer. *His most recent novel,* Janissaries, *was published earlier this year by Ace Books, and he is also the editor of a recent anthology,* Black Holes and Other Marvels. With Stefan Possony, he wrote *The Strategy of Technology, an exploration of the role of technology in war and world affairs.*

His latest books are Footfall (with Larry Niven,) *Janissaries II,* Clan and Crown (with Larry Niven and Roland Green,) *The Legacy of the Heorat (with Larry Niven and Steven Barnes,) and* Storms of Victory (Janissaries III, with Roland Green.) He has also edited (with John Carr) *The Imperial Stars series and several other anthologies.*

Dr. Pournelle lives in Studio City, California, with his wife and four sons.

At least in the present stage of our development, we humans are torn between two imperatives: one which drives us to invent and manufacture more and more effective instruments for our own destruction, and another that whispers to us that we must either stop the self-destructive process wholly or at least control it.

Because its terms are those of hard science and hard technology, the first imperative has worked well. As I have previously pointed out, the second, because it has been crippled by the vague definitions and loose meanings that characterize the vocabulary of human relations, has resulted in little more than ritual dances.

Yet there is a deep human wish to stop war, to limit war, somehow to bring war—to bring ourselves—under rational control. In the Middle Ages, in Europe, first we had the Peace of God, which was generally observed: it declared that clergy, certain civilians, churches, and people attending divine service on a Sunday should remain unharmed. Then, a little later, the Church proclaimed the Truce of God, honored more in the breach than in the observance: no one was to make war between Wednesday evening and the morning of the Monday following, nor during certain sacred days and seasons. Generally speaking, such limiting rules worked only when no fanatical doctrines divided the combatants, or when for cultural reasons they happened to observe similar codes of honor. Nonetheless, over the centuries—often at the behest of professional soldiers—they have probably done more to ameliorate war's agonies and terrors than all our efforts to abolish war entirely.

Sun Tzu said:

Indirect tactics, effectively applied, are inexhaustible as heaven and earth . . .*

Could they be applied efficiently to ending war as well as waging it?

*The Art of War (Giles's translation)

Charles Sheffield
FIXED-PRICE WAR

As the sun set, the first line of attackers came silently over the brow of the hill. They were the scouts; shadowy figures moving with no apparent coordination down to and across the river, on to the waist-high savannah scrub on the near side. When the last man was across, the second wave appeared; a line of hover-tanks with chopper cover, advancing at no more than walking pace. The counterattack waited until the tanks had reached the river. Then a bright mesh of ruby pulsed-laser beams lanced out from the nearer hillside, probing for the soft underskirts of the hover-tanks and the chopper rotors. Yellow and red tracers replied. The air became a multicolored confusion of stabbing pencils of light, smoke from burning vegetation, and the fitful glare of crippled tanks and choppers.

Suddenly the whole hillside was lit by an intense blue-white fireball, spreading from a point close to the river bank. It grew rapidly, changing color to a greenish-yellow——

Merle Walters gave a grunt of surprise, leaned forward, and hit a button on the console in front of him. The display stopped, frozen with the fireball about forty meters across. He swiveled in his chair and pressed the intercom. "Franny, get Alex Burns on the line. I think I've finally caught him."

He waited impatiently as the connection to Redondo Beach was made, looking at his watch as he did so. Eight-thirty—that made it five-thirty in California. Alex would still be around. When the intercom buzzed, he reached out his right arm and picked it up. The left sleeve was empty, pinned to his dark jacket. As he placed the receiver to his ear, the screen lit up to show a trim, ruddy-faced man in his early forties.

"Alex, I think you've finally goofed." Walters grinned in triumph at the man on the screen. "If I had another arm, I'd be rubbing my hands together here. I'm reviewing the simulation you've done for Exhibit Three of our proposal. One of your boys has gone wild and thrown in a tactical nuke. You know that's right out."

"Mr. Walters, I invite your attention to page 57 of the Work Statement of the Request For Proposal." Burns answered in the careful speech of an Inverness Scot, unchanged after sixteen years in Southern California. "The RFP very clearly states, and I quote: 'Although nuclear weapons may not be employed, clean imploders up to 1,000 metric tons TNT equivalent may be used. No more than three such devices will be available in any single engagement.' The fireball that you are looking at in Exhibit Three is a new Morton Imploder, type four, one hundred and fifty TNT tons equivalent."

Alex Burns face showed the slightest trace of a smile. Merle Walters looked at the display screen, thumbed rapidly through his copy of the Request For Proposal, and swore. "Alex, you Gaelic bastard, you did that on purpose. Don't deny it. I've known you too long not to recognize your touch there. Tell your lads the simulations are damn good—but I'd like them a lot better if you'd put some faces on the attackers. All I can see is blobs."

Burns nodded gloomily. "I know, Mr. Walters. I feel the same way. But the people at GSA won't say who we're fighting, and I can think of at least four possibles. Maybe you can get something for me at the bidders' conference."

"I'll give it a try, Alex—but don't hold your breath waiting for it. I'll be honest with you—that won't be my top priority at this bidders' session. There's something else I have to get an answer on. The Contracts Office has been like a bunch of clams on this one. Jack's trying a little line of his own to get information—we'll tell you tomorrow how it works out."

Burns nodded again. "Good night, Mr. Walters. Maybe I could suggest that you should call it a day. You're looking very tired. Trouble with the résumés?"

"As usual. We need two or three good production men—

all we can find is a bunch of retired colonels and generals. Keep up the good work on the simulations, Alex, and I'll call you about noon—our time—tomorrow."

Merle Walters broke the connection and leaned back in his chair. He rubbed his hand over the top of his bald, furrowed forehead. Alex was right. He was damn tired. Alex couldn't usually catch him that way. And with just ten days to go before the proposal was due, with all the costing still to be done, he'd better keep something in reserve for next week. He spoke again into the intercom.

"Franny, I'm cutting out. Pull a bunch of those résumés together for me as bedside reading, will you? Remember, I won't be in first thing in the morning. Jack and I will be down at Eighteenth and E Streets, at the Bidders' Conference. I can't be reached there."

He levered himself to his feet and walked to the outer office, limping slightly. He could disguise it if he tried, but it was pointless in front of Franny. She knew him better than he knew himself. She had the résumés all ready for him—probably had them ready two hours ago. Her plump, pretty face was set in what he thought of as her "take your medicine like a good little boy" expression.

"Mr. Walters, I discussed this earlier with Mr. Tukey." She held out a locator. "If you'd carry this about with you, it would be so much easier for us to get messages to you. Look, this new one only weighs an ounce—and it's only an inch wide. It wouldn't be any trouble."

He looked at it, then peered at Franny from under his thick, grizzled eyebrows—his sternest expression. "Franny, I've told you once and I'll tell you again. I'm not going to wear a damned beeper. It's an invasion of privacy. When you see Jack Tukey tomorrow, you tell him exactly what he can do with that thing. Tell him it's only an inch wide, so he shouldn't have any trouble." His gray eyes twinkled beneath the bushy brows. "Good night, Franny, and thanks for another day."

He went slowly out into the chilly November evening. Ten minutes later, Franny locked up and left also. The Washington office of WAWD Corporation was closed for the night.

The Bidders' Conference was scheduled for 9:00 A.M. in the biggest Conference Room of the old Interior building.

Merle Walters was there by 8:45, watching the arrivals. About a hundred people. Say two per company. So fifty groups interested in the procurement. Merle knew the real competition like the back of his hand. Three groups—and WAWD. The other forty-six were innocents, flesh-peddlers, or companies looking for subcontract work. When Tolly Suomi of VVV Industries arrived at 8:58, Merle followed him in and sat in the same row. Suomi looked his way and inclined his head. Merle had no doubt that Tolly knew the real score as well as he did.

Biggest Conference Room, so more than a $20 million job. Coffee served, so more than $50 million. Merle read the signs almost subconsciously, the pricing signals that only the pros could read. Then Petzell would be running the government side, for a job over $500 million.

Merle was sitting smugly on that train of thought when the senior government man came forward to the podium. Instead of Petzell, it was his deputy, Pete Wolff. Merle sat up and took notice. What the hell was going on? He'd been tracking this procurement for a year, sniffing it and sizing it. He'd been pegging it at about a billion-two. Surely they couldn't have missed the mark so badly. He leaned forward to catch the opening remarks, ignoring the stab of pain in his left side.

"Good morning, ladies and gentlemen." Wolff looked around at the sea of faces—old friends and old enemies. "I want to begin by running over the procedures we will be following on question and answers. First, though, I should tell you that I'm deputizing today for Howard Petzell." He looked around with a slight smile. "He is home today with a bad case of the flu."

Merle leaned back, then looked across at Suomi. He was sitting there with a half-smile on his face, stroking his gray beard with one finger. Chalk one up to VVV's intelligence service. Suomi had known about Petzell's illness in advance.

Wolff closed the opening preamble with the usual warning about staying away from the technical men in the government until the award was announced. Well, why not? Anybody who didn't have all his sources lined up well before the Request For Proposal hit the streets was a dead duck anyway.

Wolff came at last to the guts of the meeting. "We will now answer the questions from prospective bidders. All questions have been submitted in writing in advance. All answers will be given in writing to all attendees. Will you please identify yourselves as you read your questions. First question, please."

"Jim Peters, Consultec. How will you be applying the Equal Employment Opportunity Clause in this job?" The speaker was well known to Merle. From his Baltimore offices, Peters could be relied on to find a few hundred talented mercenaries for any job.

"As far as feasible. We know it's not easy for any of you. We don't expect an exact split, but we do want to see some WASPs in there. We can't accept a bid that's all blacks and Puerto Ricans. And we'd really like to see some minorities up near the top of your team, not just a bunch of retired West Pointers. That answer it?"

Peters shrugged. Wolff and the other government men knew his problem well enough.

"Next."

"Oral Jones, Rockdonnell Industries. It's not clear from the Request For Proposal how much Government Furnished Equipment we should assume. Can you give us any guidance?"

"It's been left open. It's up to you. Use GFE for anything; weapons, food, medical supplies, if you want to. Bid it yourselves if you think you can get it cheaper. We'll be happy to give you our price lists so you can see what we pay."

Merle sniffed. Dumb question. Nobody could undercut government prices on supplies, unless they were buying stolen goods. GSA insisted on the best prices in town from everybody. Merle waited for the real action to start.

"Warren McVittie, Lockheed. I have a question on types of bid."

Merle noticed that the Lockheed and the Rockdonnell reps were sitting in pairs. Jack Tukey was over on the left-hand side, well away from Merle, where he could keep an eye on Suomi's crack salesman, Vince Menoudakis, and also on the men from Lectron Industries and Lockheed. He and Merle were careful to remain well apart, to get independent views of the meeting, and Tolly Suomi and

Vince Menoudakis followed the same logic. Merle also
noticed that the Lectron and Lockheed men were not
their most senior reps. Suomi's presence confirmed Merle's
own feelings—that this meeting was going to be a real
groundbreaker. Top men should be there. Score one point
against Lectron and Lockheed.

"The bid request is not clear," went McVittie. "On page
24 of the RFP, there's a note to say that bidders may
choose to quote cost-plus or fixed-price. That's a new
clause for this kind of procurement. Are you actually invit-
ing fixed-price bids for the whole job?"

The action had arrived. Merle Walters leaned forward
intently. This was one of the questions he had come to
hear an answer to. Wolff looked a little uneasy, and paused
before he replied.

"Just what it says. Bid it cost-plus-fixed-fee, cost-plus-
incentive-fee, or fixed-price. It's up to you. I think I
should tell you that, other things being equal, fixed-price
bids will be favored." He stopped, then apparently felt
obliged to add another comment. "I know it's new, but
this will probably be our policy in the future on this type
of project."

Fixed-price. A whole new set of parameters to worry
about. Merle sat deep in thought, until he was roused by
Jack Tukey's voice.

"Jack Tukey, WAWD Corporation. I'd like to ask about
deliverables, especially in view of what you said about a
preference for a fixed-price contract. What are the project
deliverables, and how will they be evaluated?"

"If you bid fixed-price, there's only one real deliverable.
The overall tactical position at the end of the contract
period must be acceptable in territorial holdings. We realize this gives you problems in bidding, since we can't at
this time reveal to you the exact area where the engagement will be fought. However, this deliverable will be
developed in detail during the final contract negotiation,
when a vendor has been selected."

Nasty. In other words, you're bidding it blind, fellers.
And if you won't play the fixed-price game, you probably
lose outright. Some smartie in the government was being
super-tricky. Merle tried to fit it together.

"Vince Menoudakis, VVV Industries." The voice was

soft, with a slight trace of a stammer. Merle awakened again from his trance. He always liked to see an artist at work, and Vince was one of the great ones. "Mr. Wolff, the geography makes a big difference to the cost of the action. You know that just as well as we do. Now, wouldn't it save the government money if the bidders could be told the fighting area? There would be less work for you in negotiation, more precise bids from each of us, and a bigger effort on our part to get the really best strategies for the terrain. Where will the project be located, Mr. Wolff?"

Merle smiled to himself. In five or six sentences, Vince had somehow done his usual stroking job. How did he do it? Wolff was smiling and nodding, responding to some mysterious warmth in the questioner. If he were available, Menoudakis would really be a catch for WAWD. Earlier tries proved that Tolly Suomi knew it. He had Vince pretty well locked in.

"Yes, it would certainly save time later. Our main area—" Wolf actually began a reply before he realized what he was doing. He stopped. "Our main area is—roughly in the latitude range 15 to 25 degrees, as it says in the Request For Proposal. That is as far as I can go—after all, Mr. Menoudakis, war has not yet been declared. We don't want to start an international incident here, do we?"

Nice try, Vince. Pulling an area out of Wolff wouldn't have helped VVV much—everybody else would share the information. Suomi had gone along with it just to rub into the rest of them what a master Vince Menoudakis was. Jack Tukey had hit the nail on the head the first time he had met Menoudakis at a debriefing. "I don't remember what he said to me, Merle, but if he'd asked me to marry him, I'd probably have agreed."

The meeting broke up at about 11:30. Merle and Jack Tukey shared a cab back to the WAWD offices on Wisconsin Avenue. They had lots to talk about. Jack had news on the evaluation procedure, straight from the horse's mouth: Petzell's secretary.

"Do you realize I was in the Embers with Lottie Mitchell until two o'clock this morning? I'm telling you, she nearly drank me under the table. I should be getting danger money for my liver. I had seven bourbons and then I just lost count—and Lottie didn't have a hair out of place. Then we went on over to her apartment, and you won't believe this, but at half-past three, I found myself doing—"

"Jack, I should get money from you for introducing you to Lottie in the first place," interrupted Merle. "Stop stringing me out and get to the point. I'm well aware that you do it on purpose."

Jack Tukey grinned. It was a pleasure to see Merle rise to the bait. "All right, if you've got no romance in your soul. It's going to be a four-man review board. Technical evaluation will count 40 points, price 60 points. Now for the bad news. This one's going fixed-price, or nothing. Lottie says there's no way they'll give it out on a cost-plus basis. Where does that leave us, Merle?"

Walters looked out at the leafless November trees on Pennsylvania Avenue. "In deep shit, my boy. In up to our necks." He spoke quietly, almost abstractedly. "You know, we've never tried to be the low-dollar man on these bids. WAWD offers quality. But I don't know if we can do it this time. Six outfits can underbid us. They'll not be a patch on us technically. But you heard those deliverables. Completely undefined. Have the status halfway right after a year, and you'll get paid. And an option to renew for another two years. Doesn't matter how shaky the field position is, as far as I can tell." He fell silent as they drove through the rutted streets of Georgetown. "I'm telling you, Jack. Some half-wit's dreamed this one up to make his name in the government. We've got to think of some way round it. Fixed-price war, is it? What's our edge now?"

He was silent again for a few minutes, then nodded. "When we get to the office, Jack, call up Lottie and make a date for tonight. Most of all, I have to know *where* this war will be fought. That's the top priority. Location—and combatants. We've got a six-month job ahead of us, and two weeks to do it in. You'll have to risk your kidneys again. And one other thing. I need to know how they'll be auditing this one. If it's genuine fixed-price, there shouldn't be any government audit of it at all."

Merle sat slumped in the car seat, staring into space. His right hand rubbed the shoulder of his empty sleeve, and his blunt features were twisted in thought. Jack thought how much the old man was aging, how ill he looked. Maybe this effort was just too much to ask of him.

Merle glared at him, suddenly alive again.

"Stop gawping at me like a half-wit, Jack. When we get to the office, I want to talk to CBS and NBC. You handle ABC. Here's the way it goes."

Jack felt a surge of relief as Merle outlined his plans. Down but not out. As usual, Merle seemed to have found his angle.

"Can we price it low enough, Merle?"

"If it works out the way I'm hoping, we can underbid everybody in the business. I want you to fly out to the West Coast tomorrow night and bounce the main ideas off Alex Burns. He's key to this. I'll find somebody else to woo Lottie in your absence. Maybe I'll recruit Vince Menoudakis for the job."

Jack sniffed. "You'll be doing Lottie a disservice. You know these high-power sales types. Lots of promises—until it's time to deliver. Then they don't have what it takes. Tolly Suomi—he's the man for my money."

"You don't have that much money, Jack. Here, give me a hand to get my stiff leg out of the cab. I feel like Pinocchio today."

The air was full of gray sand and black smoke, blinding the soldiers and blotting out the fierce desert sun. Tanks were barreling forward through the dust, a group of men with combat lasers following each one. The long, high scream of an omni-projector was approaching along a dry wadi, and a Clarke neutralizer was turning to meet it, lobed antennae moving into exact phase for cancellation. The operators of the neutralizer were tunneling deep into narrow trenches in the sand, reading the strength of the omni-projector signal on the dials set in their helmet displays.

"Mr. Suomi calling on line one, Mr. Walters."

"At last." Merle grunted in satisfaction. He left the screen display running, reached over, and picked up the receiver. Tolly Suomi's bland, unlined face appeared on the intercom screen.

"Perhaps I am calling at an inopportune time, Merle. It sounds as though you are tuned to the NBC news reports. Should I call back later?"

"No. I've been trying to reach you all day. I asked your office to find you and give you the message to call me. Where are you, Tolly?"

"Newark, New Jersey."

"Can you be here in Washington—tonight?"

As usual, Suomi's face betrayed no curiosity or surprise. "I can. By seven o'clock at the latest—perhaps by six-thirty."

"I'll be here." Merle broke the connection and leaned back in his chair, looking for a comfortable position.

On the screen, the Clarke neutralizer had been homed on by a seeking missile and was out of action. The omni-projector was advancing again. Men fell before it, flopping and convulsing like landed fish as the vibrations tuned to their central nervous system frequencies.

Merle watched as the NBC newscaster summarized the day's fighting, the advances and retreats. It was on the nose with his own scratch-pad estimates. He placed a call to Alex Burns and sketched out a scenario. Alex objected to some of the ideas, and they went at it hammer and tongs for the rest of the afternoon. When Suomi arrived, they were still arguing. Merle waved him to a seat, fired a final salvo, and cut the connection.

"Never try and argue with a Scotsman, Tolly. Stubborn as donkeys. Must be the oatmeal."

Suomi smiled, smooth white in smooth ivory. "Alex Burns?"

Merle nodded. "You know him, do you? He's right again, blast him." He leaned back, his voice a bit too casual. "Had any chance to see much of Alex's work? I was wondering what you think of him."

"The same as you do, Merle. Not just the best, the very best." Suomi smiled the Tolly smile, a fraction-of-an-inch elevation of the corners of his mouth. "Don't let's be coy, Merle. You know quite well I've tried to hire Alex Burns from you. Probably as many times as WAWD has tried to steal Vince Menoudakis—and with the same success. Nothing."

"Tolly, I don't own Alex. His job does. Get ahead of us on the simulations, and Alex would take a job with VVV tomorrow to find out how you do it. I couldn't hold him a day."

"And how to do that, when Alex Burns leads the world

on simulation mock-ups." Suomi waved his arm at the display screen. "He's an artist with that thing. He can make it more real than reality. Burns is a artist the way Disney was, posing as something else. I'll tell you, Merle, I've needed an Alex in the past six months."

Merle nodded, his eyes averted. "Aye, it's been a hard time for all of us, Tolly."

The reaction was a Suomi maximum. One eyebrow raised a fraction of an inch. The sign of strong emotion. "Hard? When you've won the last four war jobs in a row? Merle, I'm not here for social reasons. I dropped everything to get here today—just as you knew I would. We've been running in circles since the November bidders' conference, trying to find out how you can price the way you do and still make money. We've got our sources in Contracts Departments, same as you—and we still don't know how you do it."

Merle smiled, rubbing his left shoulder in his habitual gesture. "You're not a poker player, Tolly. You show your hand."

"I'm a chess player, Merle. I can tell when somebody is planning seven moves ahead and the rest of us are playing six. We've been competitors for a long time, the two of us. For fifteen years we've been neck and neck. Now, what's your secret?"

"You know, don't you, that we sewed up the TV rights for the Trucial War with NBC? That was a twenty-million-dollar deal, just for special footage."

"I know. It was a neat idea, putting it on the same basis as the Olympics—but I know that's not your trick. We caught on to that last Christmas, and now we use it in our bids, too." Suomi placed his hands flat on the desk between them. "The real thing, Merle. What will it cost me to get it? You know I'll find out anyway, if I stick at it. And VVV won't go broke without it. But you have to know what it feels like to lose four big ones in a row. Name your price, I'll pay it."

A lengthening silence. Merle looked out at the gardens far below, dusk falling over the bursting azaleas of early May. "You seem sure of yourself, Tolly. Got an insider in our accounting department?"

"I don't need that, Merle. Look at this office." He

gestured at the furniture. "The better you're doing, the cheaper and lousier the fixtures. I daren't sit down too hard on this chair in case it falls apart. Come on, Merle, let's get to it. What's your price?"

"I've got my price, Tolly. Here's the ticket I'm selling." He reached into his suit pocket and pulled out his wallet. From it he took a sheet of paper about seven inches square. "That came to me yesterday."

Tolly Suomi read through it, caught his breath, and read it again, slowly. At last he lifted his head and looked Merle Walters straight in the eye. "How long, Merle?"

"You tell me. The medics can't seem to agree. One month, six months, two years. From now on, it's a game of roulette. Good thing Jack Tukey's ready. He'll make a good president for WAWD." He paused expectantly. "Don't you agree, Tolly?"

Suomi hesitated, for the beat of a hummingbird's wing. "An excellent president, Merle. He has a good business head, he eats work, and he can pick the right people—and keep them, too. Jack will make a good president for WAWD—a great president. In ten years' time." His voice raised a little. "You see, Merle, we've met—what? Thirty or forty times over the past fifteen years? Most people wouldn't say we're close. But I think I know you as well as you know me. Jack Tukey has one failing, but it's one you can't live with. Jack doesn't hate war—yet—as Merle Walters hates it. He doesn't hate the stupidity of it, the cruelty of it, the very idea of it."

Merle bowed his head. "I'm a war hero, Tolly—didn't you know that? To a lot of people in this country I'm Mister War himself. Generals are proud to shake my hand. I got this"——he gestured at his empty sleeve and left leg—"being a hero, forty years ago in the Pacific. Fighting your countrymen. No, it's Tolly Suomi who really hates war, I would say. You remember World War Two, Tolly?"

"I was eight years old when it finished, Merle. I remember it. I lost no arm, no leg. But I was on holiday in the country, when my family were home in Nagasaki. I remember that. And other things. I remember your cost-benefit study, showing that napalm is not a cost-effective weapon of war. How much did that study cost you, Merle?"

"Enough so no one would question our results. And

VVV Industries' analysis, showing that antipersonnel fragmentation bombs aren't a good investment of war capital. How much did that one cost you, Tolly?

"As you say, Merle, enough. Vince did a marvelous sales pitch on that one."

"The next president of VVV, Tolly? Would Vince want it?"

Suomi looked quizzically at Walters and waved the thought away. "You don't hire Liszt and ask him to move pianos. Vince is an artist, too. He has something we can't analyze—no place for it in chess or poker. People like him; he likes them; he sells them. Never fails. He's right where he is."

Merle nodded quietly, rubbing the side of his face with his hand. The two men sat in silence for several minutes. Finally Merle spoke.

"So now you can guess my price, Tolly. The price for the secret, the way we can underbid the market, every time, on the fixed-price war jobs. Only one way I'll accept payment." He gestured at the photograph of Lyndon Johnson, hanging on the wall. "Know why I've got that picture up there, Tolly? I'll tell you. He's the man who turned me from a hawk to—what I am. I lost two sons in Vietnam. Two boys, too young to vote, to feed the ego of a man who wouldn't ever admit he was wrong.

"Merger, Tolly. Merger, with you at the top. Vince Menoudakis as VP of Sales, Alex Burns as VP of Production. And Jack Tukey as Executive VP, waiting in the wings. Your time will come too, Tolly, and Jack has to be ready. And maybe I'll be around here for a while yet, as a high-priced easy-life consultant for you—when you need stirring up a bit. Life's not chess and life's not poker, but there's some of both in it. Merger, Tolly. Let's talk terms."

Suomi sat, face expressionless, one hand stroking his beard. "Perhaps. Perhaps. Would Jack Tukey work for me?"

"He thinks you walk on water, Tolly. So does Alex."

"Suppose I agree, find out how you operate, then back out?"

"That's tough titty for Merle Walters. A man either goes along with his judgment of people, or he's got nothing. That's the least of my worries, Tolly."

Suomi was nodding slowly. "My ancestry and education prepared me for this, Merle. There has been something that year by year has bound our fortunes tighter together— two caterpillars in one cocoon." He held out his hand. "Agreed in principle—details to be worked out. I hope we both live to see an end—to the lawyers putting the groups together. It will take a while. You control a stock majority, I hope?"

Merle nodded. "As you do. I did a little tracing of the lines on VVV this morning."

"Then it can be done. So now, Merle, tell me. Tell me something that has been on my mind every spare minute for six months. You are bidding fixed-price and you are thirty percent lower than the rest of us. How are you doing it?" Suomi was leaning forward intently.

Merle opened the credenza behind him, pulled out a bottle and two glasses. "Champagne, Tolly. Let me savor the moment. You'll have to open it. It takes two hands."

"You were that sure of yourself?"

"Either way, I would drink the champagne. Take a look at this, Tolly."

He turned on the display screen. The picture filled with scenes of battle, again in the desert. The heat, the smoke, the noise, the chaos, almost the smell seemed to spring from the screen.

"Now, Tolly, what are you seeing?"

"The Trucial War. I don't know which action. Last week's, maybe, up on the border."

Merle smiled and raised his glass. "You've got a great eye, Tolly. It's the Trucials, it's even a border skirmish— but it's next week, not last week. You said that Alex Burns is a genius. I agree. Half the battles in that war never happen. They're Alex's simulations. We ship the footage to NBC—they pay for it—and they weave the commentary around it. Much better for them—they don't have to keep a camera team out in the field. About half the footage is genuine fighting. The rest is Alex."

Suomi's eyes were flicking from the screen to Merle and back again. He was running rapidly through the difficulties, the possibilities. "How can you meet the deliverables? How can you pass an audit?"

"No audit. Fixed-price war, remember? Deliverables?

We maintain the lines we promised—you know, these aren't wars to win, they're to hold the status quo. We find the bidders on the other side, as early in the game as we can. We agree what will be fought, what will be simulated. They buy the simulations they need from us—a tidy profit there for WAWD. We have to mix it up, in case there are parties of journalists or junketing politicians. They see genuine battles. How can somebody tell if the other battles they see n the screen are real?"

"And you make a profit?"

"Thirty-five percent. No matter how much the simulations cost, or how much it takes to keep things going smoothly, *nothing* costs as much as a war—even a small one. One other thing, Tolly. Go and take a look at the war hospitals. There are still deaths because there are still battles. We stopped the worst maiming a while back, the two of us, when we got rid of the worst weapons. Now, the injuries are down again—and WAWD gets credit for tactics and brilliant fighting."

Merle Walters raised his glass again. "Here's to the merger of WAWD Corporation and VVV Industries—the war leaders. You'll have to keep up the struggle now, Tolly, until someday, maybe, we'll get some sense. I'm not optimistic. We're aggressive animals, the lot of us. But here's to war, damn its soul."

Tolly Suomi was thoughtful. He flexed his shoulders, feeling a new weight there. At last, he too, raised his glass. "To the merger. And to our motto: War is much too serious a thing to be left to the government."

The glasses clinked. On the screen in front of them, the battle raged.

Dr. Sheffield is past President of the American Astronautical Society and of the Science Fiction Writers of America. He is a scientist and a Director of Earth Satellite

Corporation. He is a theoretical physicist, born in England and educated at Cambridge University, and is a Fellow or Member of several scientific societies here and in the United Kingdom.

Since 1963, he has been continuously involved with the U.S. Space Program, as a NASA investigator, as a consultant to NASA Headquarters, and most recently as an invited advisor to Congress.

He began to write science fiction in 1976, has published many stories and six novels. His non-fiction includes some forty papers in the fields of general relativity, gravitational field analysis, orbit computation, largescale computer systems, earth resources, and nuclear physics.

Scheduled for 1988 publication are the novels Trader's World, Procteus Unbound, *and* The Judas Crisis.

One of the persisting dangers inherent in winning a hard-fought war is that men can come to power who are poorly suited to nurture peace, men who do not understand its necessities, men with little sympathy for the freedoms it should bring. Only too often, victorious generals have become weak and inept heads of state. Only too often, erstwhile liberators have turned suddenly into tyrants. This has been a hazard throughout history, and it will continue to be one as long as we have wars—perhaps as long as men are men.

Poul Anderson

MARIUS

It was raining again, with a bite in the air as the planet spun toward winter. They hadn't yet restored the street lights, and an early dusk seeped up between ruined walls and hid the tattered people who dwelt in caves grubbed out of rubble. Étienne Fourre, chief of the Maquisard Brotherhood and therefore representative of France in the Supreme Council of United Free Europe, stubbed his toe on a cobblestone. Pain struck through a worn-out boot, and he swore with tired expertise. The fifty guards ringing him in, hairy men in a patchwork of clothes—looted from the uniforms of a dozen armies, their own insignia merely a hand-sewn Tricolor brassard—tensed. That was an automatic reaction, the bristling of a wolf at any unawaited noise, long ago drilled into them.

"*Eh, bien,*" said Fourre. "Perhaps Rouget de l'Isle stumbled on the same rock while composing the 'Marseillaise.' "

One-eyed Astier shrugged, an almost invisible gesture in the murk. "When is the next grain shipment due?" he asked. It was hard to think of anything but food above the noise of a shrunken belly, and the Liberators had shucked military formalities during the desperate years.

85

"Tomorrow, I think, or the next day, if the barges aren't waylaid by river pirates," said Fourre. "And I don't believe they will be, so close to Strasbourg." He tried to smile. "Be of good cheer, my old. Next year should give an ample harvest. The Americans are shipping us a new blight-preventive."

"Always next year," grumbled Astier. "Why don't they send us something to eat now?"

"The blights hit them, too. This is the best they can do for us. Had it not been for them, we would still be skulking in the woods sniping at Russians."

"We had a little something to do with winning."

"More than a little, thanks to Professor Valti. I do not think any of our side could have won without all the others."

"If you call this victory." Astier's soured voice faded into silence. They were passing the broken cathedral, where child-packs often hid. The little wild ones had sometimes attacked armed men with their jagged bottles and rusty bayonets. But fifty soldiers were too many of course. Fourre thought he heard a scuttering among the stones; but that might only have been the rats. Never had he dreamed there could be so many rats.

The thin, sad rain blew into his face and weighted his beard. Night rolled out of the east, like a message from Soviet lands plunged into chaos and murder. *But we are rebuilding*, he told himself defensively. Each week the authority of the Strasbourg Council reached a civilizing hand farther into the smashed countries of Europe. In ten years, five perhaps—automation was so fantastically productive, if only you could get hold of the machines in the first place—the men of the West would again be peaceful farmers and shopkeepers, their culture again a going concern.

If the multinational Councillors made the right decisions. And they had not been making them. Valti had finally convinced Fourre of that. Therefore he walked through the rain, hugging an old bicycle poncho to his sleazy jacket, and men in barracks were quietly estimating how many jumps it would take to reach their racked weapons. For they must overpower those who did not agree.

A wry notion, that the feudal principle of personal loyalty to a chief should have to be invoked to enforce the decrees of a new mathematics that only some thousand minds in the world understood. But you wouldn't expect the Norman peasant Astier or the Parisian apache Renault to bend the scanty spare time of a year to learning the operations of symbolic sociology. You would merely say, "Come," and they would come because they loved you.

The streets resounded hollow under his feet. It was a world without logic, this one. Only the accidents of survival had made the village apothecary Étienne Fourre into the *de facto* commander of Free France. He could have wished those accidents had taken him and spared Jeanette, but at least he had two sons living, and someday, if they hadn't gotten too much radiation, there would be grandchildren. God was not altogether revengeful.

"There we are, up ahead," said Astier.

Fourre did not bother to reply. He had never been under the common human necessity of forever mouthing words.

Strasbourg was the seat of the Council because of location and because it was not too badly hit. Only a conventional battle with chemical explosives had rolled through here eighteen months ago. The University was almost unscathed, and so became the headquarters of Jacques Reinach. His men prowled about on guard; one wondered what Goethe would have thought could he have returned to the scene of his student days. And yet it was men such as this, with dirty hands and clean weapons, who were civilization. It was their kind who had harried the wounded Russian colossus out of the West and who would restore law and liberty and wind-rippled fields of grain. Someday. Perhaps.

A machine-gun nest stood at the first checkpoint. The sergeant in charge recognized Fourre and gave a sloppy salute. (Still, the fact that Reinach had imposed so much discipline on his horde spoke for the man's personality.) "Your escort must wait here, my general," he said, half-apologizing. "A new regulation."

"I know," said Fourre, Not all of his guards did, and he must shush a snarling. "I have an appointment with the Commandant."

"Yes, sir. Please stay to the lighted paths. Otherwise you might be shot by mistake for a looter."

Fourre nodded and walked through, in among the buildings. His body wanted to get in out of the rain, but he went slowly, delaying the moment. Jacques Reinach was not just his countryman but his friend. Fourre was nowhere near as close to, say, Helgesen of the Nordic Alliance, or the Italian Totti, or Rojansky of Poland, and he positively disliked the German Auerbach.

But Valti's matrices were not concerned with a man's heart. They simply told you that given such and such conditions, this and that would probably happen. It was a cold knowledge to bear.

The structure housing the main offices was a loom of darkness, but a few windows glowed at Fourre. Reinach had had an electric generator installed—and rightly, to be sure, when his tired staff and his tired self must often work around the clock.

A sentry admitted Fourre to an outer room. There half a dozen men picked their teeth and diced for cartridges while a tubercular secretary coughed over files written on old laundry bills, flyleaves, any scrap of paper that came to hand. The lot of them stood up, and Fourre told them he had come to see the Commandant, chairman of the Council.

"Yes, sir." The officer was still in his teens, fuzzy face already shriveled into old age, and spoke very bad French. "Check your guns with us and go on in."

Fourre unbuckled his pistols, reflecting that this latest requirement, the disarming of commanders before they could meet Chairman Reinach, was what had driven Álvarez into fury and the conspiracy. Yet the decree was not unreasonable; Reinach must know of gathering opposition, and everyone had grown far too used to settling disputes violently. Ah, well, Álvarez was no philosopher, but he was boss of the Iberian Irregulars, and you had to use what human material was available.

The officer frisked him, and that was a wholly new indignity, which heated Fourre's own skin. He choked his anger, thinking that Valti had predicted as much.

Down a corridor then, which smelled moldy in the autumnal dankness, and to a door where one more sentry was posted. Fourre nodded at him and opened the door.

"Good evening, Étienne. What can I do for you?"

The big blond man looked up from his desk and smiled. It was a curiously shy, almost a young smile, and something wrenched within Fourre.

This had been a professor's office before the war. Dust lay thick on the books that lined the walls. Really, they should take more care of books, even if it meant giving less attention to famine and plague and banditry. At the rear was a closed window, with a dark wash of rain flowing across miraculously intact glass. Reinach sat with a lamp by his side and his back to the night.

Fourre lowered himself. The visitor's chair creaked under a gaunt-fleshed but heavy-boned weight. "Can't you guess, Jacques?" he asked.

The handsome Alsatian face, one of the few clean-shaven faces left in the world, turned to study him for a while. "I wasn't sure you were against me, too," said Reinach. "Helgesen, Totti, Alexios . . . yes, that gang . . . but you? We have been friends for many years, Étienne. I didn't expect you would turn on me."

"Not on you." Fourre sighed and wished for a cigarette, but tobacco was a remote memory. "Never you, Jacques. Only your policies. I am here, speaking for all of us—"

"Not quite all," said Reinach. His tone was quiet and unaccusing. "Now I realize how cleverly you maneuvered my firm supporters out of town. Brevoort flying off to Ukrainia to establish relations with the revolutionary government; Ferenczi down in Genoa to collect those ships for our merchant marine; Janosek talked into leading an expedition against the bandits in Schleswig. Yes, yes, you plotted this carefully, didn't you? But what do you think they will have to say on their return?"

"They will accept a *fait accompli*," answered Fourre. "This generation has had a gutful of war. But I said I was here to speak to you on behalf of my associates. We hoped you would listen to reason from me, at least."

"If it is reason." Reinach leaned back in his chair, cat-comfortable, one palm resting on a revolver butt. "We have threshed out the arguments in council. If you start them again—"

"—it is because I must." Fourre sat looking at the scarred, bony hands in his lap. "We do understand, Jacques, that

the chairman of the Council must have supreme power for
the duration of the emergency. We agreed to give you the
final word. But not the *only* word."

A paleness of anger flicked across the blue eyes. "I have
been maligned enough," said Reinach coldly. "They think
I want to make myself a dictator. Étienne, after the Second War was over and you went off and became a snug
civilian, why do you think I elected to make the Army my
career? Not because I had any taste for militarism. But I
foresaw our land would again be in danger, within my own
lifetime, and I wanted to hold myself ready. Does that
sound like . . . like some new kind of Hitler?"

"No, of course not, my friend. You did nothing but
follow the example of de Gaulle. And when we chose you
to lead our combined forces, we could not have chosen
better. Without you—and Valti—there would still be war
on the eastern front. We . . . I . . . we think of you as our
deliverer, just as if we were the littlest peasant given back
his own plot of earth. But you have not been *right*."

"Everyone makes mistakes." Reinach actually smiled. "I
admit my own. I bungled badly in cleaning out those
Communists at—"

Fourre shook his head stubbornly. "You don't understand, Jacques. It isn't that kind of mistake I mean. Your
great error is that you have not realized we are at peace.
The war is over."

Reinach lifted a sardonic brow. "Not a barge goes along
the Rhine, not a kilometer of railroad track is relaid, but
we have to fight bandits, local warlords, half-crazed fanat-
ics of a hundred new breeds. Does that sound like
peacetime?"

"It is a difference of . . . of objectives," said Fourre.
"And man is such an animal that it is the end, not the
means, which makes the difference. War is morally simple: one purpose, to impose your will upon the enemy.
Not to surrender to an inferior force. But a policeman? He
is protecting an entire society, of which the criminal is also
a part. A politician? He has to make compromises, even
with small groups and with people he despises. You think
like a soldier, Jacques, and we no longer want or need a
soldier commanding us."

"Now you're quoting that senile fool Valti," snapped Reinach.

"If we hadn't had Professor Valti and his sociosymbolic logic to plan our strategy for us, we would still be locked with the Russians. There was no way for us to be liberated from the outside this time. The Anglo-Saxon countries had little strength to spare, after the exchange of missiles, and that little had to go to Asia. They could not invade a Europe occupied by a Red Army whose back was against the wall of its own wrecked homeland. We had to liberate ourselves, with ragged men and bicycle cavalry and aircraft patched together out of wrecks. Had it not been for Valti's plans—and, to be sure, your execution of them—we could never have done so." Fourre shook his head again. He would *not* get angry with Jacques. "I think such a record entitles the professor to respect."

"True . . . then." Reinach's tone lifted and grew rapid. "But he's senile now, I tell you. Babbling of the future, of long-range trends—Can we eat the future? People are dying of plague and starvation and anarchy now!"

"He has convinced me," said Fourre. "I thought much the same as you, myself, a year ago. But he instructed me in the elements of his science, and he showed me the way we are heading. He is an old man, Eino Valti, but a brain still lives under that bald pate."

Reinach relaxed. Warmth and tolerance played across his lips. "Very well, Étienne," he asked, "what way are we heading?"

Fourre looked past him into night "Toward war," he said quite softly. "Another nuclear war, some fifty years hence. It isn't certain the human race can survive that."

Rain stammered on the windowpanes, falling hard now, and wind hooted in the empty streets. Fourre glanced at his watch. Scant time was left. He fingered the police whistle hung about his neck.

Reinach had started. But gradually he eased back. "If I thought that were so," he replied, "I would resign this minute."

"I know you would," mumbled Fourre. "That is what makes my task so hard for me."

"However, it isn't so." Reinach's hand waved as if to

brush away a nightmare. "People have had such a grim
lesson that—"

"People, in the mass, don't learn," Fourre told him.
"Did Germany learn from the Hundred Years' War, or we
from Hiroshima? The only way to prevent future wars is to
establish a world peace authority: to reconstitute the United
Nations and give it some muscles, as well as a charter
which favors civilization above any fiction of 'equality.'
And Europe is crucial to that enterprise. North of the
Himalayas and east of the Don is nothing anymore—howling
cannibals. It will take too long to civilize them again. We,
ourselves, must speak for the whole Eurasian continent."

"Very good, very good," said Reinach impatiently.
"Granted. But what am I doing that is wrong?"

"A great many things, Jacques. You have heard about
them in the Council. Need I repeat the long list?" Fourre's
head turned slowly, as if it creaked on its neckbones, and
locked eyes with the man behind the desk. "It is one thing
to improvise in wartime. But you are improvising the
peace. You forced the decision to send only two men to
represent our combined nations at the conference planned
in Rio. Why? Because we're short on transportation, cleri-
cal help, paper, even on decent clothes! The problem
should have been studied. It may be all right to treat
Europe as a unit—or it may not; perhaps this will actually
exacerbate nationalism. You made the decision in one
minute when the question was raised, and would not hear
debate."

"Of course not," said Reinach harshly. "If you remember, that was the day we learned of the neofascist coup in
Corsica."

Corsica could have waited awhile. The place would have
been more difficult to win back, yes, if we hadn't struck at
once. But this business of our U.N. representation could
decide the entire future of—"

"I know, I know. Valti and his theory about the 'pivotal
decision.' Bah!"

"The theory happens to work, my old."

"Within proper limits. I'm a hardhead, Étienne, I admit
that." Reinach leaned across the desk, chuckling. "Don't
you think the times demand a hard head? When hell is
romping loose, it's no time to spin fine philosophies . . . or

try to elect a parliament, which I understand is another of the postponements Dr. Valti holds against me."

"It is," said Fourre. "Do you like roses?"

"Why, why . . . yes." Reinach blinked. "To look at, anyway." Wistfulness crossed his eyes. "Now that you mention it, it's been many years since I last saw a rose."

"But you don't like gardening. I remember that from, from old days." The curious tenderness of man for man, which no one has ever quite explained, tugged at Fourre. He cast it aside, not daring to do otherwise, and said impersonally: "And you like democratic government, too, but were never interested in the grubby work of maintaining it. There is a time to plant seeds. If we delay, we will be too late; strong-arm rule will have become too ingrained a habit."

"There is also a time to keep alive. Just to keep alive, nothing else."

"Jacques, I don't accuse you of hardheartedness. You are a sentimentalist: you see a child with belly bloated from hunger, a house marked with a cross to show that the Black Death has walked in—and you feel too much pity to be able to think. It is . . . Valti, myself, the rest of us . . . who are cold-blooded, who are prepared to sacrifice a few thousand more lives now, by neglecting the immediately necessary, for the sake of saving all humankind fifty years hence."

"You may be right," said Reinach. "About your cold souls, I mean." His voice was so low that the rain nearly drowned it.

Fourre stole another look at his watch. This was taking longer than expected. He said in a slurred, hurried tone: "What touched off tonight's affair was the Pappas business."

"I thought so," Reinach agreed evenly. "I don't like it either. I know as well as you do that Pappas is a murderous crypto-Communist scoundrel whose own people hate him. But curse it, man, don't you know rats do worse than steal food and gnaw the faces of sleeping children? Don't you know they spread plague? And Pappas has offered us the services of the only efficient rat-exterminating force in Eurasia. He asks nothing in return except that we recognize his Macedonian Free State and give him a seat on the Council."

"Too high a price," said Fourre. "In two or three years we can bring the rats under control ourselves."

"And meanwhile?"

"Meanwhile, we must hope that nobody we love is taken sick."

Reinach grinned without mirth. "It won't do," he said. "I can't agree to that. If Pappas' squads help us, we can save a year of reconstruction, a hundred thousand lives—"

"And throw away lives by the hundred millions in the future."

"Oh, come now. One little province like Macedonia?"

"One very big precedent," said Fourre. "We will not merely be conceding a petty warlord the right to his loot. We will be conceding"—he lifted furry hands and counted off on the fingers—"the right of any ideological dictatorship, anywhere, to exist: which right, if yielded, means war and war and war again; the fatally outmoded principle of unlimited national sovereignty; the friendship of an outraged Greece, which is sure to invoke that same principle in retaliation; the inevitable political repercussions throughout the Near East, which is already turbulent enough; therefore war between us and the Arabs, because we *must* have oil; a seat on the Council to a clever and ruthless man who, frankly, Jacques, can think rings around you—No!"

"You are theorizing about tomorrow," said Reinach. "The rats are already here. What would you have me do instead?"

"Refuse the offer. Let me take a brigade down there. We can knock Pappas to hell . . . unless we let him get too strong first."

Reinach shook his head goodnaturedly. "Who's the warmonger now?" he said with a laugh.

"I never denied we still have a great deal of fighting ahead of us," Fourre said. Sadness tinged his voice; he had seen too many men spilling their guts on the ground and screaming. "I only want to be sure it will serve the final purpose, that there shall never again be a world war. That my children and grandchildren will not have to fight at all."

"And Valti's equations show the way to achieve that?" Reinach asked quietly.

"Well, they show how to make the outcome reasonably probable."

"I'm sorry, Étienne." Reinach shook his head. "I simply cannot believe that. Turning human society into a . . . what's the word? . . . a potential field, and operating on it with symbolic logic: it's too remote. I am here, in the flesh—such of it as is left, on our diet—not in a set of scribbles made by some band of long-haired theorists."

"A similar band discovered atomic energy," said Fourre. "Yes, Valti's science is young. But within admitted limitations, it works. If you would just study—"

"I have too much else on hand." Reinach shrugged. A blankness drew across his face. "We've wasted more time than I can afford already. What does your group of generals want me to do?"

Fourre gave it to him as he knew his comrade would wish it, hard and straight like a bayonet thrust. "We ask for your resignation. Naturally, you'll keep a seat on the Council, but Professor Valti will assume the chairmanship and set about making the reforms we want. We will issue a formal promise to hold a constitutional convention in the spring and dissolve the military government within one year."

He bent his head and looked at the time. A minute and a half remained.

"No," said Reinach.

"But—"

"Be still!" The Alsatian stood up. The single lamp threw his shadow grotesque and enormous across the dusty books. "Do you think I didn't see this coming? Why do you imagine I let only one man at a time in here, and disarm him? The devil with your generals! The common people know me, they know I stand for them first—and hell take your misty futures! We'll meet the future when it gets here."

"That is what man has always done," said Fourre. He spoke like a beggar. "And that is why the race has always blundered from one catastrophe to the next. This may be our last chance to change the pattern."

Reinach began pacing back and forth behind his desk. "Do you think I like this miserable job?" he retorted. "It simply happens that no one else can do it."

"So now you are the indispensable man," whispered Fourre. "I had hoped you would escape that."

"Go on home, Étienne." Reinach halted, and kindness returned to him. "Go back and tell them I won't hold this against them personally. You had a right to make your demand. Well, it has been made and refused." He nodded to himself thoughtfully. "We will have to make some change in our organization, though. I don't want to be a dictator, but—"

Zero hour. Fourre felt very tired.

He had been denied, and so he had not blown the whistle that would stop the rebels, and matters were out of his hands now.

"Sit down," he said. "Sit down, Marius, and let us talk about old times for a while."

Reinach looked surprised. "Marius? What do you mean?"

"Oh . . . an example from history which Professor Valti gave me." Fourre considered the floor. There was a cracked board by his left foot. Cracked and crazy, a tottering wreck of a civilization, how had the same race built Chartres and the hydrogen bomb?

His words dragged out of him: "In the second century before Christ, the Cimbri and their allies, Teutonic barbarians, came down out of the north. For a generation they wandered about, ripping Europe apart. They chopped to pieces the Roman armies sent to stop them. Finally they invaded Italy. It did not look as if they could be halted before they took Rome herself. But one general by the name of Marius rallied his men. He met the barbarians and annihilated them."

"Why, thank you." Reinach sat down, puzzled. "But—"

"Never mind." Fourre's lips twisted into a smile. "Let us take a few minutes free and just talk. Do you remember that night soon after the Second War, we were boys freshly out of the Maquis, and we tumbled around the streets of Paris and toasted the sunrise from Sacre Coeur?"

"Yes. To be sure. That was a wild night!" Reinach laughed. "How long ago it seems. What was your girl's name? I've forgotten."

"Marie. And you had Simone. A beautiful little baggage, Simone. I wonder whatever became of her."

"I don't know. The last I heard—No. Remember how bewildered the waiter was when—"

A shot cracked through the rain, and then the wrathful

clatter of machine guns awoke. Reinach was on his feet in
one tiger bound, pistol in hand, crouched by the window.
Fourre stayed seated.

The noise lifted, louder and closer. Reinach spun about.
His gun muzzle glared emptily at Fourre.

"Yes, Jacques."

"*Mutiny!*"

"We had to." Fourre discovered that he could again
meet Reinach's eyes. "The situation was that crucial. If
you had yielded . . . if you had even been willing to
discuss the question . . . I would have blown this whistle
and nothing would have happened. Now we're too late,
unless you want to surrender. If you do, our offer still
stands. We still want you to work with us."

A grenade blasted somewhere nearby.

"You—"

"Go on and shoot. It doesn't matter very much."

"No." The pistol wavered. Not unless you—Stay where
you are! Don't move!" The hand Reinach passed across his
forehead shuddered. "You know how well this place is
guarded. You know the people will rise to my side."

"I think not. They worship you, yes, but they are tired
and starved. Just in case, though, we staged this for the
nighttime. By tomorrow morning the business will be
over." Fourre spoke like a rusty engine. "The barracks
have already been seized. Those more distant noises are
the artillery being captured. The University is surrounded
and cannot stand against an attack."

"This building can."

"So you won't quit, Jacques?"

"If I could do that," said Reinach, "I wouldn't be here
tonight."

The window broke open. Reinach whirled. The man
who was vaulting through shot first.

The sentry outside the door looked in. His rifle was
poised, but he died before he could use it. Men with black
clothes and blackened faces swarmed across the sill.

Fourre knelt beside Reinach. A bullet through the head
had been quick, at least. But if it had struck farther down,
perhaps Reinach's life could have been saved. Fourre wanted
to weep, but he had forgotten how.

The big man who had killed Reinach ignored his commandos to stoop over the body with Fourre. "I'm sorry, sir," he whispered. It was hard to tell whom he spoke to.

"Not your fault, Stefan." Fourre's voice jerked.

"We had to run through the shadows, get under the wall. I got a boost through this window. Didn't have time to take aim. I didn't realize who he was till—"

"It's all right, I said. Go on, now, take charge of your party, get this building cleaned out. Once we hold it, the rest of his partisans should yield pretty soon."

The big man nodded and went out into the corridor.

Fourre crouched by Jacques Reinach while a sleet of bullets drummed on the outer walls. He heard them only dimly. Most of him was wondering if this hadn't been the best ending. Now they could give their chief a funeral with full military honors, and later they would build a monument to the man who saved the West, and—

And it might not be quite that easy to bribe a ghost. But you had to try.

"I didn't tell you the whole story, Jacques," he said. His hands were like a stranger's, using his jacket to wipe off the blood, and his words ran on of themselves. "I wish I had. Maybe you would have understood . . . and maybe not. Marius went into politics afterward, you see. He had the prestige of his victory behind him, he was the most powerful man in Rome, his intentions were noble, but he did not understand politics. There followed a witch's dance of corruption, murder, civil war, fifty years of it—the final extinction of the Republic. Caesarism merely gave a name to what had already been done.

"I would like to think that I helped spare Jacques Reinach the name of Marius."

Rain slanted in through the broken window. Fourre reached out and closed the darkened eyes. He wondered if he would ever be able to close them within himself.

———————————————

Poul Anderson is the author of more than fifty books and two-hundred-and-some short pieces. Besides science fiction, these include fantasy, mystery, historical, juvenile, and here-and-now fiction; nonfiction; poetry, essays, translations, criticism, etc. His short stories and articles have appeared in places as various as the sf magazines, Boy's Life, Playboy, *the Toronto* Star Weekly, National Review, Ellery Queen's, *and the now defunct* Jack London's Magazine. *His novels, nonfiction books, and short stories have appeared in fifteen foreign languages.*

He is a former regional Vice-President of Mystery Writers of America and former President of the Science Fiction Writers of America, and he has had several Hugo and Nebula Awards, the "Forry" Award of the Los Angeles Science Fantasy Society, a special issue of The Magazine of Fantasy and Science Fiction, *the Macmillan Cock Robin Award for the best mystery novel, and others. Among his most popular books are* Brain Wave, The High Crusade, The Enemy Stars, Three Hearts and Three Lions, The Broken Sword, *and* Tau Zero. *More recent titles are* There Will Be Time, The People of the Wind, A Midsummer Tempest, *and* Fire Time *(a Hugo nominee).*

Poul Anderson lives in the San Francisco Bay Area with his wife Karen. Their daughter Astrid is married to fellow writer Greg Bear and has presented them with a grandson.

Two factors militate against any precise forecast of the nature and power of weapons in future warfare: the first is the necessary secrecy veiling so much weapons development; the second, probably no less important, is the rapidly increasing effectiveness and sophistication of weapons-associated instruments.

Where weapons power is concerned, I know of no better way of demonstrating what has happened, is happening, and is bound to happen than to quote from a 1964 study on weapons lethality prepared for the United States Army:*

WEAPONS

Sword, pike, etc.	20
World War I machine gun	12,730
French 75-mm gun	340,000
World War II medium tank	2,203,000
One-megaton nuclear airburst	661,500,000

What we have here is a rapidly ascending geometrical progression, characteristic of any well-funded application of science and technology. We can easily extrapolate from the few figures I have given, taking into consideration assorted ICBMs, orbital weapons, beam weapons, possibly neuroelectronic weapons, chemical and biological weapons—you name it.

My own opinion is that many sf writers have erred on the side of being too conservative, too earthbound, and have failed to give adequate consideration to this progression; not only where weapons are concerned, but also with regard to the associated instruments (of transport and control, for instance) mentioned above.

Finally, there is a third curve or set of curves, the most difficult of all to extrapolate, governing the appearance of completely new and unanticipated weapons and instruments.

Here Roger A. Beaumont and R. Snowden Ficks explore some of the possibilities.

*Historical Evaluation and Research Organization, "Historical Trends Related to Weapon Lethality," 1964.

Roger A. Beaumont
and R. Snowden Ficks

WEAPONS IN FUTURE WARFARE

Awareness of the military advantage offered by space has been prominent, in science fiction and during the age of actual exploration. Of course, the Outer Space Treaty of 1967—the "Mother Treaty"—prohibited military activity in space. Although the Soviet Union signed it, its space activities have remained basically military in nature from the first. Russian space launches are conducted by the Rocket Forces, and major Soviet efforts in the 1960s were aimed at development of an orbiting bomb-carrying satellite—FOBS, fractional orbiting bombardment system— followed by a "killer satellite" program. At the same time, the United States tried to keep space exploration a civilian affair, allowing the world press and the public to attend U.S. space shots; and while the creation of NASA was a step away from armed service control, military involvement was unavoidable due to shared technology and personnel needs. (The preponderance of military pilots in astronaut roles has been the focus of recent debate.) In that respect, it is interesting to note that much space aboard the Space Shuttle has been allocated to the U.S. Air Force.

In any event, those roseate visions of a conflict-free cosmos are gone. War in space is now being planned openly; and if a broad definition is applied, inner space— the zone between the Earth and Moon—is already a theater of operations and has been since the early 1960s, with a myriad of spy satellites scattered among 4,000 pieces of orbiting hardware, freely carrying out strategic missions. If this is the first step, what will be the second?

101

The Evolving Context

At the time of this writing, in late 1978, the stationing of a bombardment platform in inner space, carrying nuclear missiles, lasers, or charged-particle weapons, is openly discussed, and is not beyond the scope of contemporary technology or strategic thinking. Yet such a system, manned or automated, is really only a slight extension of contemporary military systems and policy, and does not truly represent war in space. This will also be the case in related military space operations in the next decade or so, with space serving not so much as an independent zone of conflict, but as a component in an Earth-based strategic equation. Presuming the millennium is not at hand, and total peace does not arrive, space conflict of the kind envisioned in such works as Haldeman's *The Forever War* will not be seen until man moves well out into the solar system, establishing mining and industrial colonies, and when distance and time, combined with technology, create conditions for independent action, unrelated to the security or perhaps even the perceived interest of terrestrial states.

The Immediate Future

Initial combat in space would at this point be analogous to WWI air operations with fragile, primitive craft operating over limited areas, with the exception that many first generation space fighters might well be unmanned drones. Space weaponry in the immediate future will draw heavily on current or designed aircraft and antiaircraft systems. At the present time, the shift from passive to active forms of strategic space hardware is led by direct-energy weapons, in the form of the laser, whose main application so far has been range-finding, but which has also been examined as an instrument for ballistic missile defense. Since 1968, U.S. high-energy laser research has been classified, with occasional reports of experimental weapons under development emerging from time to time. The canceled B-1 bomber was reported to have carried a laser gun as defensive armament. Among types of lasers now in the forefront of military discussion, according to the 1978 edition of *Jane's Weapons Systems*, are carbon-dioxide gas dynamic and carbon-dioxide electric. Development of beam weapons is also under-way, as are refinements in propulsion, guidance, reconnaissance techniques, and attendant technical systems.

The complex of change has already eroded the nearly pristine view of the solar system and space as a kind of simplistic mechanical model. More and more subtleties and nuances, such as the Van Allen Belts and LaGrange libration points, are filling in the "map" of space and reducing the ability to extrapolate and anticipate with any sense of surety. Innovation in technology produces pressure to adapt in the realm of policy and doctrine. Controllers tend, as they have in terrestrial warfare during the Industrial Age, to lag behind in their visualizing the future and altering systems to maximize potential. The interaction between the forces of inertia and change in modern organization is laden with high drama, sometimes farce, and occasionally tragedy. As cyberneticians are aware, an increase in numbers and sophistication in a system increases the range of possibilities rather more geometrically than arithmetically.

The Dilemma of Perception

The difficultues of conceptualizing such changes in any kind of perspective are evident in the vagueness of description of battles between spacecraft in militarily oriented science fiction. While undoubtedly a testament to the Duke of Wellington's observation that he would as soon describe a battle as a ball, many of the actions in science fiction are treated broadly, metamorphically, or take place in a two-dimensional matrix on the surface of planets, rather than in the fluid and shifting context of space. The fixation, in recent space-opera, on fighter aircraft and tactics, slightly extrapolated from the models of World War II is one example of that problem.

The craft in *Star Trek*, *Star Wars*, and *Battlestar Galactica* are designed to fight in a two-dimensional plane, have individual pilots, no evident problem from solar glare, or from the incredibly high gravitational stresses depicted. They fly in formations oriented to a gravitational plane even in deep space, and yet somehow seem able to monitor the 360-degree environment in which they operate, without great concern for jamming, spoofing, or jinking, all in the spirit of *Wings*, *Hell's Angels*, *Dawn Patrol*, *Fighter Squadron*, and *Baa, Baa, Black Sheep*.

The Tactical Spectrum

Given the scarcity of resources and repair facilities in space, one might well expect to see tactics conform to some variant of the pattern seen in desert warfare in the twentieth century, in which scavenging and refitting enemy equipment for one's own use became a major dimension, and in which tactical brilliance was offset by communication and supply factors. Similarly, targeting could be expected to minimize damage, to compartmentalize it, leaving the targeted system with capacity to barely function, perhaps only with the assistance of the attacker, thus assuring the support of the conquered in a unique way. The design of operations to maximize apparent threat rather than inflict damage would conform to the pattern of increasing precision and diminishing collateral damage seen in conventional wars since 1970. In this respect, the use of insidious radiological or chemical warfare, vibration, electromagnetic waves, or poison might well become the focus of development.

The Implicit Redefinition of Leadership

Given these implicit complexities, an arms-control analyst might well ask, "Is it worth it?" and beyond that, "Is it possible?" A number of quandaries could arise as the military considerations begin to influence living patterns. Perhaps rigid selection or genetic alteration would produce a warrior subrace with the demands of conflict handled by direct human-battle computer links. A critical question that emerges from this is: how much of the control as well as the fighting might be handled by artificial intelligence? It is difficult—if not impossible—to imagine weapons systems free of the contest of command-and-control acting with total independence, but this will be a main question imposed by the arrival of superintelligent machines. In some tactical systems, machines already have been delegated the option of opening fire. A fear of artificial intelligence seizing the upper hand and overdependency of humans on mechanisms is laced through the corpus of science fiction, e.g., E.M. Forster's *The Machine Stops*, Harlan Ellison's "I Have No Mouth and I Must Scream," and Fred Saberhagen's *Berserker*.

Whatever type of weapon is used—solid or explosive missile, using magnetic, electromagnetic, chemical, or ki-

netic propulsion, beam weapons, mines, or abalative clouds—
its deployment or use in space poses problems of perception
and control which, as with the leap from two-to three-dimensional arrays of force, transcend in complexity most
Earthly conflict situations. This effect will be compounded
by several factors. Velocities and stresses of directional
change will be much greater, placing tremendous demands
on reflexes, the human body and spacecraft structure.

To add to the complexity, the operational matrix of
space is a sphere. The traditional two-dimensional planar
orientation to the Earth's surface will be gone. Although
pilots now operate in three-dimensional situations, land
reference and the role of gravity as orienting factors are
close at hand. In seeking adaptation to this new milieu,
crew selection and development techniques may move
toward genetic screening, and perhaps engineering, as
well as to more sophisticated selection, as demands on
crews increase with the scope and range of action. Opti-
mizing duty-tour periods and crew rotation would obviously be critical. Levels of rest-and-recuperation could be
programmed, varying in degree, to gradually reduce physiological tensions and then reintroduce them. It is fairly
obvious that new drugs and meditative techniques would
merit exploration, to enhance crew power and reduce
fatigue generated by the tension and physical demands of
space combat.

Further along, while human capabilities may initially
dictate the design of spacecraft and systems, more and
more of the actual fighting may be done by drones, controlled from and housed in the parent craft, or prepositioned
and actuated from a distance. In the way of yet further
complications, a weapon of any type fired in space will go
on until deflected by magnetic fields, radiation, or gravity
emanating from planets or stars, or until it collides with
gas clouds, dust, or meteors. The visions, so common in
science fiction from Buck Rogers to Lupoff's *Space War
Blues*, of ships and fleets blasting away wildly at each
other in virtual *art deco* Trafalgars, will give way to more
restrained vectors of fire. Ships, unless well out into deep
space, will be constrained by the background of satellites,
colonies, drones, other ships, and base planets. Maneuvering for maximum restricted background and hiding in

the sun's glare will be at a premium. The danger of their weapons' destructive effects continuing on beyond targets may see them reduced to but one (and not necessarily the most desirable) weapon in a diverse arsenal. Self-destruction or braking to zero-velocity of missiles will have to be considered, and the control of arrays of remotely actuated firing drones and stations may well emerge as alternatives. In this regard, it is interesting to note how combat information display systems and weapons portrayed in science-fiction films and television programs remain two-dimensional in presentation format.

The Naval Analogy

Another problem related to all this is that noted by F. W. Lanchester in 1914 in *War in the Air*, his well-known theoretical analysis of the implications of air war, in which he suggested that success in war went to the side that massed its units and went for the enemy's center. He hypothesized further that, all other things being equal, the relationship between opposing forces' firepower was a relationship of the *square* of the units of fire. A debate currently rages in respect to this problem over naval force mix; the problem is that many small units provide more targets, but are also more likely to be eliminated by first-round kills than are armored ships. This debate may well be expected to continue in regard to extraterrestrial force balance, which underlies the structural similarity between space war and naval war. Sailors in action must stay in one place physically and fight their part of the ship, analogous to cogs in a machine. Commanders share danger with their subordinates and in the way of a further parallel the crew live as shipmates the rest of the time. Science-fiction writers from Doc Smith on through Larry Niven and Jerry Pournelle have noted this, and have used naval forms of rank, usage, and organization in describing space forces-fleets-armadas-navies. (Perhaps the fact that Robert Heinlein went to the U.S. Naval Academy is worth mentioning at this point.)

As true spaceships develop, and form follows function, battle craft built in orbital construction yards will not resemble the cylindrical (some might suggest phallic) and unnecessarily aerodynamic configurations of science-fiction vessels. Yet, as science-fiction writers have noted, as these ships move out into space, the organizational model of the space forces will more resemble naval rather than an air-force analogy, or at least be a fusion of the two, whether operational conditions dictate large cruisers, a destroyer flotilla approach, or a spectrum analogous to the fleets of the world wars. Most combat will occur in space, and planetary actions will be limited and precise, akin to marine-commando operations and, at this point, it is hard to better the perspective of Heinlein in *Starship Trooper*.

The Weapons Possibility

What weapons will fleets of the more distant future carry into battle? The range of weaponry will be varied and complex, as will their methods of defense and protection. There will be limited application of weapons derived from existing concepts. Rotary cannon such as the U.S. Vulcan type and other aerial guns could have applications, but they would be limited by the consumable nature of their ammunition and resupply difficulties. This is also true for missiles of various sizes and types, be they explosive or solid. The role of missile weapons—versus—beam weapons tends to be minimized in visions of future space combat, perhaps because of the limited range of such weapons on earth.

Propellant Possibilities

Weapons design will be influenced by technologies tangential to that area of research; e.g., metallurgy, hydraulics, ballistics, physics, and so forth. An overview of such currently evolving fields as explosive optics suggests the complexities that will be encountered in the long run, while reducing a sense of certainty in forecasting. Similarly, parallel developments in micropowder metallurgy and related work on enhanced chemical explosives is now producing a "new ball game" in an area that sat on the back shelf from World War II until the 1970s. There are many possible configurations for firing missile weapons beyond the use of rockets, whose propellants and explosives would constitute a high battle-damage risk. That suggests that a premium would be placed on developing instantaneous mixing systems, in which the relatively inert ingredients would be separate until actual deployment, already seen as a working principle in chemical-warfare systems. The development of ethnic-specific enzyme destruction agents may be of more significance to terrestrial than space conflict in the near future, but should not be ignored in terms of their implications. Since rockets also present problems of weight and bulk, perhaps research may move toward centrifugally impelled solenoids, or even torsion- or spring-powered propellant systems; perhaps firing ice, or very small particles of solids which offer low radar profile. Similarly, there are more than a few ways to skin the cat of beam-weapon generation. Even at the present time, work is underway on a variety of counter-inductance generator systems, capacitor technologies, jet-driven generators, and a number of other approaches.

Missile Weapons

Variants of missile weapons offer some possibilities in terms of reaching very high velocities, unaffected by air drag or gravity. One example is the "HARP" satellite launching system developed in the early 1960s by the Canadians, employing large-caliber American naval guns firing shells boosted by rocket motors, a technique which has continued to be the focus of research. By the mid-1960s, such a system applied to a smaller gun was reportedly able to fire 175mm shells a distance equaling that from Philadelphia to New York, albeit with crude accuracy. The "light gas" gun suggests another possibility; a system in which a volatile gas is detonated in a chamber closed by a thin metal shield, which, when the pressure mounts to a high enough level, ruptures and frees the gas to work against a piston, firing a projectile at speeds above 8,000 feet second—almost three times the speed of a hunting rifle, and higher than contemporary tank guns. Such a system, hybridized with a HARP technique, could produce hypervelocity missiles with microminiaturized homing systems.

The Nuclear Dimension

The use of nuclear weapons in space has already been closely examined within the framework of antiballistic missile systems, with particular interest shown in their ability to generate X rays and thereby damage ICBMs in high trajectory. Nuclear testing in its final phases included high-altitude detonations which showed spectacular auroras and ionization. In deep space, then, radiation, electromagnetic pulse, and immediate damage within a fireball would be the principal means of wreaking havoc, since heat and blast damage would not play destructive roles at the distances which they do on Earth against unhardened targets. In a related vein, a concept under evaluation currently for possible use as an anti-ICBM and satellite weapon in the near future is "junk," or chaff—small pieces of metal, plastics or other solids. To protect a spacecraft moving at sixty miles a second into a floating cloud of such material would require an armoring system or sophisticated warning and maneuvering apparatus.

Replenishments

More emphasis will be placed on renewable weapons, whose exhaustion of "propellant" or "change" will not easily deplete a ship's ammunition store. Such systems might include beam weapons whose forces can be derived from shipboard power generating systems and collected from external sources. In some cases, energy of nearby sun-stars could be applied by means of collection, reflection and focusing mechanisms.

Configurations of Fragmentation

Calling to mind again the great volume of territory that will be the maneuver ground of space fleets, it would be impossible to operate without supplementary equipment. Minefields could be sown for both offensive and defensive roles. These mines might take the form of giant hand grenades, since blast effect is greatly reduced in space by a lack of atmosphere. Damage is best assured by particles, across a range of sizes. Nuclear weapons could be jacketed in cases containing a myriad of shrapnel, actuated by either command or by remote sensing of targets that conform to a preprogrammed profile. While blast effect would be minimal unless it activated directly in contact with a target, particles and radiation would be the instrument of damage. Multistage aerosol might provide a tamping medium for concentrating blast.

Shielding

While development of wide-spectrum defenses would be imperative due to the great value of both ships and their highly trained crews, defensive design considerations would be more easily expressed than in any previous form of fighting vehicle. Free of gravity and tension stresses, vessels could be constructed in linked modules, or shielded with multihulls, or surrounded by aerosol or microsolid "clouds." Stable man-made, superheavy elements, now only projected as to "exist" by physicists, could provide defense against various forms of weapons radiation and missile damage, as well as from natural sources—e.g., solar flares and meteors. Further shielding could be obtained through plasma and aerosol technology, which would abrade or diffuse the effects of such obstacles, mines, "junk" or chaff clouds, and beam weapons, as well as predetonating contact and proximity-fused missiles. By cloaking a vessel in a cloud of suitable material, it would be possible to monitor, deflect, and reflect light stimulation and particle weapons. In a related vein, electronic countermeasures (ECM), which have developed along with military dependency on electronics, will be a key factor in both offensive and defensive space operations. Whether generated from manned ship or stationary mobile drones, the technique of providing false and confusing information will increase with the volume and complexity of space operations.

Space, Lag, and Command-and-Control

Beyond projections of existing or immediately anticipated technology lies a broad landscape of theoretical possibility. The hypothesis that a weapon is anything which can be used to defeat an enemy implies that skills in management, intelligence and deception cannot be ignored as elements of a weapons system. Not immediately obvious is the fact that as military forces extend themselves into space, strategic planning will undergo a virtual reversal in thinking, since due to the factors of volume and time, commanders will have an autonomy of command not seen since the age of fighting sail. The theory of relativity will become the fact of relativity, as command-and-control links begin to move out of phase with the pattern of the electronic age on Earth, where, while weapons systems move with relative degrees of sluggishness, electric and electronic communications are virtually instantaneous.

In space, distance will see speed-of-light communications and weapons facing increasing lag, which will produce command and targeting problems. Consider, for example, the simple case of a duel between two ships each traveling at 25,000 miles per hour at a range of 25,000 miles. First, each ship would not be able to sense the enemy ship's firing of speed-of-light weapons in time to adjust or change course. Next there would be limits on a ship's "jinking" ability, due to strains on structure, human crews, and the drain on fuel supplies. Moreover, such an encounter would require randomization of course and speed to confound an enemy's firing pattern, which would, in turn, try to maximize chances of a hit within a cone of probability. Such uncertainties would virtually randomize tactics in a manner reminiscent of the Battle of the Atlantic in World War II, where mutual code-breaking merely produced mutual uncertainty and groping.

To pursue the scenario a bit further, a laser would take about .13 seconds to transit. Radar pulses going and returning would take twice as long, leaving the actual location of a target problematical, since the target could vary course slightly and at a randomly oscillating speed. To complicate the problem, it should be noted that braking a spacecraft is not as simple a problem as it might seem, and it does consume energy. In any case, even with no computers or mechanical tracking time in the firing sequence, at least half a second would elapse between a ship's sensing enemy radar tracking and receiving a hit.

The development of hyperlight weapons and communication systems, while apparently impossible, may attract attention from research and development experts, at least as something more than a topic of parlor discussion. In the meantime, the limitations of radar for conning and combat, analyzed at some length by James Oberg in *Space Wars*, will place a premium on optical systems which, in addition to passivity, offer a chance to halve the response time of radar's to-and-from mode of operation. It will be possible to construct optical systems in space with resolution capacity well beyond that of Earth-bound telescopes. Stereoptical-parallax sensitive systems would obviously be invaluable. Computer enhancement and response would be preferable to human-operated systems, which would have lag and error built into them. Problems of identification, countersystems employing dazzle, overload, camouflage, and cloaking would all devolve from the use of such systems, as would the equipping of spacecraft, manned and unmanned, with low visibility to optical or radar scan and, conversely, low-signature sensors.

Command-and-Control

There are also problems related to command-and-control. It is sometimes hard to keep in mind that the headquarters is part of a general "weapons system." The hampering of subordinates, the ignoring of warnings, the problems of authority and coordination are all part of the implicit paradox of hierarchical organization, as is the development of the "headquarters syndrome," in which mission becomes subordinated to ego, whim, and the dynamic of the organization as a social system rather than as delivery system. In the wars of the twentieth century, progress in radiocommunications moved senior commanders farther and farther to the rear until, in the air war over Vietnam and in the *Mayaguez* affair, immediate battlefield decisions were made in the Office of the President, cases in which apparent political advantage outweighed conventional wisdom, or some might suggest, common sense. Such centralizing of command at a distance will tend to fade as elements are dispersed farther from Earth, and subsequently from nonterrestrial subordinate headquarters. If the lag is not fully appreciated, and subordinate commanders are not allowed discretion and comprehensive intelligence capability, the forces that result will be unable to make plans or decisions in far-flung tactical crises.

Intelligence, Propaganda, and Systems Vulnerability

Intelligence gathering and analysis, always vital, will be no less essential in space military operations. Distance and the dispersion of force will put a special premium on optimum application of available forces; for no matter how many units a power may possess, they will become dramatically finite in an expanding infinity. Because deceptions are not truly weapons does not necessarily mean they are ineffective in that role. Black or gray propaganda would fall into this area, as would alterations in space ecology such as fusion-triggered solar flares or redirection of meteorites and comets. Even in the first phase of the militarization of space, the danger of attack from an unidentified source emerges as a new and somewhat unique problem. The identification of friend and foe was already a thorny matter in World War II. It has become more serious in the nuclear age, and presents a new order of complexity in space. Militarization of space requires rethinking the problem of protecting the infrastructure of societies against the impact of accurate and powerful weapons of uncertain origin and location. The "signature" of nuclear weapons can be "read" quickly to identify components and probably source. Conventional explosives and beam weapons would not be so easily traced.

The vulnerability of the sinews and arteries of industrial societies was revealed in World War II, when raids by Allied bombers in the last few months of the European war against German synthetic-oil plants and transportation caused a plunge in German productive capacity, as well as a blunting of its air defense systems. In the Eisenhower era, stockpiling of crucial raw materials, an expanded civil-defense program and plans for dispersing the construction of new industry as well as moving strategic facilities out of major cities became policy for a time, reflecting an anxiety about their vulnerability. After the Cuban missile crisis and the shift to a "counterforce" strategy and the preoccupation with Vietnam, such programs faded from sight. The concern for vital modes of communication and the need for dispersion and shielding remained alive in the airborne command-post system and the MX missile complex. It is still hard for many to understand that the loss of a few key technical or communication elements may be more serious than the destruction of much larger combatant units. In "The Perfect Weapon," Poul Anderson suggested another dimension of the *querschnitt* (vulnerable subcomponent) effect in suggesting that the dissolving of paper would render a modern military bureaucracy harmless. Today, neutralizing their computer terminals or photocopy machines might do just as well. Apocryphal stories abounded of computer cards swelling in the heat of Vietnam.

Quasi-War

Conflict in space may eventually evolve to forms which are not easily discerned as warfare. Perhaps technological and cultural advances will heighten understanding of the fact that destruction is not victory, and the ultimate weapon may therefore not be one of violence, but rather a complex of alteration and conversion; e.g. synchronous satellite television and radio broadcasts of propaganda, as well as subliminal transmissions and scientific rumor generation. This effect was referred to in the eighteenth century by Marshal Saxe when he observed that the "object of war is not a pyramid of skulls." More recently, Robert Asprey, in *War in the Shadows*, suggested a transition from "battle-and-victory" to "pressure-and-gain."

Another exotic "weapons system" examined from a variety of perspectives by science fiction writers is the alteration of time and space, to allow a close approach to an enemy permitting tactical surprise, such as concealing vulnerable targets in other epochs, etc., a theme treated lightly in Reg Bretnor's "The Gnurrs Come from the Voodvork Out."

The Organizational Constants

In essence, policymakers and fabricators and controllers of weapons in space will face many problems hitherto encountered in essence in military history. The politics of weapons choice will certainly be evident, interacting with the bureaucratic politics of the armed services and related organizations. Unless human beings are somehow magically transformed, one can expect to see tension between rational choice and maintenance of the social systems, the interests of elites, factions, cliques, advocates, Young Turks versus Old Guard, corruption, and service rivalry, even within the framework of a National Space Command. The problems of overspecialization of force, of balance, of overruns, and of faddism are not likely to disappear.

The Challenge of Systems Balance

Science-fiction writers since the Second World War have

described systems in which research-and-development interacts with the traditional warrior ethos, variations on a theme of futuristic *bushido,* such as Gordon Dickson's Dorsai in *Soldier, Ask Not* and *The Genetic General.* Dickson's descriptions of battles, usually focused on ground action (an exception being The Battle of Newton in the latter work) touch on basic principles. His mercenaries carry less than the last word in weapons, trading off destructive power against designs that offer the least possibility of being jammed or blocked; e.g., spring-loaded rifles firing nonmetallic slivers, requiring no maintenance and free from fouling. Such danger implicit in overcommitting to high technology is often referred to as the "KISS principle" in the American military; KISS is the acronym for "Keep it simple, stupid." There are also references to a need for having systems designed by geniuses to be used by idiots. In 1950 Arthur C. Clarke examined this effect at some length in "Superiority," a short story in *The Magazine of Fantasy and Science Fiction,* in which the narrator tells of a war between interplanetary powers. The side that uses lots of good solid, simple technology in ever-larger numbers overwhelms opponents who keep leaping from what seems to be one high-tech panacea project to another. Each leap presents a variety of bugs and unanticipated side-effects which fall short of the expected goal, generating hysterical frenzies, and further pratfalls. Looking at the story in the aftermath of Vietnam may create a sense of poignance in some readers and irony in others. Yet Clarke merely transposed Lanchester's "laws" into a futuristic context.

The Arms Control Factor

Beyond the questions of weapons system and hardware choice, in the immediate future one may expect to see a continuation of the disarmament dialogue evolving since the coming of "high technology" war in the middle of the nineteenth century. Much of what has gone on in that area seems to the cynical to be wheel-spinning and a mask for deception, intelligence gathering, and weapons development. The generation of World War II spoke of the Washington Naval Conference through clenched teeth, and some contemporary analysts have seen the SALT talks as a sop to public wishful thinking, as camouflage for espionage, or as empty gestures toward a shaky détente. Yet others have seen them as the hope of the future and evidence of a growing if grudging realization of the futility of major war in the nuclear age.

With the expansion into space, this pattern is likely to continue. Politicians on both sides will maintain a rhetoric of peace and that ethic will impact from time to time on weapons choice, as well as supporting a consciousness of the danger of war in nations which allow open discussion of such matters; an effect which critics suggest makes disarmament conferences merely a weapon in the arsenal of psychological warfare of totalitarian states. The militarization of space has not yet become an agenda item in SALT, which may be a by-product of lag in perception due to the special complexity of the problem. In that sense, time will tell.

The quickly changing perspectives regarding military developments in space are beginning to cause public discussion and may well intrude themselves into any future SALT-type conferences. Yet whatever controls are developed, they may be less like dams holding back military technological innovation, and rather more like rocks over which rapids ultimately break.

Epilogue

This review of possibilities is necessarily based on extrapolations from existing knowledge, just as in the early days of the genre, science fiction focused on rather close projections of existing military technology, and a fairly heavy fixation on threats from obvious terrestrial enemies, as noted by I. F. Clarke in *Voices Prophesying War*. Erskine Childer's *The Riddle of the Sands* and Hector Bywater's *The Great Pacific War* were rather more like proto-RAND scenarios than science fiction in the projective sense, written without access to classified information, and without awareness of the full range of existing technology, as would be any essay on the subject. The breakneck developments in crystallography alone promise a complex of variants well beyond "reasonable" speculation. Science fiction has played the role of vanguard in tracing out possibilities and trends; a fact now recognized in the employment by futurologists of science-fiction plots in a kind

of modified Delphi technique. The result of such prognos-
tications, however, often seems to underline the truism
that one must kill to dissect. Ultimately, there will be
developments, like hypnosis, electromagnetism, nuclear
fission, and the transistor, which will appear and recast
frameworks and paradigms. As Arthur Clarke noted at the
dawn of the true Space Age, the high technology of one
culture may appear as magic to a less developed culture;
e.g., the cargo cults born of the Second World War among
Pacific islanders who saw ships and planes as the vehicles
of gods. This problem has been nibbled at by Charles
Fort, and by Bergier and Pauwels in *The Morning of The
Magicians*. A mixture of anxiety and wonder has served as
the yin-yang of science fiction, a distinction notable in, for
example, the titles of such studies as Sam Moskowitz's *A
Sense of Wonder* versus Kingsley Amis's *New Maps of
Hell*.

As Robert Ardrey argued in *African Generals*, the development of weapons may be as valid a means of tracing
man's technological development as his use of tools,
insomuch as many of the latter have been designed to
build the former, a theme carried on in different forms by
A. E. Van Vogt in *The Weapon Makers* and Arthur Clarke
in several of his works. If humans are not by nature
predators, they do show at least a love-hate relationship
with weapons and violence, marked enough to make such
peaceful tribes as the Arapesh and the Eskimos a small
exception to a broad rule. Indeed, the least-expected possibility in both science fiction and public policy related to
space is that Tennyson's visions of a parliament of man will
be made flesh. Whatever the successive realities, we can
expect science fiction to continue to play and to grapple
with possibilities, and steer into the fact of Wittgenstein's
caution: "Whereof we cannot know, thereof we should not
speak."

Yet at this point, it is easy to conclude in surveying all
these possibilities that the sheer scope of space and the
complexity of waging war in it truly dwarfs mankind's
pretensions. One finds, however, that a similar sense of
gigantism stimulating visions of peaceful idylls and utopias
was born of the discovery of the Americas. In spite of our
current apprehension and the intimidating sense of scale,

human enterprise will then probably rise to the occasion, in the curious synthesis of pride, inventivity, assertiveness and bloody-mindedness that has characterized man's evolution on the planet which seems now more and more to be only an incubator for his ultimate destiny.

Roger Beaumont holds a Ph.D. from Kansas State and a bachelor's and master's from Wisconsin. He has taught at Kansas State, at the University of Wisconsin-Oshkosh and Marquette, and has taught history at Texas A. & M. since 1974. He has also served as Associate Director of the Center for Advanced Study in Organization Science, an executive development "think-tank" at U. of Wisconsin-Milwaukee.

In his main field of academic interest, military affairs, Beaumont has written for such journals as the U.S. Naval Institute Proceedings, Military Affairs, The Royal United Service Institution Journal, *and the* Military Review. *He has lectured at the U.S. Dept. of Agriculture Graduate School, at the Industrial College of the Armed Forces, and at the U.S. Army Command and General Staff College.*

Beaumont is the author of Military Elites *and* The Sword of the Raj: The British Army in India, *and co-editor of* War in the Next Decade. *He is also American editor of* Defense Analysis, *a professional quarterly published at the University of Lancaster in England.*

R. Snowden Ficks' previous writing has been in the field of political commentary and military technology, and has co-authored a science fiction novel. He is a Marine Corps veteran and an alumnus of Milton College, and is presently an associate of an investment banking firm in Milkwaukee, Wisconsin, where he lives with his wife and two children.

The effectiveness of weapons is determined not only by their sophistication and destructive power. Much depends also on the skill with which they are employed: on the disposition and vulnerability of the objective, on surprise, on timing. Primitive though it is, a gurkha kukri can be terrifying and deadly in the stillness of the night; a shotgun, only slightly more sophisticated, can be more impressive than a machine gun several miles away. In war, all possibilities must be considered and prepared for.

In this story, Mr. Beaumont considers a rather chilling one which most superweapon-oriented people dismiss too lightly.

Roger A. Beaumont

SCENARIO FOR THE FALL OF NIGHT

OFFICE OF THE COMMANDING GENERAL
PROVISIONAL WESTERN COMMAND
PLANS AND OPERATIONS DIVISION
HAVANA, CUBA

14 October 1983

SUBJECT: Conduct of Operation RECLAMATION (After Action Report)
Chairman Military Division
Secretariat
Central Committee of the Communist Party USSR

The following initial after-action report is submitted for use in compiling the official history and for action by the Central Committee in respect to decorations and awards. (Casualty lists and statistical analyses will follow as Annex B through M.)

1. The inception of Operation RECLAMATION in 1953
was at the instigation of Marshal Konev who attempted, through its design as a theoretical project,
to give impetus to wide-scale staff planning, which
had suffered in the Stalinist era and under the demands of war. The exercise of a dozen staffs of officers of all ranks was held each year, 1953-61, at the
headquarters of each major command, focusing on
the problem of a military attack upon the United
States without the employment of nuclear weapons.
The results of each exercise were centralized at the
Suvorov Academy and analyzed by the General Staff
and the Military Division of the Central Committee.
The initial fruits of the program gave rise to the
formation of a special permanent planning staff in
1955.

2. The special staff, RECLAM, under Colonel Vorov,
proceeded to harden the operational plan of RECLA-
MATION and forward duplicate copies of all orders
and plans which it evolved to the Central Committee. At the same time, the existence of the staff and
its work were virtually unknown to all but a few in
the security, personnel and pay branches. Special
studies were also made by GRU, on request, of intelligence aspects of the problem.

3. As the plans developed, the Central Committee
considered them in detail, approving, rejecting and
making suggestions. The concept was simple. The
United States was to be attacked by conventional
forces in such a way that nuclear retaliation was
out of the question, and with the goal of decisively
diminishing U.S. strategic isolation and invulnera-
bility. By dovetailing the results of the many field
exercises, the plan evolved to an employable state
in 1958. The first step had been defined as a bridge-
head in Latin America from which subversive activities would be employed to topple the already deteriorating U.S. posture in South and Central America. The subsidy and support of the rebel Castro in
Cuba was authorized a considerable increase.

4. At the same time, the usual overtures concerning disarmament were maintained, with constant emphasis on Soviet developments in the areas of nuclear capabilities. Upon the entry of Castro into HAVANA, step two began: the training of the cadre of the Latin armies. This was undertaken at former labor camp sites in Western Siberian regions. The Red Army Training Corps worked in this area in cooperation with KGB and GRU. The Bay of Pigs fiasco was an unexpected opportunity as was the furor over "nuclear" weapons in Cuba. It was most advantageous at that point for the US to misread our intentions. The elaborate "backdown" on the part of the Soviet government, followed by the disarmament treaty, created a new confusion in U.S. policy.

5. The third stage, and the most critical, was the securing of a foothold in Mexico in which we were assisted by the scaling down of U.S. foreign-aid programs. The most valuable catalyst, although certainly unforeseen, was the great North American earthquakes of 1980. The rescue forces which we sent into Mexico at a time when the U.S. was preoccupied with its own vast damage problems were able to develop virtual enclaves in the form of "rescue stations" distributed along both coasts. By moving aggressively and deftly in this period of disorganization, we were able to undercut Mexican right and centrist political forces, while General Tutin, director of rescue services, was able in this period to pre-position fuel, food, and ammunition caches extensively in the north Mexican frontier provinces, most of which survived the aftershocks of 1981. Most important, of course, was the extent to which our presence was accepted and even demanded by the general population as a source of order and materiel.

During this period, the coming to power of other sympathetic regimes, politically and militarily, made it possible to organize three military commands on the frontiers of the United States using various dimensions of anti-American feelings and interests. The first, under General Brekinsky with headquarters in HAVANA, was given the "target area" WASHINGTON, D.C.-NEW ORLEANS. The second, General Tutin's headquarters, VERACRUZ. oversaw the district SAN FRANCISCO-NEW ORLEANS. The third, under Marshal Vorov, with the goal of landing in JAMES BAY, began training in the WHITE SEA two years before the actual operation. All logistics and military control from this point on were handled through the General Staff.

6. Conditions for the actual assault were laid down at a full meeting of top staffs with the Central Committee on 10 January 1982, 18 months prior to the actual commitment. They were:

a. Recruitment and three months' training of Latin American elements of a 10-brigade force to deploy along the RIO GRANDE, 20 percent to be Soviet personnel (all mobile elements involving air-ground liaison, signals, indirect artillery support, airlift and support forces) to be called the Latin American People's Army.

b. A highly trained strike force of three airborne and three amphibious divisions in Cuba (10 percent Soviet).

c. An air fleet of 800 close support bombers and 800 fighters in range of all target areas.

d. (1) Capability of Red Navy submarine forces to unload four divisions of helicopter-hovercraft troops in JAMES BAY area within 12 hours, plus antiaircraft rocket and air support sites in these areas.

(2) Deployment of "freighters" bearing Free Quebec flats in normal shipping traffic to position helicopter-borne strike forces off major coastal cities.

e. Arrangements by KGB and GRU to activate

sleeper strike forces at key U.S. military bases and
cities, supplemented by dissident elements.

   f. Guarantee by each commander of exact timing
and full deploymemt of forces by attack hour plus
one.

The conditions were met at attack day minus two
months, and the concept was presented to the Central Committee formally three weeks before execution.

7. The actual operation began at 0400, 1 July
1983. The Mexican-based force struck along the
axis TIJUANA-BAKERSFIELD-SACRAMENTO (two armored, two mobile and two infantry divisions)
toward FORT WORTH-DALLAS and HOUSTON (two
armored, two mobile and three infantry divisions).
Two mobile divisions moved directly east toward
NEW ORLEANS to link up with the one airborne and
one amphibious division attacking from Cuba. The
remainder of the Cuban forces was deployed as follows: one airborne and one amphibious division at
MIAMI; one airborne brigade at JACKSONVILLE; and
pre-positioned "trawler"-borne amphibious brigades,
each moving against MOBILE, CHARLESTON, and
SAVANNAH. In the northern sector, the four hover-
craft divisions began to move south at dawn with an
average speed of eighty kilometers per hour and, by
noon of the second day, had contacted small units of
the Canadian and U.S. Army two hundred miles
north of TORONTO. At the same time, GRU and KGB
sleeper units in the United States and Canada attacked telephone switchboards, power plants, police
departments, telegraph offices, rail switch points,
key road overpasses, airfields, and military bases at
280 points, delaying American response to the attack 18 hours. Air activity against our advancing
forces the first day was sporadic. Soviet air units
smashed American air on the ground at 37 different
bases with moderate losses. Key targets were airborne troop vehicle transport concentrations. For-
tunately, the dismantling of U.S. surface-to-air missile

batteries around major cities led to a loss of only 24
aircraft on the first day. By nightfall of the 1st, our
forces in the West had secured LOS ANGELES, isolated the Marine bases, and were passing through
BAKERSFIELD on the way north.

Farther east, SAN ANTONIO, CORPUS CHRISTI, and
GALVESTON fell; and NEW ORLEANS was isolated by
the airborne troops of General Mirsky's division.

8. The second day saw stiffening resistance in California and Texas. Tutin found it necessary to strike
north against the U.S. 101st Airmobile Division's
flank with his New Orleans force. The greenness of
the Latin American troops began to show, particularly with supply difficulties and U.S. airmobile flexibility. MONTEREY and MODESTO were reached in
California; elements of the U.S. 4th and 6th Divisions were recognized here, and some reserve units.
Our supply artery, the main north-south highway in
California, was cut by small U.S. Marine armor units
on the night of 2 July. Seven of our airfields were
destroyed, with a loss of over 200 aircraft; however,
our strikes against 15 more U.S. airdromes paid
dividends. In the north, General Vorov's advance
units began to shell TORONTO at sundown on the
2nd, coinciding with the capture of MIAMI and
JACKSONVILLE.

The drawing in of the U.S. 82nd Airborne, as well as
piecemeal deployment of U.S. armor, aided our forces
in blunting enemy counterattacks. A dozen major
U.S. cities had been taken, and the counterattack
had failed to more than moderately slow the assault.
The Mexican ambassador approached the U.S. government with an ultimatum which, above all, blocked
U.S. use of nuclear weapons. The world publicity
given a Mexican demand for return of its stolen
provinces, and a plebiscite for all-American minor-
ity groups who might prefer their own state, was
skillfully presented. He also informally indicated
American citizens in the captured areas would be

considered "nuclear hostages." While he was chat-
ting with the President, the fall of DALLAS-FORT
WORTH to our forces was announced.

9. At this point, coordinated direction was imple-
mented by this headquarters. Air attacks were ordered against SEATTLE and PORTLAND, SALT LAKE
CITY, ST. LOUIS, CHICAGO, WASHINGTON and PHIL-
ADELPHIA. Our "trawler" and "freighter"-based
fleet Marine battalions went ashore at NEW YORK,
NEWARK, PHILADELPHIA, SAN FRANCISCO, SEAT-
TLE and 12 other cities close to the coast which had
been paralyzed by our sleeper net. The GRU grace-
fully agreed to throw its precious sabotage sleeper
net into the balance, and communications were suc-
cessfully crippled again in 23 northern American
cities. A total of 7,218 comrades died in these two
great subversive attacks against the capitalist mo-
nolith, but not in vain. A brigade of Brekinsky's airborne group in HAVANA hastily assaulted CHARLES-
TON, and the movement of the amphibious division
from MIAMI by night on fast torpedo boats under
the direct orders of Premier Castro turned the tide.
By nightfall of the 3rd, the boats had, with some loss,
advanced a brigade against AUGUSTA. TORONTO,
ROCHESTER, HAMILTON, and DETROIT all came under fire on the 3rd as well. At this point, our attacking forces began to show serious signs of fatigue.
Consolidation was necessary, but living off the rich
American resources aided in keeping motor transport at a much higher percentage of operativeness
than expected. In the West, SAN FRANCISCO and
SACRAMENTO were secured on the night of 3-4 July,
and a brigade left the now-reduced Marine bases to
occupy LAS VEGAS and prepare for joining with the
Texas group. U.S. air strikes materialized against
road transport and airfields within the U.S. and
against airfields in Mexico and Cuba. At this point,
the home Soviet Air Force and rocket units stood at
constant alert, since casualties had reduced our
effective strength to two divisions in the northeast, still bravely attacking; 20 divisions in Cali-

fornia-Texas, with heavy unarmored vehicle losses;
and four divisions in the East. This headquarters
then issued orders for a concentration of forces into
cohesive defense enclaves in the areas LOS ANGE-
LES–SAN FRANCISCO–CHARLESTON–NEW ORLEANS–
MOBILE, assuring that the submarine resupply operations could proceed and that increasing U.S. air
activity would be of less avail. All military facilities,
waterworks, transportation facilities, airfields, and
bridges were to be destroyed in evacuated areas. It
was with great bitterness that we ordered Vorov's
small force to attempt to break out again to JAMES
BAY the morning of the 6th. We had already lost five
of the submarines standing by. Since the Americans
were still in the dark concerning our activities, we
requested the Central Committee to proceed with its
offer to return the seized American cities in exchange for the Mexican demands; i.e., the cession of
New Mexico, Arizona, California south of LODI, Texas
west and south of the BRAZOS, and Cuban garrisons
in MIAMI and KEY WEST.

10. At this point, our military situation was precarious. We had lost two-fifths of our original attack
force, over half of our vehicles, and half of our committed air forces. (This was, however, being quickly
remedied by ferrying through sympathetic African
states and Brazil and then north. But it was clear
that it would take at least two weeks to get up to
strength.) Also, our men were tired. The green Latin
troops, never fully stable, began to panic and desert.
But, as we know now, the Americans were not doing
well either. DETROIT, CLEVELAND, PITTSBURGH and
CHICAGO were in turmoil; our brave sleeper agents
still held MADISON, MILWAUKEE, MINNEAPOLIS, and
TACOMA's main facilities; WASHINGTON, D.C. was
an empty city, as was NEW YORK. The American
military's hasty realignment of forces had cost them
dearly in terms of response and maintenance. Their
Air Force generals were demanding permission to
attack the USSR. The general confusion and lack of

stability weighed in our favor. On the night of 5 July, after the remainder of our air units struck again at American fields and transport with heavy losses on both sides, the President called for an armistice and agreed to terms. By noon on the 6th, all was quiet, and regular supply vessels were able to put in at our U.S. ports. The rest of the story is diplomatic history.

11. The final account on the military side will naturally not be available until interviews with key participants and unit journals are analyzed and weighed. The main lessons stand out. The Americans were not ready militarily or psychologically for direct attack on their homeland. No provision had been made to secure vital installations, even on most military bases. There is no doubt that, if we had committed our forces more judiciously after more training, the final result might have been immediately decisive. All in all, however, there is also no doubt that Operation RECLAMATION was a success in terms of world opinion, consolidation of Latin American support, and in shattering American confidence. Its full fruits have not yet been gathered.

In addition to his nonfiction, previously mentioned, Roger Beaumont has been a member of the Science Fiction Writers of America since 1973, and has published in Analog *and* Futures.

Science fiction, basically, is a literature of what ifs, of alternate futures and different universes; and one variety of these is the future where history has taken a different track, or where the laws of nature, as we know them, do not hold true.

Randall Garrett writes of a world that shares our origins but neither our history nor our view of causes and effects. In his world, kings and emperors rule, and what we today call magic is an exact science with its own precise technologies. Yet even there, men are still driven by ambition, by envy, by love and hatred, by courage and fear and loyalty. And they continue to fight wars—in which magic also is a weapon.

Readers familiar with Garrett's Lord Darcy stories will be happy to encounter Lieutenant Darcy and Junior Sergeant Sean O Lochlainn.

Randall Garrett

THE SPELL OF WAR

The Lieutenant lay on his belly in the middle of a broad clearing in the Bavarian Forest, on the eastern side of the Danau, in a hell of warfare many miles from Dagendorf.

He was eighteen years old, and his fingers, clawlike, had dug into and were holding on to the damp earth on which he lay.

Ahead of him, far out of sight beyond the trees, the Polish artillery thundered and roared. It had begun only thirty seconds before, and already it seemed as though it had been going on forever.

Next to him, lying equally flat, was Superior Sergeant Kelleigh. The Sergeant was more than twice the Lieutenant's age, and had seen long service in the Imperial Army.

"What do you think, sir?" he asked in a hushed voice.

The Lieutenant swallowed. "Damned if I know," he said evenly. He was surprised at how calm his voice sounded. It betrayed nothing of what was inside him. "Where are those damned shells going?"

"Over our heads, sir. Hear that whistling burble?"

"I do indeed, Sergeant. Thank you."

"Pleasure, sir. Never been in an artillery barrage before, sir?"

"No, I haven't. I'm learning."

Kelleigh grinned. "We all learn, sir. You faster than most."

"Thank you again, Sergeant." The Lieutenant put his field glasses to his eyes and did a quick survey of the surrounding terrain. Too many trees.

A hundred yards to their rear, the shells from the big guns were exploding, making a syncopated counterpoint to the roar of the artillery pieces.

"I hope Red Company got out of that," the Sergeant muttered. He was looking back toward the area where the shells were landing. "Damn, that's good shooting!" He touched his chest, where his bronze identification sigil rested beneath his combat jacket. "I'd think they were using a clairvoyant, except I believe our sorcerers are better than theirs."

"Don't worry, Sergeant; as long as you've got your sigil on you, you can't be seen physically." The Lieutenant was still looking through his field glasses. "If there are any infantry in that wood, I don't see them. I wonder if—"

Spang-ng-ng-ng!

The bullet sang off a rock not ten inches from the Lieutenant's head.

"That's the Polish infantry, sir. Let's move it."

"Right you are, Sergeant. Roll."

Staying low and moving fast, the two men performed that maneuver known to the science of military tactics as *Getting The Hell Out*. In the twenty-five yards they had to move, several more bullets came close, but none hit anything but earth.

They rolled down the sharp declivity that was protecting the rest of Blue Company, and hit bottom hard enough to take the breath from them.

The Lieutenant gasped twice, then said, "Where the Hell were they firing from?"

"Damned if I know, sir. Couldn't tell."

"Well, they're out there in the woods somewhere. That's why all the artillery shells are going over our heads."

There was no more small-arms fire, though the big guns kept up their intermittent roar.

"We seem to be safe enough for the moment," the Lieutenant said. Further down the ravine, the could see the rest of Blue Company.

"Aye, sir." The Sergeant was silent for a moment, then said: "Been meanin' to ask you, sir, if you'll not consider it an impertinence . . ." He paused.

"Go ahead, Sergeant. The worst I'll do is refuse to answer if it's too personal."

"Thank you, sir. Been meanin' to ask if you were any kin to Coronel Lord Darcy."

"He's my father," said Lieutenant Darcy.

"It's a pleasure knowin' you, sir. I remember you as a kid—I served under the Coronel ten years ago. A great officer, sir."

Lieutenant Darcy suddenly found tears in his eyes. He brushed them away with a sleeve and said: "Then you're Sergeant *Brendon* Kelleigh? My father has spoken of you often. Says you're the finest NCO in His Imperial Majesty's forces. If I ever see him again, I'll tell him of your compliment. He'll be honored."

"I'm the one who's honored, sir." The Sergeant's voice was a little choked. "And you'll see him again, sir. You've only been with Blue Company for a week, but I've seen enough of you in action to know you're the survivor type."

"That's as may be," said the Lieutenant, "but even if I make it through this mess, I may not see him again. You were with him in Sudan, I believe."

"When he got the bullet through his chest? I was, sir."

"It clipped his heart. Now his condition is deteriorating, and the Healers can do nothing. He'll not live out the year."

After a short silence, Superior Sergeant Kelleigh said: "I'm sorry to hear that, sir. Very sorry. He was a fine officer."

The Lieutenant nodded wordlessly. Then he said: "Let's move south, Sergeant, back to Blue Company. Keep low."

"Aye, sir."

They moved down the ravine.

Thirty yards or so down, the two men met Captain Rimbaud, commander of Blue Company.

"I saw you two move back," he said harshly. "What the Hell happened? None of that artillery is hitting around us."

He was a big man—two inches taller than Lieutenant Darcy's six feet, and a good stone heavier. He had a blocky face and hard eyes.

"Small-arms fire, sir," the Lieutenant said.

"From somewhere out in those woods."

The Captain's hard eyes shifted to the Sergeant. "That right, Kelleigh?"

Lieutenant Darcy let his young face go wooden. He said nothing.

"Aye, sir," the Sergeant said stiffly. He, too, had recognized the slight on the young Lieutenant. "They're out there, sir; no question of it. First shot came within a foot of us."

Captain Rimbaud looked back at the Lieutenant. "Did you see any of them?"

"No, sir." No excuses. He didn't explain about the woods. Rimbaud should be able to figure that out for himself.

The artillery was still thundering.

The Captain turned and climbed carefully up the eastern slope of the ravine. A quick peek over the edge; then he slid back down. "No wonder. This slight breeze is bringing the smoke in from those cannon. You two were in the clear. I hope they choke."

"Agreed, sir," said Lieutenant Darcy.

"I think—" began the Captain. He didn't finish. There was a noise and a tumble of earth and small stones, and a man came rolling down the western slope of the ravine. Both officers and the noncom had spun around and had their .44 Morleys out and ready for action before the man hit the bottom of the ravine and splashed into the water.

Then they relaxed. The man was wearing the uniform of their own outfit; the Duke of Burgundy's 18th Infantry.

As the square-jawed, tough-looking little man came to his feet, Captain Rimbaud said: "You almost got yourself shot, coming in that way Sergeant. Who the Hell are you?"

The little Sergeant threw him a salute, which the Captain returned. "Junior Sergeant Sean O Lochlainn, sir, commanding what is left of Red Company." His Irish brogue was thick.

After a moment, Captain Rimbaud found his voice. *"What is left of Red Company?"*

"Aye, sir. The artillery got us. Wiped out the Captain, the Lieutenant, and both Senior Sergeants. Out of eighty men, there's at most fifteen left." He paused. "I don't know if they'll all make it here, sir. There's small-arms fire out there, too."

"Mary, Mother of God," the Captain said softly. Then: "All right, let's move down. If one of their observers can get word to their artillery, there will be shells dropping in here pretty soon."

Blue Company was another thirty-five yards down the ravine. They were warned to watch for Red Company, and during the next few minutes, eleven more of them came in. Then there were no more.

There were seventy-five men of Blue Company and twelve of Red in that ravine now, all of them wondering what in Hell was going on out in those woods. For some reason, no artillery fire fell in the ravine. Either Blue and Red hadn't been spotted, or the observer couldn't get through to the guns.

While Captain Rimbaud and Sergeant Kelleigh checked out the troops, the young Lieutenant sat down next to Sergeant O Lochlainn for a breathing space.

"Queer war it is," said Sean O Lochlainn. "Queer war, indeed."

Soldiers love to talk, if they have the time and opportunity. In combat, it is the only form of entertainment they have. In a hard firefight, their minds are on their precious lives; but as soon as there is a lull and they are sure the enemy cannot hear them, they will talk. About anything. Family, wives, sweethearts, women in general, booze, beer, parties, bar fights, history, philosophy, clean and dirty jokes—

You name it, and a soldier will talk about it if he can find a buddy interested in the same subject. If he can't he'll change the subject. But he'll talk, because it's almost the only release he has from the nervous tension of the threat of sudden dismemberment or death.

"All wars are queer, Sergeant," said Lieutenant Darcy. "What's so exceptional about this one?"

"I'd say, sir, because it is exceptionally stupid, even for a war." He glanced at the Lieutenant. "Aye, sir; all wars are stupid. But this one is stupider than most. And, for once, most of the stupidity is on the other side."

The Lieutenant was beginning to like the stout little Irishman. "You think, then, that King Casimir is stupid?"

"Not as an overall thing, no, sir," the Sergeant said thoughtfully. "But His Slavonic Majesty has done a few stupid things. Wants to be a soldier, like his late father, and can't cope with it—if you see what I mean, sir."

"I do indeed, Sergeant. Your analysis is cogent."

From 1922 to 1937, Casimir VIII had expanded the Polish hegemony into Russia, and Poland now controlled it from Minsk to Kiev. But now the Russians showed signs of banding together, and the notion of a United Russia was one that nobody wanted to face; so Casimir VIII had wisely abandoned Polish expansion toward the east. Had he remained king, it might well be that the present war would never have taken place, for that cagey old fox had known better than to attempt an attack westward against the Anglo-French Empire.

But his son, Casimir IX, who had ascended the throne in 1937, knew no such wisdom. He saw the threat of the Russias and decided to move west into the Germanies; not realizing, apparently, that Henry X, by the grace of God King of England, France, Scotland, and Ireland, Lord Protector of the New World, King of the Romans and the Germans, and Emperor of the Holy Roman Empire, would have to protect the Germanies. When Polish troops entered Bavaria, Prince Hermann of Bavaria had called to his liege lord for help, and King Henry had sent it.

Casimir IX wanted to be the military leader his father was, but he was simply not up to it.

Lieutenant Darcy wondered for a moment if that was the flaw in his own character. Coronel Lord Darcy had been a fine soldier and had won many honors in the field. *Am I*, the young Lieutenant thought, *trying to be the soldier my father was?* Then: *Hell, no, I never wanted to be a soldier in the first place! I'm out here because the King needs me. And as soon as he doesn't need me any-*

more, I'm shucking this uniform and getting the Hell back home.

"It's like Captain Rimbaud," said Sergeant O Lochlainn.

Lieutenant Darcy blinked, bringing his mind back to the conversation. "Beg your pardon, Sergeant? *What's* like Captain Rimbaud?"

"Meanin' no disrespect, sir," said the stout little Irishman, "but Captain Rimbaud's father was General Ambrose Rimbaud, of whom ye have no doubt heard, sir."

"I have," said the Lieutenant. "I didn't know that Captain Rimbaud was his son."

"Oh, that he is, sir. Again meanin' no disrespect, sir, but the Captain is well known throughout the battalion as a glory hunter."

"I'll reserve judgment on that, Sergeant," said the Lieutenant.

"Aye, sir. I'll say no more about it."

The Lieutenant edged his way up the slope of the ravine and took a quick look over the top.

He said: "Good God!" very softly.

"What is it, sir?" asked the tough little Irish sergeant.

"Take a look for yourself, Sergeant," Lieutenant Darcy said. "The place is alive with Polish soldiers."

A bullet from a Polish .28 Kosciusko rifle sang across the edge of the ravine, splattering earth over the two men. Then another.

Lieutenant Darcy slid back down the slope.

"With your permission, sir," said the stout little Irishman, "I'd just as soon not take a look now."

Lieutenant Darcy couldn't help but grin. "Excused, Sergeant. They've got us spotted." The grin faded. "There must be at least thirty of them up there in those woods. Probably more, since that smoke is obscuring a lot of them. And there must be even more, up and down the line." He frowned. "There's more smoke out there than one would think, considering how far back the artillery must be."

"I've seen it before sir," said the Irishman. "It's more fog than smoke. On a cold, damp day like this, the smoke particles seem to make a fog condense out of the air."

The Lieutenant nodded. "That accounts for the fact that the Polish infantry can stay inside that cloud and still breathe." He paused, then: "The cloud is getting denser, and it's moving this way. It will be drifting over this ravine in a minute or two. Get down to the Captain and tell him what I saw. I'll stay here and try to make them think there's still a large force in this part of the ravine."

"Aye, sir." The Sergeant moved south.

Lieutenant Darcy found an eighteen-inch piece of broken branch half in the rivulet that ran down the center of the ravine, and moved north about ten yards. Then he climbed up the bank again.

He took off his helmet, put it on the end of the branch, and drew his .44 Morley. Lifting the helmet with his left hand, he fired over the edge with the pistol in his right. He didn't care what his aim was; all he wanted to do was attract attention.

He did.

The bullet whanged off the crown of his helmet, knocking it off the stick into the brooklet.

Damn good shot, the Lieutenant thought as he slid back down the embankment.

He retrieved his helmet. There was a shiny streak on the top, but no dent. He put the helmet back on in spite of the wetness. By then, the smoky fog was drifting over the top of the ravine.

The Lieutenant found himself a little jittery. *Have a smoke,* he told himself. *Relax.* The cloud over the ravine would mask the smoke from his pipe.

He took the stubby little briar from his backpack. It was already filled with tobacco for emergencies just such as this. It took three flicks of his thumb to get his lighter aflame.

And then he found that his hand was shaking so badly that he could not light the pipe. He almost threw the lighter into the stream a few feet away.

He put out the flame and shoved both pipe and lighter back into his backpack.

Get hold of yourself, dammit! he thought. He was thankful that no one had seen him betray his fear that way. He was particularly thankful that Coronel Everard, the battalion commander and an old friend of his father's, hadn't seen him.

He was suddenly aware of the silence. The artillery had

stopped. Now there was only the sporadic *crack!* of small-
arms fire. He got to his feet and moved quickly south,
toward the rest of Blue Company. The sun overhead shone
sickly through the yellow-brown haze.

He almost tripped over the body that lay sprawled on
the slope. The rivulet gurgled over the dead man's boots.
The soldier was face down, but the bullet hole in the small
of his back showed that the slug had gone right through
him. The Lieutenant stepped over him, choking, and went
on.

Blue Company, and what was left of Red, were up on
the eastern slope of the ravine. They had scooped out
toeholds in the bank in order to stay near the top, but
were keeping their heads down.

Captain Rimbaud saw Lieutenant Darcy and said; "Your
diversion didn't work, Darcy. They know where we are.
How they can see us through this smoke, I don't know."

"Nor do I, sir. Can you see anything?"

"Not a damn thing. I can see them moving occasionally,
but not for long enough to get a shot at any one of them.
Have you any ideas?"

Lieutenant Darcy tried to ignore the three bodies lying
at the bottom of the ravine. "Can we move farther south,
sir? That would put us closer to where the rest of the
battalion is."

The Captain shook his head. "The terrain slopes off
rather rapidly, and this ravine gets shallow and disappears.
The stream flows out into a flat meadow and makes a bog
of it. They'd still have us in their sights, and we'd never
make it across that bog."

The Lieutenant nodded. "Yes, sir. I can see that."

The troops were firing sporadically into the fog, not with
the hope of hitting the occasional flitting shadow that was
visible behind the rolling fogbank, but with the hope that
they could keep the Polish troops back.

Sergeant Arthur Lyon, second ranking noncom of Blue
Company, came running up from the right. He stood six-two
and was solidly built. He was usually smiling, and the lines
in his face showed it, but there was no smile on his face now.

"Sir," he said, addressing the Captain, "they're moving
in to the north of us. If they get into this ravine, we'll have
enfilade fire raking us."

"Mary, Mother of God," the Captain said with a growl in his voice. He looked at Darcy. "Any suggestions, Lieutenant?"

The Lieutenant knew this was a test. Captain Rimbaud had been testing him ever since he had joined Blue Company. "Yes, sir. Apparently, they have us outnumbered. And the cessation of the artillery fire seems ominous to me."

Rimbaud narrowed his eyes. He did not like damp-behind-the-ears lieutenants who used words like "cessation" and "ominous."

"In what way?" he asked.

"They've been lobbing those shells over the woods, sir. They hit Red Company's line and nearly wiped them out. Why haven't they shelled us? I think it's because we're too close, sir. They can't elevate their guns enough to get over those trees and drop shells on us. An observer's messenger has been sent back to tell the Poles to pull their artillery back a hundred yards so they can get at us. In that case, sir, their infantry is merely trying to scare us; they won't come down this far for fear of their own artillery."

"What would you do, Lieutenant?" Rimbaud asked.

"Do we know the characteristics of the cannon they're using, sir?" Lieutenant Darcy asked.

"The six-inch Gornicki? I don't, personally; I'm not an artilleryman."

"But our artillery officers would?"

"Certainly."

"Very well, sir," the Lieutenant said decisively. "Our artillery is southwest of here. If we go to the southern end of this ravine and head back that way, we can report what we know. The Polish guns won't go back any farther than they have to in order to lob shells into us. Knowing the characteristics of the Gornicki, the artillery officers can figure out where the guns *must* be when the shells start hitting this ravine, and they can lay down a barrage on the Poles."

The Captain's eyes narrowed. When he spoke, his voice was heavy with a mixture of sarcasm and scorn. "I see. On the basis of pure guesswork, you would have us *retreat*? Not while *I* am Captain of this Company, we won't." He turned his head to look up and eastward, though he could see nothing but the sky and the upper portions of trees. "If they haven't come here after us in exactly ten minutes, this Company is going over the edge of this damned ravine and straight through them. Got that?"

"Yes, sir," said the Lieutenant. Such a charge would be suicide, and the Lieutenant knew it.

"Lieutenant, north of here this ravine narrows down for a few yards. Then it makes a slight curve to the east. Three men could hold off anyone coming down through there. Take Sergeant Lyon and Sergeant O Lochlainn with you. Grab some rifles from the dead; they won't be needing them, and a rifle is better for that sort of work than a handgun. Don't forget to take ammo. Now, get moving. Be back here in five minutes."

Silently, the three men obeyed.

They stayed low, and as close to the eastern bank of the ravine as possible.

It was autumn now, and the dry summer had left little water running down the ravine, but it was obvious that, come spring, when the winter snows melted, the water would be much higher. What was now a trickle would become a flood.

Now, the banks were six to eight feet above the water level, but in spring the ravine would be close to full.

"The Captain has a lot of nerve," Sergeant O Lochlainn said quietly. There was a touch of sarcasm in his whispered voice.

"That's not nerve," said Sergeant Lyon. "Charging through that line is idiocy."

" 'Tis not what I meant, Sergeant," Sean O Lochlainn said. "What I meant was, he'd got a lot of nerve ordering me around; I didn't relinquish command of Red Company to him, but he assumes it."

"Then why did you obey?" Lyon asked.

"Habit, I guess. Habit." Sergeant O Lochlainn sounded as though he were unhappy with himself.

They came to the narrow part of the ravine. Here the clay walls had been eroded back to uncover two huge slabs of rock, one on each side. They were almost perpendicular to the bottom, giving sheer walls seven feet high on the eastern side and nearly eight feet on the western. The gap between them was only three feet.

"I think the Captain was right about this, sir," said Sergeant Lyon. "Three men with rifles can hold off anything that tries to come through there."

Lieutenant Darcy glanced at his wristwatch, then looked down the narrow corridor. It was straight for some thirty yards, then swerved northwest as the banks became clay again. "We can do it, I think," he said. "But watch out for grenades. I doubt if they have anyone who can lob a grenade that far up and over, but they might. Let's back up to that last bend. We can still pick them off if they try to come down that narrow gap, and there'll be less chance of anyone dropping a fistful of high explosive on us."

When they got into position, Lieutenant Darcy said: "If you would, Sergeant O Lochlainn, guard our rear and keep an eye on the eastern parapet—just in case the Poles try to cut us off from the rest."

"Aye, sir."

They waited. The minutes passed slowly.

"You're not a career man, are you, sir?" Sergeant Lyon asked.

"No. I saw enough of the Army when I was a boy. My father was a career man."

"Would that be the Coronel Lord Darcy that Sergeant Kelleigh always talks about?"

"Yes. Kelleigh was my father's top-kick in the old days. Are you career?"

"No, sir. When this mess is over, I'm taking my discharge as soon as I can get it."

Behind them, Sergeant O Lochlainn's voice said: "What're ye goin' to do, once ye get out, Sergeant?"

"Well, I used to think I had a call for the priesthood," Lyon said, "but I'm not sure of it; and as long as one isn't sure, one oughtn't to try it. I think I'll try out for Armsman. Being an Officer of the King's Peace is a job I think I can handle and one I *am* sure of. What about you, O Lochlainn?"

"Well, now, that's a thing I'm sure as sure of," the stout little Irishman said. "I'm going to be a Master Sorcerer."

"Indeed?" said Lieutenant Darcy. "Have you been tested for the Talent, then?"

"Why, sir, I already have me Journeyman's ticket in the Guild."

"You do? Then what the Hell are you doing in the Army? You could have got a deferment easily enough."

"So could you have, sir, I daresay. But *somebody's* got to fight this bloody war, sir. I volunteered for the same reason you did, sir." He paused. Then: "The Empire expects every man to do his duty, sir."

The Lieutenant glanced at his wristwatch. Two minutes to go, and no sign of enemy activity. *Yes*, he thought, *the Empire* does *expect every man to do his duty*.

The Anglo-French Empire had already lasted longer than the ancient Roman Empire. The first Plantagenet, Henry of Anjou, had become King of England in 1154, taking the title of Henry II. His son, Richard the Lion-Hearted, had become King upon the death of Henry II in 1189. Richard I had been absent from England during most of the first ten years of his reign, establishing a reputation as a fighter in the Holy Land. Even today, Islamic mothers threaten their children with *Al Rik*, a most horrendous *afreet*.

Richard had been hit by a crossbow bolt at the Siege of Chaluz in 1199, and after a long bout with infection and fever, had survived to become a wise and powerful ruler. His younger brother, John, died in exile in 1216, so when Richard died in 1219 the crown had gone to Richard's nephew, Arthur, son of Geoffrey of Brittany. Known as "Good King Arthur," he was often confused in the popular mind with King Arthur Pendragon, of ancient Kymric legend.

During Arthur's reign, St. Hilary of Walsingham had produced his monumental works which outlined the theory and mathematics of Magic. But only those with the Talent could utilize St. Hilary's Laws of Magic.

Even today, such people were rare, and Lieutenant Darcy felt that it was a waste to allow Sean O Lochlainn to expose his God-given Talent to the sudden death that could come from combat.

Every man must do his duty, yes. But what was the duty of a Sorcerer?

"Someone comin' from the rear," said Sergeant O Lochlainn.

"Watch ahead, Lyon," the Lieutenant said sharply. He turned to see what was coming from behind.

It was Senior Sergeant Kelleigh.

"What is it, Sergeant?" the Lieutenant asked.

Kelleigh swallowed. "Sir, you are in command. Captain Rimbaud is dead."

The Lieutenant looked at his wristwatch. One minute left, and no one had come down that corridor. "Let's move," he said in a quiet, calm voice. "Back to the Company. Keep down."

It was not true calmness, the Lieutenant knew; it was numbness, overlying and masking his fear. Fear of the artillery, fear of death and dismemberment, had been suddenly supplemented by a fear that was akin to, but vastly greater than, stage fright.

He? *He?* In command?

Mary, Mother of God, pray for me!

He was younger than any other man in the outfit, and he had less combat experience than most of them. And yet the burden of command had fallen on *him.*

He knew he dared not show his inner self; he dared not crack. Not for fear of showing himself a coward, but because of what it would do to the men. In a properly trained army, when the officers are taken out of action, the noncoms can carry on. Death is expected; it may come as a shock, but not as a surprise.

But for a commander to go into a panic of fear—to show the yellow—is more demoralizing than sudden death.

Consciously or subconsciously, rightly or wrongly, a soldier always feels that his superiors know more about what is going on than he does. Therefore, if an officer cracks up, it must be because he knows something that the men don't.

And fear of the unknown can cause more despair than fear of the known.

So the fear of causing catastrophe to his troops (*his troops!*) overrode all the other fears as he led the three sergeants back to the rest of the men while the irregular *crack!* of small-arms fire punctuated the air.

The Captain's body lay a few feet from the rivulet that ran down the ravine. It was covered by a blanket. Lieutenant Darcy knelt down, gently lifted the covering, and looked at his late commander. There was a bullet wound in his chest, just to the left of the lower tip of the sternum.

"Went right through 'im, it did, sir," said a nearby corporal. Whittaker? Yes—Whittaker.

The Lieutenant carefully turned the body on its side. The exit wound near the spine, between the fifth and sixth ribs, was larger than the entrance wound, as might be expected. From the trajectory, the Lieutenant judged it must have gone right through the heart. *Probably died before he knew he'd been hit*, he thought. He replaced the blanket and stood up.

"How long do you think it will be before the Poles get their guns back in position, Sergeant?" he asked Kelleigh.

Kelleigh looked at his wristwatch. "Another five minutes is all we can depend on, sir." He looked at the Lieutenant and stood expectantly, awaiting his orders. So were the other two sergeants.

Without saying anything, the Lieutenant went over to where the late Captain had dropped his pack. He opened it and took out the little collapsing periscope. Then he climbed up the slope of the ravine wall and eased the upper end of the periscope over the top. The Captain had carried the device because regulations said he should, but he never used it because he thought it a coward's gadget. Lieutenant Darcy believed there was a difference between caution and cowardice.

After half a minute, he said: "Sergeant Kelleigh, what are the men shooting at?" Most of the foggy smoke had cleared away, and the Lieutenant could see nothing but woods out there. There wasn't a Polish soldier in sight.

Kelleigh climbed up the slope and took a quick look over the top. "Why—at those Polish troops out there, sir. They're behind those trees, shootin' at us." His voice had a touch of bewilderment in it, as though he were afraid the young Lieutenant had lost his reason.

The Lieutenant moved up and looked over the edge. He could see them now. Some were lying prone, some standing behind trees, and now and then one would move from one tree to another in the background. He slid down a little and used the periscope again. No one. The woods were empty.

"Sergeant O Lochlainn!" he snapped.

"Aye, sir!"

"Come up here for a minute. Sergeant Kelleigh, tell the men to cease fire and get ready to move out."

"Yes, sir." He slid down and was gone.

The stout little Irish sergeant clambered up to where the Lieutenant was. "Aye, sir?"

"Take a look at those woods through the periscope. Then take a look over the top. And don't think like a soldier, think like a sorcerer."

Sergeant O Lochlainn did as he was told without saying a word until he was done. But when he brought his head down, he looked at Lieutenant Darcy. "Shades o' S'n Padraeg! You're right, sir. 'Tis an illusion. There's no troops out there. It's a psychic effect that registers on the mind, not on the eye, so it isn't visible in a mirror."

"And it's being projected through that haze?"

"Aye, sir; it's needed for a big illusion like that."

Lieutenant Darcy frowned. "We can't say there isn't *anybody* out there. Someone is shooting at us."

"Aye, sir. And a pretty good shot, too."

"Can you dispel that illusion, Sergeant?"

"No, sir; not with the equipment I've got with me. Not in a minute or two." He paused. "If we could locate the sniper—"

Lieutenant Darcy was back at the periscope. "He must have us spotted here by now. Three of us have looked over that edge, but he can't know if it's the same man or not, so—" He stopped suddenly. "I think I see him. No wonder he's so good at spotting us."

"Where, sir?"

"Up in that big tree to the northwest. About thirty-five feet off the ground. Here—take the periscope."

The Sergeant took it and, after a moment said: "Aye, sir. I see him. I wonder if there's any more about."

"I don't think so. Have you noticed the wounds of the men who have been hit were always high on the left side of the body?"

"Now that I think of it, sir. But I thought nothing of it."

"Neither did I until I saw that those Polish troops are illusions. Then I realized that whoever was doing the shooting was high up and to the northeast. Then everything was obvious."

"That's how you knew which tree to look at, sir?"

"Yes, I—" He stopped, listening to the silence. The order to cease fire had been relayed to his troops.

Sergeant Kelleigh approached and looked up the slope

at his new commander. "Sir, the troops are ready to march. We'd best get started if we're going to get out of here, sir; that artillery can start any minute now."

The Lieutenant slid down the bank of the ravine. "Who are your two best riflemen, Sergeant? Your best shots."

"Corporal Whittaker and Senior Private Martinne, sir."

"Let's go. Come along, Sergeant O Lochlainn."

The remainders of Blue and Red Companies were waiting for them, packs on, rifles at the ready.

The Lieutenant said, "At ease" before they could come to attention, then said: "I want all of you to listen very carefully because we only have time for me to say it once. Sergeant Kelleigh, take this periscope and get up there and tell me what you see. Don't stick your head up; use the 'scope. While he's doing that, the rest of you pay attention.

"Sergeant O Lochlainn, here, has a ticket as a Journeyman Sorcerer. He and I have discovered that sorcery is being used against us. Not, I think, strictly Black Magic, eh, Sergeant?"

"Not at all, sir," said the Irishman. "An illusion is meant to confuse, but it does no direct harm. Not Black Magic at all."

"Very well, then," the Lieutenant continued. "But we've been pinned down here by—"

Senior Sergeant Kelleigh came back down the slope, his eyes wide, his face white. "There's nobody up there," he said softly.

"Almost nobody. We've been pinned down by a lone sniper. All those Polish troops we've been firing at are illusions produced by sorcery. But you can't see them in a mirror.

"The sniper is in that big tree to the northeast, about thirty-five feet up. Corporal Whittaker, Private Martinne, the Senior Sergeant tells me you're crack shots. Take the periscope and spot that sniper. Then both of you keep up a steady fire. Kill him if you can, but at least make sure he stays down. The rest of us are going to go over the top and head for those woods while you keep up cover fire for us. As soon as we get there, we'll all cover for you, and you come running. Everybody got all that?"

"Yes, sir," came the ragged chorus.

"Now, I want you to realize one important thing: the Poles haven't got much infantry around. If they did, they'd use them, instead of relying on one man and a set of illusions, They have damned few men to move, fire, and protect those fieldpieces.

"So we, lads, are going through that woods and take those fieldpieces away from them."

Grins broke out on the soldiers' faces.

"It's going to be hard, but I want you to keep in mind that the soldiers you'll see when you get out there are only illusions. They can't hurt you. All the firing for the past quarter hour has been done by us and that sniper. Notice how quiet it is now. It has been so noisy in this ravine that we didn't realize *we* were making all the noise. But now we'll have to get out of here before the *real* noise starts."

Whittaker and Martinne were already up at the lip of the ravine. After a moment, the Corporal said: "We've got him spotted, sir."

"Fire when ready."

The two men cut loose.

"Let's go, men," said the Lieutenant.

And up and over they went.

Lieutenant Darcy, in the lead, threw a swift glance at the tall tree that held the sniper. Bullets from the rifles of Whittaker and Martinne were splashing bark off the trunk and the limb where the sniper was hiding. Good enough.

They moved fast, keeping low and spread out. It was possible that there might be more than one sniper around, though the Lieutenant didn't think so, and playing it cautiously was the order of the day.

Ahead of them, the illusory Polish infantrymen still moved about, but they no longer seemed real. They were flickering phantoms that receded and faded as the Imperial troops moved toward them.

"Where's Kelleigh goin', sir?" Sergeant O Lochlainn's voice came from a few yards to Lieutenant Darcy's left. The Lieutenant took a quick glance.

Instead of going straight for the woods, Kelleigh had cut off to the left at an angle. Covered by the rifle fire from Whittaker and Martinne, he was headed straight for the sniper's tree!

"He's going to get that sniper," Lieutenant Darcy said

sharply. *The damned fool!* he added to himself. He hadn't ordered Kelleigh to do that. On the other hand, he hadn't ordered him not to—simply because it hadn't occurred to him that Kelleigh would do anything like that. *And it should have,* he told himself. *It* should *have!*

But now was no time to say anything.

The remains of Blue and Red Companies reached the woods.

"Get down!" the Lieutenant snapped. "Lay some covering fire on that tree so that Whittaker and Martinne can get over here!"

The order was obeyed, and the two men came up and over just as the Polish Gornickis exploded into thunder, launching their six-inch shells toward the ravine.

Whittaker and Martinne were only a few yards from the edge of the ravine when the first salvo exploded at the bottom of it. If the shells had landed that close on level ground, the men would have died then and there; but the walls of the ravine directed most of the blast upward. Both men were knocked flat, but they were up again and running within seconds.

Then there was the crack of a rifle shot from the sniper's tree, and Martinne fell sprawling, his left eye and temple a smashed ruin. Whittaker kept coming.

The Lieutenant snapped his head around to look at the tree.

Sergeant Kelleigh was still a few yards from it. The sniper hadn't seen Kelleigh yet; he had moved around to the north side of the tree, to another branch, and had seen the two men running. One shot, and Martinne was dead.

Then the sniper saw Superior Sergeant Kelleigh. He had to make a snap decision and a snap shot. Kelleigh, obviously hit, stumbled, fell, and rolled.

But he was behind that tree, and the sniper couldn't adjust his precarious position fast enough to get his rifle to bear a second time. Kelleigh, flat on his back, had his .44 MMP out and firing. Two shots.

Even as the sniper fell, Kelleigh hit him with one more shot in mid-air.

Seeing all this from a distance, Lieutenant Darcy gave the order to cease fire. Then: "Sergeant Lyon, you are senior NCO now. Send someone out to look at Martinne. I think he's dead, but make sure. Sergeant O Lochlainn, will you come with me?"

The thunder of the guns went on, the shells fell screaming into the ravine to spend their explosions uselessly against the clay of the walls and other, equally lifeless clay.

The Lieutenant and Sergeant O Lochlainn ran northward to where Sergeant Kelleigh lay.

He was still flat on his back, eyes closed, right hand clasping his .44 Morley to his chest. It rose and fell with his chest. Beneath it, blood flowed steadily.

The Lieutenant knelt down. "Kelleigh?"

The Sergeant opened his eyes, focusing them unsteadily on the young face. "You know," he said distinctly.

The Lieutenant nodded.

"Don't tell the Coronel."

And then, very quietly, he died.

With his thumbs, the Lieutenant pulled the eyelids down, held them for a few seconds, Sergeant O Lochlainn made the Sign of the Cross and murmured an almost inaudible prayer. The Lieutenant made the same Sign in silence, letting the stout little Irishman's prayer do for both of them.

Then Sergeant O Lochlainn went to the body of the sniper. The Pole had fallen on his face and was very definitely dead. The Irishman opened the sniper's backpack and began rummaging through it.

"Here! What are you doing?" Lieutenant Darcy asked. Robbing the dead was not a part of civilized warfare—if such a thing existed.

"Well, sir," said Sergeant O Lochlainn without looking up from what he was doing, "this man here was a sorcerer of some small ability, and he might have the paraphernalia I need. Ah! Just the thing! Here we are!"

"What do you mean?" the Lieutenant asked.

"Well, sir," the Sergeant said, looking up with a grin, "if we're going to take those fieldpieces away from the Poles, it might be better if they're attacked by a battalion instead of the bob ends of two companies. And believe me, sir, I'm a better sorcerer than he was."

Lieutenant Darcy tried to return the grin. "I see. Very well, Sergeant; carry on."

The artillery thundered on.

Lieutenant Darcy picked up his small group of men and moved eastward with them. The soft breeze brought the smoke and stench of the thundering guns directly toward them; but it drifted slowly, and it was not dense enough to make the men cough.

There was a grim smile on Sergeant O Lochlainn's face as they neared the eastern edge of the woods. Beyond was a clear space half a mile or so square.

Sergeants Lyon and O Lochlainn and Lieutenant Darcy lay flat on their bellies watching the battery of eight Gornickis blast away. The Lieutenant watched through his field glasses for a full minute, then said: "Fifteen, maybe sixteen infantrymen with rifles. The rest are all gun crews. Range about eight hundred yards." He took the binoculars from his eyes and looked at the Irish sergeant. "Where do you have to be to set up our phantom battalion, Sergeant?"

"I'll have to set it up right about here, sir. But I can establish my focal point, and then get out, leaving it to operate by itself."

"Good. Because when they see your illusions coming, those gunners are going to depress their barrels and fire point-blank. Can you set up the illusion so that some of them will fall when shells explode around them?"

"Nothin' to it, sir."

"Fine. The rest of us will move south to those woods flanking them. Give us ten minutes to get there before you start the phantoms moving in. Then run like hell to get down with us before they start firing straight in here instead of over our heads. From their flank, we can enfilade them and wipe them out before they know what's happening."

"It's goin' to tear hell out of these trees," was all the Sergeant said.

The Lieutenant and Sergeant Lyon led the men south through the woods and then turned eastward again, well south of the clearing where the Polish artillery blasted away.

"All right now, lads," the Lieutenant said, "set your sights for three hundred fifty yards. Keep low and try to make every shot count. We won't see the phantoms, but the Poles will. We will be able to tell when they see the illusion by the way they behave; their infantry will start firing their rifles toward those trees to our left, and the gunnery crews will stop their barrage and frantically start depressing the muzzles of their pieces. As soon as their infantry begins to fire, so do we. But—mark this!—*no volleys!*"

"If we all fire at once, they'll spot us. Now, I'm going to count you off, and I want you to remember your number. Whatever your number is, I want you to listen for that many shots from here before you fire. After that, you may fire at will, slow and steady. We're getting low on ammo, so don't be wasteful. Got it?"

They did. The Lieutenant counted them off.

For a minute or two, nothing happened. Then everything happened. There were shouts and sounds of excitement from the Polish lines. The infantrymen threw themselves prone and began firing at nothing the Imperial forces could see. The gunners began frantically spinning the wheels that would lower the aim of their guns.

The Lieutenant, who had given himself no number and was therefore automatically Number Zero, took careful aim and fired. A man dropped limply, and the Lieutenant swallowed a sudden blockage in his throat. It was the first time he had ever deliberately fired at and killed a man.

The rest of the men, in order, began firing steadily.

Very rarely do battles go as one expects them to, but this was one of the rare ones. The Poles, to the very end, never did figure out where that death-dealing fire was coming from. The distraction of the phantoms advancing toward them in numberless hordes kept them from even thinking about their left flank. The action was over in minutes.

"Now what, sir?" asked Sergeant Lyon. "Shall we go out and take over those guns?"

"Not yet. Battalion can't be over a couple of miles south of here. Send a couple of runners. We'll wait here, just in case more Poles come. We'll be safer here in these woods than out there, standing around those fieldpieces. Have the runners report directly to Coronel Everard and get his orders on what to do with those things. Move."

"Yes, sir." Sergeant Lyon obeyed.

Lieutenant Darcy sat down on a nearby fallen log, took out his pipe, tamped it lightly, and fired it up. Sergeant O

Lochlainn came up and sat beside him. "Mind if I join you, sir?"

"Not at all. Welcome."

"Nice piece of work, sir."

"Same to you, Sergeant. I don't know what those Poles saw, but it must have been something to see. Panicked the Hell out of them. Congratulations."

"Thank you, sir." After a pause, the Sergeant said: "Sir, may I ask a question? Maybe it's none of me business, and if so ye've but to tell me, and I'll never think of it again."

"Go ahead, Sergeant."

"What was it Sergeant Kelleigh didn't want you to tell Coronel Everard?"

The young Lieutenant frowned and puffed solemnly at his pipe for nearly half a minute before he said: "To be perfectly honest, Sergeant, I don't know of anything he would want me to keep from Coronel Everard. Not a thing."

No, he thought. *Nothing he had wanted to keep from Coronel* Everard. *He didn't want me to tell Coronel* Darcy. *And I shan't. Kelleigh made a terrible mistake, but he paid for it, and that's an end of it.*

"I see, sir," the Irishman said slowly. "He was dying and likely didn't know what he was saying. Or who he was talkin' to."

That could be, Lieutenant Darcy said.

But he knew it wasn't so. He had known since he saw the Captain's body that Kelleigh had shot him. The bullet had gone straight through, parallel to the ground, not from a high angle. And the hole had been made by a .44 Morley, not by a .28 Kosciusko.

It would have been simple. Men in a firefight don't pay any attention to what is going on to their right or left, and what is one more shot among so many?

Kelleigh had felt that the Captain's decision to charge the Polish line was suicidal, and that Darcy's planned retreat was the wiser course.

When he found that the Polish troops were an illusion, he had paid for his crime in the best way he knew how. Captain Rimbaud had been going to do the right thing for the wrong reason, and Kelleigh could no longer live with himself.

There would be no point in telling anyone. Kelleigh was dead, and the only evidence—Rimbaud's body—had been blown to bits in the first Polish salvo to hit the ravine.

But—however wrongly—Kelleigh had given Lieutenant Darcy his first command. The Lieutenant would never forget that, but he would always wonder whether it had been worth it.

The Hell with it, he thought. And knocked the dottle from his pipe.

Randall Garrett is the author of a great deal of fiction, mostly in short story form. His novels include Unwise Child *and* Anything You Can Do, *and he has written two nonfiction books: a book on the lives of the saints called* A Gallery of the Saints *and a biography entitled* John XXIII: Pastoral Prince. *With Robert Silverberg, he co-authored* The Shrouded Planet *and* The Dawning Light, *and with Laurence M. Janifer, three "happy novels,"* The Impossibles, Brain Twister, *and* Supermind, *all involving "The Queen's Own FBI."*

Randall is perhaps best known for his Lord Darcy series, in which our story belongs. The first, "The Eyes Have It," was published in Analog *in 1964, and was followed by many more stories and one novel,* Too Many Magicians.

After serving in the Marine Corps in World War II, he took his degree in chemistry, supplementing his income with regular sales to Analog, *and finally writing full-time. He is married to fellow writer Vicki Ann Heydrou.*

Where, in future warfare, will a weapon end and a vehicle—a means for moving men and/or weapons from here to there—begin? In former times, a war-horse was itself a weapon, so was a chariot, many a ship of war, kamikaze planes; and certainly, in a future when remote control may very well be the rule rather than the exception, the distinction between a weapon and its means of transport will become less and less clear-cut. The expression of destructive force in war has, until now at least, always gone through five phases:

1. Preparation. *Industrial production, organization, training*
2. Logistics. *Movement "out of action"*
3. Maneuver. *Movement "in action"*
4. Weapons, *primary radius of expression*
5. Weapons, *secondary radius of expression*

The two weapons phases are perhaps best illustrated by an artillery shell: the primary phase refers to its flight from gun to target; the secondary, to the effective radius of whatever it happens to be loaded with.

Today, in war on land and sea (and through near space), certain vehicle-weapons (or weapon-vehicles) appear to have virtually eliminated the second and third phases. At the same time, progress in weapons design is eliminating or threatening to eliminate vehicles too vulnerable or too cost-ineffective, very much as the development of rifled naval guns eliminated the wooden fighting ship. Therefore the game today is to determine which will be found obsolete, which will not be found obsolete until too late, and what new vehicles will most effectively take their places.

In his article, Ing plays the game well, and I think the reader will enjoy playing it with him.

Dean Ing

MILITARY VEHICLES: INTO THE THIRD MILLENNIUM

Long before the first ram-tipped bireme scuttled across the Aegean, special military vehicles were deciding the outcomes of warfare. If we can judge from the mosaics at Ur, the Mesopotamians drove four-horsepower chariots thundering into battle in 2500 B.C.; and bas-reliefs tell us that some Assyrian genius later refined the design so his rigs could be quickly disassembled for river crossings. In more recent times, some passing strange vehicles have been pressed into military service—Hannibal's Alp-roving elephants and six hundred troop-toting Paris taxicabs being two prime examples. Still, people had seen elephants and taxis before; application, not design, was the surprise element. Today, military vehicle design itself is undergoing rapid change in almost all venues: land, sea, air, space. Tomorrow's war chariots are going to be mind-bogglers!

What will military vehicles of the immediate future—of the next few generations—be like? It is possible to list a few primary considerations for the design of any military vehicle without naming specific functions. It should have higher performance than previous vehicles; it should be more dependable; and it should be cost-effective. Those three criteria cover a hundred others including vulnerability, speed, firepower, maintenance, manufacturing, and even the use of critical materials. Any new design that doesn't have to trade off one of these criteria to meet others is going to be very, very popular.

Before taking a cut at designs of some specific new craft just on our horizon, it might be well to look at the power plants and materials that should be popular in the foreseeable future.

Power Plants

Internal combustion engines may be with us for another generation or so, thanks to compact design and new fuel mixtures. Still, the only reason why Indianapolis racers don't use turbines now is that they are outlawed by Indy officials: too good, too quiet, too dependable. Turbines can be smaller if they can operate at higher temperatures and higher RPM. Superalloy turbine blades may be replaced by hyperalloys or cermets; oiled bearings may be replaced by magnetic types. And automated manufacturing could bring the cost of a turbine power plant down so low that the unit could be replaced with every refueling. In short, it should be possible to design the power plant and fuel tanks as a unit to be mated to the vehicle in moments.

The weapons designer won't be slow to see that high-temperature turbines can lend themselves to MHD (magnetohydrodynamics) application. If a weapon laser needs vast quantities of electrical energy, and if that energy can be taken from a hot stream of ionized gas, then the turbine may become the power source for both the vehicle and its weapons. Early MHD power plants were very heavy, and required rocket propellants to obtain the necessary working temperatures.[1] Yet there are ways to bootstrap a gas stream into conductive plasma, including previously stored electrical energy and seeding the gas with chemicals. If the vehicle needs a lot of electrical energy and operates in a chemically active atmosphere—oxygen will do handily—then a turbine of some sort may be with us for a long time to come.

Chemically fueled rockets are made to order for MHD. If the vehicle is to operate in space, an MHD unit could be coupled to a rocket exhaust to power all necessary electrical systems. The problem with chemical rockets, of course, is their ferocious thirst. If a vehicle is to be very energetic for very long using chemical rockets, it will consist chiefly of propellant tanks. And it will need careful refueling, unless the idea is to junk the craft when its tanks are empty. Refueling with cryogenic propellant—liquid hydrogen and liquid fluorine are good bets from the stored-energy standpoint—tends to be complicated and slow. So when oxidizer is available in the atmosphere, the turbine is a popular choice. It goes further on a tank of fuel, it is very dependable, and its support equipment is relatively cheap.

By the end of this century, rocket-turbine hybrids could be used for vehicles that must flit from atmosphere to vacuum and back again. The turbine could use atmospheric oxidizer while the craft stored its own for use in space.

There is reason to suspect that simpler air-breathing jets, such as the Schmidt pulsejet, could also operate as ramjets by clever modifications to pulse vanes and inlet geometry. In this way, sophisticated design may permit a small have-not country to produce air-breathing power plants that challenge those of their richer neighbors. A pulsejet develops thrust at rest and could boost a vehicle to high subsonic velocity where the ramjet becomes efficient. Supersonic ramjets need careful attention to the region just ahead of the inlet, where a spikelike cowl produces exactly the right disturbance in the incoming air to make the ramjet efficient at a given speed. A variable-geometry spike greatly improves the efficiency of a ramjet over a wide range or airspeeds, from transsonic to Mach 5 or so. We might even see pulse-ram-rocket hybrids using relatively few moving parts, propelling vehicles from rest at sea level into space and back.

For a country where cost-effectiveness overshadows all else, then, the simplicity of the pulse-ram-rocket could make it popular. Since a turbine is somewhat stingier with fuel, a turbine-rocket hybrid would yield better range. The choice might well depend on manufacturing capability.

As MHD technology develops lightweight hardware, it will be possible to use megawatt quantities of electrical energy directly in power plants.[2] An initial jolt from fuel cells or even a short-duration chemical rocket may be needed to start the MHD generator. Once in operation, the MHD unit could use a combination of electron beams and jet fuel to heat incoming air in a duct, and at that point the vehicle could reduce its expenditure of tanked oxidizer. We might suspect that the MHD generator would need a trickle of chemical, such as a potassium salt, to boost plasma conductivity especially when the MHD unit is idling. By the year 2050, MHD design might be so highly developed that no chemical seeding would be necessary under any conditions. This development could arise from magnetic pinch effects, or from new materials capable of withstanding very high temperatures for extended periods while retaining dielectric properties.

It almost seems that an MHD power plant would be a perpetual-motion machine, emplaced in an atmosphere-breathing vehicle that could cruise endlessly. But MHD is an energy-conversion system, converting heat to electricity as the conductive plasma (i.e., the hot gas stream) passes stationary magnets.[3] The vehicle would need its own compact heat generator; perhaps even a closed-loop gaseous uranium fission reactor for large craft. A long-range cruise vehicle could be managed this way, but eventually the reactor would need refueling. Still, it would be risky to insist that we will never find new sources of energy which could provide MHD power plants capable of almost perpetual operation.

For propulsion in space, several other power plants look attractive. Early nuclear weapons revealed that graphite-covered steel spheres survived a 20-kiloton blast at a distance of 30 feet. The Orion project grew from this datum, and involved nothing less than a series of nuclear bombs detonated behind the baseplate of a large vehicle.[4] As originally designed by Ted Taylor and Freeman Dyson, such a craft could be launched from the ground, but environmentalists quake at the very idea. The idea is not at all farfetched from an engineering standpoint and might yet be used to power city-sized space dreadnaughts of the next century. Incidentally, the intermittent explosion drive was tested by Orion people, using conventional explosives in scale models. Wernher von Braun was evidently unimpressed with the project until he saw films of a model in flight.

The mass-driver concept is also simple in principle, using magnetic coils to hurl small masses away at high speed, producing thrust against the coils. Gerard O'Neill has demonstrated working models of the mass driver.[5] In space, a mass driver could be powered by a solar array or a closed-cycle reactor, and its power consumption would not be prohibitively high. The thrust of the device is modest— too low for planetary liftoff as currently conceived. Its use in an atmosphere would be limited, power source aside, by aerodynamic shock waves generated by the mass accelerated to hypersonic velocity within the acceleration coils. For fuel mass, O'Neill suggests munching bits from a handy asteroid; though almost any available mass would do. The mass need not be magnetic since it can be accelerated in metal containers, then allowed to continue while the metal "buckets" are decelerated for reuse.

Solar plasma—the stream of ionized particles radiated by stars—has been suggested as a "solar wind" to be tapped by vast gossamer sails attached to a space vehicle. It seems unlikely that a craft could move effectively into a solar wind as a sailboat tacks against moving air. The interstellar yachtsman has an advantage, though: he can predict the sources of his "wind." He cannot be sure it won't vary in intensity, however, which leads to scenarios of a craft becalmed between several stars until one star burns out—or bcomes a nova.

It takes a very broad brush to paint a military operation on such a scale that solar sails and mass drivers would be popular as power plants. These power plants are very cost-effective, but they need a lot of time to traverse a lot of space. By the time we have military missions beyond Pluto, we may also have devices which convert matter completely into photons, yielding a photon light drive. In the meantime, nuclear reactors can provide enough heat to vaporize fuel mass for highthrust power plants in space. So far as we know, the ultimate space drive would use impinging streams of matter and antimatter in a rocket thrust chamber. This is perhaps the most distant of far-out power plants, and presumes that we can learn to make antimatter do as we say. But a vehicle using an antimatter drive would be able to squander energy in classic military fashion.

The power plants we've discussed so far all lend themselves to aircraft and spacecraft. Different performance standards apply to land- and water-based vehicles, which must operate quietly and slowly—at least during docking stages. Turbines can be quiet, but they produce strong infrared signatures, and they use a lot of fuel, limiting their range. When you cannot be quick, you are wise to be inconspicuous. This suggests that electric motors might power wheeled transports in the near future, drawing power from lightweight storage batteries or fuel cells. The fuel cell oxidizes fuel to obtain current, but the process generates far less waste heat than a turbine does. The fuel cell also permits fast refueling—with a hydride, or perhaps hydrogen—which gives the fuel cell a strong advantage over conventional batteries. However, remember that the fuel cell "burns" fuel. No fair powering a moon-rover or a submarine by fuel cells without a oxidizer supply on board!

When weight is not a crucial consideration, the designer can opt for heavier power plants that have special advantages. The flywheel is one method of storing energy without generating much heat as that energy is tapped. A flywheel can be linked to a turbine or other drive unit to provide a hybrid engine. For maximum emergency power or for brief periods when a minimal infrared signature is crucial, the vehicle could operate entirely off the flywheel. Fuel cells could replace the turbine in this hybrid system. Very large cargo vehicles might employ reactors; but the waste heat of a turbine, reactor, or other heat engine is always a disadvantage when heat-seeking missiles are lurking near. It's likely that military cargo vehicles will evolve toward sophisticated hybrid power plants which employ heat engines in low-vulnerability areas, switching to flywheel, beamed power, or other stored-energy systems producing little heat when danger is near. As weapons become more sophisticated, there may be literally almost no place far from danger—which implies development of hybrid power plants using low-emission fuel cells and flywheels for wheeled vehicles.[6]

Materials

Perhaps the most direct way to improve a vehicle's overall performance is to increase its payload fraction; i.e., the proportion of the system's gross weight that is devoted to payload. If a given craft can be built with lighter materials, or using more energetic material for fuel, that craft can carry more cargo and/or can carry it farther, faster.

Many solids, including metals, are crystalline masses. Entire journals are devoted to the study of crystal growth because, among other things, the alignment and size of crystals in a material profoundly affect that material's strength. Superalloys in turbine blades have complex crystalline structures and are composed of such combinations as cobalt, chromium, tungsten, tantalum, carbon and re-fractory metal carbides.[7] These materials may lead to hyperalloys capable of sustaining the thermal shock of nuclear weapons at close range.

More conventional alloys of steel, aluminum, and tita-nium may be around for a long time, with tempering and alloying processes doubling present tensile strengths. When we begin processing materials in space, it may be possible to grow endless crystals which can be spun into filament bundles. A metal or quartz cable of such stuff may have tensile strength in excess of a million pounds per square inch. For that matter, we might grow doped crystals in special shapes to exacting tolerances, which could lead to turbine blades and lenses vastly superior to anything we have today.

Vehicle structures are bound to make increasing use of composite materials as processing becomes more sophisti-cated. Fiberglass is a composite of glass fibers in a resin matrix, but sandwich materials are composites, too. A wide variety of materials can be formed into honeycomb structures to gain great stiffness-to-weight characteristics. An air-breathing hypersonic vehicle might employ molyb-denum honeycomb bonded to a hyperalloy inner skin form-ing an exhaust duct. The honeycomb could be cooled by ducting cool gas through it. On the other side of the honeycomb might be the craft's outer skin; say, a compos-ite of graphite and high-temperature polymer. Advanced sandwich composites are already in use, and show dra-matic savings in vehicle weight. The possible combinations in advanced sandwich composites are almost infinite, with various layers tailored to a given structural need. Thirteen years ago, an experimental automobile bumper used an advanced composite of stainless steel mesh between layers of glass and resin to combine lightness with impact resis-tance.[8] A racing car under test that year had a dry weight of 540 pounds, using a chasis built up from a sandwich composite with a paper honeycomb core. Today, some aircraft use aluminum mesh in skins of epoxy and graphite fiber. The next such composite might be titanium mesh between layers of boron fiber in a silicone polymer matrix.

The chief limitation of composites seems to be the adhesives that bond the various materials together. It may be a long time before we develop an adhesive that won't char, peel, or become brittle when subjected to temperature variations of hypersonic aircraft.

Several fibers are competing for primacy in the search for better composites; among them boron, graphite, acetal homopolymer, and aramid polymers. Boron may get the nod for structures that need not sustain very high temperatures, but graphite looks like the best bet for elevated temperature regimes. Sandia Laboratories has developed a system to test graphite specimens for short-term, high-temperature phenomena including fatigue, creep, and stress-rupture.[9] The specimens are tested at very high heating rates. If the Sandia system isn't looking into antilaser armor, it almost certainly will be—and soon.

Before leaving the topic of materials, we might pause to note the research into jet fuels. A gallon of JP-4 stores roughly 110,000 Btu, and some new fuels pack an additional 65,000 Btu into a gallon.[10] Even if the fuel is slightly heavier, the tank can be smaller. The result is extended range. It seems reasonable to think that JP-50, when it comes along, will double the energy storage of JP-4.

Vehicle Configurations

With the advent of microminiaturization comes a new problem in defining a vehicle. We might all agree that a vehicle carries something, but begin wrangling over just how small the something might be. An incendiary bullet carries a tiny blazing chemical payload: but is the bullet then a vehicle? In the strictest sense, probably yes. But a bullet is obviously not a limiting case—leaving that potential pun unspent—when very potent things of almost *no* mass can be carried by vehicles of mosquito size.

The payload of a very small vehicle could be stored information, or it might be a few micrograms of botulism or plutonium, intended for a specific human target. Ruling out bats and insects as carriers, since they are normally rather slapdash in choosing the right one among possibly hundreds of targets of opportunity, we could develop extremely small rotary-winged craft and smarten them with really stupendous amounts of programming without exceeding a few milligrams of total mass. Fleets of these inconspicuous mites would be expensive to produce, but they just may be the ultimate use for "clean room" technology in which the United States has a temporary lead. The mites would be limited in range and top speed, so that a hypersonic carrier vehicle might needed to bring them within range of the target—like a greyhound with fleas. It would then slow to disgorge its electromechanical parasites. One immediately sees visions of filters to stop them, and special antifilter mites to punch holes through the filters, and sensors to detect antifilter mite action, and so on.

There is no very compelling reason why the mites couldn't actually resemble tiny flies, with gimbaled ornithopter wings to permit hovering or fairly rapid motion in any direction. There may be a severe limitation to the absolute top speed in air, depending on the power plant. Perhaps a piezoelectrically driven vibrator could power the minuscule craft; it might be simpler than a turbine and tougher to detect. Whatever powers the mite, it would probably not result in cruise speeds over 100 miles an hour unless an antimatter drive is somehow shoehorned into the chassis. But even with the velocity limitation, the mites could probably maneuver much more quickly than their organic counterparts—which brings up a second dichotomy in vehicles.

Information storage is constantly making inroads into the need for human pilots in vehicles, as the Soviets proved in their unmanned lunar missions. A military vehicle that must carry life-support equipment for anything as delicate as live meat, is at a distinct disadvantage versus a similar craft that can turn and stop at hundreds of 'g's. Given a human cargo, vehicle life-support systems may develop to a point where bloodstreams are temporarily thickened, passengers are quick-frozen and (presumably) harmlessly thawed, or some kind of null-inertia package is maintained to keep the passenger comfortable under 500-gravity angular acceleration. During the trip, it's a good bet that the vehicle would be under computer guidance, unless the mission is amenable to very limited acceleration. In short, there will be increasing pressure to "depersonalize" military missions because a human being is a tactical millstone in the system.

Possibly the most personalized form of vehicle—and surely one of the most complex per cubic inch—would be one that the soldier wears. Individualized battle armor, grown massive enough to require servomechanical muscles, could be classed as a vehicle for the wearer. The future for really massive man-amplifying battle dress doesn't look very bright, though. If the whole system stands twenty feet tall it will present an easier target; and if it is merely very dense, it will pose new problems of traction and maneuverability. Just to focus on one engineering problem of the scaled-up bogus android: if the user hurls a grenade with his accustomed arm-swing using an arm extension fifteen feet long, the end of that extension will be moving at roughly Mach 1. Feedback sensors would require tricky adjustment for movement past the transsonic region—and every arm-wave could become a thunderclap! The user will have to do some fiendishly intricate rethinking when he is part of this system—but then, so does a racing driver. Man-amplified battle armor may pass through a certain vogue, just as moats and tanks have done. The power source for this kind of vehicle might be a turbine, until heat-seeking missiles force a change to fuel cells, or, for lagniappe, a set of flywheels mounted in different parts of the chassis. The rationale for the several prime movers is much the same as for the multi-engined aircraft: you can limp home on a leg and a prayer. Aside from this redundancy feature, power transmission can be more efficient when the engine is near the part that moves. Standing ready for use, a multi-flywheel battle dress might even sound formidable, with the slightly varying tones of several million-plus rpm wheels keening in the wind.

No matter how cheap, dependable, and powerful, a military vehicle must be designed with an eye cocked toward enemy weapons. Nuclear warheads already fit into missiles the size of a stovepipe, and orbital laser-firing satellites are only a few years away. A vehicle that lacks both speed and maneuverability will become an easier target with each passing year. By the end of this century, conventional tanks and very large surface ships would be metaphors of the Maginot Line; expensive fiascos for the users.

Despite its popularity with the Soviets, the conventional

tank seems destined for the junk pile. Its great weight
limits its speed and maneuverability, and several countries
already have anti-tank missile systems that can be carried
by one or two men. Some of these little bolides penetrate
all known tank armor and have ranges of several kilometers.[11] Given the huge costs of manufacturing and maintaining a tank, and the piddling costs of supplying infantry
with tank-killing hardware, the future of the earthbound
battle tank looks bleak. This is not to suggest that the tank's
missions will be discarded, but those missions will probably
be performed by very different vehicles. We will take up
those vehicles under the guise of scoutcraft.

More vulnerable than the tank, an aircraft carrier drawing 50,000 tons on the surface is simply too easy to find,
too sluggish to escape, and too tempting for a nuclear
strike. It seems more sensible to build many small vessels,
each capable of handling a few aircraft.[12] Ideally, the aircraft would take off and land vertically. Such carriers could
be spread over many square miles, reducing vulnerability
of a squadron of aircraft. A pocket aircraft carrier might
draw a few hundred tons while cruising on the surface.
Under battle conditions, the carrier could become an air-
cushion vehicle, its reactor propelling it perhaps 300 miles
an hour with considerable improvement in maneuverability. Its shape would be aerodynamically clean during high-
speed operation—perhaps with variable-geometry catamaran
hulls to permit surface cruise.

Undersea craft are harder to locate. Radar will not reveal a submerged vehicle, and sonar—a short-range detection system—must deal with the vagaries of ocean temperature and pressure gradients as well as pelagic animals.
There may be a military niche for large submersibles for
many years to come—perhaps as mother ships and cargo
vessels.

A submerged mother ship would be an ideal base for a
fleet of small hunter-killer subs. These small craft could
run at periscope depth for 1,000 miles on fuel cells, possibly doubling this range with jettisonable external hydride
tanks. A small sub built largely of composites would not be
too heavy to double as an air-cushion vehicle (ACV) in
calm weather, switching from ducted propellers to ducted
fans for high-speed cruising. From here, it is only a step to

the canard swing-wing craft shown in Figure 1. Snorkel and communication gear are mounted on the vertical fin, and the craft carries a pair of long-range missiles on its flanks just inside the ACV skirts. The filament-wound crew pod could detach for emergency flotation. High-speed ACV cruise mode might limit its range to a few hundred miles. The swing wings are strictly for a supersonic dash mode at modest altitude, using the ducted fans and perhaps small auxiliary jets buried in the aft hull, drawing air from the fan plenum.

Heavy seas might rule out the ACV mode, but if necessary, the little sub could broach vertically like a Poseidon before leveling off into its dash mode. With a gross weight of some 30 tons, it would require some additional thrust for the first few seconds of flight—perhaps a rocket using hydride fuel and gaseous oxygen. The oxygen tank could be replenished during undersea loitering periods. Since the occupants would pull a lot of 'g's when reentering the water in heavy seas, the nose of the craft would be built up with boron-plastic honeycomb in its composite structure. The idea of a flying submersible may stick in a few craws—until we reflect that the SUBROC is an unmanned flying submersible in development for over a decade.

On land, military cargo vehicles will feature bigger, wider, low-profile tires in the effort to develop all-terrain capability. Tires could be permanently inflated by supple closed-cell foams under little or no pressure. If the cargo mass is distributed over enough square feet of "footprint," the vehicle could challenge tracked craft in snow, or churn through swamps with equal facility. The vehicle itself will probably have a wide, squat profile—the tires may be as high as the cargo section—and for added maneuverability, the vehicle can be hinged in the middle. All-wheel drive, of course, is *de rigeur*. It's a popular notion that drive motors should be in the wheels, but this adds to the unsprung portion of the vehicle's weight. For optimal handling over rough terrain, the vehicle should have a minimal unsprung weight fraction—which means that the motors should be part of the sprung mass. Relatively little research has been done on torque transmission via flexible bellows. When designers realize how easily a pressurized

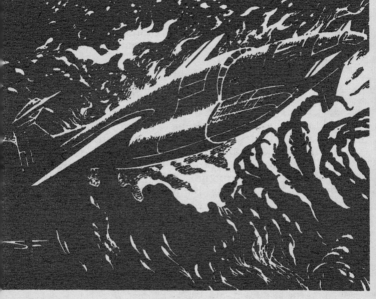

Figure 1

bellows can be inspected, they may begin using this means to transmit torque in cargo vehicles.

The suspension of many future vehicles may depart radically from current high-performance practice. Most suspensions now involve wishbone-shaped upper and lower arms, connecting the wheel's bearing block to the chassis. A rugged alternative would be sets of rollers mounted fore and aft of the bearing block, sliding vertically in chassis-mounted tracks. The tracks could be curved, or adjustable and slaved to sensors so that, regardless of surface roughness or vehicle attitude above that surface, the wheels would be oriented to gain maximum adhesion. Turbines, flywheels, fuel cells, and reactors are all good power plant candidates for these wheeled vehicles.

Some cargo—including standoff missiles, supplies, and airborne laser weapons—will be carried by airborne transports. In this sense a bomber is a military transport vehicle. Here again, advanced composite structures will find wide use, since a lighter vehicle means a higher payload fraction. Vertical takeoff and landing (VTOL), or at least very short takeoff and landing (VSTOL), will greatly expand the effectiveness of these transports, which will use variable-geometry structures including leading and trailing edges, not only on wings but on the lifting body. Figure 2 shows a VSTOL transport with its triple-delta wings fully extended for maximum lift at takeoff. Long aerodynamic "fences" along the wings guide airflow, and the lower fences provide fairings for landing gear. The wing extensions telescope rather than swing as the craft approaches multimach velocity, and for suborbital flight the hydrogen-fluorine rocket will come into operation at around 100,000 feet. In its stubby double-delta configuration the craft can skip-glide in the upper atmosphere for extended range, its thick graphite composite leading surfaces aglow as they slowly wear away during reentry. During periodic maintenance, some of this surface can be replaced in the field.

As reactors become more compact and MHD more sophisticated, the rocket propellant tanks can give way to cargo space although externally the VSTOL skip-glide transport might seem little changed. Conversion from VSTOL to VTOL could be aided by a special application of the mass-driver principle. In this case the aircraft, with ferrous

Figure 2

metal filaments in its composite skin, is the mass repelled by a grid that could rise like scaffolding around the landing pad. This magnetic balancing act could be reversed for vertical landing—but it would take a lot of site preparation which might, in turn, lead to inflatable grid elements that would rise as a torus around the landing site.

Once the antimatter drive is developed, the transport might become little more than a streamlined box with gimbaled exhaust nozzles near its corners. Such a craft could dispense with impediments like lifting surfaces, but would still need heat-resistant skin for its mile-a-second flights inside a planetary atmosphere.

Among the most fascinating military vehicles are those designed for scouting forays; surveillance, pinpoint bombing sorties, troop support, and courier duties are salient uses. Nazi Germany briefly rescued Mussolini with a slow but superb STOL scoutcraft, the Fieseler Storch. Our SR-71 does its scouting at Mach 3; and the close-support A-10 loiters at a tenth that speed.[13] Now in development in the United States, Britain, and Germany is a family of remotely piloted scoutcraft that may become the next generation of scouts, combining the best features of the Storch and the SR-71. Figure 3 is a rough cut at a fourth-generation scout.

The general shape of the scoutship is that of a football flattened on the bottom, permitting high-speed atmospheric travel and crabwise evasive action while providing a broad base for the exhaust gases of its internal ACV fans. The ship is MHD powered and draws inlet air from around the underlip of the shell just outboard of the ACV skirts. The skirt petals determine the direction of deflected exhaust for omnidirectional maneuvers, though auxiliary jets may do the job better than skirt petals.

The scout would use thick graphite composite skin and would sport small optical viewports for complete peripheral video rather than having a single bubble up front. The multiple videos offer redundancy in case of damage, they permit a stiffer structure, and they allow the occupant—if any—maximum protection by remoting him from the ports.

The question of piloting is moot at the moment. Grumman, Shorts, and Dornier are all developing pilotless observation platforms, but a scoutcraft of the future would

Figure 3

probably have a life-support option for at least one occupant.[14] The design shown in Figure 3 has an ovoid hatch near the trailing edge. For manned missions, an occupant pod slides into the well-protected middle of the craft—and could pop out again for emergency ejection. For unmanned missions, the occupant pod could be replaced by extra fuel, supplies, or weapons. Some version of this design might inherit the missions of the battle tank, but with much-improved speed and maneuverability.

We have noted that the craft could be highly maneuverable, and that it should have a graphite composite skin. Given supersonic speed and automated evasion equipment, it might be the one hope of outrunning an orbital laser platform's weapon!

Of course, this scout doesn't exceed lightspeed. What it might do, though, is survive a brief zap long enough to begin a set of evasive actions. Let's say the enemy has an orbital laser platform (OLP) fairly near, not directly overhead but in line-of-sight, 400 miles from the scout, which is cruising at Mach 1. The laser is adjusted perfectly and fires.

What does it hit? A thick, polished carapace of graphite composite, the filaments aligned to conduct the laser's heat away from the pencil-wide target point. Sensors in the scout's shell instantly set the craft to dodging in a complex pattern, at lateral accelerations of about 10 'g's. At this point, the occupant is going to wish he had stayed home, but he should be able to survive these maneuvers.

Meanwhile, the OLP optics sense the change of course— but this takes a little time (roughly two milliseconds) because the OLP is 400 miles away. Re-aiming the laser might take only ten milliseconds or it might take considerably longer. Then the OLP fires again, the new laser burst taking another two millisec to reach the target.

But that's fourteen millisec—and the scout is moving roughly one foot per millisec, and is now moving to one side. Its change of direction is made at well over 300 per second, over 4 feet of angular shift before the next laser shot arrives. The scout's generally elliptical shell might be 20 feet long by about 10 feet wide. Chances are good that the next laser shot might miss entirely; and in any case it would probably not hit the same spot, by now a glowing scar an inch or so deep on the scout's shell. Discounting luck on either side, the survival of the jittering scout might depend on whether it could dodge under a cloud or into a steep valley. It might, however, foil the laser in open country by redirecting a portion of its exhaust in a column directly toward the enemy OLP. The destructive effect of a laser beam depends on high concentration of energy against a small area. Beam spread can scatter that concentration if the laser must travel very far through fog, cloud, or plasma. Assuming that the scout could hide under a tall, chemically seeded column of its own exhaust for a few moments while staying airborne, it would have a second line of defense. And we must not forget that the laser's own energy against the target creates more local plasma which helps to spread and attenuate the beam.

One method of assuring more hits on a scout would be to gang several laser beams, covering all the possible moves that the scout might make. The next question would be whether all that firepower was worth the trouble. The combination of high-temperature composites, MHD power, small size, and maneuverability might make a scoutship the same problem to an OLF that a rabbit is to a hawk. All the same, the hawk has the initial advantage. The rabbit is right to quake.

An unmanned scout, capable of much higher rates of angular acceleration, would be still more vexing to the OLP. If the OLP were known to have a limited supply of energy, a squadron of unmanned scouts could turn the tide of battle by exhausting the OLP in futile potshots. It remains to be seen whether the jittering scout will be able to dodge, intercept, or plain outrun a locally fired weapon. But given a sufficiently compact reactor, or antimatter drive, the scout could become a submersible. The broad utility of such a craft might obsolete most other designs.

Having discussed vehicles that operate on land, sea, in air, and in space, we find one venue left: within the earth. Certainly a burrowing vehicle lacks the maneuverability and speed of some others—until the burrow is complete. But under all that dirt, one is relatively safe from damn-all. Mining vehicles already exist that cut and convey 10 tons of coal a minute, using extended-life storage batteries for power. One such machine, only 23 inches high, features a supine driver and low-profile, high-traction tires.[15]

Perhaps a future military "mole" will employ seismic sensors to find the easiest path through rocky depths, chewing a long burrow to be traversed later at high speed by offensive or defensive vehicles. Disposal of the displaced dirt could be managed by detonating a nuclear device to create a cavern big enough to accept the tailings of the mole.

An Alternative To Vehicles?

As we've asserted, a vehicle of any kind is essentially a means to carry something from Point A to Point B. So it is possible that the vehicle—*as a category*—might be obsolete one day. The matter transmitter is a concept that, translated into hardware, could make almost any vehicle obsolete. True, most conceptual schemes for matter transmitters posit a receiving station—which implies that some vehicle must first convey the receiving station to Point B. But what if the transmitter needed no receiving station? A device that could transmit people and supplies at light speed to a predetermined point without reception hardware, would instantly replace the vehicle, except for pleasure jaunts. It would also raise mirthful hell with secrecy, and with any armor that could be penetrated by the transmitter beam. If the beam operated in the electromagnetic spectrum, vehicles might still be useful deep within the sea, beneath the earth's surface, or inside some vast Faraday cage.

But until the omnipotent matter transmitter comes along, vehicle design will be one of the most pervasive factors in military strategy and tactics.

NOTES

1. Ben Bova, "Magnetohydrodynamics," *Analog*, May 1965.
2. Richard Rosa, "How to Design a Flying Saucer," *Analog*, Sept. 1972.
3. Janet Raloff, "U.S.-Soviet Energy Pact," *Science Digest*, Feb. 1976.
4. John McPhee, *The Curve of Binding Energy* (New York; Farrar, Strauss & Giroux, 1974).
5. Gerard O'Neill, *The High Frontier* (New York; Bantam Books, 1978).

6. Committee on Advanced Energy Storage Systems, *Criteria for Energy Storage Research and Development* (Washington, D.C.; N.A.S. 1976).

7. Visvàldis Biśs, "Phase Analysis of Standard and Molybdenum-Modified Mar-M509 Superalloys," *J. Testing and Evaluation*, May 1977.

8. Dean Ing, "Mayan Magnum," *Road & Track*, May 1968.

9. R. H. Marion, "A Short-Time, High-Temperature Mechanical Testing Facility," *J. Testing & Evaluation*, Jan. 1978.

10. *Aviation Week & Space Technology*, Jan 1976, p.111.

11. J. I. H. Owen (ed.), *Brassey's Infantry Weapons of the World (New York;* Bonanza Books, 1976).

12. *Air Force Times*, 12 June 1978.

13. Fairchild Republic Co., Data release on A-10, 1978.

14. R. T. Pretty and B. H. R. Archer (eds.), *Jane's Weapon Systems* (London; Jane's Yearbooks, 1974).

15. *Compressed Air*, Apr. 1978.

Dean Ing was an interceptor crew chief when he first sold to Astrounding Science Fiction *in 1954. Later he became a heavy construction worker, technical writer, racing driver, research engineer, and university professor.*

Dean presently stays busy with mechanical design, vintage model aircraft, back-packing and survival studies. He has been a Hugo and Nebula runner-up, is the author of seven non-fiction books on high technology, and has another novel now on the stands. He and his wife Gina live in Oregon, and so do their two daughters. Gina's media work is heard on National Public Radio and station KSOR.

As weapons become more and more deadly and vehicles faster than ever before, and as electronic computation and control increase in effectiveness, the role of man as a wielder of weapons and direct pilot or driver of military vehicles will inevitably diminish in importance, and ultimately will probably come to an end.

But the end is not yet. As Dr. Nahin's stirring story shows, we have entered a phase of virtual man-machine symbiosis in warfare—a partnership in which man may become the more dependent of the two.

Paul J. Nahin

THE MAN IN THE GRAY WEAPONS SUIT

The warrior gently ran his hands over the cool, smooth flanks of his love. She responded not in any physical sense, but still he knew that deep within, under the flawless skin, she felt his presence. With a single flowing, graceful motion, he mounted her. She opened wide and he slipped inside. The fit was narrow: his bulk squeezed tightly against her sides. But to the warrior, it was cozy, snug, warm. The plexiglass cockpit housing slid back down over his helmeted head with barely a hissing of its electric motor.

He inserted the digital communication umbilical cable from his bio-sensor body box into the female connector on the floor and became as one with Red Striker Five.

Snapping the throat mike down against his neck, he called the Combat Information Center on the nuclear carrier. "CIC, this is Red Striker Five. All weapons stores on board, fuel topped off, and set for launch. Give me your ready-status readouts."

"Roger, Red Striker Five, we have you on first launch.

174

For your ready status—wind over the bow at forty-two knots, sea state at level three, cloud cover starts at five thousand, solid to eight thousand five hundred, and clear from there up. You are initially on weapons tight, with a required visual verify of a bogey before authorized to perform a weapon release. No voice communication in the clear allowed—perform all data transmission to the fleet on GPS LINK 99. Set your security level switch to antijam position three. Ship radars show a clear screen out to one-five-five miles. Prepare to launch."

The warrior felt the passing of a momentary irritation. *Weapons tight, with a visual verify! Damn!* His air superiority platform could detect, lock on, and track twenty-three simultaneous targets out to 300 line-of-sight miles. His frequency hopping, pulse-doppler lock-down radar could pick enemy infiltrators out of the massive clutter background echo of the ocean, even if they attempted to penetrate fleet defense by coming in 100 feet off the deck at Mach two. His "fire-and-forget" Eagle-Six missiles, with home-on-jam radiation seeker heads, could attack and kill with probability point nine, nine, nine at 170 miles, at hypersonic speed. And he had to identify a hostile visually before weapon release! Even with his electro-optical visual aid, that meant a maximum attack range of 10 miles. Maybe 15 if he used the narrow-field zoom lens with auto-video tracking. Damn! It was *his ass* on the line, not those of the political toadies who soiled their pants at the thought of a mistaken ID. Having to close that near to a potentially deadly hostile dropped his survival probability by at least 10 percent.

But maybe the hunting will be good today. The use of the Global Position System satellite, and its antijam, encrypted digital data link meant that something was up. His pulse rate elevated, and the surface of his skin wetted slightly with perspiration. Small biosensors in his body box picked these reactions up and routinely filed them away in the on-board flight computer. The gray weapons platform called Red Striker Five would need to know everything if it was to help the warrior survive.

The flight-deck tractor was already hooked up to his aircraft, and the warrior waited as the twenty-one ton Red Striker Five was attached to the steam catapult. Eight hundred feet ahead, just faintly visible in the dim, early glow of daybreak, was the edge of the flight deck. From there it was 93,000 feet straight up to his operational limit and possible death, and 90 feet straight down to certain death. No in-between. Just up or down. He briefly thought of what it would be like, sealed in his cockpit as he made that short, yet long fall into the water, and then imagined the essentially infinite inertia of the 87,000 ton CVN as its stately mass crushed him under at 30 knots. No real need to worry about that—the fall alone would kill him all by itself, without any help.

His eyes and mind turned to the red-glowing cockpit displays. Soon, as he climbed out of the cloud cover and burst into sunlight, he would turn the night-vision lights off. As the final seconds before launch slipped away, he made the last run through his checklist. Red Striker Five was ready, a deadly air and near-space machine of precise, electronically guided death. Her companion tensed as CIC warned him of launch, and he braced for the high gee acceleration that would fling them up to takeoff speed. Theoretically, it would take only a bit more than half the flight-deck length. But the warrior had witnessed launches that hadn't worked. His mouth felt dry and his heart pounded as he brought the throttle levers up to 60 percent of full military power. More than that would dangerously stress the catapult mechanism. Red Striker Five roared her pleasure as she gulped the JP5-nitro mix.

The blast of launch pressed him back into the body contour seat, the details of his peripheral sight faded in a tunnel-vision redout as blood flowed away from his optic nerves, and the edge of the flight deck rushed toward him at incredible speed. And then, as Red Striker Five lifted free of the launcher coupling, the warrior's left hand shoved the throttles forward, his right pulled back on the stick, and he accelerated up and away. Pulling a thirty-degree attack angle, he rode the twin jet engine exhausts at an initial climb rate of 20,000 feet per minute.

He could feel the whining turbine shafts under his buttocks, one cheek over each roaring monster. He used the feedback through his backside to even-up the shaft rpms to balance out the engines. Balanced engines gave better handling, less fuel consumption, and minimum vi-brational abuse to his spine.

The rear-view closed-circuit screen showed the carrier rapidly falling behind and below him. As he hurtled toward the clouds, the massive ship was soon no larger than a postage stamp, and then, as he flicked on the afterburners, it disappeared in seconds. He was riding a tornado now, each engine thundering out 42,000 pounds of thrust. At two pounds of thrust per pound of platform weight, Red Striker Five was like no aircraft that had ever flown before. Her limits were set by the endurance of the warrior, not by technology.

He punched through the top of the cloud cover with a vertical velocity vector of 30,000 feet per minute, and the airspeed needle past the Mach one line. His only indication of breaking the sound barrier in a climb was the funny behavior of the altimeter—first it lurched upward 2,500 feet, and then wiggled its way back to normal. The engine vibrations on his butt, the pounding roar in his ears, and the instant response of his craft to the stick, throttle, and foot controls gave him the same pleasures a passionate woman would have. Except no woman could ever be so perfect.

When Red Striker Five passed 30,000 feet, the warrior returned to normal engine power, as the afterburners wasted too much fuel for just cruising. He nosed the craft over gently until he was in level flight at 33,000, with an indicated airspeed of 1,200 knots.

He flipped off the night-vision lights, set the surveillance radar to its long-range search mode, and turned his MARK XII/IFF beacon transponder on. The beacon could be interrogated by coded transmissions from properly equipped observers, and Red Striker Five would automatically broadcast her mission number, altitude, bearing, and airspeed. Her echo would also be enhanced on the observer's radar screen. Failure of an interrogated aircraft to respond to such requests could bring an infrared missile up the tailpipe!

"CIC, this is Red Striker Five. I'm at start of mission run. Going now to GPS LINK 99."

"Roger, Red Striker Five, we have a solid track and now going with you to LINK 99." There was a pause, and then,

"Good hunting, Red Striker Five. Take care." The warrior heard the strange metallic bang on the voice circuit as the digital link took over—he was now in direct communication with CIC's computer. It would talk to him by audio tone cues through his headset that he could react to faster than an oral command. He was now getting the situation normal cue of a continuous up-down frequency sweep from one kilohertz to five kilohertz, each three seconds. The sound was comforting to the warrior, like the humming of a mother to a baby. He snuggled happily in his seat.

Red Striker Five flashed through the sky, serving as the eyes of the mighty naval fleet miles below and behind. Part of the always-flying combat air patrol, CAP war missions were top-priority tasks. A billion-dollar carrier, and its hundred-million-dollar companions of missile destroyers and cruisers couldn't afford to let the enemy get close enough to launch a tactical nuclear-tipped cruise missile. CAP missions extended the fighting reach of the fleet from the fifteen-mile range of naval gunfire to the hundreds of miles that were Red Striker Five's combat radius.

Ten minutes after launch, the warrior heard the audio tone cue in his ears change to a frequency sweep period of one second. The first stage alert cue. Three bogeys were beginning to edge onto his cockpit radar screen, and the preengagement weapons program in the fire-control computer switched the radar from surveillance to track-while-scan. All of Red Striker Five's radar updates were now being automatically fed up to the GPS satellite, 22,000 miles over his head, and then back to the CIC computer. There, integrated with sensor data from surface, subsurface, airborne, and space platforms, CIC had an accurate, real-time picture of everything that moved in a water-air-space volume of over 2,000,000 cubic miles.

The bogeys were flashing red on the multicolored radar screen now, the computer's visual cue to the warrior to pay attention. His left hand punched the Mark XII interrogate button—seconds later, the flashing red switched to the steady yellow of a friendly response. Good. But the enemy had been known to spoof the IFF by making recordings of friendly replies, and then retransmitting them when their penetration aircraft detected the interrogation request' The warrior went to the HOARSE GOOSE mode and hit the interrogate button again. Now a new, special coded signal was included that would *inhibit a friendly from replying. A reply would be a fake*. But these were friends, as their images on the screen now changed to green, and the audio tone cue reverted to three seconds. The radar returned to routine surveillance, the tracking computer dumped the stored trajectories of the identified bogeys, and the fire-control computer relaxed its electronic finger on the trigger. Red Striker Five streaked on.

Four hundred miles out, with the radar's constantly searching fan beam picking up nothing, the audio tone cue went into a continuous ping-ping-ping. LINK 99 was calling. The warrior pushed a red button next to the cockpit video screen, normally displaying a rear view of the aircraft. The screen cleared of the flashing sky, and an encrypted digital message streamed down from the GPS. LINK 99 was a spread spectrum, time-division multiple-access channel, with hundreds of users tied into it, on a time-sharing basis. With a spectral width of 4 gigahertz, and a signal level 40 db below the background noise, there was no way the enemy could jam it, even if he could find it in the infinite electromagnetic spectrum. Unless he was willing to devote the entire electrical output of a 2,000 megawatt nuclear power plant to the task—a highly unlikely event. The decoded message scrolled in milliseconds onto the screen:

MULTIPLE HOSTILES AT HEADING 079 SUB-SURFACE ACOUSTIC SENSORS INDICATE VE-LOCITY VECTOR OF 1450 KNOTS, AT 500 FEET, ON FLEET INTERCEPT BEARING WEAPONS FREE DOCTRINE NOW IN EFFECT ENGAGE AND DESTROY

This was more like it! This is what he was waiting for—he punched the red button again to acknowledge the message and the audio tone cue changed to a rhythmic six-kilohertz pulse, with a period of one-half second. The GPS would watch for surface-launched missiles directed at Red Striker Five, and warn the warrior by modulating the pulse rate, intensity, and tone frequency in each ear.

He put the radar in its high-power burn-through-jam, track-while-scan mode, five degrees around both sides of 079, from sea level to 1,000 feet. Eleven flashing red spots appeared on the radar screen, in a vee pointed back toward the fleet. They were 620 miles from the warrior's home ship, and 215 miles from Red Striker Five, to his left. The warrior pushed the HOARSE GOOSE button. There was little doubt: the attack pattern was characteristic of the enemy, and no friendlies would roar into the fleet in such a clearly provocative, hostile way. But he was going to kill them, and he had time to be sure. Red crosses appeared, superimposed over the flashing hostiles! They had replied to HOARSE GOOSE, thinking they were being normally interrogated. *Too bad for them,* thought the warrior. *Let's go get'm, baby!*

The warrior snapped on the power switch for his heads-up display. Normally a clear plastic shield extending from the top of his instrument panel to just below the canopy, it now became a remote projection output of the fire-control computer. Once combat started, there was no time to keep moving eyes and head between instrument display and cockpit windshield. The HUD showed the warrior the radar screen image, Red Striker Five's gun-cannon status, and projections of the proper launch envelope for the Eagle-Six missiles against all tracked enemy targets.

The warrior looked at the computed intercept course and saw he was already within attack range. He elected to go in closer. That was his only mistake.

Hitting the afterburner switch, he lit the tail of Red Striker Five and went into a sixty-degree banking turn-dive. As he passed through 20,000 he was hitting 1,900 knots and accelerating. The titanium/boron fiber skin of Red Striker Five was a dim, yet visible cherry glow. The projected intercept course, computed by the dedicated radar computer operating at a memory-cycle time of 43 nanoseconds, kept pace easily.

The warrior flipped the red plastic cover off the missile arming/firing switches with his left thumb, and threw the leftmost of three exposed toggles. He couldn't hear the cryogenic pumps, but he knew the infrared sensors on the missileseeker heads were now rapidly cooling down to the ten degrees Kelvin where they operated optimally for the terminal attack phase. He asked for a launch countdown from fire control to achieve missile intercept at approximately 70 miles range, and large numerals projected on the HUD. As the numbers flickered by, he flipped the middle target-attack toggle to designate all displayed radar tracks as hostiles. When the flashing red zero appeared on the HUD, he threw the rightmost toggle on the missile switches, and the Eagle-Six weapons came off their wing pods, two at a time, from each side.

Fump! The first double pair streaked off, each missile locked onto its own target. Guided by control signals from Red Striker Five's radar computer, they would fly their own way in on the last 2,000 meters of intercept with the infrared seekers.

Fump! The second double pair raced out and away, their exhaust trails leaving a crazy, swiftly dispersed pattern. Each missile quickly accelerated to 4,000 knots, its body glowing red-hot with the air friction. The warrior loved night-attack missions; the blazing missile skins looking like jewels. But even in the daylight he could follow them for a few split-seconds. Then they were gone.

Fump! The last three missiles launched, two from the right wing, the eleventh from the left.

The warrior watched, fascinated, as thin, spidery purple lines, marking the missile paths, weaved their way on his HUD toward the flashing red hostile symbols. At first the enemy vee stayed on course, but then their electronic warning systems picked up the inbound missiles. The vee started to break up, the pattern spreading apart. The warrior knew that some were diving, others climbing, but all were being flown by men as good as dead. An Eagle-Six missile could pull 37 gees in a chase-down manuever; greater even than Red Striker Five could take without disintegrating. And the enemy platforms were inferior to Red Striker Five. But the doomed men tried. And the warrior had no pity. They were the enemy!

One after the other, the purple filaments reached out and touched a desperately twisting, whipping, spinning red dot. And then they both slowly faded from the display. The searing explosion, the vaporizing metal, the carbonized flesh—all were reduced to a quiet decay of glowing

colored light reflected in the cold eyes of the warrior. The
tracking radar computer performed an automatic-kill assessment of each strike, looking for the highly characteristic fragmentation pattern of a successful intercept. As a
backup, for attempted kills at ranges under 100 miles, a
spectrum analyzer also examined the radiation from the
explosion fireball, looking for a suddenly enhanced carbon
line. The last blaze of glory of an enemy warrior before the
mist that was once a man's body dispersed forever. A
low-level kill assessment would bring a secondary missile
attack, but none was needed. All eleven hostile markers
had vanished. He flicked off the afterburners and let his
machine coast down to 1,000 knots. No need to waste fuel.

And then the warrior felt Red Striker Five shudder, and
his surprise was unbounded as he saw fireballs bigger than
his fist stream by his cockpit above and to the right of his
head. He'd been jumped from the rear, and was taking
high cyclic 37mm cannon fire! With his attention diverted
to the earlier attack, a twelfth enemy aircraft had somehow
avoided detection. *The bastards must have learned how to
defeat LINK 99! Maybe those were decoys I just took out!*
As he realized his peril, the right wing took two hits: one
on the tip and one on the trailing edge near the wing root.
Red-hot, searing metal fragments tore through Red Striker
Five's body, and one, the size of a man's thumb, ripped
into the warrior's right leg, just below the knee. Muscle
tissue, bone, and arterial fragments, mixed with shreds of
flight-suit fabric, splattered the cockpit, and blood gushed
from the wound. Instrument glass splinters ripped into his
body. Blinding pain tore at the warrior, and he would
have screamed but for the paralyzing shock.

The warrior knew, just before he passed out, that his
survival was out of his control. He retained enough strength
to slap the emergency combat palm switch at the side of
his seat, and then he rapidly slid into unconsciousness. It
was up to Red Striker Five to get them both home.

The palm switch activated the autonomous-combat program in the flight computer. Immediately Red Striker
Five examined all biosensor outputs on the warrior's body,
determined the presence and location of blood loss, and
pumped compressed air to the proper imbedded circular

tube in the right suit leg to create a tourniquet. The blood flow slowed to a seeping.

Simultaneously, Red Striker Five lit her afterburners, blew away all external weapons pods, and dove for the deck. The enemy war plane followed her down, too close for a missile attack, but well within gun range. It was the enemy's mistake.

Red Striker Five leveled out at 200 feet, moving at 1,500 knots, weaving, jinking, humping, in a manner determined by a random-number generator in the computer software. Desperately trying to keep those 37mm fireballs away from her warrior!

The enemy pilot was good—but Red Striker Five was better. Hurt by the loss of streamlining from the ragged metal edges where she'd been hit, Red Striker Five was melting at 1,500 knots. The enemy was 1,000 meters behind and closing at 1,600 knots. Red Striker Five dropped to 20 feet above the ocean, letting her surface following radar keep her at altitude. The enemy stayed on her tail. The enemy pilot was *very* good, rough-riding through the near-surface thermals on an attack run.

The two screaming metal bullets raced over the water; cannon bursts rocking Red Striker Five violently. The acoustic shock wave each was dragging along was incredible, and a boiling wake of dead fish bobbed to the surface long after the hunter and the hunted had passed. And then Red Striker Five fought back.

When the enemy was only 700 meters behind, Red Striker Five popped her air brakes and lost 300 knots almost immediately. Simultaneously, she pulled into a climb and did a full inside loop, coming down behind and on the tail of the snookered enemy aircraft. The defeated foe had a few milliseconds to realize his fatal error, and then Red Striker Five ripped him apart with two dozen strikes from her dual 20mm cannons. The flaming enemy debris flared out along a ten-mile track, but by then Red Striker Five, bearing her dying warrior home, was gone.

Racing for altitude, she climbed to 5,000 feet and started squawking on all clear broadcast channels:

EMERGENCY-EMERGENCY-EMERGENCY
RED STRIKER FIVE CAP

WOUNDED PILOT ABOARD
REQUEST PRIORITY LANDING
REQUIRE FLIGHT DECK MEDICAL

Over and over she transmitted her urgent message as
she bore in toward the fleet with her burden. The warrior
flickered in and out of consciousness, but knew neither
where he was or what his fate would be. He put his trust
in Red Striker Five and passed out.

She didn't fail him. The flight deck was cleared, and
with guidance signals from CIC's computer, Red Striker
Five made a perfect landing. The Navy medical personnel
gently lifted the warrior's torn body from the shattered
cockpit and placed him carefully on the deck. After emergency aid, as they prepared to take him below for permanent surgery, he temporarily regained his senses once
more.

"Take it easy, son," said the medic, "you're hurt pretty
bad, but you'll be okay. I saw it all on the radar screen—
that's some aircraft you got there. She fought her way out
and back like nothin' I ever seen!"

The warrior smiled weakly through a pale white face
lined with pain and shock. He looked up at Red Striker
Five and saw not a technological marvel of electronics,
armament, metallurgy, and computer programs. He saw
both a warm and loving creature, and a being that had
killed to save him. Killed with savagery and intelligence.
His body filled with emotion, a feeling of passion that only
later he would just barely begin to understand.

He looked at the battle-ravaged Red Striker Five, and
just before he slipped into darkness again, he knew. He
knew she'd be there when he came back. She'd wait for
him, and he loved her.

And he knew she loved him, too.

Paul J. Nahin is 47, married with three children, and an Associate Professor of electrical and computer engineering at the University of New Hampshire. Born in Berkeley, he grew up in Southern California, and all his college work was done in that state: B.S., Stanford; M.S., Caltech; Ph.D., University of California, Irvine.

He spent some years as a radar and digital systems engineer (Hughes, Beckman, General Dynamics), as a college professor (Harvey Mudd, George Washington University, and UNH), and as a military think-tank analyst (Institute for Defense Analyses, the Center for Naval Analyses, and the Naval Research Laboratory). He has been a consultant to the U.S.A.F. on automated air-to-air combat systems.

Dr. Nahin has been writing science fiction for two years, and his stories and articles have appeared in Analog, Twilight Zone *and in* Omni. *His first nonfiction book, a technical history and biography, has just been published by the Institute of Electrical and Electronics Engineers—* Oliver Heaviside: Sage in Solitude, *New York, N.Y.: IEEE Press, 1988—(Oliver appeared a few years ago as a time traveler in "The Invitation," in the* The Fourth Omni Book of Science Fiction, Zebra, 1985). *He is now writing a "semi-scholarly" book on time travel entitled* Physicists, Philosophers, Priests and Time Travelers.

For years, science-fiction writers have been exploring the theme of men against machines in war, of fighting robots with varying degrees of "intelligence" and of varying deadliness. Here Michael Coney rings a new change on the old theme. The resulting situation (though it has had its parallels in premechanical warfare) is a novel one in sf—and not beyond the bounds of possibility.

Michael G. Coney

JUST AN OLD-FASHIONED
WAR STORY

Curtain up on the war theater . . .

Bethel had laughed, slowing the vehicle and leaning out, snapping his fingers. "Here, boy!" he'd shouted, chuckling as the nose sensor on the nearest terrier swiveled toward him eagerly and the little machine made a short run, a legless scuttle. "Come to your Uncle Rob!" he'd called coaxingly. Then the terrier had stopped short, ten meters off, uttered a croak of disappointment, and glided away, scanning the horizon for more interesting heat sources.

It was a Cauk terrier, you see. It was not able to attack Rob Bethel or Dr. Leopold Wiley because they had small gadgets implanted within their forearms. These gadgets nullified the homing devices, warning the terrier that Rob and Leo were good guys, sending it elsewhere in search of bad guys.

The bad guys were known as Colls, which was a useful word to distinguish them from Cauks—since who was good and who was bad was not always clear, and *never* relevant.

Some eight kilometers from base, Dr. Wiley had failed to find any Cauk wounded to tend and bring in, and Rob Bethel had searched unsuccessfully for atrocities to photo-

186

graph in glowing 3-V (in point of fact they were both seeking the same thing) and the vehicle had broken down. After a brief discussion they decided to walk home. They were illogically reassured by the frequent sight of Cauk terriers. As always, they succumbed to the temptation to ascribe human characteristics to the diabolical little machines. They sort of felt that the terriers would protect them, if the enemy terriers came.

The enemy terriers came around noon, six of them gliding like fat stingrays over the midden of wet destruction, and the Cauk terriers ignored them. They—the Cauk terriers—were sniffing the air for the warmth of Coll humans. There was no earthly reason why Cauk terriers should be interested in the plight of Cauk humans—unlike the Coll terriers, who were interested to the point of fascination.

Two of the Coll terriers peeled off and veered left, skimming across the rain-pocked mud. The other four continued on their way, because they were not needed.

Rob Bethel ran. Dr. Leopold Wiley ran.

The two machines followed.

The gap closed as Wiley paused to snatch up the bag of medical gear, which he had dropped in his fear; closed again as Bethel later dragged Wiley from the mud where he had fallen and lay whimpering, imagining the terrier driving straight up his anus and exploding there.

The two men ran.

The terriers rose and fell as they hurdled little ridges in the devastated land; a motion quite beautiful to watch, like tiny schooners in a cross-sea; but nobody was watching. They glided on, hungry for the warmth of human flesh, mechanically contented in that they were fulfilling themselves.

Bethel and Wiley were holding hands like children as they skipped and slid and stumbled; and this was beautiful, too. It was quite possible that Bethel was man enough to have accepted that, since he would surely die, then he would die well. Which did not mean abandoning Wiley to grovel in the shit.

Their eyes were full of sweat and tears. They did not see the shallow crater before them. Suddenly they were falling, then they hit water and filth and lay gasping. They both knew there was no point in moving any more, and Wiley's anus began to crawl again as he lay face down in ten centimeters of water and tried to drown before the terriers arrived.

It was almost with despair that Wiley said, "Why the hell aren't we dead?"

Bethel picked himself up. The terriers hovered uncertainly about ten meters away at the lip of the shallow crater. On seeing him, their sensors twitched. "They're still there," he told Wiley.

Wiley stared too. "They should come for us. Why the hell don't they come for us? The bastards are programmed to attack!" His voice rose as though aggrieved. As the war had progressed he had gradually come to believe in nothing, except machines. And now they, too, were proving unreliable.

"All we need is a gun," murmured Bethel.

The terriers were sitting ducks, but the men had no guns. Incredibly, this war was fought according to rules, and the rules stated that noncombatants went unarmed. Only soldiers carried guns—but the terriers were stupid, and were unable to distinguish soldiers from medics and medics from newsmen. They were terribly good at distinguishing Cauks from Colls, however.

Bethel heard a moan and glanced anxiously at Wiley, thinking the doctor had broken down. Wiley looked back at him puzzled, then they both stared around, seeing their environment for the first time.

Two people sat nearby, watching them.

These two were Colls, the Enemy. Specifically, they were Leroy Matapasu, a terrier maintenance man, and Mary Bluestream, a lady colonel. They were wishing they had guns, in order that they might kill the fierce and powerful Cauks who had invaded their crater.

The four noncombatants flung themselves at one another and for a while they fought, while the two Coll terriers watched with mechanical indifference. The battle was inconclusive, although Matapasu sustained a bad gash on his leg from a projecting rock.

Afterward, the four humans lay in awkward silence, panting. They scrutinzed one another covertly, and possibly they felt a little ashamed. "Uh . . . if I had my bag, I could dress that wound of yours," said Wiley to Matapasu, by way of a friendly overture. "But it's over by those goddamned terriers of yours."

Matapasu smiled. "Thanks. I can get it, if you like." So saying, he stood and began to climb from the crater. "Mary, come with me, will you?"

Bethel watched them climb.

Wiley screamed, "Stop them! For God's sake, stop them, Bethel!" He hurled himself at Matapasu and Bethel grabbed Col. Bluestream, not quite knowing why. They all rolled into the bottom of the crater. "Hang onto her, Bethel!" shouted Wiley. "Don't let her go!" and Bethel obeyed, because it was a long time since he'd held a woman, and it made a pleasant change from dying.

As they lay in a heap, Wiley explained.

"That's why the terriers didn't attack us. Because these two Colls are here. They have implanted gadgets to nullify the terriers' homing devices, just like we have. So long as we stick close to them, the terriers will stay away!"

It was an interesting situation. Matapasu asked, "Just how long do you think you can hold onto us? As soon as it's dark, we'll get away from you. I take it you have no weapons?"

So they lay in the bottom of the crater, interconnected, while the two terriers watched from the lip. During the late afternoon, as darkness gathered like a stagnant pool in the crater, Bethel fell asleep but was jerked awake by Wiley. He thought about this for a while, as he held onto Col. Bluestream's wrist. What they were doing was pointless, he thought. It was merely postponing the inevitable.

He was stiff and sleepy; and much later he whispered to Mary Bluestream, "Get out of here, huh? Wiley's asleep."

So Mary Bluestream and Matapasu crawled away up the shallow crater, straight into the sensors of two nearly arrived Cauk terriers who kept their distance only because of the gadgets implanted in the sleeping Cauks down below.

The two Colls crept back into the crater and joined the two Cauks.

The four terriers watched from the crater lip.

The long night began.

*   *   *

The machines at the crater rim shifted and thought, during the night. Their thoughts were simple. Each pair of machines already knew its pair of victims, and each individual machine had now selected its individual prey—but was prevented from attacking by a nagging impediment in its mechanical brain. It would have been frustrating for anything other than a machine, but to the terriers it merely represented a geometrical problem. Computing angles, the terriers shifted and thought.

In the morning everyone was on tremendously good terms with everyone else. It was just as though there had never been a war; it was just like a picnic except for the lack of food and the two Coll terriers and two Cauk terriers who watched them from the edge of the crater. It had stopped raining.

It was barely noticeable that Matapasu and Dr. Leopold Wiley were not as all-fired happy as Col. Bluestream and Bethel—whom they suspected of having made love during the night. Bluestream and Bethel were young and full-blooded—although technically enemies—and they had been found lying slightly apart from the other two in the morning. It was a pity, this intrusion of sex into the cleanness of war, and it cast a slight shadow over the joy of the morning.

Nevertheless the four sat together in hearty companionship. After all, when men are forced together in adversity, the human being in them will shine through, will it not?

"You know," said Col. Mary Bluestream thoughtfully, "It's all the fault of these goddamned machines. The four of us—would we pretend to be enemies, if we'd met anywhere else? Of course not. We're human beings. And our enemy—the enemy of us all—is the machine."

"So what the hell are we going to do?" asked Wiley.

"So long as the four of us stick together, the machines won't harm us. I suggest that we all walk back to the Coll lines. Two of us will be taken prisoner, but at least we'll all live."

"Except we two Cauks," said Wiley. "I understand the Colls shoot their prisoners."

"That's not true!" insisted Mary Bluestream.

"Maybe not. So how about the four of us walking into the Cauk headquarters?" suggested Wiley.

Matapasu uttered a short, cynical laugh and the subject was dropped. Silence fell. Bethel and Col. Bluestream were lightly holding hands. The terriers watched. They had all the time in the world.

"I'm hungry," said Mary Bluestream. The sun was high.

It is of little relevance to note that the sun—at that moment—was shining also on a group of schoolchildren who ran laughing from their bright classrooms on the outskirts of New Lima, Peru; or that the leader of the Animal Strength Steel Band was sipping a planter's punch as he and his men rested between bouts at the Blue Horizon Holiday Environment, Jamaica. It was of little relevance to the protagonists in this neatly encapsulated, carefully limited war.

Bethel said slowly, "The terriers attack a heat source. Maybe we could provide them with a decoy heat source which would detonate them."

"We need something the same size and temperature as a man," said Matapasu thoughtfully.

The sun grew hotter; steam rose from the sodden ground. Combat Area R was situated in the tropics, which was economical from the point of view of clothing. Cautiously the four drank from the muddy pool of the crater before it all evaporated. They told one another what good people they were, and they watched the terriers, friend and foe alike, with uniform hatred. There was nothing within a fifteen-kilometer radius except pulverized mud and robots. It was as lonely as all hell.

There were two Colls and two Cauks, and two Coll terriers and two Cauk terriers. It was mathematically so perfect that there had to be a meaning, there had to be a solution. It was Matapasu who suggested the pit. Away back in his ancestry, pits had frequently been used to trap wild animals.

They scrabbled in the wet soil with their bare hands, and when their fingers got sore, they took off their shoes and dug with those. They pulled rocks from the dirt with a great sucking, they lay on their stomachs and pulled out bootfuls of warm mud, throwing it behind them. Their wrists, their arms, their shoulders, their backs ached with a fierce agony.

"The sides of the pit must be steep," said Matapasu. "Vertical, if possible."

Due to the wetness of the ground this was difficult to achieve, but they worked on. Bethel stood in the bottom of the pit, calf-deep in crud, and scooped out bootfuls of slop. Matapasu and Wiley rolled rocks, lining the pit with them to prevent the sides from falling in. Their boots fell apart and Bethel toiled on with cupped hands. Mary Bluestream packed dry soil from the crater lip into the gaps between the rocks. Rain began to fall again, heavy and permanent.

It took a long time to achieve a pit almost two meters deep and of similar diameter, but eventually it was done.

"Let's get the terriers in there," said Wiley. "We can rest after." The others groaned. They could barely move.

They clustered in a group near the rim of the crater, about twelve meters from the pit. Matapasu left the group, edged towards the pit. The Cauk terriers expressed interest, fidgeting, their ground-effect motors kicking little puffs of muddy spray. Matapasu sidled on, getting the pit between him and the machines.

A Cauk terrier dashed forward. Matapasu uttered an involuntary yelp of fear and ran for the security of the group. The terrier veered, skirting the pit. Suddenly it lost lift. It slid sideways and fell out of sight. Emboldened, Matapasu stepped forward again.

Bethel dealt similarly with the Coll machines and soon all the terriers lay in the bottom of the pit, humming. Exhausted but relieved, the humans lay about the crater, allowing the cooling rain to play on their aching bodies, trying to summon the strength to start walking. Bethel dozed, his hand resting on Col. Bluestream's thigh. The filth began to dribble away from their clothes as the rain intensified.

Eventually Wiley stirred. He rolled over, blinking away wetness, and stood. "Best be moving," he said, stirring Bethel with his foot. The others woke, peering up at him. Water lay all around them in great dancing pools. They climbed to their feet, regarded one another with shifty awkwardness, then shook hands. Together they climbed up out of the crater. The horizon had disappeared in a veil of gray wetness.

The terriers came humming up after them. The pit was full of water. The little machines had escaped, lifting themselves on the rising tide.

The sun shone briefly through a gap in the clouds, coloring the mud gold.

*   *   *

The hostess in Aisle C of the giant pleasure cruisers smiled and said, "If you will look down to your left you will see Combat Area R. In fact, I'm told that it's in use right now, as a theater in the Cauk-Coll conflict."

Anna Seberg, the actress, saw ochre mud through a gap in the clouds. "Poor goddamned soldiers," she said. The sight of tortured ground gave her an instant thirst; she pressed buttons C and 4.

"They hardly ever use human soldiers now," said Charles. "They use machines."

"Poor goddamned machines," said Anna Seberg.

The four humans sat in the bottom of the crater and regarded the doctor's bag. Now that they had retrieved it from the terriers—by walking together in tight formation through the mud—they wondered if it was worth it. Matapasu and Wiley were in charge. Wiley opened the bag and laid the instruments on a plastic sheet.

"Bring the alcohol and the bag and come away from there," said Matapasu. "We all sit on the far side of the crater, right?"

Although they were in theory united against the common enemy, they still found it difficult to trust each other. This was not due to any fault in themselves; it was the result of propaganda to which they had been subjected for a very long time. War might be hell but these people were basically okay. Nevertheless, the doctor's sharp instruments represented weapons.

Wiley poured alcohol over the bag and touched a match to it. The blue flame flickered and Bethel seized the handle. He flung the bag out of the crater. They all lay on their stomachs in the warm mud, watching the bag burning twenty meters away. Mary Bluestream thought the mud felt primeval and sexual.

The terriers of both political persuasions gathered around the bag, sensing its heat, cogitating electrically and thoroughly.

"When it begins to cool," said Matapasu, "it'll pass through a period when it's at blood heat, then maybe we'll see something."

"It's too small to fool them," said Wiley gloomily. "Anyway, they'll never all attack at once. They're programmed not to waste themselves."

In fact none of the terriers attacked. They watched the flames die, they watched the bag cool to ash and dark metal, then they lost interest and returned to their surveillance of the humans. . . .

Colonel Bluestream had last week supervised the deployment of the latest small batch of draftee foot soldiers. She stood looking across the wasteland. She couldn't quite understand where all those people had gone. It crossed her mind that the entire forces of both sides had deserted, in the unthinkable manner of a civilian strike, leaving the Combat Area to four noncombatants.

"What shall we try next?" she asked. She was a colonel, not an expert in robotics. She was young for her rank and, when clean, was quite pretty.

There was a long silence during which the men tried not to be annoyed by the question. At last Bethel spoke.

"I reckon we're all agreed that we have to forget nationalities," he said. "And the trouble with the suggestion that we all walk together to one HQ or the other is that it was nationalistic. Now, what about this. Colonel Bluestream and I, Coll and Cauk, walk to the Coll lines. You two walk the other way. The terriers will be unable to attack, because each pair of us has, between them, one anti-Cauk gadget and one anti-Coll gadget. How's that?"

"Two prisoners are taken," objected Matapasu. "That means that two of us are shot."

"It's better than four of us starving," Bethel said. "I'm willing to take the chance."

"I'm not," said Matapasu, scowling at Wiley.

They discussed the suggestion for some time, in fact until nightfall; but were unable to reach a conclusion. There was no way one member of a pair would walk all the way to certain death, merely to save the other member. Bethel was deeply disappointed, because he'd been indulging in a sweet daydream where he gave his life for Mary Bluestream, and now they wouldn't let him do it. Bethel was an unusual person, a 3-V newsman who believed in love.

Before they slept, Wiley summarized the situation. "We are four people and we're threatened by four machines," he said. "We have no means of communication with the

rest of the world. We have no food. Our pit's full of water and
we have no way of emptying it. All we have are our clothes,
the normal contents of our pockets, a few medical supplies
of the usual type and . . . our brains. Now. What do we do?"

"We pray," suggested Matapasu.

"We make love," whispered Mary Bluestream.

"We sleep on it," said Wiley. "We give our subcon-
scious a chance to work. In the morning, someone will
have the answer."

The factions fraternized as darkness fell.

"Do you think we'll ever get out of this alive?" Mary
asked Rob. It was a question designed to arouse manly
sympathy. "I mean, if *any* of us leave, we'll be killed.
There's no way we can send for help." She sat close to him
in the twilight. She was a woman, she was tough, she
knew how and when to use her sex.

"We'll think of a way." Bethel put his arm around her.

"It's not right. Noncombatants should be made immune
to these machines."

"They surely should," said Bethel.

Wiley sat talking to Matapasu. "Where are the soldiers?" the medic said. "I mean, the whole area seems
empty."

Matapasu grinned coldly. "The terriers are very efficient. Maybe they've cleaned the area out."

Wiley thought. "You understand these machines. Is there
any way we can persuade them to annihilate one another?"

"Why on earth should they want to do that?" asked
Matapasu in surprise.

They woke to find Matapasu drawing diagrams in the
mud, enormously excited. "Take a look at this," he said.
"Think of the terriers and ourselves as magnets. Unlike
poles—Coll human and Cauk terrier—attract. But like
poles repel. . . ."

"I don't get you," said Wiley sourly. He had heard
Bethel and Bluestream groaning in delight during the
night, while he could only groan with cold and fear and
hunger, which were depressing sensations to groan with.

"If you walk toward a terrier of your own nationality,"
explained Matapasu carefully, "it will retreat from your

implanted jamming gadget, maintaining a distance of some twelve meters."

"Are all terriers alike, Cauk or Coll?" asked Wiley.

"They come from the same factory," said Matapasu. "I've built them."

He continued, "You notice the way whenever we move, the terriers move also, jockeying for an optimum position. Now, what I suggest is this. We move around the interior of the crater until the terriers are evenly spaced around the rim. Then we bunch in a group, each opposite a terrier of his own nationality. Then, simultaneously we walk away from each other, out of the crater, driving each terrier before us until they are out of range of the people of the opposite nationality—probably about five hundred meters from the crater. Then we all go home. Right?"

Eventually Bethel found himself standing opposite a Cauk terrier, back to back with Wiley, with Col. Bluestream to his left and Matapasu to his right.

"Now . . ." said Matapasu softly.

Bethel walked forwards. The terrier retreated. Behind and to the sides, he assumed the other terriers were retreating. He stole a glance over his left shoulder. Mary was moving away at right angles to him, her terrier retreating too. "Goodbye!" he called.

"Bye, Rob!"

He would see her after the war, whenever that was. He walked on, correcting a tendency of his terrier to veer left by moving left too, increasing speed slightly. He caught sight of Matapasu almost running, to his right. He was about forty meters from the crater rim. Sharp buried stones in the soft mud hurt his bare feet as he shepherded the terrier along. The terrier began to veer left again, and he hurried to correct it. He heard Matapasu yelling.

Something was wrong.

Mary appeared in his field of vision, her back to him, walking away fast, but not as fast as Bethel's terrier now moved towards her. He wheeled about and saw Matapasu's terrier headed straight for him. Everyone, terriers and humans, was running in a giant circle. All the terriers had veered left and, instead of being driven, were now the pursuers. The humans fled hopelessly, circling.

"Everyone head for the crater!" shouted Matapasu. "Now!"

The circle broke as they ran for the axis, the machines close behind. Bethel dived over the rim and found Col. Bluestream in his arms, found everyone in one another's arms as—not for the first time—they discovered that they loved one another exactly as much as life itself. The machines stopped, thwarted but not discouraged. The heap of humanity remained motionless, one flesh.

It was of no interest to its occupants, but the crater in which they lay was old—even historic. It marked the point where the last antitank missile had destroyed the last tank. The tank commander's name had been Vanessa McDonald and she had died just as surely as if there had been no tank around her—which all goes to prove the futility of tanks, and the correctness of the Council of Nations' decision to outlaw armor plate in the interests of economy, and restrict offensive machinery to terriers.

"Here's an idea," said Wiley. "We move about until the terriers are positioned in pairs of the same nationality, opposite each other. Then Rob and I get between the Cauk terriers and you two. Then you, Matapasu and you, Colonel—get up on the rim. Then you close in on your own pair of terriers from either side—making sure they don't slip past you into the crater. Then you grab one, or both, and you dismantle them with my surgical instruments. Then we repeat the process on the Cauk terriers. How does that sound?"

"Any terrier will detonate on contact with a human heat source," said Matapasu. "Our implanted gadgets inhibit the homing device, that's all. A Coll can easily be killed by a Coll terrier, if he manages to get close enough. It won't work, doctor."

"Think of something yourself, if you're so goddamned smart."

During the lively exchanges which followed, Col. Bluestream moved close beside Bethel, who smiled at her. She threw an arm around his neck; the other held a glittering scalpel to his throat. "Don't anyone move," she said. "Now, Leroy. Come over here, carefully, and get a knife."

Matapasu obeyed, choosing an instrument with care. Wiley grinned sourly.

Bethel kept still. He was not unduly disappointed in

Mary Bluestream, since he understood the strain which continuous fear put on a person, particularly a fragile woman like Mary. Bethel would have made a good, stupid husband. Wiley continued to grin.

"Right," said Matapasu. "I'll tell you what we're going to do. We're going to kill you two bastards, and we're going to carry you back to our lines. That way we'll have the protection we need. Good thinking, Colonel Bluestream."

"I don't think she's so goddamned bright," commented Wiley as Matapasu approached with a knife. "If you kill us, the terriers will move in."

"How's that?"

"Our antihoming gadgets are implanted in a vein. A tiny turbine is powered by the blood flow. Arrest the flow, and you'll de-energize the gadget."

"You're lying."

"I'm a doctor," said Leopold Wiley. "I've implanted hundreds."

Later that day Wiley lay on his back in the twilight and stared at the stars, and tried to forget his hunger. Weird notions passed through his mind. It had been almost three days since he'd eaten, and he was becoming lightheaded. Soon, he feared, he would be unable to think at all, and the terrier would look like his dog Albert, and he would climb from the crater and scratch it behind the ear.

He heard Mary Bluestream say, "I'm so sorry, Rob . . ."

Then, as night fell and the secret rustlings started up nearby, while love conquered treachery, he knew the answer. He slept, fearful that in the morning his simple scheme would prove unworkable.

He awoke, knowing that it would succeed.

The sun was already hot and they were all very weak. Wiley explained his plan to them, while they tried to understand; and in the end they nodded tiredly. Nobody could find anything wrong with Wiley's idea, although they tried hard enough, being so far gone in fatigue and hunger that they scarcely cared to move themselves.

His hands trembling with weakness, Dr. Leopold Wiley sprayed the wrists of Bethel and Col. Bluestream with local anaesthetic. Then he took up his scalpel and made an incision in each wrist. He sprayed a coagulant as the blood began to pump and, working clumsily but fast, he removed the antihoming gadgets.

The terriers fidgeted on the lip of the crater—but Wiley's and Matapasu's antihoming gadgets were still operative.

Dr. Leopold Wiley made minute adjustments to each gadget to allow for an estimated differential in rate of flow.

Then he implanted Bethel's gadget in Col. Bluestream's wrist, and Col. Bluestream's gadget in Bethel's; and he sewed them up.

Bethel and Col. Bluestream kissed, and everybody shook hands and forgot all their previous difficulties. They arranged to meet one another after the war, on the first of September next after the cease-fire, in the Anaconda Bar on Bargas, Brasilia. The date happened to be Matapasu's birthday, and the bar was where Bethel once celebrated a victorious soccer game and got picked up by the police.

Everybody wept.

Then Leroy Matapasu and Col. Mary Bluestream climbed out of the crater and began to walk east, towards their headquarters, secure in the knowledge that between them they had one gadget that would protect them from Coll terriers, and one gadget that would protect them from Cauk terriers.

Similarly, Bethel and Wiley began to walk west.

The terriers moved also, but without conviction. Eventually, as though from force of habit, the two Coll terriers again began to dog the footsteps of Bethel and Wiley, and the two Cauk terriers likewise followed Matapasu and Bluestream, at a distance of around ten meters.

It was good to see those devilish machines defeated by human ingenuity.

Dr. Leopold Wiley was weak and slow and Rob Bethel was weak too, but had the advantage of a superior physique. Nevertheless Bethel's stomach hurt and his feet hurt and his heart hurt too; and he turned around and looked after his Mary, and waved.

Col. Bluestream turned also, and saw the two Cauk terriers inexplicably closing in on her and Matapasu, and she screamed.

Wiley and Bethel watched from a distance of around three hundred meters. The terriers moved like cheetahs, a bounding glide over the rough terrain. They homed in on

Col. Bluestream and Matapasu and exploded between their legs, lifting them gently from the ground and dumping them quietly on their backs.

Wiley said, "Too bad. Their anithoming gadgets must have malfunctioned."

Bethel tried to blink the shock from his eyes, tried to blink the sight from his mind, and saw Wiley standing there, smiling.

"*One* of their gadgets malfunctioned," Bethel said very slowly. "When you switched my gadget with hers, you sabotaged it." The two bodies lay on the torn ground in the distance; they stared at the sky together like lovers on an outing. "You killed them," said Bethel.

"They're goddamned Colls, Rob."

"Listen, I'm going to kill you, Wiley," said Bethel, weeping.

Dr. Leopold Wiley backed off and slid the scalpel from his pocket. He'd expected difficulty with Bethel, so he'd come prepared. Bethel couldn't be expected to understand. Wiley had implanted hundreds of gadgets in Cauk soldiers and civilians to protect them. A Cauk was not secure, was not *complete*, until he'd been doctored by Wiley.

And the Colls? They were the Enemy, of course. So they had to be killed. Hell, that was what war was all about, wasn't it? The rules were laid down; a man might not agree with them, but he had to obey them.

"Back up, Rob," said Wiley. "I don't want to hurt you."

The Coll terriers hovered close, humming.

Bethel tried to reason with himself. He tried to think himself back in time four days, to remember that he'd been a complete and content and well-adjusted person before he'd met Mary. Then he saw Wiley again, standing there with a crazy grin and a glittering scalpel. He turned away and walked off.

Then suddenly he broke into a run, and began to laugh wildly, while the tears fell.

Behind him, Doctor Leopold Wiley started to scream.

Wiley pounded across the slippery ground. The sun was high but it had rained again during the night, and the landscape steamed. Bethel was drawing away from him, strong legs pumping. Wiley slipped, recovered and ran on. Implanted in his wrist was a gadget that repelled Cauk terriers—but he was being pursued by Coll terriers, against which he had no defense except prayer. He tried *that* too, mumbling breathlessly as he ran, but it didn't seem to help.

Then he slipped and fell, and lay waiting.

Bethel stopped, turned, and looked back.

The terriers stopped, a meter from Wiley, held at bay by the gadget in Bethel's wrist. To complete the geometry of Wiley's terror, Bethel stood nine meters away.

"Help me," whispered Wiley, lying on his stomach.

"Go fuck yourself," said Bethel, and took one slow careful step away.

Wiley felt a bump against his hip, then felt nothing more.

Bethel saw the body skid like a toboggan, then he turned and walked towards his headquarters.

Ten meters behind, the remaining Coll terrier followed him like a faithful hound or maybe hyena. Hours later, the concrete block of headquarters loomed above him.

The Cauk terriers came to meet him, a glittering pack fresh from the manufacturer's warehouse. They'd been dispatched to look for Colls, but in their mechanical minds Bethel was an adequate substitute.

After all, he had no defense against them. The gadget in his wrist was now a Coll gadget.

He was tired and soon fell. A terrier nuzzled against him affectionately.

Michael G. Coney was born in Birmingham, England, in 1932. After qualifying as a Chartered Accountant, he spent most of his life doing other things: running an English pub for three years, managing a hotel and night club in Antigua, West Indies, for another three, and since 1972, when he moved to Canada, working for the British Columbia Forest Service as a management specialist. He is married, with three children and one grandson.

Mr. Coney started writing around 1968, and has published about a dozen novels and some thirty short stories, most of the latter in The Magazine of Fantasy and Science Fiction.

Science fiction has often asked the question of how far the man/machine symbiosis can be carried, especially in war. In "The Private War of Private Jacob," Joe Haldeman— who is especially well known for his The Forever War and other tales of conflict in the future—provides one answer.

Joe Haldeman

THE PRIVATE WAR OF PRIVATE JACOB

With each step your boot heel cracks through the sun-dried crust and your foot hesitates, drops through an inch of red talcum powder, and then you draw it back up with another crackle. Fifty men marching in a line through this desert and they sound like a big bowl of breakfast cereal.

Jacob held the laser projector in his left hand and rubbed his right in the dirt. Then he switched hands and rubbed his left in the dirt. The plastic handles got very slippery after you'd sweated on them all day long, and you didn't want the damn thing to squirt out of your grip when you were rolling and stumbling and crawling your way to the enemy, and you couldn't use the strap, noplace off the parade ground; goddamn slide-rule jockey figured out where to put it, too high, take the damn thing off if you could. Take the goddamn helmet off too, if you could. No matter you were safer with it on. They said. And they were pretty strict, especially about the helmets.

"Look happy, Jacob." Sergeant Melford was always all smile and bounce before a battle. During a battle, too. He smiled at the tanglewire and beamed at his men while they picked their way through it—if you go too fast you get tripped and if you go too slow you get burned. He had a sad smile when one of his men got zeroed and a shriek, a happy shriek when they first saw the enemy and glee when an enemy got zeroed—and nothing but smiles smiles smiles through the whole sorry mess. "If he *didn't* smile, just once," young-old Addison told Jacob, a long time ago. "Just once he cried or frowned, there would be fifty people waiting for the first chance to zero that son of a bitch." And Jacob asked why and he said, "You just take a good look inside yourself the next time you follow that crazy son of a bitch into hell and you come back and tell me how you felt about him."

Jacob wasn't stupid, that day or this one, and he did keep an inside eye on what was going on under his helmet. What old Sergeant Melford did for him was mainly to make him glad that he wasn't crazy too, and no matter how bad things got, at least Jacob wasn't enjoying it like that crazy laughing grinning old Sergeant Melford.

He wanted to tell Addison and ask him why sometimes you were really scared or sick and you would look up and see Melford laughing his crazy ass off, standing over some steaming roasted body, and you'd have to grin, too, was it just so insanely horrible or? Addison might have been able to tell Jacob, but Addison took a low one and got hurt bad in both legs and the groin and it was a long time before he came back and then he wasn't young-old anymore but just old. And he didn't say much anymore.

With both his hands good and dirty, for a good grip on the plastic handles, Jacob felt more secure and he smiled back at Sergeant Melford.

"Gonna be a good one, Sarge." It didn't do any good to say anything else, like it's been a long march and why don't we rest a while before we hit them, Sarge or, I'm scared and sick and if I'm gonna die I want it at the very first, Sarge: no. Crazy old Melford would be down on his hunkers next to you and give you a couple of friendly punches and josh around and flash those white teeth until you were about to scream or run but instead you wound up saying, "Yeah Sarge, gonna be a good one."

We most of us figured that what made him so crazy was just that he'd been in this crazy war so long, longer than anybody could remember anybody saying he remembered; and he never got hurt while platoon after platoon got zeroed out from under him by ones and twos and whole squads. He never got hurt and maybe that bothered him, not that any of us felt sorry for the crazy son of a bitch.

Wesley tried to explain it like this: "Sergeant Melford is an improbability locus." Then he tried to explain what a locus was and Jacob didn't really catch it, and he tried to explain what an improbability was, and that seemed pretty simple but Jacob couldn't see what it all had to do with math. Wesley was a good talker though, and he might have one day been able to clear it up but he tried to run through the tanglewire, you'd think not even a civilian would try to do that, and he fell down and the little metal bugs ate his face.

It was twenty or maybe twenty-five battles later, who keeps track, when Jacob realized that not only did old Sergeant Melford never get hurt, but he never killed any of the enemy either. He just ran around singing out orders and being happy and every now and then he'd shoot off his projector but he always shot high or low or the beam was too broad. Jacob wondered about it but by this time he was more afraid, in a way, of Sergeant Melford than he was of the enemy, so he kept his mouth shut and he waited for someone else to say something about it.

Finally Cromwell, who had come into the platoon only a couple of weeks after Jacob, noticed that Sergeant Melford never seemed to zero anybody, and he had this theory that maybe the crazy old son of a bitch was a spy for the other side. They had fun talking about that for a while, and then Jacob told them about the old improbability-locus theory, and one of the new guys said he sure is an impertubable locust all right, and they all had a good laugh, which was good because Sergeant Melford came by and joined in after Jacob told him what was so funny, not about the improbability locus, but the old joke about how do you make a hormone? You don't pay her. Cromwell laughed like there was no tomorrow and for Cromwell there wasn't even any sunset, because he went across the perimeter to take a crap and got caught in a squeezer matrix.

The next battle was the first time the enemy used the drainer field, and of course the projectors didn't work and the last thing a lot of the men learned was that the light plastic stock made a damn poor weapon against a long knife, of which the enemy had plenty. Jacob lived because he got in a lucky kick, aimed for the groin but got the kneecap, and while the guy was hopping around trying to stay upright he dropped his knife and Jacob picked it up and gave the guy a new orifice, eight inches wide and just below the navel.

The platoon took a lot of zeros and had to fall back, which they did very fast because the tanglewire didn't work in a drainer field, either. They left Addison behind, sitting back against a crate with his hands in his lap and a big drooly red grin not on his face.

With Addison gone, no other private had as much combat time as Jacob. When they rallied back at the neutral zone, Sergeant Melford took Jacob aside and wasn't really smiling at all when he said: "Jacob, you know that now if anything happens to me, you've got to take over the platoon. Keep them spread out and keep them advancing, and most of all, keep them happy."

Jacob said, "Sarge, I can tell them to keep spread out and I think they will, and all of them know enough to keep pushing ahead, but how can I keep them happy when I'm never very happy myself, not when you're not around?"

That smile broadened and turned itself into a laugh. You crazy old son of a bitch, Jacob thought and because he couldn't help himself, he laughed too. "Don't worry about that," Sergeant Melford said. "That's the kind of thing that takes care of itself when the time comes."

The platoon practiced more and more with knives and clubs and how to use your hands and feet but they still had to carry the projectors into combat because, of course, the enemy could turn off the drainer field whenever he wanted to. Jacob got a couple of scratches and a piece of his nose cut off, but the medic put some cream on it and it grew back. The enemy started using bows and arrows so the platoon had to carry shields, too, but that wasn't too bad after they designed one that fit right over the projector, held sideways. One squad learned how to use bows and arrows back at the enemy and things got as much back to normal as they had ever been.

Jacob never knew exactly how many battles he had

fought as a private, but it was exactly forty-one. And actually, he wasn't a private at the end of the forty-first.

Since they got the archer squad, Sergeant Melford had taken to standing back with them, laughing and shouting orders at the platoon and every now and then loosing an arrow that always landed on a bare piece of ground. But this particular battle (Jacob's forty-first) had been going pretty poorly, with the initial advance stopped and then pushed back almost to the archers; and then a new enemy force breaking out on the other side of the archers.

Jacob's squad maneuvered between the archers and the new enemy soldiers and Jacob was fighting right next to Sergeant Melford, fighting pretty seriously while old Melford just laughed his fool head off, crazy son of a bitch. Jacob felt that split-second funny feeling and ducked and a heavy club whistled just over his head and bashed the side of Sergeant Melford's helmet and sheared the top of his helmet off just as neat as you snip the end off a soft-boiled egg. Jacob fell to his knees and watched the helmet full of stuff twirl end over end in back of the archers, and he wondered why there were little glass marbles and cubes inside the gray-blue blood-streaked mushy stuff and then everything just went.

Inside a mountain of crystal under a mountain rock, a tiny piezoelectric switch, sixty-four molecules in a cube, flipped over to the OFF position and the following transaction took place at just less than the speed of light:

UNIT 10011001011MELFORD
DEACTIVATED.
    SWITCH UNIT 1101011100
JACOB TO CATALYST STATUS.
    (SWITCHING COMPLETED)
    ACTIVATE AND INSTRUCT
UNIT 1101011100JACOB.

and came back again just like that. Jacob stood up and looked around. The same old sun-baked plain, but everybody but him seemed to be dead. Then he checked and the ones that weren't obviously zeroed were still breathing a bit. And, thinking about it, he knew why. He chuckled.

He stepped over the collapsed archers and picked up Melford's bloody skull-cap. He inserted the blade of a knife between the helmet and the hair, shorting out the induction tractor that held the helmet on the head and served to pick up and transmit signals. Letting the helmet drop to the ground, he carefully bore the grisly balding bowl over to the enemy's crapper. Knowing exactly where to look, he fished out all the bits and pieces of crystal and tossed them down the smelly hole. Then he took the unaugmented brain back to the helmet and put it back the way he had found it. He returned to his position by Melford's body.

The stricken men began to stir and a few of the most hardy wobbled to their hands and knees.

Jacob threw back his head and laughed and laughed.

Joe Haldeman, Oklahoma born, spent a year as a foot soldier in Vietnam, where he was wounded. On his return, he sold his first science fiction story, then wrote his first novel, War Year, *a non-sf book about Vietnam. His first science fiction novel,* The Forever War, *won the Hugo, Nebula, and Ditmar awards for best novel of the year 1975. It too was based on his Vietnam experience.*

Joe has a B.A. in physics and astronomy and a M.F.A. in English. His latest novels, at this writing, are Worlds *Worlds Apart, and* Tools of the Trade.

He lives in Gainesville, Florida, with his wife Gay.

Though weapons have been getting speedily more and more lethal, as a general rule, campaigns and combat have not. Of every thousand men during the Civil War, 62 died of disease each year; by the Spanish-American War, this had been reduced to 25.6; by World War I, to 16.5; and during World War II and the Korean War, to 0.6 and 0.3 respectively. The death rate for those wounded (not counting killed in action) showed a similar drop—from 13.3 per hundred in the Civil War to 2.5 per hundred in Korea.

The reason, of course, was the progress in military medicine, surgery, and sanitation. It closely paralleled civilian trends, and indeed made significant contributions to the progress of medicine as a whole. At least where conventional weapons are concerned, we can expect this to continue. (The introduction of nuclear or other radical weapons would, naturally, result in a set of new and largely unpredictable equations.)

In many respects, the weaponry with which the military medical man fights death and injury and disease is developing as rapidly and astonishingly as the weapons with which wars are fought. Military medicine now has as its allies all the physical and biological sciences, to provide new techniques and instruments hitherto undreamed of— except, perhaps, in science fiction. The military medical man can think and plan today in terms which would have been unthinkable a year or two ago, and tomorrow—

Well, no man in the sf field is better qualified to discuss what military medicine may do tomorrow than Alan E. Nourse, M.D.

Alan E. Nourse

ONE FOOT IN THE GRAVE: MEDICINE IN FUTURE WARFARE

One of the cruel realities we have always had to live with is that our bodies, in themselves, are not very respectable fighting machines beyond the level of throwing rocks and clubbing opponents to death with tree limbs. We don't have teeth, claws, or hooves that are very useful for fighting. We don't have the inch-thick protective hides possessed by most animal predators. We don't have decent night vision, and we can't smell anything at *all*, for God's sake. Our liver, kidneys, spleen, bowels, and genitals are wide open to easy assault; vital organs such as lungs and heart have only the flimsiest of bony cages for protection. True, our brains—the only *effective* natural weapons we have—are protected a little more cleverly than the rest of us, housed in a solid bony vault, yet that protective vault with all its vital support conduits is stuck up on a soft five-inch-diameter stalk that any enterprising barbarian could cut through with a dull flintstone.

This, of course, is one major reason that warfare has always been such a *messy* business for individual humans throughout history. Armor to protect the soft, vulnerable organism inside has never really worked: it has merely slowed the soldier down and made him easier to catch. Every time somebody thought up better, stronger, lighter armor, somebody else would think up more violent projectiles, better explosives, or more effective ways to pry it open, infiltrate it or disable it.

This is also why the more modern individual dogface soldier, no matter how fine his mind might be, has counted for so little on a thousand battlefields. His only real contribution in most cases has been collective, as one of a mass of bodies, of which a certain (usually high) percentage are expected to be sacrificed to achieve any given objective. Of course, there are special situations—frogmen mining destroyers, for example, or small commando squads blowing strategic bridges—in which each individual plays a vital role, but such actions are always clandestine, fast-strike-and-get-out operations, extremely dangerous to each individual, and under circumstances where they have *no* support, medical or otherwise, in the field. The massed-bodies-hurled-against-guns has been far the more common pattern in recent centuries, and you don't need too many resounding disasters such as Pickett's Charge to become convinced that massed human bodies do not necessarily solve the military problem.

Considering how *in*effective massed bodies have proven in fairly unsophisticated past warfare, it's puzzling how many fine science fiction novels (Haldeman's *The Forever War*, Heinlein's *Starship Trooper* and Busby's *Rissa Kerguelen* spring instantly to mind; there are a million others) continue to present whole armies of individual dogface soldiers fighting en masse as vital factors in very sophisticated future warfare. Certainly in future wars involving planets, star systems, or galaxies, this concept is going to have to be reexamined. The sheer logistics of transporting whole armies of men *plus* their bewildering array of weaponry *plus* their life-support systems from Earth to Xenora I, 47 light-years away, with the notion that they are going to do anything effective when they get there makes the whole idea just short of laughable; especially if we're going to adhere to the principles of Einsteinian physics as we understand them and put aside such fantasies as space-warps, faster-than-light travel, time-contraction-suppressors and other fanciful delights. (Okay, we might—conceivably—have these things one day, but if the Xenorians are suddenly coming after us, we'd sure better not *plan* on having them).

Of course future wars *may* be conducted on the same idiotic principle of massed bodies hurled at the enemy which has prevailed in past wars—in which case, future military medicine, as in the past, will have to concentrate on salvaging the one soldier out of a thousand who isn't torn completely to ribbons. But there is a much more likely form of warfare in which medicine could play a far more constructive role. Already we see definite moves toward this concept: turning the fighting over to machines and getting the men off the battlefield. In future conflicts in distant areas of space or time, rather than sending out huge armies of cannon fodder, it seems more likely that warfare would involve sending out a very few superbly trained, superbly supported, and superbly protected humans to oversee the deployment of huge numbers of machines that do the actual fighting.

These few humans would *not* be expendable—anything but. There might not be many of them, but they would be the ones that kept the war afloat. With ever more sophisticated fighting machines equipped with ever more sophisticated computers for guidance and direction and a thousand other dynamic functions, we wouldn't *need* huge numbers of men in the field—they would just get in the way and get killed—but the few that we had we would *really* need to supply the judgemental decisions, interpretations, assessments, reconsiderations and all the other beyond-computer functions of the human brain. These few would be scattered about in far-flung places, and they would have to have the things they needed to keep alive right out there with them. And it is here that medicine would be able to play a vital role in future warfare.

Soldier as Physician

Medicine has three main functions during warfare, as far as combat troops are concerned: (1) *Field treatment of injuries* to preserve life; (2) *Restoration* of the fighting man's physical integrity; and (3) *Rehabilitation* of the soldier to combat readiness or retirement from the field, as the case may be. In the case of future warfare, item (1) may present some peculiar problems that will require some ingenious solutions.

Problem: You have a lone man or woman soldier in a ship or on a station, far removed from any others and charged with operating and deploying an army of mechanical juggernauts throughout half a star system. The soldier is light-years away from any support system and far out of reach of even effective communication with base medical resources. How then do you field-salvage that soldier in event of severe injury—or even in event of relatively minor injury which might develop into a life-threatening or fatal situation? (Consider that in such a case something like a crushed thorax, a lacerated femoral artery or a sublethal exposure to neutron radiation might qualify as "a relatively minor injury." Presumably he's not playing for peanuts out there.)

Solution: You field-salvage the victim by making him his own physician with his own complete, personal medical center literally built into his body, or within easy reach of it.

This does not mean handing the soldier a box of Band-aids and saying, "There you are, Bud, it's up to you"—the common technique of twentieth-century warfare. Nor does it mean sending every soldier to medical school—in which case he'd be of far more value working back in a Restoration Center than out in the field. It *would* mean, first, giving each front-line soldier brief but highly concentrated training in life-support techniques, anatomy, physiology and hold-the-fort type medicine, using the most effective forced-learning techniques you have available at the time; and second, equipping him one way or another with all the medical technology necessary to use that knowledge when he needs it to save his own life or others. Some of the technology could be built directly into his various support systems (pressure suit, ship, pillbox or what-have-you). Some, however, would better be built into *him*.

External support systems would, for example, need to contain miniaturized but functionally effective cardiopulmonary resuscitation mechanisms sufficient to maintain life (respiration and heart function) for a prolonged period, and triggered to go into operation instantly upon physiological evidence of need—decreased or absent respirations; decreased cardiac output; decreased, irregular or absent pulse; a drop in constantly monitored hematocrit; and so forth. In everyday life there is unfortunately a life-threatening lag between somebody's calling the aid car and the aid car's getting to where it's needed. That lag is a killer. Once the aid car gets there, the salvage rate is remarkably good—but you cannot resuscitate a dead man. In future warfare, our soldier can't afford that lag; the medical goal must be resuscitation every time. With external support ready to move instantly when he needs it and wherever he is, the future soldier can be in a position to survive primary assault long enough to be able to do something to help himself later, whatever his injury.

External support could be continued in other areas as well. Shock solutions and stimulants could be in place and ready for automatic use on the basis of sensory or physiological triggers. Whole blood or packed red cells could also be on standby. Problems of long-term blood storage should long since have been solved. The problem of cross-matching could be handled before the soldier is sent out—or better yet, obviated completely by prior collection and storage of his own blood. This is already a ridiculously simple state-of-the-art procedure, except for the preservation problem: essentially, you draw two units of the soldier's blood, wait three weeks, then return one unit to the body and draw two more. This gives you three units. Wait three more weeks, return the oldest unit to the body, and draw two more. This gives you four units in storage. Put three in permanent preservative, return one to the body and draw two more. Keep this up until you have whatever supply you want in permanent preservative. Then, much later, when blood is needed, zip, in it goes—the soldier's own blood, no transfusion reactions, no pyrogenic reactions, no nothing.

Certain built-in support systems could supplement these external supports in a variety of ways and, assuming the achievement of certain technologies we do not yet have, could add a whole series of additional dimensions to front-line warfare medicine in the future. One simple example would require only minor refinement and enhancement of existing technology: a whole built-in pharmacopoeia of basic medicines, drugs, and hormones implanted within the soldier's body for release in basic-dosage increments whenever the occasion demanded. Implant capsules could be rendered permeable or impermeable either by soldier-controlled electrical charge or triggered by the release of drug-specific synthetic activating hormones. The implants themselves could be located anywhere—there's lots of excess storage space in the human body (abdomen, thigh, pelvis, thorax, etc.) Release controls, much like tiny pocket-calculator keyboards or combination lock dials, could be carried under the skin of the chest (cf. present-day pacemakers), flank, or thigh.

Standard drugs might include analgesics to deal with moderately severe pain, hypnotics to help with rest, diuretics, and antihistamines; nitroglycerin, digitoxin and propranolol; anti-inflammatories, antibiotics and antivirals—make up your own list. For special problems, the pharmacopoeia could contain eye drops for glaucoma, insulin for diabetics, T3 and T4 for hypothyroids, uricosurics for gout, hormones for contraception in event of team operations, even the ubiquitous cyanide for fates worse than death (although one might hope that might be triggered from a separate keyboard to prevent mistakes). Quite aside from sparing the harried soldier the indignity of trying to chase escaped pills around a free-fall cabin, such a system would keep a wide range of medications available precisely where they were needed in the exact increments that they were needed in.

Such a system, too, could lend itself to greater and greater sophistication and usefulness as the technology—and our knowledge of basic physiology, biochemistry, and endocrinology—evolves. It stands entirely to reason that the extraordinary demands of front-line fighting in future war could place extraordinary demands upon the front-line soldier—incredible energy demands, hyperactive mental acuity, extraordinary demands for cell repair, hormonal function, biochemical activity, all prolonged far beyond the normal human capacity to hang together and keep functioning. Conceivably, the same built-in system used for dispensing medications could be used to trigger the hormonal and biochemical supplements needed to render the soldier a superfunctioning human when the need was present, to keep him functioning at extraordinary levels as long as necessary, and then to repair and restore him when the crisis point is past and the "superfunctioning" soldier collapses like a rag doll. Ideally, such a system might have a dual triggering capacity with voluntary triggers to be used by the soldier when he is able to use them and recognizes the need, backed up by a fail-safe system of hormonal triggers to be activated automatically when the soldier's body is signaling needs that he doesn't recognize, or when he has lost the capacity for voluntary triggering.

Soldier as Self-Surgeon

Such systems would have one serious disadvantage: they would not have direct access to the soldier's brain or nervous system at all. So far we have not found any way to achieve direct electronic-neuronal contacts or hookups effectively juxtaposing nonliving electromagnetic machine with living nerve tissue (short of electroshock therapy, which might perhaps be a little coarse for real usefulness in future warfare). The problem of making such contacts of sufficient delicacy is going to be a mean one, but there is no fundamental law of nature that says it can't ultimately be done down to any degree of delicacy you might want. There is just not that much difference between electronic impulses and neurochemical impulses, and ultimately, direct contacts and feedbacks will be achieved.

When they are, built-in support systems of far greater basic value to the front-line soldier would be possible. Consider that the human brain is perhaps the most remarkable portable medical center in existence. With direct electronic-neuronal contacts, using pushbutton or dial controls under his direct control, the soldier could, in cases of overwhelming, agonizing or continuing pain, trigger endorphin production for as long as necessary. Hunger could be turned off for prolonged periods by electronic tickling of nerve centers in the brainstem. Thirst could be "quenched" and body fluids preserved for days on end by stimulating antidiuretic hormone production in the pituitary. (The kidneys might not be too happy about that, but it might keep the soldier alive). If the soldier needs sleep— real *sleep*, fast and deep, between assaults, he can dial S for sleep and bang, he's out like a poleaxed mule—with a pre-set timer, of course, to wake him up again. If he wakes up and needs to be moving in top form and *fast*, he has access to the epinephrine-norepinephrine system. If he's hurt, or infected, or hammered with hypothermia, or baking hot, or radiation-exposed, and has to keep moving no matter what, he can flag the adrenocortical system. And, perhaps equally useful, he can have direct control over emotional centers in much the same fashion; there may be times when getting really mad can save his life.

A similar machine-brain contact could have an even more interesting application, assuming that the soldier had

had that prior basic medical training we spoke of earlier. It's reasonable to assume that the vast majority of nondeath casualties among front-line soldiers in future war will be *surgical* casualties—lacerations, penetrating wounds, fractures, or burns of thermal, lasar or radiation origin. We can also assume that there will be no M*A*S*H-type field surgery units within easy reach (unless, of course, 20 light-years is "within easy reach," which seems unlikely). But suppose the soldier has a small brain-machine connection built in, analogous to a tiny telephone jack, perhaps located at the base of the skull, which will accept some sort of prerecorded communication device—call it a "recording cube"—with microcomputer capacity to respond and select according to the soldier's own input via remote-control switching and microphone. Then suppose that his support system carries a library of such recording cubes packed with person-to-person directions recorded by expert surgeons to guide the soldier through the performance of his own life-saving surgery, from diagnosis of the procedure that needs to be done to completion of the operation.

Let's say the soldier has a right femur which has been shattered at mid-shaft and must be pinned. Other medical-support systems have kept him alive long enough for him to reach his recording-cube bank. Now, with the proper cube or cubes jacked in, the surgeon first directs stimulation of brain endorphins plus sufficient suitable counterirritation of the back of the left hand to produce effective deep anesthesia of the right leg from the groin down, pausing at each logical branch-point for the soldier to signal satisfactory response or performance. Then the surgeon would direct the soldier to the external landmarks, direct the incision he is to make, direct hemostasis with the proper clamps and electrocoagulation, then stimulate physiological arteriospasm of the femoral artery directly through the brain.

The artery seems to be intact—but it must not be severed or torn, or a different kind of crisis altogether will be precipitated, so the surgeon by preplanning of the recording cube enters into a running dialogue with the soldier— perhaps something like this:

Surgeon (per cube): You've got to find and protect the artery. First of all, gently separate the large bundles of the quadriceps muscle with those dull, rounded Silverberg retractors. Go easy, don't tear the muscle. Signal when done.

Soldier (voice over to cube): Okay, they're separated.

Surgeon Now secure the retractors so the muscles stay separated. Use those Niven hooks to hold them apart.

Soldier They're secured.

Surgeon Fine. Now you should be able to feel the femoral artery deep down in the wound. Put your finger on it and respond when you feel it.

Soldier I can feel it.

Surgeon How fast is it pulsating?

Soldier It isn't pulsating.

Surgeon Is there lots of blood coming up in the wound? Respond.

Soldier Hardly any. It's pretty dry.

Surgeon Then you haven't found the femoral artery. Or else it's completely severed and retracted way up into the groin. Do you feel a big lump in the groin? Signal.

Soldier No.

Surgeon Then feel and look into the wound again for a pulsating artery. Signal.

Soldier I don't feel anything—wait. Yes. It's buried under a smaller vessel and a pink cordlike thing.

Surgeon The smaller vessel is the femoral vein and the pink structure is the femoral nerve. Tell me how fast the artery is pulsating.

Soldier About sixty per minute.

Surgeon Okay, it's intact. Now use those blunt Bova separators to loosen the whole vessel bundle for about seven or eight inches up and down. Very gently, just free it up. Signal when done.

(Long pause)

Soldier I think it's done.

Surgeon Can you see the fracture underneath?

Soldier Yes, it's right under there. A sharp bone edge just cut my glove.

Surgeon Then stop everything and change gloves. (Pause) Now go back to the femoral artery again. Take the Nourse shield and curve it in under the whole freed-up length of that bundle of vessels. Wrap it around loosely. Signal when done.

Soldier That's done.

Surgeon Now bring the elastic end of the shield clear around and tack it to the back of your leg with a Bretnor biter. You want those vessels out of the way, *clear* out of the way. Signal.

Soldier It's done.

Surgeon Okay, now you're ready to tackle the bone itself—

Ultimately, in this fashion of self-surgery, the femur is pinned and glued, the unharmed blood vessels and nerve released, the muscles replaced, the wound closed and the healing begun—and a soldier in a future war will soon be back fighting whereas he otherwise very probably would have died. Never mind that the surgeon who spent eight solid months structuring that one single particular computerized recording cube has been dead for 200 years, or that standard treatment of that injury at a major hospital center at that time might involve total replacement of the femur with a better-than-natural artificial one, with full ambulation the day after surgery—that wouldn't help the soldier a bit. In the field he must use what he has, and this is just one possible type of support system he might have available.

Resurrection and Reconstruction

Of course, in terms of future warfare, everything we have been talking about so far, up to and including an open self-reduction of a fractured femur in the field, falls strictly into the category of First Aid. It all goes on far from home, far from doctors, far from hospitals, far from *any* kind of definitive medical backup. The soldier under field conditions in future war is going to have one foot in the grave from the very start; the best that medical innovation can possibly do is try to help him keep the other one out. The goal will be to patch him up, keep him going, get him back to fighting if at all possible or, barring that, keep him alive long enough to get him to *real* medical help.

The job of *real* medical help will be to take whatever is

left when it gets back (which may be precious little) and either resurrect it or reconstruct it—whichever is more appropriate in any given case. If what comes back is essentially an externally maintained heart-lung preparation with a few shreds of nervous tissue still connected, the decisions will be far different than if the soldier has merely had his entire body avulsed at the level of the 5th dorsal vertebra (and hopefully has brought the avulsed part back with him in a perfusion tank).

Precisely how such injuries would be dealt with would obviously depend on the level of medical and bioengineering technology available at the time. Salvage or nonsalvage might well depend upon just which war you were in—or even on which end of the same war you were in. We know, for example, that 45,000 U.S. soldiers died of tetanus during World War I, but only 13 during World War II. Similarly, high percentages of wounded died of shock during World War II, while shock losses were much lower in Korea and lower still in Vietnam—all because of advancing technology.

Given a basic living organism to work with, however, a great deal may be possible, utilizing various techniques and materials for reconstruction. In just the past few decades, enormous strides have been made in the preparation and insertion of human prosthetic parts, and this technology is certain to progress rapidly. Currently on the shelf we have prosthetic replacement hips, knees, ankles, wrists, elbows, finger joints, and toe joints—although one must admit than not one of these is exactly *perfected* as yet. We have artery reconstruction materials, implantable heart valves and penile prostheses, all state-of-the-art. We can surely foresee implantable prosthetic hearts, implantable artificial kidneys, tracheas. esophagi, large and small intestines, Fallopian tubes, uteri (presumably functional) and so forth. Later, prosthetic livers and lungs may follow to help reconstruct damaged bodies, and whole-bone or whole-limb prostheses will replace piecemeal joint reconstruction. A facsimile visual organ is already on the drawing board; a true functioning, implantable prosthetic eye will have to wait for direct electronic-neuronal connections and a few biochemical miracles as well, but sooner or later may well be achieved.

A word of caution should be said, however, about using prosthetic parts, particularly if one has the idea of using them to "improve" the human body in the manner of the 12-Billion Dollar Man (due allowance being made for inflation). There can be serious problems involved in giving human flesh and blood extraordinary powers through prosthetic tampering. Let a man leap suddenly into the air with those jet-driven, superpowerful prosthetic legs and his liver will be shoved straight down through Poupart's ligament and lodge somewhere in his calf—and then when he *lands* from that leap, hoo, boy, what a mess! Both legs driven up into his chest. Give him an X-ray eye, and the scatter radiation is liable to fry his brain the first time he uses it unless he's provided with ¾-inch lead shielding. Even today, with all the experience orthopedic surgeons have had, total hip replacements still have a nasty way of eroding through the patient's pelvis and "wandering" up into his abdomen after a few months' use. Unfortunately, prosthetic materials are not always as soft, pliable, and resilient as *living* materials. And, for this very reason, surgeons in the future may, in the long run, much prefer live-organ replacements for restoration of the war-maimed than any prosthetics we might imagine.

But here we come up against a different problem: a physiological law of nature which may well prove to be just as stubborn and unmodifiable as Einstein's physical speed-of-light law—the law of Self vs. not-Self. Organ heterografts aren't going to work. For all that have been tried, the only ones with a halfway decent *serious* record have been kidney transplants (and, of course, blood transfusions). A few heart transplants have survived, but the endurance record is nothing to cheer about. More to the point, in terms of future warfare, the heterografts that work at all do so thanks only to continual, carefully monitored-immunosuppression techniques which, in effect, render the graft recipient a lifelong immunological cripple— certainly not the stuff that effective future soldiers will be made of.

The truth is that the body doesn't like anything but itself. There is no other physiological and/or biochemical principle that I know of which seems to be so universally true and so doggedly applicable to virtually all living organisms. Not-Self is poison, and Self will literally destroy itself trying to throw out not-Self. Thus, in the long run, it seems most probable that surgeons seeking serious replacements for destroyed or missing parts or organs are going to come to organ *homografts*. We are going to have to replace missing pieces of Self with replacement pieces of Self.

The name of that game is cloning, and once we have a better grip on the physiology and microtechniques of cloning, it's not going to be all that tough. Every soldier in future wars—in fact, just about every*body*, period—could easily have snippets of tissue stored in permanent banks, the tissues chosen being those that keep best for cloning purposes. There won't be any grisly scenes in the jungle with helpless Indian women raped of their ova and then used as human incubators. Ordinary epithelial cells could be sucked free of their nuclear content, the clone genetic material inserted and the whole thing grown like Chicken Little in a tank of soup. Frequently required parts could be severed at the stage of embryonic differentiation and nurtured separately. True, the injured soldier might have to be life-supported for months or years until needed replacement parts are grown to the necessary stage of maturity, but time may not be of the essence when it takes half a lifetime to get to the site of battle. And above all, the replacement parts would be Self and nothing else, with no rejection problems.

The Mind/Machine

There will, of course, be cases in which the damage is so gross or so total that even homograft replacement will not be able to do the job. If the soldier's brain has been destroyed, for instance, I think the medics are going to be up a tree—technology or no technology. Even if techniques for direct neuronal connections with a cloned brain were possible, you would still have a human organism with a chicken dumpling for a brain until you had devoted years to teaching it something—and even then, considering human development time, you'd be likely to have a happy but useless child-adult on your hands. Everything in the original brain would obviously be irrevocably lost. If all of the soldier *except* the brain were destroyed, you might have better going, but you'd still have to wait half a lifetime for a clone-grown body to mature—and it would be anybody's guess what might happen to the brain psychologically in the meantime.

An alternative, the ultimate prosthetic repair or creation of a cyborg, *might* be plausible provided the problem of direct electronic-neuronal connections can be solved. Although we discussed this earlier, it deserves a word or two more at this point. Next to the solution of the Self/not-Self problem (if it is inherently soluble, which I doubt), it seems to me that the problem of the direct E-N connection is one of the most massive challenges that medicine faces in the future, not only in terms of future warfare but in terms of future evolution of human capability. In the simplest possible terms, we have brains and nervous systems which operate on neurochemical impulses mediated by hormones, enzymes, amino acids, fatty acids, and so forth. Those brains and nervous systems are enormously subtle and sophisticated in their function. On the other hand, we have ever more subtle and sophisticated electronic machines—computers, switches, recording devices, broadcasting devices, receivers, etc.—which operate on electrical impulses mediated by electromagnetic forces. We understand the electronic systems pretty well, but we cannot join the two systems together into interconnecting, functioning units because we don't understand the neuronal system worth sour green apples. We can join the two systems only indirectly through our human senses, which are our windows to the outside-Self world. We see a signal on a screen and signal back by means of the gross motor intervention of pushing a button, thus altering the electronic system. It's clumsy and terribly inadequate, however much it may have advanced us technologically. And it's going to remain clumsy and inadequate until we learn how to join electronic and neuronal systems into fully integrated, functioning, intercommunicating units. Only with this can man and machine become man/machine and begin exploring his/its mutual potential.

This, of course, would be the ultimate cyborg. This would be an advanced way of restoring war-ravaged human individuals to continuing effective life and usefulness. This would also be a way of pooling the capacity of man and machine so that each could potentiate the other into a supercapable entity with more-than-human potential, but with the human qualities intact because they are part of the machine (and vice versa). In terms of future warfare, this would be a means of transforming ordinary, soft, easily squashed human beings into formidable fighting machines, a step beyond biomedical science. Whether it would be the right step—or a good step—might depend on the nature of the future war.

Certainly this is a staggering challenge to biomedicine now and in the future, and for better or for worse, two things might safely be said about it:

(a) When a way is found to make mind/machine connections, it is going to change the nature of every human life, war or no war.

(b) We've got our work cut out for us, finding out how.

Alan E. Nourse started pre-medical studies at Rutgers in 1945, but interrupted them to serve two years in the Navy's hospital corps. Afterwards he returned to Rutgers for his B.S., and took his M.D. at the U. of Pennsylvania Medical School in 1955. He interned in Seattle, and then devoted two years to freelance writing before entering general practice at North Bend, Washington in 1958. In 1963, he returned to full-time writing.

His first national publication was a short story, "High Threshold," published in Astrounding in 1951, and this was followed by some sixty short stories and novelettes which appeared in virtually all the magazines of the time. In addition, he published a short novel, A Man Obsessed and, in collaboration, wrote The Invaders Are Coming (both for Ace). His writing helped to pay for his medical education and, of course, reflects a strong medical orientation.

Dr. Nourse has published fifty or so works of fiction and nonfiction, including a dozen or so juveniles and three volumes of short stories. Two of his latest titles are The Fourth Horseman, a science fiction novel (Harper and Row 1983,) and The Elk Hunt, a nonfiction work on coronary heart disease. (Macmillan 1986.)

The promise of the medical and biological sciences is, unfortunately, not confined to the healing of the sick and injured, nor to preventing the human tragedy of the physically deformed or mentally twisted. Bioengineering and genetic manipulation for military purposes have become commonplace science-fiction themes, so that we have cloned soldiers, and soldiers who are half-man, half-machine, and soldiers who are hybrids undreamed of since the first beast-man myths came to disturb our sleep.

Edward Bryant's "Shark" falls into this last category. It is a strong story, a tragic story. But it is more than a story of the extremes men will go to to destroy other men. I myself see it as a profound allegory of what war can do to the minds of many men and many women.

Edward Bryant

SHARK

The war came and left, but returned for him eighteen years later.

Folger should have known when the clouds of smaller fish disappeared. He should have guessed, but he was preoccupied, stabilizing the cage at ten meters, then sliding out the upper hatch. Floating free, he stared into the gray-green South Atlantic. Nothing. With his tongue, he keyed the mike embedded in his mouthpiece. The sonex transmitter clipped to his tanks coded and beamed the message: "Query—Valerie—location." He repeated it. Electronics crackled in his ear, but there was no response.

Something moved to his right—something a darker gray, a darker green than the water. Then Folger saw the two dark eyes. Her body took form in the murk. A blunt torpedo shape gliding, she struck impossibly fast.

It was Folger's mistake, and nearly fatal. He had hoped she would circle first. The great white shark bore straight in, mouth grinning open. Folger saw the teeth, only the teeth, rows of ragged white. "Query—" he screamed into the sonex.

Desperately he brought the shark billy in his right hand forward. The great white shape, jaws opening and closing, triangular teeth knifing, whipped past soundlessly.

Folger lifted the billy—tried to lift it—saw the blood and the white ends protruding below his elbow and realized he was seeing surgically sawed bone.

The shock made everything deceptively easy. Folger reached behind him, felt the cage, and pulled himself up toward the hatch. The shark flowed into the distance.

One-handed, it was difficult entering the cage. He was half through the hatch and had turned the flotation control all the way up when he blacked out.

Her name, like that of half the other women in the village, was Maria. For more than a decade she had kept Folger's house. She cleaned, after a fashion. She cooked his two meals each day, usually boiled potatoes or mutton stew. She loved him with a silent, bitter, unrequited passion. Over all the years, they had never talked of it. They were not lovers; each night after fixing supper, she returned to her clay-and-stone house in the village. Had Folger taken a woman from the village, Maria would have knifed both of them as they slept. That problem had never arisen.

"People for you," said Maria.

Folger looked up from his charts. "Who?"

"No islanders."

Folger hadn't had an off-island visitor since two years before, when a Brazilian journalist had come out on the semiannual supply boat.

"You want them?" said Maria.

"Can I avoid it?"

Maria lowered her voice. "Government."

"Shit," said Folger. "How many?"

"Just two. You want the gun?" The sawed-off twelve-gauge, swathed in oilcloth, leaned in the kitchen closet.

"No," Folger sighed. "Bring them in."

Maria muttered something as she turned back through the doorway.

"What?"

She shook her matted black hair. "One is a woman!" she spat.

Valerie came to his quarters later in the afternoon. The project manager had already spoken to Folger. Knowing what she would say, Folger had two uncharacteristically stiff drinks before she arrived. "You can't be serious," was the first thing he said.

She grinned. "So they told you."

He said, "I can't allow it."

The grin vanished. "Don't talk as though you owned me."

"I'm not, I'm just—" He floundered. "Damn it, it's a shock."

She took his hand and drew him down beside her on the couch. "Would I deny your dreams?"

His voice pleaded. "You're my lover."

Valerie looked away. "It's what I want."

"You're crazy."

"You can be an oceanographer," she said. "Why can't I be a shark?"

Maria ushered in the visitors with ill grace. "Get along," she said out in the hallway. "Señor Folger is a busy man."

"We will not disturb him long," said a woman's voice.

The visitors, as they entered, had to duck to clear the doorframe. The woman was nearly two meters in height; the man half a head taller. Identically clad in gray jumpsuits, they wore identical smiles. They were—Folger searched for the right word—extreme. Their hair was too soft and silkily pale; their eyes too obviously blue, teeth too white and savage.

The pair looked down at Folger. "I am Inga Lindfors," said the woman. "My brother, Per." The man nodded slightly.

"Apparently you know who I am," said Folger.

"You are Marcus Antonius Folger," Inga Lindfors said.

"It was supposed to be Marcus Aurelius," Folger said irrelevantly. "My father never paid close attention to the classics."

"The fortune of confusion," said Inga. "I find Mark Antony the more fascinating. He was a man of decisive action."

Bewildered, Maria stared from face to face.

"You were a component of the Marine Institute on East Falkland," said Per.

"I was. It was a long time ago."

"We wish to speak with you," said Inga, "as representatives of the Protectorate of Old America."

"So? Talk."

"We speak officially."

"Oh." Folger smiled at Maria. "I must be alone with these people."

The island woman looked dubiously at the Lindfors. "I will be in the kitchen," she said.

"It is a formidable journey to Tres Rocas," said Per. "Our airboat left Cape Pembroke ten hours ago. Unfavorable winds."

Folger scratched himself and said nothing.

Inga laughed, a young girl's laugh in keeping with her age. "Marcus Antonius Folger, you've been too long away from American civilization."

"I doubt it," said Folger. "You've obviously gone to a lot of trouble to find me. Why?"

Why?

She always asked him questions when they climbed the rocks above the headland. Valerie asked and Folger answered and usually they both learned. Why was the Falklands' seasonal temperature range only ten degrees; what were quasars; how did third-generation computers differ from second; how dangerous were manta rays; when would the universe die? Today she asked a new question:

"What about the war?"

He paused, leaning into a natural chimney. "What do you mean?" The cold passed into his cheek, numbed his jaw, made the words stiff.

Valerie said, "I don't understand the war."

"Then you know what I know." Folger stared down past the rocks to the sea. How do you explain masses of people killing other people? He could go through the glossary—primary, secondary, tertiary targets; population priorities; death-yields—but so what? It didn't give credence or impact to the killing taking place on the land, in space, and below the seas.

"I don't know anything," said Valerie somberly. "Only what they tell us."

"*Don't question them*," said Folger. "*They're a little touchy.*"

"*But why?*"

"The Protectorate remembers its friends," said Per.

Folger began to laugh. "Don't try to snow me. At the peak of my loyalty to the Protectorate—or what the Protectorate was then—I was apolitical."

"Twenty years ago, that would have been treason."

"But not now," said Inga quickly. "Libertarianism has made a great resurgence."

"So I hear. The boat brings magazines once in a while."

"The years of reconstruction have been difficult. We could have used your expertise on the continent."

"I was used here. Occasionally I find ways to help the islanders."

"As an oceanographer?"

Folger gestured toward the window. "The sea makes up most of their environment. I'm useful."

"With your talent," said Per, "It's such a waste here."

"Then too," Folger continued, "I help with the relics."

"Relics?" said Inga uncertainly.

"War surplus. Leftovers. Look." Folger picked up a dried, leathery rectangle from the table and tossed it to Per. He looked at the object, turning it over and over.

"Came from a killer whale. Got him last winter with a harpoon and shaped charge. Damn thing had stove in three boats, killed two men. Now read the other side."

Per examined the piece of skin closely. Letters and numerals had been deeply branded. "USMF-343."

"See?" said Folger. "Weapons are still out there. He was part of the lot the year before I joined the Institute. Not especially sophisticated, but he had longevity."

"Do you encounter many?" said Inga.

Folger shook his head. "Not too many of the originals."

The ketch had been found adrift with no one aboard. It had put out early that morning for Dos, one of the two small and uninhabited companions of Tres Rocas. The three men aboard had been expecting to hunt seal. The fishermen who discovered the derelict also found a bloody axe and severed sections of tentacle as thick as a man's forearm.

So Folger trolled along the route of the unlucky boat in his motorized skiff for three days. He searched a vast area of choppy gray water, an explosive harpoon never far from his hand. Early on the fourth afternoon, a half-dozen dark-green tentacles poked from the sea on the port side of the boat. Folger reached with his left hand for the harpoon. He didn't see the tentacle from starboard that whipped and tightened around his chest and jerked him over the side.

The chill of the water stunned him. Folger had a quick, surrealistic glimpse of intricately weaving tentacles. Two eyes, each as large as his fist, stared without malice. The tentacle drew him toward the beak.

Then a gray shadow angled below Folger. Razor teeth scythed through flesh. The tentacle was cut; Folger drifted.

The great white shark was at least ten meters long. Its belly was uncharacteristically dappled. The squid wrapped eager arms around the thrashing shark. The two fish sank into the darker water below Folger.

Lungs aching, he broke the surface less than a meter from the skiff. He always trailed a ladder from the boat. It made things easier for a one-armed man.

"Would you show us the village?" said Inga.

"Not much to see."

"We would be pleased by a tour anyway. Have you time?"

Folger reached for his coat. Inga moved to help him put it on. "I can do it," said Folger.

"There are fine experts in prosthesis on the continent," said Per.

"No thanks," said Folger.

"Have you thought about a replacement?"

"Thought about it. But the longer I thought, the better I got without one. I had a few years to practice."

"It was in the war, then?" asked Inga.

"Of course it was in the war."

On their way out, they passed the kitchen. Maria looked up sullenly over the scraps of bloody mutton on the cutting board. Her eyes fixed on Inga until the blonde moved out of sight along the hall.

A light, cold rain was falling as they walked down the trail to the village. "Rain is the only thing I could do without here," said Folger. "I was raised in California."

"We will see California after we finish here," said Inga. "Per and I have a leave. We will get our antirad injections and ski the Sierras. At night we will watch the Los Angeles glow."

"Is it beautiful?"

"The glow is like seeing the aurora borealis every night," said Per.

Folger chuckled. "I always suspected L.A.'s future would be something like that."

"The half-life will see to the city's immortality," said Inga.

Per smiled. "We were there last year. The glow appears cold. It is supremely erotic."

In the night, in a bed, he asked her, "Why do you want to be a shark?"

She ran her nails delicately along the cords of his neck. "I want to kill people, eat them."

"Any people?"

"Just men."

"Would you like me to play analyst?" said Folger. She bit his shoulder hard. "Goddammit!" He flopped over. "Is there any blood?" he demanded.

Valerie brushed the skin with her hand. "You're such a coward."

"My threshold of pain's low," said Folger. "Sweetie."

"Don't call me Sweetie," she said. "Call me Shark."

"Shark."

They made love in a desperate hurry.

The descent steepened, the rain increased, and they hurried. They passed through a copse of stunted trees and reached the ruts of a primitive road.

"We have flash-frozen beefsteaks aboard the airboat," said Inga.

"That's another thing I've missed," Folger said.

"Then you must join us for supper."

"As a guest of the Protectorate?"

"An honored guest."

"Make mine rare," said Folger. "Very rare."

The road abruptly descended between two bluffs and overlooked the village. It was called simply the village because there were no other settlements on Tres Rocas and so no cause to distinguish. Several hundred inhabitants lived along the curve of the bay in small one-story houses, built largely of stone.

"It's so bleak," said Inga. "What do people do?"

"Not much," said Folger. "Raise sheep, hunt seals, fish.

When there were still whales, they used to whale. For recreation, the natives go out and dig peat for fuel."

"It's quite a simple existence," said Per.

"Uncomplicated," Folger said.

"If you could be anything in the sea," said Valerie, "what would it be?"

Folger was always discomfited by these games. He usually felt he chose wrong answers. He thought carefully for a minute or so. "A dolphin; I suppose."

In the darkness, her voice dissolved in laughter. "You lose!"

He felt irritation. "What's the matter now?"

"Dolphins hunt in packs," she said. "They gang up to kill sharks. They're cowards."

"They're not. Dolphins are highly intelligent. They band together for cooperative protection."

Still between crests of laughter: "Cowards!"

On the outskirts of the village they encountered a dozen small, dirty children playing a game. The children had dug a shallow pit about a meter in diameter. It was excavated close enough to the beach so that it quickly filled with a mixture of ground-seepage and rainwater.

"Stop," said Per. "I wish to see this."

The children stirred the muddy water with sticks. Tiny thumb-sized fishes lunged and snapped at one another, burying miniature teeth in the others' flesh. The children stared up incuriously at the adults, then returned their attention to the pool.

Inga bent closer. "What are they?"

"Baby sharks," said Folger. "They hatch alive in the uterus of their mother. Some fisherman must have bagged a female sand tiger who was close to term. He gave the uterus to the kids. Fish won't live long in that pool."

"They're fantastic," Per breathed. For the first time since Folger had met him, he showed emotion. "So young and so ferocious."

"The first one hatched usually eats the others in the womb," said Folger.

"It's beautiful," said Inga. "An organism that is born fighting."

The sibling combat in the pit had begun to quiet. A few sand-tiger babies twitched weakly. The children nudged

them with the sticks. When there was no response, the
sticks rose and fell violently, splashing the water and mash-
ing the fish into the sand.

"The islanders hate sharks," Folger said.

*She awoke violently, choking off a scream and blindly
striking out at him. Folger held her wrists, pulled her
against him, and then began to stroke her hair. Her
trembling slowly subsided.*

"Bad dreams?"

She nodded, her hair working softly against his jaw.

"Was I in them?"

"No," she said. "Maybe. I don't know. I don't think so."

"What happened?"

*She hesitated. "I was swimming. They—some people
pulled me out of the water. They put me on a concrete slab
by the pier. There was no water, no sea—" She swallowed. "God, I want a drink."*

"I'll fix you one," he said.

*"They pulled me out. I lay there and felt the ocean drain
away. And then I felt things tear loose inside me. There
was nothing supporting my heart and liver and intestines
and everything began to pull away from everything else.
God, it hurts—"*

Folger patted her head. "I'll get you a drink."

"So?" said Per. "Sharks aren't particularly aggressive,
are they?"

"Not until after the war," said Folger. "Since then there's
been continual skirmishing. Both the villagers and the
sharks hunt the same game. Now they've started to hunt
each other."

"And," said Inga, "there has been you."

Folger nodded. "I know the sea predators better. After
all, that was my job."

The children, bored with the dead shark pool, followed
the adults toward the village. They gawked at the Lindfors.
One of the more courageous boys reached tentatively
toward Inga's hair as it blew back in the wind.

"Vayan!" shouted Folger. "All of you, move!" The children reluctantly withdrew. "They're accustomed to whites,"
he said, "but blondes are a novelty."

"Fascinating," said Inga. "It is like an enclave of a
previous century."

The road widened slightly and became the village's main street, still unpaved, and winding down along the edge of the sea. Folger saw the aluminum bulk of an airboat tied to a pier, incongruous between two fishing ketches. "You come alone?" he said.

"Just the two of us," said Inga.

Per put his hand lightly on her wrist. "We're quite effective as a team," he said.

They passed a dark-stone house, its door swung open to the wind. Rain blew across the threshold.

"Abandoned?" said Inga.

"Quaint old island custom," said Folger. "Catholicism's a little diluted here. Priest comes only twice a year." He pointed at the open door. "The man who lived there died at sea a couple days ago. Family'll keep the door open, no matter what, for a week. It's so his soul can find shelter until it's shunted to heaven or hell."

Per said, "What happened to the man?"

"He was fishing," Folger said. "Friends saw it all. A great white shark got him."

Closer now:

"Dolphin!"

"Shark!"

They lay together.

"I wish we had more time," said Inga. "I should like to hunt a shark."

"Perhaps on some future leave," said Per.

"And that's about it for the village," said Folger. "There isn't much more to see, unless you enjoy native crafts like dipping tallow candles or carding wool."

"It's incredible," said Inga. "The only time I have seen anything remotely like this was in prereconstruction America."

Folger said, "You don't look that old."

"I was barely into puberty. The Protectorate brought our father from Copenhagen. He is a design engineer in hydroelectrics. He worked on the Oklahoma Sea projects."

They stood on a rough plank pier beyond one horn of the crescent of houses. Per tapped a boot on the wood to shake loose some of the mud. "I still can't see how you endure this place, Folger."

Half-asleep, Folger said, "Someday when the war is

*over, we'll get a place by the ocean. There's still some
great country north of San Francisco. We'll have a house
among the trees, on a mountainside overlooking the beach.
Maybe we'll make it a stone tower, like Robinson Jeffers
built."*

Close to his ear, Valerie said, "A tower would be nice."

*"You'll be able to read all day, and swim, and we'll
never have any visitors we don't want."*

"It's a fine dream for you," Valerie whispered.

"I came as jetsam," Folger said.

The three of them stood silently for a few minutes,
watching clouds darker than the water spill in from the
west. Triangular shapes took form on the horizon. Folger
squinted. "Fishermen are coming in." After another minute he said, "Tour's over."

"I know," said Inga.

"—hoping. I kept hoping." Folger raised himself on one
elbow. "You really are going to go through with it."

The fishing boats neared the breakwater. Folger and the
others could hear the faint cries of the crewmen. "Why are
you here?" he said.

Per Lindfors laid a comradely hand on Folger's shoulder. "We came here to kill you."

Folger smiled. What other response could there be?

"Tell me how it works," said Valerie.

*They paused on a steel catwalk overlooking the catch
pens. In the tank immediately below, two divers warily
manhandled a five-meter great blue in an oval path. If
water weren't forced over the shark's gill surfaces, the fish
would suffocate. The water glittered in the glare of arc
lights. Beyond the pens, the beacon on Cape Pembroke
blinked its steady twelve pulses per minute.*

"I know the general techniques," said Folger. "But it's
not my specialty. I'm strictly mapping and logistics."

"I don't need apologies," said Valerie.

"Excuse me while I violate the National Security Act."
Folger turned to face her. "Most of the technology is
borrowed from the brothers upstairs on the orbital platforms. Everybody's been doing secret work with cyborgs.
Somewhere along the line, somebody got the bright idea of
importing it underwater."

"The Marine Forces," said Valerie.

"Right. The bureaucrats finally realized that the best weapons for fighting undersea wars already existed in the ocean. They were weapons which had been adapted for that purpose for more than a hundred million years. All that was needed were guidance systems."

Valerie said wistfully, "Sharks."

"Sharks and killer whales; squid; to a degree, dolphins. We're considering a few other species."

"I want to know how it's done."

"Primarily by direct transplant. Surgical modification. Nerve grafts are partially electronic. Is that what you wanted to know?"

She stared down at the docile shark in the tank. "There's no coming back, is there?"

"We'll probably use your old body to feed the new one."

"So kill me. Do I rate a reason why?"

"Not if your execution had been scheduled now," said Inga. "It would not have been merciful to alert you in advance. Such cheap melodrama is forbidden by Protectorate codes."

Folger snorted. "Isn't all this overly Machiavellian?"

"Not at all. We were given considerable latitude on this assignment. We wished to be sure of doing the right thing."

"—come down to the point of whether or not I'll stop you from doing this." Wind off the headland deadened his words.

"Can you stop me?" Valerie's voice was flat, without challenge.

He didn't answer.

"Would you?" Valerie kissed him gently on the side of the throat. "Here's a Hindu proverb for you. The woman you love, you must not possess."

He said in a whisper, without looking at her, "I love you."

"If you're not going to kill me," Folger said, "I've got work to do."

"Folger, what is your fondest wish?"

He stared at her with enigmatic eyes. "You can't give it to me."

"Wealth?" said Per. "Recognition? You had a considerable reputation before the war."

"When we leave," said Inga, "we want you to return with us."

Folger looked slowly from one to the other. "Leave the island?"

"A center for deep Pacific studies is opening on Guam," Inga said. "The directorship is yours."

"I don't believe any of this," said Folger. "I'm in my fifties, and even considering the postwar chaos, I'm a decade behind my field."

"Some refresher study at the University of San Juan," said Per.

Inga said, "Reconstruction is not all that complete. Genius is uncommon. You are needed, Folger."

"Death or a directorship," said Folger.

Folger spoke to the project manager in a sterile cubicle off the operating theater. "What are her chances?"

"For survival? Excellent."

"I mean afterwards."

The project manager drew deeply on his extinguished pipe. "Can't say. Test data's been spotty."

"Christ, Danny!" Folger swung around. "Don't double-talk me. What's that mean?"

The project manager evaded Folger's eyes. "A high proportion of the test subjects haven't returned from field trials. The bio boys think it may have something to do with somatic memory, cellular retention of the old nonhuman personality."

"And you didn't tell us anything about this?"

"Security, Marc." The project manager looked uncomfortable. "I never know from day to day what's under wraps. You know, we haven't had radio reception for twelve days now. Nobody knows—"

"I swear, Danny, if anything happens to her—"

The pipe dropped from the project manager's open mouth. "But she's a volunteer—"

It was the first time Folger had ever struck another human being.

"Elections are approaching on the continent," said Inga.

"Free?"

"Of course," said Per.

"Reasonably," said Inga. "Within the needs of reconstruction."

A crowd of children scampered past. Further down the beach, the fishermen began to unload the day's catch.

"Do you remember a man named Diaz-Gomide?" said Per.

"No."

"He is a Brazilian journalist."

"Yes," said Folger. "About two years ago, right?"

Per nodded. "He is not only a journalist, but also a higher-up in the opposition party. He is their shadow minister of information."

"Señor Diaz-Gomide has proved a great embarrassment to the present administration," said Inga.

"The same regime that's been in power for a quarter century," said Folger.

Inga made a noncommittal gesture. "Someone had to keep order through the war and after."

"The point is," said Per, "that this Diaz-Gomide has been disseminating historical lies on behalf of his party."

"Let me guess," said Folger. He walked slowly toward the end of the pier and the Lindfors followed. "He has disclosed terrible things about the government in connection with the Marine Institute on East Falkland."

"Among other fabrications," said Per.

Folger stopped with his toes overhanging the water. "He alleged that inhuman experiments were carried on, that the brains of unwilling or unknowing subjects were transplanted into the bodies of sea creatures."

"Something like that, except he couched it in less clinical language."

"Down the rabbit hole." Folger shook his head slowly. "What do you want from me—a disclaimer?"

Inga said, "We suspect Diaz-Gomide grossly distorted your statements in the interview. It would be well if you set the record straight."

"The Marine Forces experiments have been greatly exaggerated," said Per.

"Probably not," said Folger.

They stared at each other.

Folger floated in the center of the holding tank. The whisper of the regulator sounded extraordinarily loud in his ears. He turned to follow the great white shark as it slowly circled, its eye continually focused on Folger. The shark—he found difficulty ascribing it her name—moved fluidly, weaving, head traveling from side to side slowly with the rhythm of its motion through the water.

She—he made the attempt—she was beautiful; implacably, savagely so. He had seldom been this close to a shark. He watched silently her body crease with a thousand furrows, every movement emphasizing musculature. He had never seen beauty so deadly.

After a time, he tried the sonex. "Valerie—inquiry—what is it like?"

The coded reply came back and unscrambled. "Marc—never know—mass & bulk & security—better."

He sent: "Inquiry—happy?"

"Yes."

They exchanged messages for a few minutes more. He asked, "Inquiry—what will they do with you?"

"Assigned soldier—picket duty—Mariana Trench."

"Inquiry—when?"

"Never—never soldier—run away first."

"So," said Folger. "Recant or die?"

"We would like to see you take the directorship of the research center on Guam," said Inga.

Folger found the paper among other poems scattered like dry leaves in Valerie's room:

"In the void, inviolate
  from what she was

is
  and will be"

He went outside to the catch pens. From the catwalk he looked into the tank. The shark circled ceaselessly. She swung around to his side and Folger watched the dark back, the mottled gray and white belly slide by. He watched until darkness fell.

"Do I get time to consider the offer?" Folger asked.

The Lindfors looked at each other, considering.

"I was never good at snap decisions."

"We would like to tidy up this affair—" said Per.

"I know." Folger said. "Skiing the Sierras."

"Would twelve hours be sufficient?"

"Time enough to consult my Book of Changes."

"Do you really?" Inga's eyes widened fractionally.

"Treason," Per said.

"No. No more. My mystical phase played through."

"Then we can expect your decision in the morning?"

"Right."

"And now it is time for supper," said Inga. "Shall we go to the boat? I remember, Folger. Very rare."

"No business during dinner?"

"No," Inga promised.

"Your goddam girl," said the project manager. *Soaked through with sea water and reeking of contraband liquor, he sloshed into Folger's quarters. "She got away."*

Folger switched on the lamp by the bunk and looked up sleepily. "Danny? What? Who got away?"

"Goddam girl."

"Valerie?" Folger swung his legs off the bed and sat up.

"Smashed the sea-gate. Let loose half the tanks. We tried to head her off in the channel."

"Is she all right?"

"All right?" The project manager cupped his hands over his face. "She stove in the boat. Got Kendall and Brooking. You never saw so much blood."

"Christ!"

"Hell of it was," said the project manager, "we really needed her in the morning."

"For what?"

"Really needed her," the project manager repeated. He staggered out of the room and disappeared in the hall.

Folger answered his own question the following day. Through devious channels of information, he learned that Valerie had been scheduled for vivisection.

That night, Folger climbed the mountain above his house. He felt he was struggling through years as much as brush and mud. The top of the mountain was ragged, with no proper peak. Folger picked a high point and spread his slicker over damp rock. He sat in the cold and watched the dark Atlantic. He looked up and picked out the Southern Cross. A drizzle began.

"Well, hell," he said, and climbed back down the mountain.

Folger took an Institute launch out beyond the cape and anchored. He lowered the cage, then donned his scuba gear. He said into the sonex: "Query—Valerie—location."

Later that morning, Folger suffered his loss.

Maria shook him awake in the morning. Folger awakened reluctantly, head still full of gentle spirals over glowing coral. The water had been warm; he had needed no suit or equipment. Endless, buoyant flight—

"Señor Folger, you must get up. It has been seen."

His head wobbled as she worried his shoulder with insistent fingers. "Okay, I'm awake." He yawned. "What's been seen?"

"The big white one," Maria said. "The one that killed Manuel Padilla three days ago. It was sighted in the bay soon after the sun rose."

"Anybody try anything?" Folger asked.

"No. They were afraid. It is at least ten meters long."

Folger yawned again. "Hell of a way to start a morning."

"I have food for you."

Folger made a face. "I had steak last night. Real beef. Have you ever tasted beef?"

"No, Señor."

Maria accompanied him down the mountain to the village. She insisted upon carrying some of the loose gear; the mask, a box of twelve-gauge shells, a mesh sack of empty jars. Folger filled the jars with sheep's blood at the village butcher shop. He checked his watch; it was seven o'clock.

The skiff was tied up at the end of the second pier. The aluminum airboat glittered in the sun as they passed it. Inga Lindfors stood very still on the bridge. "Good morning, Folger," she called.

"Good morning," said Folger.

"Your answer?"

Folger appraised her for a moment. "No," he said, walking on.

The carcinogenic spread of the war finally and actively engulfed the Falkland Islands. The systemic integrity of the Institute was violated. Many components scattered; some stayed to fight.

Folger, his stump capped with glossy scar tissue, had already said his good-byes.

Suspended in the cold gray void, Folger realized he was hyperventilating. He floated free, willing himself to relax, letting his staccato breathing find a slower, smoother rhythm. Beside him, a line trailed up to the rectangular

blur of the skiff's hull. Tied to the nylon rope were a net
and the unopened jars of sheep's-blood bait.

Folger checked his limited arsenal. Tethered to his left
wrist was the underwater gun. It was a four-foot aluminum
tube capped with a firing mechanism and a waterproof
shotgun shell. A shorter, steel-tipped shark billy was fixed
to a bracket tied to the stump of Folger's right arm.

Something intruded on his peripheral vision and he
looked up.

Arrogant and sure, the two deadly shadows materialized
out of the murk. The Lindfors wore only mask, fins, and
snorkel. They appeared armed only with knives.

Folger saw them and raised the shark gun in warning.
Per Lindfors grinned, his teeth very white. With slow,
powerful strokes, he and his sister approached Folger from
either side.

Disregarding Inga for the moment, Folger swung the
muzzle of the shark gun toward Per. Per batted it aside
with his free hand as Folger pulled the trigger. The con-
cussion seemed to stun only Folger. Still smiling, Per
extended his knife-hand.

Inga screamed in the water. Per disregarded Folger's
weak attempt to fend him off with the billy and began to
stroke for the surface. Folger turned his head.

A clownish face rushed at him. Folger stared at the
teeth. The pointed nose veered at the last moment as the
shark brushed by and struck at Per. The jaws cleanly
sliced away Per's left arm and half his chest. The fish
doubled back upon itself and made another strike. Per's
legs, separate and trailing blood, tumbled slowly through
the water.

Then Folger remembered Inga. He turned in the water
and saw half her torso and part of her head, a swatch of
silky hair spread out fanlike behind the corpse.

He looked back at the shark. It turned toward him
slowly and began to circle, eerily graceful for its immense
size. A dark eye fixed him coldly.

Folger held the metal billy obliquely in front of his
chest. The tether of the shark gun had broken with the
recoil.

The shark and Folger inspected each other. He saw the
mottled coloration of the shark's belly. He thought he saw

a Marine Forces code branded low on the left flank. He keyed the sonex:

"Query—Valerie—query—Valerie."

The shark continued to circle. Folger abruptly realized the shark was following an inexorably diminishing spiral.

"Query—Valerie—I am Folger."

"Folger." An answer came back. "Valerie."

"I am Folger," he repeated.

"Folger" came the reply. "Love/hunger—hunger/love."

"Valerie—love."

"Hunger—love." The shark suddenly broke out of her orbit and drove at Folger. The enormous jaws opened, upper jaw sliding forward, triangular teeth ready to shear.

Folger hopelessly raised the billy. The jaws closed empty and the shark swept by. She was close enough to touch had Folger wished. The shark drove toward the open sea and Folger swam for the surface.

He tossed the yarrow sticks for an hour. Eventually he put them away, along with the book. Folger sat at the table until the sun rose. He heard Maria's footsteps outside on the stone walk. He listened to the sound of her progress through the outside door, the kitchen, and the hall.

"Señor Folger, you didn't sleep?"

"I'm getting old," he said.

Maria was excited. "The great white one is back."

"Oh?"

"The fishermen fear to go out."

"That's sensible."

"Señor, you must kill it."

"Must I?" Folger grinned. "Fix me some tea."

She turned toward the kitchen.

"Maria, you needn't come up tonight to fix supper."

After his usual meager breakfast, Folger gathered together his gear and walked out the front door of the house. He hesitated on the step.

You become what you live.

She lived shark.

He said into the wind. "What do you want me to do? Carve a cenotaph here on the mountain?"

"What, Señor?" said Maria.

"Let's go." They started toward the trail. "Hold it," said Folger. He walked back to the house and opened the front door to the wind and rain. He chocked it with a rock. Then he climbed down the path to the sea.

———————————————————

1979 is Edward Bryant's eleventh year as a professional writer. His first story was sold to Again, Dangerous Visions *in 1968 at the first Clarion Workshop. Since then, he has published the books* Among the Dead, Phoenix Without Ashes, *and* Cinnabar, *and has edited* 2076: The American Tricentennial. *He denies that he is a shark fetishist: "I respect sharks," he says, "and find them fascinating, but I don't keep one in the tub." Nonetheless, he plans to finish a shark novel,* Triburon, *in which the protagonists of his story "Shark" appear.*

Born a New Yorker, he was reared in the west. Ranching and one-room schools and small town are all in his background. His military experience he describes as "minimal and vicarious." Some experienced war-gamers hustled him into a medieval game; he kept thinking of air power, positioned his archers on hills, and slaughtered the enemy. He won, they sulked, and he "decided to retire from war games with a winning record."

He now lives in Denver, Colorado.

I really do not know whether this story should have preceded "Shark" or followed it, for they both deal with the use—or should we say misuse?—to further the ends of war of those life sciences Alan Nourse considered in his article.

David Langford

TRAINING

A mantrap took my foot off, so I dropped to inspect the damage. Five years ago, I'd have fainted as a million volts of pain came searing up the nerves: now it was just an irritation. Uncomfortable, like the knobby rocks I'd landed on in the instinctive dive for cover. I fixed the tourniquet with my left hand and teeth—you *never* let the gun slip from the right hand when in action, even if it's only the training ground. I was about to stick my head up for a quick look at the objective, but just then there was a popping and crackling as an IR laser drew a line of bright sparks through the air. Superheated rockdust burst where it struck; one fragment scored my forehead and filled my eyes with blood. The hypnos soaked up the pain, but I wasted more seconds tying a kerchief over the wound with one hand only.

An electric-discharge laser would need seconds to recharge. I hoped it wasn't a gasdynamic or chemical job—and stuck up my head. Nothing hit me during the quick look I allowed myself, so I tossed a grenade and a smoke bomb as far as I could towards the laser bunker and started hopping, slightly off the direct line of approach. The guess about the laser was wrong, though, for straightaway another dotted line of ionization sparks came probing through the smoke, shattering rocks in a continuous explosion. A good shot now could smash the directing mirror

244

and put the damn laser out of action, but even a Forceman can't aim too well one-legged, and I didn't care to drop again right now. Instead I pulled more smoke bombs from my belt and threw them way to the right of the first cloud, while I came in from the left. I planned to shove a grenade right through their firing slit. They saw me, though, and the crackling line came tracking back toward me, and I threw myself forward to the base of the pillbox where the beam couldn't aim—or so I hoped. Then I saw the little vents in the concrete right by my eyes, and realized that not only were the bastards using a chemical laser, but they pumped the deadly hydrogen-fluoride exhaust out right here, specially for goddam idiots like me. Then the HF gas was stripping the skin from my face, scarring my windpipe and filling my lungs with bloody froth, and after a little while I died, again.

The thing about the training ground is that you *can't* win. It goes on and on until you're dead. This may sound terrifying if like most people you're a virgin where Death is concerned; but to Forcemen, deaths are just part of our lives. The logic is pretty simple, after all: anyone laden with gut-fears and unbalancing hormones is thinking about himself instead of about the fighting, and can't do his job objectively. Poker players keep emotion out of their faces; we keep ours out of our glands.

So I lay there in the tank and watched my foot grow. The regenerator fluid is thick, yellowish and murky, but I could see I'd already sprouted a fine bunch of tarsal bones, coated with the jelly of re-forming flesh. The fluid filled my mouth and nostrils and lungs, which no doubt were healing at a good rate. The only quarrel I have with regeneration is that it's boring: the process takes hours. Once I was cut clean in half by a riot gun and spent five days growing new me, from the belly down, like some stupid flatworm. It's all necessary, though. Like they told us, deep down in the genes we've got this locked-in program that shrieks *survive!* when death's about, and shrieks it so loud that you can't hear your other thoughts. Only way to stop it is to get used to dying . . . and then maybe you get your promotion.

That had been my forty-sixth death. I reckoned I was used to it.

They let me out of the sickbay in the end, and I marched off on my own two tender feet (the treatment leaves you uncalloused, like a baby), feeling ready to rush that laser again and this time smear the crew. I'd been in some of those bunkers myself, of course—sooner or later, the crew always gets smeared. Next day we'd be starting a fresh course on how to improvise your own nukes—the trick being to shape your charge of plute-oxide fuel before the poisoning gets to you. No need to catch up on studies that night, so I wandered into the bar for a juice and sat down by Raggett, a new guy with only half-a-dozen deaths. He still wore the death-pips on his arm: I gave up the decorations when they reached double figures, myself.

"Chess?" I said to be sociable. "Or we could grab a room for a bit of wargaming, if that doesn't sound too much like work."

"I thought I'd go into town," said Raggett. He is a ratty little fellow, and he looked really furtive as he said this. Men from the Force can go into town anytime they don't have classes or training—it's supposed to be a compliment—the brass trust us. But somehow there's a sort of feeling, not quite strong enough to be an unwritten rule, that the real pros don't leave camp. So I gave Raggett a twitch of my eyebrow, and he said, "I could use a woman."

At that I remembered my last woman, maybe only two deaths into training, and I also remembered Mack, the long-server who'd taken me into town back then out of sheer kindness (it had been his first time in years) and warned me where I'd likely be rolled, or poxed, or both. Mack, poor guy, was wasted in an overseas raid: no pickup for recycling.

"Why don't we go together?" I said. "I think I know the good places."

"Well . . . thanks, Jacklin! Can I get you another?"

I let him get me a juice I didn't really want, and he told me the latest stats, which I knew already, only I was feeling friendly. Seventy-two percent of the new intake had dropped out on their first combat trial. Psych discharge: some people just can't take dying. It made me feel closer to Raggett, even with all those D's of seniority.

"—great stuff," he was saying. "The vocal solos are out of this world. You heard it?"

I blinked. "Heard what? A new tape? Uh, sorry, friend, but music doesn't do anything for me. I used to follow the charts, but I never get time these days."

"I was wondering about that," Raggett said. "I've noticed that seniors mostly keep out of the audio room, and I mean, you know, is this some goddam unwritten rule I don't know about?"

I told him I didn't know about it either. "After I'd been in the Force a while, the things I did before didn't seem too important. You get this feeling of being really in touch here, on the ball, keeping ahead of classes and scoring high in combat trials. Especially those. I mean, it feels better than music and such."

Raggett frowned a little, and I wondered whether he was planning to give up his piddling hobbies right away. I wondered a couple of other things too.

"Let's get into town," I said.

The streets were the same; the lights were different. The route through the back streets came to me as we went along, and soon we were walking down alleys where the lighting was just about nonexistent. I remember thinking this part of town had gone downhill since my last time . . . and then, as our footsteps sounded grittily in one quiet and smelly spot, there was a scraping of other feet, and three punks jumped us. It turns out the Force technique of not caring about getting dead or injured works fine in unarmed combat, too: I was a wide-open target as my fingers went in a V into the first punk's eyes and my boot into the second's groin, while whatever Raggett did to the third left him a screaming lump until I kicked him to sleep. I came out of it with a dislocated finger, which, thanks to the conditioning, didn't hurt much as I reset it.

"Hope they're not maimed for life," said Raggett as we went on. I guessed two of them were and that the third wouldn't feel well for close on a week: so what? they put themselves up as targets, and we knocked them down. Good practice, too.

Then we were at the House, a place like any dingy

house in these slums if you didn't know. I pressed the
doorcom button and said "Two guys here looking for company." There was a pause while (I guessed) a black-light
camera looked us over; then the door clicked open. Inside,
it was like the foyer of any small and dingy hotel. An
ugly-looking receptionist who probably knew something
about unarmed combat himself asked us our preferences.

"Blonde," said Raggett eagerly. "Not over thirty."

I remembered a name from that visit so long ago. "Cathy,"
I said.

We slapped down the oversized wads of money he
demanded, took keys like any hotel keys and climbed the
stairs.

What the hell am I doing here? I thought. I turned the
key in the lock and choked in stale perfume. It wasn't the
Cathy I remembered, but she was just as efficient, coming
to me with a smile and kissing me and gently taking off my
clothes. I like efficiency: she was an expert in her trade
just like I was in mine. In no time at all we were lying
together on the huge bed while I looked very closely at
her gray eyes and pale yellow hair and decided *quite
attractive, really*.

We talked a while. She said professionally nice things
about how I was big and strong and so on, and I told her
she looked good, and I was a Forceman who hadn't been
into town for five years. She gave me a funny look then.

"We don't get many old-timers here," she said.

"I'm not thirty yet," I said, grinning.

"Well, you know what they say about the Forcemen
who've been there a while."

I didn't know what they said about them, and asked.
She twisted her face into a funny little frown, and said,
"You maybe paid to talk all night? Can't you do that in
your very own cell or whatever they keep you in?"

"Okay, let's get on with it." I put my arm around her,
and her hands started doing things up and down me and it was
all very pleasing, soft and warm. She stroked me for maybe
a quarter of an hour and I stroked her right back, with a little
of my mind away thinking about improvised nukes and next
day's course, and by and by she stopped. She just lay there
with her head on my chest and sniffed. I felt a damp spot on
my chest then, and lifted up her head. She was crying.

"Something wrong?" I asked.

"Something wrong with you. You . . . you Forcemen! You're not men, you're not. For Christ's sake, don't you ever get it up?"

I remembered then that that was part of it all, and thought this was funny since I'd had a hard-on only that morning while rushing the laser bunker. But now I'd hurt her professional pride or something, so I told her I was tired and would try harder, and she stroked me and sucked me and tickled me without anything special happening. In the end I got out of there and waited in the foyer until Raggett came down with a big smile.

I thought about it all on the way back, and decided that maybe when you get used to dying and everything, then you get above all the little weaknesses. I felt that I'd really matured. Next day I put in for promotion.

David Langford has a degree in physics from Brasenose College, Oxford, and is employed as a physicist by Her Majesty's Government. His first story sale, "Heatwave," was to Ken Bulmer's New Writings in SF *in 1974, and he has since sold the other British markets such as* Ad Astra, Andromeda, Aries, *and* Pulsar. *He contributed a considerable part to Colin Wilson's and George Hay's study of* The Necronomicon. *His first book,* War in 2080: The Future of Military Technology, *was published this year, by Westbridge in the United Kingdom and by Morrow in the U.S. "Training" is his first American story sale.*

He lives with his wife (whose degree in Egyptology "almost enables her to read his writing") in Berkshire.

Finally, what will happen if and when mankind out-grows war? When all the aggressive instincts inherited from the cave, the jungle, the Roman amphitheater, and a hundred thousand battlefields have been bred out of us, or culturally discarded?

What may happen if, isolated here on Earth, having given up the adventure into space, we finally learn to live at peace with one another?

What will the last soldiers left do then?

Rick Rubin

FINAL MUSTER

Coming out of stasis is a peculiar sensation. Life returns first to your brain, and for a second you are aware that the rest of you is dead—not just asleep but actually without life. You are standing there in your stasis cubicle, heavily loaded with equipment, and your body is dead. But you don't fall down, and the juice returns to the big muscles of your legs and arms and chest and then to all of the minor muscles and blood to veins and arteries and finally to every tiny capillary. Then you are awake, and you step out into the world.

The sun was halfway up the east side of the sky, and across the parade ground I could see the barracks and ordnance buildings and mess halls and other structures of Fort Morris shimmering in the rising heat waves. Lieutenant Rolf Baker, my platoon leader, was standing in front of the bank of cubicles that held myself and three other sergeants. I threw him a salute.

"Good morning, Sergeant Oskowski," he said.

"Good morning, sir," I said. "They woke us late this time."

"Later than you think, Sergeant. Three hundred years late. It's 2516."

"You don't say! Three hundred years without a war. Who finally upset the applecart, sir?"

"I'm afraid I don't know. I don't even know who we're fighting."

"It's pretty unusual for them not to tell us right off."

"There's supposed to be a formation in an hour, Oskowski. We'll find out then. Better go wake your men."

To my left the other three Sergeants were coming out of their stasis cubicles. Around us the whole Regimental Combat Team was coming to life, 5000 officers and men stepping out of deep-freeze, ready and able to fight anybody's war. We mobilize down through the ranks—Colonel Moss our C.O. is unfrozen by the civilian authorities, he wakes four Lt. Colonels, they wake four more each, and so on down through Majors to Captains to Lieutenants to squad leaders like myself, who wake their squads. We come out of our stasis cubicles fully armed and in prime condition, ready to be fed, briefed and move in less than an hour if necessary.

In the old Greek myth, the man planted dragon's teeth, and fighting men sprang up out of the ground. I can never quite get the analogy out of my mind, seeing the regiment come out of their stasis cubicles. The difference is that in the myth the soldiers fell to fighting among themselves, while the 45th Regimental Combat Team comes out a disciplined unit.

Unfreezing consists of throwing just one switch per man. I went down the row that held my squad throwing the switches, then sat down in front and started checking over my tommygun. Of course it wasn't actually a tommygun, the old twentieth-century weapon. More properly, it was a rapid fire blaster, Model 2079—a cross between a flame thrower and a junior-size atomic cannon with a miniaturized back pack for power and a rifleshaped nozzle—but somehow calling it a tommygun makes it more personal to me.

My squad started to step out and form up. I let them stretch and yawn and make their tired old jokes. At the far end I noted that two new men had replaced Miller and Chavez, killed at the tag end of the Afro-Asian war 300 years before. I made a note to see if either of the replacements had come in lately. They might throw some light on

those 300 long years of apparent peace when we'd stood
cold and dead in our stasis cubicles without a war to fight.

Those inexplicable 300 years faintly disturbed me. At
least, something disturbed me, for this muster day felt
somehow different from the ones in the past. The time
before there had been 75 years between wars—by far the
longest period of peace since the founding of the stasis army,
but the war we had come out to fight had been the roughest,
too. The armies of the Western Hemisphere had fought all
of Afro-Asia for three bloody years. It was during the Afro-
Asian thing that I got my third stripe and rocker and a squad
of my own. Seventy-five years before that, as a corporal, I'd
fought Brazuritina, the four-country block of southern South
America. And before that the intervals had been shorter yet;
fifteen years, seven years, twenty years, ten years.

So something must have changed out there in the civilian world, or else they must have found another way to
fight their wars. In the bright sun of this 300-year-late
muster day, it would have been nice to know what had
happened. But why should a soldier care? A war is a war.
You die as dead from anyone's weapon, and one war is
pretty much like another.

That typical soldier's attitude, I suppose, was why they
began to store us away between wars. Soldiers make lousy
citizens in peacetime. And a good peacetime soldier is
likely as not to make a lousy wartime one. So they perfected the system of stasis, and we volunteered to wait out
the between-war intervals in our steel and plastic cubicles,
each man with name and service record on his cubicle
door, waiting for the bands to begin to play.

My squad formed up rapidly, standing sharp in a ramrod-
straight row. I walked to one end and passed in front of
them, making a casual sort of inspection.

"Good morning, Staff-Sergeant Oskowski," Filippi the
rocket and missile man said. "Did you enjoy your beauty
rest?"

"Yes thank you Private First-Class Filippi," I said. "I've
slept ever so much better since I moved out of range of
your snoring."

"Hullo, Sarge," Orozco said. He was the flame thrower,
a broadfaced boy of Mexican descent, quiet and shy but
efficient.

"Hello Orozco," I said. "How's your cigarette lighter?"

"Hey, Sarge," Corporal Ryan the demolition man said. "What's with the music?"

The funny thing was that I hadn't, until Ryan mentioned it, even noticed the music. For the P.A. system was serenading us with sounds of violins and muted horns, soft chamber orchestra music instead of the marches and war songs we customarily woke to.

"I don't know, Ryan," I said. "And that's not all I don't know. It's a strange muster day—that's for sure."

"What else?" Yamamoto, our vehicle and engineering man, said.

"I don't know who we're supposed to be fighting," I said. "All I know is what year it is."

They waited to hear. I walked down the rest of the line, past Johnson, the other tommygunner, and the two new men, Bill Chestnut, a Sioux Indian and the new squad sniper, and Charles LaBonte, a thin-faced, black-haired man, older than most recruits, assigned to us as a corpsman.

"It's 2516," I said finally. "You boys have had a nice three-hundred-year nap."

I got the effect I was aiming for. They gasped, almost in unison. Then they started to buzz, guessing among themselves what was up, until I told them to knock it off. Around us other squads were forming up, and platoons, and companies, and battalions, and finally, if you could see it all as one unit, the entire Regimental Combat Team. Dust rose into the midmorning air and orders were barked and men scratched and belched and shuffled into lines. The Lieutenant came over.

"Any news, sir?" I said.

"Nothing, Sergeant," he said. "Your squad all right?"

"All present and accounted for sir. Nobody skipped into town last night I guess."

We both chuckled at the hairy old joke about the soldier slipping out after stasis check and coming back a doddering old man the next morning. He would have been a hell of an old man this time, after 300 years.

The Lieutenant inspected my squad, then sent us off to the mess hall for breakfast. I double-timed the boys over, getting the kinks out, and we filed in and went through the line.

The cooks were civilians. A soldier's job, after all, is to fight. Not to cook or clean up or any of the other menial jobs they used to have soldiers do, but to stick to his trade. Civilians do those things.

Civilians—We don't dislike them and we don't love them. They're another kind of people. Peace lovers, family men, businessmen. Day-to-day people, who live life in any dull, boring way that it comes. They aren't interested in excitement, in proving themselves under fire and learning the final truth that you can only learn in combat. They just want to live. In a way they're sane and we're crazy. But we are what we are.

So we fight their wars. After the war is over we have a big party and celebrate. And that time the civilians start being glad that we're going back into stasis soon. We're not particularly delicate about our pleasures. We take women where we find them, and of course, they're often somebody else's woman. We get drunk and we raise hell and then the civilians hate our guts and they're glad when we go back into deep-freeze. But a few minor indignities are worth the service we perform of fighting their wars for them.

By the next time they've forgotten how much they hated us, or else they are a whole new bunch of civilians. They're glad we're coming back out to fight their wars. They feed us a real good breakfast that first muster-day morning out of deep-freeze.

This is as good a time as any to mention that of course it's not really deep-freeze. It's a combination of temperature and electricity and intravenous drugs and radiation, all wrapped into one package. Which doesn't matter in the least. You stand in the cubicle, and it feels like going to sleep very fast; and when you wake up, no matter how much later, it's like tomorrow. But in another way it's not like tomorrow. You're vaguely aware, in stasis, of the time going by. Not bored, not restless, just vaguely aware. The years roll by and the world changes around you. They keep you dusted, and they keep all of the buildings in vacuum, and the world changes around you. Then someone flips Colonel Moss's switch, and we come out to fight their wars. To fight because it's our job and because that's the one thing that we all love, we slightly crazy soldiers who could never adjust to humdrum peacetime lives.

During that fine civilian-cooked breakfast, eggs and ham and flapjacks and preserves and juice and toasted muffins and coffee, I talked to the two new men.

From Bill Chesnut, the sniper, I could learn little. He'd come into the outfit only a couple of years after we went back into stasis in 2198. He had a pretty typical story. He was a wild kid, always getting into trouble and when he was nineteen he killed a man in a street fight. It wasn't particularly Chesnut's fault, or the other man's either, for that matter, but he was tried and sentenced to 30 years in the penitentary. Then they offered to let him join the army instead. He jumped at the chance.

A lot of the men come in that way, and in the army it's never held against them. The army, nowadays, is about the only remaining place for a man with a combative nature.

Anyway, Chesnut enlisted and went through basic training, a year of being taught the tricks of the trade by veterans too old to be worth cold storage. Chesnut even liked training, which is no snap, better than he liked civilian life. That's the best sign of the making of a soldier and I knew that I had a man who would pull his weight.

Charles LaBonte, the new corpsman, was a different matter. His trouble was restlessness rather than wanting to fight, but it made him unfit for civilian life no less. Born in 2291, he'd found the world a dull place. Adventure was dead; the world was calm and uneventful. From the time that he got out of school until he was thirty, he wandered around, trying to find a place where he fitted in. In 2322 he enlisted in the army, figuring it as the only place where there might be some excitement.

"It was a stainless-steel world out there," he said. "Everything was worked out and nothing ever happened. No wars, no revolutions, no big changes. Ever since the Afro-Asian war, the people kept anything interesting from happening."

"Sounds pretty bad," I said.

"It was. One year after another, everything the same. People just moved along on the same level; never sad, never happy, never excited."

"Well, they must not be getting along so well now," I said. "If they were they wouldn't have called us out."

"That's right. Besides, it's been nearly two hundred

years since I came in. Lord, think of that! Two hundred years. Everybody I knew is dead. My family is long gone. I feel alone in the world."

"We're your family now," I said. I could remember when I felt the same way, after the first time in stasis, just a kid of twenty and suddenly twenty-three years younger than my old friends. Even so, my friends had at least still been alive. LaBonte's were dust by now.

The bugle blew assembly and we came out of the mess hall and walked back to the parade ground and formed up with the rest of Able Company. The regiment drew up in a long line, like on parade, facing a platform that had been set up near the center of the field. On the platform were Colonel Moss, the C.O., a couple of generals probably down from division or corps, two or three light colonels and four civilians dressed in limp gray and brown and pastel-colored clothes that I took to be the current civilian style.

Colonel Moss introduced one of the civilians to us, a Mr. Karonopolis, the mayor of the nearby city of Linkhorn. From Colonel Moss's first words I detected a tension of some sort. He made the introduction in almost insultingly few words, biting off each syllable as if it were bitter. Then he stepped back, very stiff and soldierly, and stood in a ramrod sort of parade rest.

Mr. Karonopolis took over the microphone.

"Make yourselves comfortable, gentlemen," he said. Nobody moved of course.

"On behalf of the local and federal government, the civil population, and of myself I wish to make you welcome to the year 2516," he said. "We of the twenty-sixth century feel that we know you men, even though you do not yet know us. In school we have studied your brave exploits of the past."

So he continued. It was all very kind and pleasant, but we had heard the same things, or variations of them, every time we had come out of stasis. He didn't say anything we didn't know until he began to describe the events since we went into cold-storage.

He told of a world of social, scientific and philosophic progress, of cultural and intellectual advances and internation accord. The world he described ran smoothly. Nations were at peace with nations, individuals with other individuals. It was a world that had no need for an army—even a stasis one.

He was leading up all through the speech to what he said next, and yet the idea was so difficult to grasp that when he finally said it in plain words it was as though he had dropped a bomb on us.

He told us that we were to be decommissioned and returned to civilian status.

I think he expected us to cheer. He was a civilian, and had no understanding of soldiers' minds.

A murmuring grew in the ranks, and I was a part of the murmuring, arguing to myself the impossibility of returning to a civilian world, a strange and incomprehensible civilian world 300 years more advanced than the last one I had seen, returning from war and excitement and the only trade I knew or wanted to know to a humdrum civilian world made of foam rubber and stainless steel.

The Colonel stood on the platform in the blazing sun, his face a mask. The music tried to soothe us, soft and calm. And the murmuring grew louder.

A soldier stood out of the ranks in the next company, a tommygunner like myself, waving his weapon in the air. "Like hell!" he shouted. "Like hell I'll become a civilian. What do you think I am? You're crazy!"

His Sergeant ordered the tommygunner back into ranks but the order lacked the conviction that any order needs. So the man stood and shouted at the civilian and the murmur grew, like angry bees.

"Who do you think you're talking to?" a voice shouted.

"Damn fool civilian," another roared.

"You can't do away with war," my Lieutenant said, half to himself. "There'll always be wars. It's human nature."

On the platform the civilians registered first surprise and then dismay. In their lifetimes none of them had ever met a soldier. How could they be expected to understand them? And probably they had never heard any of the soldierly language that was pouring at them now.

They put their heads together in a conference, and then Mr. Karonopolis stepped over to the Colonel and spoke to him. The Old Man stood at his rigid parade rest and only shook his head negatively. The Mayor spoke again, more strongly it seemed to me. This time the Colonel ignored him entirely.

They tried whatever they had tried on Colonel Moss on the two Generals from higher headquarters but got no better response. Then another of the civilians stepped to the microphone.

"Gentlemen, please," he said. "There is no value in this. What is the good of an army without wars? Surely you don't want to remain in stasis forever, waiting for a war that will never come?"

The murmur grew to a roar.

"We don't intend to thrust you naked into a hostile world," he said. "You will be retrained into any field you want. Or you can simply live, not work at all. You can have homes and wives and cars. You can enjoy life now—you've earned enjoyment."

Then his voice was blotted out by the angry buzzing of the men. Even the men of my own squad were shouting. "We're soldiers—we don't want to be anything else," Ryan yelled.

"You can't abolish wars," Filippi screamed.

"Go to hell!"

"Shut up you bastard!"

And standing there at attention I tried to picture myself as a civilian, living out the rest of my life, forty or fifty years probably, for I was only twenty-eight, living a humdrum day-to-day existence with no excitement or danger but only the routine of a civilian's soft life.

And yet the civilians were right. What use was there for an army if there were to be no more wars? Could they really have abolished wars?

The civilians on the platform huddled together in conference again and then the Mayor approached the Colonel, and this time the Colonel nodded his head to whatever the Mayor said.

I will say this for the civilians—they were facing soldiers for the first time in their lives, and they were obviously surprised by the reaction they'd gotten but through all of the shouting and swearing they had shown no sign of fear. Perhaps it was the bravery of men facing something that they don't know is dangerous. In any case, after the Colonel had agreed to whatever they had asked they left the platform and climbed into a groundcar—a smooth-skinned bug without any wheels or visible motor and drove away.

The Colonel approached the microphone, and the roar dropped to complete silence in a second and we could hear the soothing music again.

"Fall the troops into the barracks," the Colonel said. "Set up for garrison duty."

So we marched across the parade grounds to the barracks, 5,000 strong. Somewhere up the line, someone started cadence count and the entire regiment joined in; 5,000 bass voices drowning out the music of the P.A. system. And somehow it did not sound like the last time we would march.

The barracks were just as we had left them, not even dusty after 300 years in a vacuum. I had the men break out their barracks bags and set up their gear. By the time that was done, the word came down to choose three men for overnight pass. I let Filippi and Ryan and Orozco go, while the rest of us settled down to spend the afternoon at poker and talk.

After a while, Johnson and Chestnut and I went over to the P.X., which the civilians had opened, and joined the beer drinkers in the slop chute. The main topic of conversation, naturally, centered around what the civilians had said and what was going to happen.

"They're nuts if they think they've done away with wars," Sergeant Mangini from Charlie Company said. "Wars are human nature. You can't change that."

"They say there haven't been any in three hundred years," I reminded him.

"So what? There've been other times when there weren't any wars for a long time. But they always ended. They'll need us again."

"Maybe we'll have to start our own war," Sergeant Olivier from H.Q. Company said. "If these civilians have gotten so soft, maybe we'll have to wake them up a little. For the good of the species, you know?"

"You're darn right," Chestnut said. "We'll just have to start our own war."

"You're getting pretty salty for a guy just out of Basic," I said.

"Look Sarge, if they send us back to civilian life, you know where I'll be? In prison. They'll make me serve out my sentence."

"We'll all be in prison soon enough," Mangini said. "We're not suited for civilian life—not one of us. We'll be too wild and violent for them, and they'll end by putting us all behind bars."

"They said they'd reeducate us," I defended.

"They can't reeducate us any more than they can teach civilians how to be soldiers," Mangini said. "A man's born a soldier, he dies a soldier. He just can't be taught to live like a civilian."

After a while, I drifted back to the barracks. I found orders from the Captain saying that Tuesday (I have no idea what day it actually was—we always call muster day Monday) we were to start regular training schedule.

After supper I came back to the barracks and lay on my bunk trying to think the thing through. All over the barracks the men were talking about the demobilization, and soon they had something new to talk about. Long before any self-respecting soldier would have come in off of an overnight pass, the men who had been in town started drifting in. Everyone started talking about what they'd seen that had driven them back so early.

At ten, Filippi and Orozco came into the barracks.

"C'mere, Filippi," I said.

He ambled over and sat on the side of my bunk.

"It's a hell of a world out there Sergeant," he said.

"Let's hear about it," I said.

"It's not that it looks so very different. Their cars and choppers and airplanes are about the same—a little smoother and quieter, but you can still tell which is which. Mostly the whole thing is just quieter. And the city seems smaller. More parks, more trees, everything moving slow and easy like in a small town."

"What about the people?"

"They've changed. They're relaxed and easygoing. They don't seem to ever hurry, and they don't have a care in the world. Everyone just walks around talking and taking it easy. And you can't get them mad or start a fight to save yourself."

"You tried to start a fight?"

"Sure. All of us tried. But no one could get the civilians riled up. Say something to them, and they'd smile and pat you on the back and talk about it like it was a specimen under a microscope. And if a soldier just walked up and took a swing, a couple of civilians would hold him and talk to him until he didn't want to fight anymore."

"Maybe they're just a bunch of cowards. That doesn't prove anything."

"Well, the women are different too, Sarge. That ought to prove something. You try to pick one up, and she doesn't get mad or scared. She just smiles and says she'd rather not. Or, if she's willing, it's nothing like you expect. If she feels like making love, she does it and then says thank you and just goes away. No trauma, no love, no crying and wailing about virtue."

Filippi went off to tell the rest of the men about what he'd seen in Linkhorn, and I lay on my sack and thought about what he'd said. I'd been brought up to believe that people don't change, but if what Fililppi had said was true it looked like maybe I was taught wrong. I made up my mind to take a pass into town Tuesday night and see for myself.

The next morning we woke to the same soothing music, but we breakfasted and started training, trying to drown out the music with our shouts. We marched and practiced squad tactics and ran the infiltration and obstacle courses and fired our weapons. About three in the afternoon, we knocked off and another three men from each squad were allowed to go on pass. I put on my Class A summer uniform, still well pressed and dapper from 300 years earlier, and took the bus into Linkhorn.

As Filippi had said, the city seemed to have shrunk. Not in area exactly, and perhaps not even in population, but the buildings were lower and there were more trees and grass and parks. The machines were less noticeable. Not that there weren't any, but you just didn't notice them. The cars were sleek and mild colored, moving smoothly along without wheels or motor sounds, the copters rose on silent rotors, everything seemed muted. The moving sidewalks—the pride of Linkhorn the last time I'd been there—were gone, and the citizens seemed to actually enjoy walking, strolling arm-in-arm, talking and laughing together. The town was so peaceful that it made me nervous.

Of course I had to try to start a fight. I walked into a civilian going full tilt and knocked him to the pavement.

"Why the hell don't you watch where you're going?" I said.

He picked himself up and dusted himself off. "Come now," he said, "We're both aware that you ran into me on purpose."

"You want to make something of it?"

"On the contrary. But tell me, you're a Sergeant, aren't you? I'm rather unfamiliar with the rating system. I haven't had a chance to talk to one of you men yet."

"I'm a Staff-Sergeant."

"How interesting. That's a position of some authority, isn't it?"

"Yeh, I command a squad."

"A squad? Oh yes, the basic small unit of a military force."

"That's right, eight men."

"That must be challenging. Tell me, how much of the decision-making function do you exercise in the field?"

I was starting to answer when I caught on to what he was trying to do, but he seemed so sincerely interested in me that it was hard not to go along with him. "Quit trying to change the subject," I said.

"Why, certainly, if you wish. But I really am interested."

"I think I'll knock your teeth down your throat."

"I hope you won't," he said. "And after all, it wouldn't prove much. I quite agree that you're a better fighter than I am."

"What'dya mean by that?" I said. I kept looking for fear in his face, or anger, even, but there was none. He spoke slowly and evenly and seemed really more interested in what I was saying than in saving his skin.

"I'm a fairly decent athlete," he said, "But quite untrained as a fighter."

"You're a coward," I said.

"I suppose that in your frame of reference I do seem a coward. I don't want to fight and I won't be angered. But from my standpoint, Sergeant, I'm not a coward at all. I'm simply not disturbed by what you've said. I know myself too well—my faults, my weaknesses, my strengths—and your accusations haven't added any new perceptions about myself. And if they had, I would be more likely to thank you than fight you."

I wasn't getting anywhere and my heart wasn't in it anymore anyway. Somehow, although he wasn't more than a few years older than me, he managed to remind me of my father, or of how my father should have been. I moved on. I had to try a girl to satisfy myself about what Filippi had said about them.

It was twilight by then, and I was walking through one of the rolling green parks that dotted the city. The girl was small and slim with long brown hair worn straight down her back, her face young and pert.

"Hi-ya, babe, let's you and me go off somewhere and make it," I said.

She laughed a tinkling sort of laugh and said, "My name is Jodi."

"I'm Kenny Oskowski," I said. "Want to try a real man for a change?"

"I would like to know you better, if that's what you mean."

"Sure, babe. Let's find a hotel and get acquainted."

"I'd rather go for a walk. It's an awfully nice evening. Wouldn't you just as soon go for a walk?"

"Okay, we'll walk," I said. "I'm in no hurry."

We walked. We had a milkshake together. (Me—a milk-shake! But somehow I didn't need whiskey with her, though she wouldn't have minded if I'd wanted one.) We went bowling and walked some more and ended by sitting on a bench holding hands and listening to a band concert in the park.

At 10:30 I walked her home, and she was like my little sister instead of the pickup I'd tried for. I walked her to her door, feeling warm and kind and hoping for a single chaste good-night kiss.

"Would you like to stay all night with me, Kenny?" she said.

"I didn't think you were that kind of girl, Jodi," I said.

"What kind of girl? I like you. I enjoy your company."

"But what about love?"

"I suppose that is love. Love isn't something you can pin down."

"Do you want to get married?"

"No, why? I like you now, or maybe love you, but that doesn't necessarily have anything to do with living with you for the rest of my life."

So in the end we made love and I stayed with her all night, but gently and pleasantly, for its own sake and for our own. And in the morning I went back to the army, feeling as I had never felt before after an overnight pass, happy and at peace with the world, without a hangover or a sense of guilt or any bawdy stories to tell the troops.

And at Fort Morris I found the soldiers still talking war. Demanding that a war be made for them, or that Colonel Moss lead them against the civilians.

We trained all that day—more firing range, more squad tactics, more physical conditioning. In the afternoon all of the men who had not had their passes yet were given them and sent into Linkhorn.

They came straggling back, bitter and angry and frustrated, most of them before ten o'clock, having been unable to start any fights or cause any trouble. In the barracks they joined in little groups to talk of what they had seen and what they wanted to do to the civilians.

"Man, they're dull," Sergeant Olivier said. "Nicest thing we can do for them is to shoot them up a little and wake them up."

"You can't even start a fistfight with one of them," I said. "How the hell do you expect to start a war?"

"Close up we have to talk to them," he said. "You don't have to talk to start a war. You just go in shooting."

"But why do you want to start a war? What have they done to you?"

"When did you start being a peace lover?" Olivier said.

"Maybe last night. It seems a pretty happy world out there. Why should we destroy it?"

"Because it's our job. You think a society like that one can last? Hell no. They'll fall apart from sheer inertia."

"I doubt it. But anyway, why should you care?"

"I'm a soldier."

"Not any more. You're going to be a civilian now, Sergeant Olivier."

"You think I could stand to live like that? Day after day without any excitement? I'm a soldier and I've got to fight."

"There aren't any more wars."

"There will be. If not now, eventually. Without us this fool country will be defenseless. It's our duty to wake them up."

Olivier spoke for all of them. Their faith in the future of wars was unshakable. War could no more be outgrown than sex.

"I see it this way," Filippi said. "Colonel Moss will get fed up with waiting and move us against the city. After the city, the state. We'll join up with the rest of the army and get this world back into the old groove."

I quit arguing with them. I suddenly saw that I was the only one who didn't think that it was our duty to destroy the society outside. And as Olivier and Filippi and the others talked of their plans for starting a war I realized that I was going to be fighting against them if they did. I retreated to my bunk to think.

Down the room I saw LaBonte, the new corpsman, doing the same. After a while I got up and walked down and sat on his bunk.

"What do you think?" I said.

"Think about what, Sarge? I was just resting."

"No, LaBonte, you were thinking. You're not a soldier like those guys. You came in for excitement, not blood. You're thinking the same as I am."

"How's that, Sarge? How are you thinking?"

I looked around the room carefully. Speaking my mind was dangerous in a barracks full of soldiers looking for a fight. But no one was near, and I felt pretty sure of LaBonte.

"I'm thinking that if these guys move on the civilians, I'll have to be on the civilian side," I said.

"You're crazy," he said.

"I don't know if I could stand living like they do, but this society looks pretty sane and honest to me. I think they really have outgrown war. I'm going into town tonight and warn the civilians. And if worse come to worse, I'm going to help them defend themselves."

"That's treason," LaBonte said. "Don't talk treason to me."

"I thought you might want to come along."

"All right, maybe I do feel like you do, Sarge. But if we went in there and the army started a war, they'd gun us down on sight as traitors."

"You're probably right. But I'm going anyway. I've got to try to help."

"Not me."

"I'm going tonight. Are you going to report me?"

"No. I won't do that. Not until tomorrow at least."

"All right. But if you tell, I'll kill you for it."

"I won't tell."

I walked back to my bunk and lay there working over my plan and thinking and waiting for lights out. Across the room the buzz of war talks continued. Taps blew at 11:00 and the men began to sack out and slowly the talk died and the barracks became still. I lay and waited and stared at the ceiling until 2:00, waiting for the last whisper to die out and the last man to fall asleep. Then I got up and dressed silently. I took my tommygun and Filippi's rocket launcher and some of Ryan's demolition equipment, fuses and explosives, and tiptoed out of the barracks, watching LaBonte as I passed to see if he would make an alarm. But he lay still.

There were two guards on duty at the gate, lazing around with cigarettes hanging out of their mouths.

"Where'ya heading with all that stuff, Sarge?" one of them asked. I recognized him as Don Carpenter from Charlie Company, a balding overaged corporal, back down to private for about the tenth time since the last war.

"Going into town to stir up a little excitement, Carp," I said.

"Going to get the jump on the rest of the boys, huh?"

"That's right. Start a little war of my own before the real one."

"Aw, Sarge, you know there ain't going to be any more wars. The civilians told us so."

"That's right. I forgot."

"I ought to check your pass, Sarge. And I ought to make you leave that hardware here."

"You ought to, but you won't."

"Nope. It's too quiet for me. If you can stir up some action, I'm for it."

So I passed out through the gate and marched down the road under the cool midnight sky, staggering under the tools of war.

I was almost to the center of Linkhorn before I saw anyone. Then it was what looked like policemen, two of them in a city car, but they carried no weapons that I could see and they didn't talk like cops.

"Hello, soldier," one of them said. "Nice night."

"Take me to whoever runs this town, will you?" I said.

"We'll be happy to. But what's the rush, Sergeant? Let us buy you a cup of coffee or a drink. We'd like to hear about the army."

"Look," I said, "this is pretty urgent."

"I'm sure it is," the cop said. "You wouldn't be walking into the city this late at night with all that equipment unless you had a pretty important reason. Why not tell me about it? Perhaps I can help you."

"Turn off the psychology," I said. "I'm on your side— you don't have to soothe me down. I came to warn you that the army is likely to attack you. I want to help you defend yourself."

"Why that's certainly kind of you, but I wouldn't imagine that the army will do anything this late at night. Come on and have a drink and rest."

I turned my tommygun toward him. "Goddamn it," I said, "Take me to whoever runs this place and quit psychoanalyzing me or I'll start the war right here and now."

He just sat there and grinned at me, cool and brave and yet friendly. After a minute I lowered the tommygun and grinned back.

"You were taking a hell of a chance," I said.

"I don't think so. You came in to help us. If you'd come looking for a fight, I would have reacted differently."

"Have it your own way. But remember that I do want to help. And that army isn't going to sit out there forever, waiting for a war."

I climbed in the patrol car and they drove me to an all-night restaurant. We sat for a while shooting the breeze. Once again, like the man I'd talked to, they seemed genuinely interested in me personally. After an hour they drove me to a hotel and got me a complimentary room. No one made any attempt to relieve me of my weapons, and before the cop left, he promised that a city official would be by to talk to me in the morning.

I didn't even try to sleep. I lay on the hotel bed and thought about what I'd done and what was likely to follow until the horizon showed rose and pink and the sky got blue and things began to move in the city around me.

The sun was well up before the city official called for

me. He introduced himself as Stephen French, a short man in his middle forties, well built, gray at the temples and mild-mannered. The city council, he told me, was sitting in session, considering the army situation. He could conduct me to them so that I could tell them what I knew. In a few words, he made me feel very important.

We stopped downstairs for breakfast in the hotel dining room and over bacon and eggs Mr. French told me what he knew of the situation.

The army was not fully unfrozen all over the country. About a third of the units had been taken out of stasis to be decommissioned. The civilians had wanted to do it slowly in order to prevent the sudden influx of men from unbalancing society.

The plan to decommission the army had been brewing for some years but they had waited to make sure that war was actually no longer a threat. That the soldiers would not want to become civilians (and all over the country it was the same) had been something they hadn't foreseen. A gap in their logic, Mr. French admitted with a wry smile. So now, all over the country, they were faced with angry, rebellious soldiers.

"What sort of weapons do you have, sir?" I asked.

"None. We gave up using weapons years ago. Even the police don't use weapons anymore. But then we haven't a crime problem anymore. About all the police do is help cats out of trees and look for stray children."

"You must have some sort of weapons. Or at least machines to make them."

"Yes, probably we could produce them. But even with weapons, we're not soldiers. We couldn't stand up against the army."

"Couldn't you produce one big bomb and wipe them out?"

He gave me a strange look. "No, I don't think we'll do that. That isn't our way."

"You won't have any way if you don't. They'll wipe you out. What about a defensive weapon? Something to stop tanks from running and guns from shooting?"

"Yes, I believe we could produce something like that. But it wouldn't solve anything. Your soldiers could wipe us out in hand-to-hand combat."

I gave up on the weapon angle. "Society has certainly changed since the last war," I said. "What happened?"

What he told me was too complicated to put down here. Basically, after the West had defeated the Afro-Asians, the Easterners had turned away from machinery and returned to an emphasis on meditation, the mind and philosophy. And, then, from the defeated, these things had swept the world, creating a worldwide society that used machines but was not very concerned with them. The important things became thought, self-analysis, and meditation, integrated with the Western behavioral sciences.

The change had grown from within rather than by law. Finally the time had come when everyone was concerned with improving himself, with dominating his own ego, and seeking individual perfection rather than dominating others. Everyone could look back on a happy childhood, where formerly bad childhoods had always bred the dangerous people. Competition for gain and power died away and what remained was competition for the pleasure of measuring yourself against others, rather than to feed your ego.

Emotions were as highly respected as the intellect as long as they did not hurt others. People grew beyond the need for constant external entertainment. They found their pleasures in learning and creating. Of course, psychology and the other behavioral sciences advanced tremendously. What the soldiers had run into when they tried to pick fights were competent lay-psychoanalysts.

"But that won't save you from the army," I told Mr. French. "You can't talk to an army."

"We realize that now," he said. "We aren't underestimating the danger of the situation we've gotten ourselves into."

We came to the city hall, a modest stone and glass building set in the center of a park, and Mr. French led me in. It was all very casual. He took me to a man sitting at a desk by a tall set of doors and said, "I've brought the soldier who came in from the Fort last night."

"Take him right in," the man at the desk said. There were no guards or messengers or feverish conferences, and I was still carrying my weapons when we walked through the doors and found ourselves in the council chambers, a wide room with lots of windows and a large round table in the middle around which sat a group of simply dressed men and women.

"Welcome," the man at the head of the table said. I recognized him as Mr. Karonopolis, the Mayor. "We appreciate your having come to help us."

"I want to do anything I can," I said.

"Please sit down," he said. "We would like to ask a few questions."

I sat. Mr. Karonopolis introduced me to the other members of the council and then they began to question me.

"What do you think are the feelings of most of the soldiers?"

"They're angry," I said. "They want to remain soldiers, to fight. They're afraid that you'll force them to be civilians."

"But why is it that they don't want to become civilians?"

"It's just not their life. They're soldiers. They look down on civilian life as dull and boring and insignificant."

"But you feel differently?"

"No, not really. I just don't think the army has a right to destroy this society. I don't want to live in it, but it seems too good to destroy."

"Would the other soldiers be willing to destroy it?"

"Yes, sir, I think so."

A murmur ran through the chamber. "How do their officers feel?"

"I don't really know, but I think they pretty much agree."

"Do you think they will decide to attack?"

"That's up to Colonel Moss. The Regiment moves when the Colonel tells it to. Until he decides, they'll just stew."

"And if the Colonel decides not to move?"

"They'll do only what he tells them. They're soldiers."

They lost interest in me after that and began to talk among themselves.

"May I say something?" I said.

"Certainly Sergeant Oskowski," the Mayor said.

"Don't you want me to tell you about troop disposition and firepower and that sort of thing?"

"No, I don't think that would help us much," the Mayor said.

"I'm glad you don't, of course. I wouldn't like to have to

tell you. I'd feel even more like a traitor. But it seems to me that you aren't taking the right line of defense. All you're interested in is how the soldiers feel. And I can tell you that they feel like starting a war.

"You've got to figure out a defense. I brought in a few weapons. You should be able to improvise more. But you'll be facing five thousand trained soldiers with every kind of modern weapon. You'll never beat them in the open.

"The way I see it, the best thing is to attack them before they attack you. Send out a few carloads of booze and let them get themselves drunk, then go out there in the middle of the night with knives and clubs, picking up their weapons as you kill them.

"I don't know if it will work, but it's the only way to save your society. I can teach you how to use their weapons and tell you how the camp is laid out. I feel like a traitor, but I'll do it anyway. Because if you don't attack first, your society is finished."

I stood there, after my speech—waiting for applause, I suppose. The council members smiled at me, softly and sadly, and finally Mayor Karonopolis said, "Thank you very much for your expression of loyalty, Sergeant Oskowski. But I am afraid that we can't do any of the things you suggest. You say that we have to defend our society or they will destroy it. But you see, if we do what you suggest, we will have destroyed it ourselves."

I sat down, feeling at the same time like a complete fool and the only sane man in the room. The discussion moved back and forth, mostly concerning itself with whether and how soon the Regiment would attack. Occasionally one of the councilmen would ask me a question, but mostly they spoke to each other, like scientists rather than politicians, illustrating their points with case histories from other societies dating back to before the Greeks.

Finally it was decided to send another delegation, to see the Colonel alone this time and feel out his attitude.

Mr. French, the man who had brought me to the council, told me that I was free to do as I wished, but that he would be happy to show me around the city if I wanted. I accepted his offer and he got a car out of the pool.

He showed me manufacturing plants and colleges and

private homes and museums, and yet somehow the tour
was less interesting than I had expected. Most of the
changes since last I'd seen the city had been inside of the
people. The machines were there, of course, doing all of
the arduous work, and the new buildings and new products. But the people considered them only necessary, not
important. The buildings—in fact, the entire style of
architecture—was designed to emphasize people, rather
than the buildings themselves.

Passing an athletic field, Mr. French and I started talking about track records, and I got a shock. I'd looked upon
the civilians as relatively soft and weak, misjudging their
pacifism as weakness. But I discovered that the current
record for the mile was 2 minutes, 3.8 seconds, and the
hundred-yard dash was run in 6 seconds flat. Schoolboys
polevaulted over 16 feet. They had given up distance
javelin throwing when the throws had become so long that
the wind was more of a factor than the thrower. Now they
threw flat, at targets 250 feet away, almost as far as the
record distance when I was young. And nearly everyone
participated in one sport or another. Mr. French said that
they attributed the fantastic records to control of the mind,
for the people weren't any larger or heavier muscled than
before. But excellent physical condition was the rule rather
than the exception, and the people in general were actually in better shape than my fellow soldiers.

As for the colleges, they no longer issued degrees. People studied for knowledge and took courses on and off
during their lives. Classes had become lecture series, and
the newspapers printed lists of which lecture series were
starting and who was speaking.

Late in the afternoon, Mr. French got word by his
pocket radio that the delegation to Fort Morris had returned, so we went back to the city hall to hear the news.

Mr. Kolar, the man who had headed the delegation,
analyzed the Colonel as feeling himself caught in a dilemma.

"He is trained to accept civilian control," Mr. Kolar
said, "To do what the civilian authorities tell him. But we
have told him to become a civilian himself, and that is a
command that falls outside of his frame of reference."

"How do you think he will decide?" Mayor Karonopolis
said.

"Right now he's wavering between waiting to see what will happen and launching an immediate attack. He instinctively feels that we are wrong, that our society is deluding itself in thinking that there will be no more wars."

"Pardon me, Mr. Kolar," I said, "But perhaps if I returned to the Fort, I could convince the troops about your society."

"No," he said, "They know what you've done, and they think of you as a traitor. You would only start bloodshed, perhaps even tip them into action."

"It seems," the Mayor said, "That we shall have to solve the Colonel's dilemma for him. Mr. Fitzgerald, the proposed plan was yours. Do you feel prepared to try to implement it?"

"But do we have the right to manipulate them?" a Councilwoman asked.

"Perhaps we don't," the Mayor said, "But in the long run it seems the only way to protect themselves. And after all, the soldiers have the avowed purpose of protecting society. Mr. Fitzgerald, what do you say?"

A tall, bony-faced man with horn-rimmed glasses stood up at the end of the table. "Yes, Mr. Mayor," he said, "I'll be happy to try."

The tall man chose two others to accompany him and they left the room.

"You might as well stay here," the mayor said. "Mr. Fitzgerald has a portable radio transmitter in his coat and we'll be able to listen."

We made ourselves comfortable and waited for the technicians monitoring Fitzgerald's transmission to cut him in to the wall loudspeaker.

"You'll have to make a decision yourself if our plan succeeds," the Mayor said. "You must decide whether your loyalty is to the Fort or to us."

"I don't see that there's much choice. I can't go back."

"Still, this will mean for the rest of your life. Perhaps we could arrange it so that you could return to the Fort with honor."

"No, sir, I'm afraid that I've already made my choice. I think I'll just have to learn to live here and like it."

"It won't be easy. It's a pleasant society for us, but we

all grew up in it. You will miss the excitement and conflict. I doubt if you can ever entirely adjust to our mild way of life."

"I'll just have to try, sir. But you seem pretty sure that you can solve the problem of the army. Can you be that sure? What's your plan?"

"It's a psychological one, and you'll hear it soon enough. Of course there's always an area of doubt. We must wait and see, and hope."

We sat and sipped coffee and waited, the minutes dragging slowly by, until the loudspeaker on the wall crackled into life. It broke into the middle of a conversation between Colonel Moss and Councilman Fitzgerald.

"Colonel, we can't thank you enough for saving us from the plot," Mr. Fitzgerald was saying.

"Long experience has shown that war is human nature," the Colonel said.

"Yet the traitors had us convinced."

"They would have disbanded the army, waited a few years, and then struck when you least expected it."

"We see that now, sir."

"The army stands ready to march, Mr. Fitzgerald."

"The time isn't right yet, sir. Our enemies are not prepared to attack. It will be three years at the minimum, and we don't believe in attacking first."

"Yes, that is the weakness of democracy. But a noble weakness."

"I suppose that it's best for you to spend those years in training?"

"No, no," the Colonel said. "Three years of garrison duty would soften the men."

"Then what do you propose?"

"We shall return to stasis. You must keep a careful watch and alert us just before hostilities commence. We can be ready to march in an hour, if necessary, but a few days or a week's notice is best."

Councilman Fitzgerald and the Colonel talked for a few minutes more, completing plans for the imaginary future war against the traitors, and then the Councilman took his leave, and the radio crackled into silence.

"I suppose that it's unfair to us," the Mayor said next to me.

"You knew that they would choose to return to cold storage, didn't you?"

"Yes, Sergeant. Fitzgerald's plan was predicated on their dislike of garrison duty and their faith in war as a part of human nature. It wasn't too difficult to predict with our knowledge of psychology. Actually, Colonel Moss symbolically repeated the original decision of the army to go into stasis. Do you think that we've done wrong by your comrades?"

"No, sir. I think you've done the best you could."

"We can try waking them one at a time in the future," he said.

"Yes, sir. But they still won't choose civilian life."

And so the next day I rode a helicopter out and watched the Regiment muster on the parade grounds and march back to their cubicles. It was too far to see who was marching my squad. Corporal Ryan, I suppose. They marched back and disbanded, not into civilian life but into perpetual stasis.

Of myself, during the years since then, there isn't much to tell. I wandered around the country. I studied a little at a couple of colleges and tried to find a place and an interest for myself. But there wasn't any, for I was still a soldier. I was restless and lonely and not very adjustable—an old soldier at thirty without a war to fight.

That's why I came back here to Fort Morris and took over maintaining the Fort. Not that a man is needed, for the machines do the work, but it seems more personal for me to care for my old comrades in arms. I check the vacuums of the barracks and ordnance buildings and other buildings and I see to it that the cubicles of my former comrades are dusted and clean, as though they might want to look out of their plastic and steel cubicles. To keep a watch for the enemy, for the war they silently await.

I have watched myself—and listened—for news of the foe, but I have not seen him approach. Years in this time and place have convinced me that, indeed, war and violence have been winnowed out of the human heart and mind. Yet who can say that all the universe is as peaceable as Earth is now? That somewhere, sometime, there will not be beings of this world or some other, bent on doing battle, and only my silent, waiting warrior brothers to oppose them?

As for myself, I live, and therefore daily die. And sometimes stop to look into the cubicle marked *Staff-Sergeant Kenneth Oskowski, Squad Leader, 2nd Platoon, Able Company, 3rd Battalion, 45th Regimental Combat Team*.

The vacant cubicle.

————————————

Rick Rubin, now 56, "lives in constant delight with a wonderful woman" in Portland, Oregon, "in an old house half a mile from the old house he grew up in." He attended Lewis & Clark College and Stanford University, and "fought the Korean War from a heavily guarded crypto room in Naples, Italy, where he ruthlessly destroyed every North Korean who approached."

Since then he has been writing steadily, "with occasional lapses into ski bumming and traveling exotic lands," and when necessary working in a variety of jobs: welfare caseworker, tavern handyman, etc. His short stories have appeared in Playboy, Esquire, Argosy, and a great many other crime and mystery, men's, and science fiction magazines.